LIBBY TANNER

Better than Gelato

THE FIRST TASTE OF LOVE IS THE SWEETEST

Better than Gelato

THE FIRST TASTE OF LOVE IS THE SWEETEST

LIBBY TANNER

CITY OWL
PRESS

This book is a work of fiction. Names, characters, places, and incidents either are products of the author's imagination or are used fictitiously. Any resemblance to actual events or locales or persons, living or dead, is entirely coincidental and not intended by the author.

BETTER THAN GELATO
The First Taste of Love is the Sweetest

CITY OWL PRESS
www.cityowlpress.com

All Rights reserved. Except as permitted under the U.S. Copyright Act of 1976, no part of this publication may be reproduced, distributed, or transmitted in any form or by any means, or stored in a database or retrieval system, without the prior consent and permission of the publisher.

Copyright © 2025 by Libby Tanner.

Cover Design by MiblArt. All stock photos licensed appropriately.

Edited by Tee Tate.

For information on subsidiary rights, please contact the publisher at info@cityowlpress.com.

Print Edition ISBN: 978-1-64898-511-9

Digital Edition ISBN: 978-1-64898-512-6

Printed in the United States of America

To my husband, Justin, who makes our whole life feel better than gelato.

Chapter One

I'm not scared. I'm not even nervous or uneasy. The man next to me is terrified. His huge dark hand squeezes the armrest so tight I see the sharp peaks of each knuckle. He tightens the seat belt another millimeter, the blue vinyl fabric straining against his bulk. I've never seen a man big enough to wrestle grizzly bears look like he wants to curl into a ball and suck his thumb.

A flight attendant walks down the narrow aisle and gives him a reassuring smile. He turns away from her toward the small oval window. As he shifts, the sleeve of his T-shirt comes up, revealing a tattoo across his large right biceps. It says FEARLESS in bold, jagged letters. I look at the hunch of his massive shoulders, and the irony is too much for me. I try to smother a giggle, but I'm unsuccessful.

"Something funny?" he asks in a low voice.

"Absolutely not," I say. It comes out with a British accent, which is unfortunate because I'm not British. I sometimes accidentally switch into accents when I'm nervous.

His eyes bore into me, and the muscles in his jaw tighten. I clear my throat and continue in my regular California accent.

"Okay, maybe a *little* funny. Big tough guy, scared of flying, ironic tattoo..."

He does not look amused.

"It's definitely less funny now that you're looking at me like you wish me bodily harm." I discreetly look for a flight attendant. Maybe it's not too late to change seats.

"You can stop shaking, Blondie. I'm not going to break your arm."

I'm not really shaking, just tapping my feet on the worn blue carpet.

"But if I feel my Big Mac coming up," he continues, "I'm not grabbing that motion sickness bag. It's going right on your shoes."

I can tell from the slant of his eyes he's not joking. "Did you just threaten to vomit on a total stranger?" I ask.

"Did you just make a grown man feel like a sissy-baby-chicken-head?" he snaps back.

"Sissy baby what?" *What is this guy talking about?*

"According to my kids, that's the worst thing you can be called," he replies.

My eyebrows shoot up. "You have kids?"

"Yep. Two of 'em. But I tell you what, I got that Fearless tattoo before they came along. Being a dad brings a whole new kinda fear into your life."

"How old are they?" I ask.

"My boy Samuel is nine and my little girl Tanya is six."

"That's like my girl!"

He gives me a once-over. "How old are you? There's no way you got a six-year-old daughter."

"Well, no." My cheeks heat up. "I'm twenty. But I'm a nanny. I mean I'm going to be. And the little girl is six."

"A nanny huh? Do you have any younger brothers or sisters?" he asks.

"No," I shake my head. "All older."

"Ever spent much time with a six-year-old girl?" he prods.

"No," I repeat, irritation creeping into my voice. "There were surprisingly few six-year-olds living in my college dorm."

"Well, good luck," he says with a smirk.

The plane starts shaking as we accelerate down the runway and my seatmate mutters under his breath. I can't tell if he's praying or swearing. He has the same look my best friend Maggie had when I convinced her to go on the Zipper at the county fair. I had to sing the Star-Spangled Banner at the top of my lungs to keep her from puking. We were twelve.

I'm not going to sing for this guy, but I could try to take his mind off things. I do love the shoes I'm wearing.

"So, why are you going to Milan?" I ask. The plane picks up speed.

"Work." He looks down at the runway flying past.

"What do you do?"

"Business consulting." He takes a couple of fast breaths.

"I'm a business major myself!" I say. "I was supposed to take a bunch of obscenely dull classes this semester but fate has intervened. An opportunity fell right into my lap. Like it was meant to be, you know?"

I look at his blank face. He doesn't know. I continue undeterred.

"I heard about this nanny gig from my Italian professor. I called the family that very day, and they hired me and bought me a ticket to Milan."

I'm waiting for him to cheer at my good luck, but he doesn't. He just stares at the back of the seat in front of him as sweat trickles down his temple.

"So now, instead of dying a slow death from human resources management, I'm going to wander down cobblestone streets taking pictures and eating gelato."

The plane has leveled off now and the shaking is mostly over. He turns to look at me.

"If you hate business classes, why are you majoring in business?" His face is still flushed, but his breathing sounds better.

"Doesn't matter," I reply. "The point is, I've miraculously escaped all of that for a year."

He tips his head to the side. "And what about when the year's over?"

"Then I slog through two more years and graduate."

"And then?" he presses.

"Then I move back to my suffocatingly small hometown and run the family dry cleaning business." The thought is so depressing my toes curl up, but I try not to let it show.

"And who came up with this plan?"

"My dad."

His lips dip into a frown. "I see. And do you always let other people make your choices for you?"

This guy sounds less like a business consultant and more like a therapist.

"It's not like that." I reply automatically.

"If you say so," he says, with an annoying shrug.

This conversation is the worst. I should have just let him puke on me.

I spend the flight reassuring myself that my seatmate doesn't know what he's talking about. After all, I made this decision, didn't I? And sure, I've never worked with kids, or been to Italy, or even left the US. But I have a *feeling,* deep in my bones, that I'm meant to do this.

After what feels like days, the flight attendant tells us to prepare for landing. Even over the scratchy intercom, the Italian sounds incredible. I hang on every vowel, get lost in the up and down cadence. I know she's telling me to fasten my seatbelt and put my tray up, but it sounds like she's telling me to embrace life and live to the fullest. And also that she likes my hair.

When our plane lands, I walk down the narrow hallway and out into the main airport. I'm in Italy. *Actual* Italy. I close my eyes and soak up this feeling-this certainty that the best year of my life has officially started.

I follow the crowd of travelers and make my way to baggage claim. I'm trying to walk normally, like my carry-on isn't that heavy, but the truth is, it *is* that heavy. My hands are sweaty, and I'm trying to make them not be sweaty, but that's not a thing I know how to do. I arrive at the baggage carousel and feel a moment of panic. How will I find my new boss?

I look frantically from unfamiliar face to unfamiliar face, feeling more anxious by the second. Then I see a man holding a sign that says Juliet Evans. He has wildly curly black hair and a full face. Next to him is a woman and a little girl. The three of them look just like the photo Marco sent me.

Relief washes over me and my whole body tingles with excitement. I walk over, grinning like an idiot and say, "This is me."

"Julietta! So happy to meet you! I am Marco Rossi." He's speaking faster than my Italian teacher, and it takes my brain an extra moment to match his words to their English counterparts.

"This is Sofia, my wife," he says motioning to a slender woman with glowing olive skin and glossy dark hair. I wonder what miracle products she uses to make her hair shine that way. She kisses my cheeks and says, "*Benvenuta.*" I'm at least four inches taller than her and she has to stand on her tiptoes to reach my cheeks.

"*Grazie,*" I say back. I probably sound like a five-year-old, but I'm so excited to speak to real Italians, I don't care.

BETTER THAN GELATO

"This is Isabella, our little *tesoro*," Marco continues. Isabella is skinny with straight brown hair that falls past her shoulders. She's missing a front tooth, but I've heard that's normal for kids her age.

She slips her hand into mine and asks, "Are you a Barbie?"

I have neither the bust nor the accessories of Barbie, but I guess being tall, blonde, and skinny is enough to get lumped into that category. I shrug and say, "Sort of." She holds my hand as we wait for my suitcases. At one point, she drops my hand, wipes the sweat onto her pants and grabs my hand again. I send a heartfelt plea to my nervous system to take the sweating down a notch.

We step outside the airport, and I let the sights and sounds and smells of Italy wash over me. At this moment that's a bunch of leering cab drivers, honking horns, and the scent of cigarettes and car exhaust. Still, it feels magical.

September in Milan is chillier than September in California, and I wish I'd grabbed my jacket from my suitcase. Marco leads us to the car, which looks like a child's toy. The fact that we all manage to fit inside of it seems to bend the laws of physics.

Marco simultaneously carries on a conversation with me, while conversing with the other drivers through his open window. His conversation with me contains fewer swear words.

"This is Isa's first year of full-day school," he says. "You'll be dropping her off at 8:00 a.m. and picking her up at 4:00 p.m. Sofia will go with you tomorrow to show you."

I nod and look out the window at the city of Milan. Beautiful old buildings, cobblestone streets, Italians nonchalantly going about their amazing Italian lives. I can't stop smiling.

Oh no, has my smiling crossed the line from friendly to manic?

It's happened before. I do my best to smile like a normal person who is pleasant and happy, instead of a lunatic who's broken free of the asylum.

"She looks tougher than the last girl," Isa says.

Sofia gives Isa a warning look, but Isa turns to me and says, "The last nanny quit."

Oh. I try to hide my surprise, but I have a terrible poker face. Sofia flushes in embarrassment and Isa giggles in delight.

"Why did she quit?" I ask Isa in a super casual, not-a-big-deal sort of way.

Isa looks at me with wide innocent eyes, and I know before she even opens her mouth that the next words she speaks will be a lie.

"I have no idea," she says. She maintains strong eye contact, daring me to ask a follow-up question. *Are all six-year-olds this intimidating?*

"Sofia and I will be home by 6:00 p.m.," Marco continues in a rush. "You're welcome to eat dinner with us, but when you meet your friends, I'm sure you'll want to go out in the evening, and that's fine too." He reaches into his briefcase and pulls out a black cell phone and hands it to me.

"The phone is on us, you can just pay to put more minutes on the card as it runs out. It's already full of numbers. There's a nice group of friends our previous nannies have spent time with, and I'm sure they'll be calling soon."

Marco pulls into a tiny parking lot full of tiny cars just like his. There are four tall apartment buildings surrounded by trees. With Marco's help, I lug my suitcases to apartment building C. The elevator is too small for all of us to go up at once, so Marco brings me up first and Sofia and Isabella follow.

As soon as Isabella walks in the door she gives me a tour, pointing out doors and windows, as if being American, I might not recognize such things. The Rossis' apartment is small, but bright. The couch is the dark red of sundried tomatoes, and the curtains are a sheer, sunny yellow. I catch a balcony to the right and a kitchen to the left before Isa drags me down the hall to my room.

It's perfect. Small and cozy, with a wardrobe tucked in one corner and bed and nightstand tucked in the other. The bed has a turquoise comforter and two giant pillows with striped pillowcases. Isa settles onto the bed and offers commentary on each item in my suitcase as I unpack. Marco is a fashion designer, and Isabella has strong opinions on clothes.

"That's a lot of jeans," she says. "Why do you have so many?"

"I wear them everywhere," I say, and Isabella furrows her brow.

"Do you work in construction?" she asks.

I laugh and shake my head. "No."

"Then you're wearing the wrong clothes," she says straight-faced. "You'll be the only one at school pick-up wearing jeans. But don't worry. I will tell you all the clothes you should be wearing instead. You're lucky to have me."

I laugh. "I think you're right."

I like this girl. She's funny and smart. This nanny gig is going to be a breeze.

"I would rather light myself on fire!"

Isa punctuates this proclamation by throwing a fistful of colored pencils all over the kitchen. Her eyes are wild, and her fine hair sticks out from her head like the halo of an angry god.

The homework page she's supposed to color lies on the dark mahogany table next to her overturned backpack.

My first full day as a nanny has been...challenging. Isa was scowly and grumbling in the morning, but who isn't? She threw a plate against the wall when Sofia put the wrong snack in her bag, but who hasn't?

Sofia edges along the counter toward Isa's position by the fridge. She moves slowly, so as not to enrage Isa further. Marco left for Portugal this morning for a fashion summit of some sort, so Sofia's on her own.

"*Mi piccolo topino*," she says, calling Isa her little mouse. "It's just one page. You can do one page. One tiny little page, *amore*?"

"I would not color those triangles if you gave me a million gazillion euros!"

Yikes. Good luck with that one, Sofia. This is when I'm glad I'm the nanny and not the mom. I tiptoe down the plush gray carpet to my room but stop at the door. *Wait. Is helping with homework supposed to be part of my job?*

I creep back down the hall and peek around the corner to make sure Sofia has it all under control. She does not have it under control. She has the eyes of a sickly wildebeest facing a hungry lion.

If my mom were here, she would whip Isa into shape in no time. She raised five kids and not a single one of us would dare raise our voice at her. But I'm not my mom, and I don't know how to whip people into shape.

I think for a minute, then zip to my room and grab the adult coloring book I brought for the plane ride. It has underwater scenes that are supposed to be relaxing to color. By the time I return to the kitchen, Isa's standing on her chair shrieking.

"*Scusi*, Isa, could I borrow a few of your pencils? I can't find mine."

Isa and Sofia look at me startled. Isa blinks.

"Maybe just three?" I ask and bend over to pick up three colored pencils from the tile floor. I make sure Isa gets a good look at the cover of my coloring book. "*Ti va bene*?" Is that okay?

Isa nods her head and goes back to screaming, but it's not quite as loud.

I walk to the living room, leaving the kitchen door open behind me so Isa can see me settle into a navy armchair, select a page and begin coloring.

"No, I won't!" She's still yelling in the kitchen, but it's clear she's distracted. "Leave me alone!" she yells at Sofia, and I hear Sofia murmur something as she leaves the kitchen and heads to her bedroom.

It takes thirty seconds for Isa to stomp over to my chair.

"*Che ci fai*?" she demands. What are you doing?

"I'm coloring," I tell her. "Thanks for lending me your pencils. They're really nice."

"That doesn't look like any of my coloring books," she says.

"It's not. It's a coloring book for grownups. My mom got it in a special store."

Her brow furrows as she works up the courage to ask for a page, but I don't make it easy for her. I keep coloring as though I don't notice her opening and closing her mouth.

Finally she asks, "Could I have a page from your book to color? *Per favore*?"

"Of course," I reply immediately. "Choose any page you'd like."

She takes her time and finally settles on an ocean scene with a tortoise and some jellyfish. She carefully pulls the page out and sets it on the black and chrome coffee table. I go back to coloring my dolphins, and she heads to the kitchen and picks up all the pencils she threw. She comes back and lays them out on the table next to her page.

We color in companionable silence for twenty minutes. In my head, I make a list of positive things about Isa.

1. She didn't cry at school drop off this morning, when most of the other kids did.

2. She's funny. Calling our bus driver a monkey face was mean, but also hilarious.

3. She's got a pretty good arm. Those pencils went everywhere.

"Do you like coloring?" Isa asks me.

"I do," I say. "It helps me calm down."

"Me too," she says.

She finishes the tortoise and shows it to me proudly.

"I think you have real talent," I say, meaning it. "I bet you could color anything and make it look awesome."

I can't tell if I'm being too obvious, so I keep my head down and color my seaweed. Out of the corner of my eye, I see her go to the kitchen and come back with her homework page.

It takes her two minutes to complete it.

"Nice pattern," I say.

"I think you should have made the dolphins bluer," she says of my picture. "All the dolphins I've seen look bluer."

"That's a good tip for next time," I say as Sofia comes into the living room.

"*Tesoro*! You finished your homework!"

Isa scowls. "Yes, I finished. It took two seconds."

Neither one of them mentions the fifteen minutes of hysterics that preceded it.

"Well, I'm headed to bed," I say. I lean over and give Isa a kiss on the head. "*Buonanotte.*" Good night.

I brush my teeth, change into my pajamas and snuggle under my turquoise comforter and check my email. I have a sweet message from my mom and dad, and an email from Sharon, my college adviser.

Sharon is a large woman, who swears a lot and hugs a lot and gets things done. I know she had to do some fast talking to get the scholarship office to sign off on this year in Milan. When the school is paying your tuition, they don't love it when you take off to Europe. Sharon pointed out that it would be a good educational experience. And I'm pretty sure she bribed them with front row tickets to all the home basketball games. Her son is the starting forward, and the team is on fire this year.

She reminds me to pick out my classes for next year and get them to her by the end of the month so they can get approved by the scholarship office. I look at the list and my eyes glaze over. I would rather swim naked with piranhas than sit through a class called Statistical Analysis of Supply Chain Economics.

I'll choose my classes tomorrow, when I've had another day to settle in.

I'm about to turn off the lamp on the nightstand when there's a soft knock on my door.

"Come on in," I call.

Sofia opens the door and takes a tiny step inside.

"I just wanted to say thank you for helping with Isa tonight," she says. "She can be pretty stubborn..."

"No problem," I say. I give her my most confident smile.

When she leaves, I admit the truth to myself: that creature hurling colored pencils and shrieking is more velociraptor than child. I turn out the light and pull the blanket all the way up to my chin. *What in the world have I gotten into*?

Chapter Two

The horns and cursing of Italian traffic are, to my ears, the sweet sounds of freedom. It's Friday night, I'm riding the tram downtown, and I've never been happier to get out of the apartment. In the last week, Isa has dumped her pasta on the floor, given me the silent treatment for twenty-four hours, and written on the living room wall with permanent marker.

When a girl named Carmen called my new cell phone and invited me to a rock concert, I eagerly accepted. Her Italian was accented with Spanish and hard to understand over the phone, but she said she'd been friends with the last two nannies, and we made plans to meet at Piazza Duomo on Friday at 7p.m.

I have no idea who Carmen is. This could all be an elaborate trap to harvest my organs. But I've spent the last five days either being bullied by Isa or wandering the city alone. I'm desperate to make some friends. *Plus, how many kidneys do I really need?*

I leap off the tram at Piazza Duomo in the heart of downtown Milan. It's a massive square, bigger than several city blocks. Dominating the space is a colossal cathedral that looks like something from a fairytale, but not where the princess lives. The spires are spiky and there's a cluster of gargoyles lurking along the roofline. It's ominously beautiful. My hands itch for my camera.

The perimeter of the piazza is lined with ornate buildings that look centuries old and way too cool to house mundane things like pharmacies and banks. But there they are, sandwiched in between designer clothing stores and restaurants with outdoor seating.

For the last week, I've felt like a giant transported to a land of tiny cars, narrow streets, and petite people. But standing in this huge piazza in the shadow of Cathedral Duomo, I feel like a pixie.

The piazza is packed with people, and it's clear that this is where everyone meets up. I can feel the energy tingling along my skin as I watch the crowd of glamorous Italians, ready to begin their glamorous Friday night activities.

I'm not sure how I'll find Carmen or how this night will go, but I know I can't go back to that apartment right now. So I pretend my hands aren't sweating, and I saunter as confidently as I can toward the steps of the cathedral where dozens of people sit waiting and chatting.

"*Ciao bionda*," an Italian guy calls. Hello blonde.

I've been in this country for less than a week and this is the fourth time this has happened. Sometimes it's Hello Blonde. Sometimes it's Hello Beautiful. Sometimes it's even Hello Beautiful Blonde. I may get tired of it one day, but that day has not arrived yet.

I give the young man a wave, then turn and walk in the other direction. I'm flattered, but also slightly terrified.

I'm nearing the edge of the piazza when someone yells, "Julieta!"

I turn and spot a small young woman waving at me from the top step of the cathedral.

"Carmen?" I ask, walking over.

"Yes!" she says, tucking a strand of wavy dark hair behind her ear. "Sorry it took me so long to find you!" I'm about to ask how she knew it was me, then I take a look around and realize I'm definitely the best candidate for American nanny.

"I'm so glad you made it!" she says and stands on tiptoe to kiss me on each cheek. I'm obsessed with the cheek kissing here and plan on doing everything in my power to start this trend in America when I go back.

"Thanks so much for inviting me," I say.

BETTER THAN GELATO 13

"Of course! We're meeting Diego, Paolo, and Valentina here too, but they're always late. Then we'll all ride over to the church together."

I'm so focused on the exotic names, I almost miss the second part of her statement.

"Ride where?" I ask.

"To the church," Carmen repeats.

"The church?" I say back stupidly.

"Yeah, the concert is at la chiesa di Sant'Ambrogio. It's a beautiful old church not far from here."

I look at Carmen's outfit. Silky black pants with stiletto boots. A flowing blouse in deep purple with a gold zipper down the front. Large gold bracelets on both wrists and a black and gold clutch.

"What kind of concert is it?" I ask, a bad feeling growing in my stomach.

"It's an opera, but not a whole opera," Carmen says, brushing a wave of hair out of her face. "Visiting performers come and perform their best songs."

"I thought it was a rock concert." I gesture lamely to my outfit. I'm wearing ripped jeans and a leather jacket with a Coldplay T-shirt. My hair is in a bunch of funky braids.

"Oh!" Carmen says, taking in my outfit. Her eyes go big. I'm hoping she'll tell me that I look fine.

"It will be pretty dark in there," she says instead.

My face heats up. *Could I make a worse first impression?*

As we wait, she gives me the scoop on Diego, Valentina, and Paolo.

"Diego is from Chile. He's been here about three years. He's like a puppy, high energy and yapping a lot, but he's a good guy."

"Valentina is from Argentina, and she's gorgeous, but also so sweet. You'll see.

"Then there's Paolo. His family still lives in Sicily, but he came up to Milan for work. I'm not sure exactly what he does...something in a bank."

Definitely the grandson of a mafia don sent up north to infiltrate the banks.

Carmen herself is from Peru and makes it clear she has no plans to go back.

"Jake is meeting us at the church," Carmen continues. "He's also here for a year. He works at a hospital outside the city, some sort of doctor. But he's American like you."

I keep my facial expression neutral, but inside I groan. *The last thing I need is a dorky American sticking to me like Velcro.*

The gang arrives and Carmen makes introductions. I try to look like a normal, cool, American girl that they would totally love to be friends with. I get a lot of cheek kisses and *benvenutas*.

"I am Paolo Zarantonella," Paolo says taking my hand and kissing it. "It is a pleasure to meet you."

Somehow, Carmen forgot to mention that Paolo is *outlandishly* handsome. Full lips, thick wavy hair, dark eyes lined with thick lashes. He's wearing fitted black slacks with a white dress shirt and cufflinks. His shoes are dark and shiny.

"Ciao," I stutter.

Paolo immediately wants to know how long I've been in town and why Carmen's been hiding me from everyone.

"I haven't been hiding her," Carmen says. "I met her tonight."

"That's no excuse," Paolo says, keeping his eyes on me and smiling in a way that makes my toes wiggle.

Diego bounces over and stands next to him. "*Ciao,* Julieta! Where are you from?" he asks. He looks younger than Paolo, and his full cheeks remind me of my three-year-old nephew.

"California," I say.

Diego's eyes light up with excitement. "Do you live by any movie stars?" he asks.

"No," I say with an apologetic smile.

"I'm going to be an actor in Hollywood one day," he says and grins. "Maybe then we can be neighbors."

"That sounds like a great plan," I tell him.

Valentina gives me a shy smile and walks over. She's wearing a simple white dress that would look plain on anyone else but looks stupendous on her. Her long dark hair is held back with a rhinestone clip.

"Welcome to Italy," she says. "And welcome to our group. Some of us are crazy," she looks over at Paolo and Diego, "but we have a good time."

We take a short bus ride and get off in front of the most gorgeous church I've ever seen. Il Duomo is impressive for its sheer size, but this little church, with stained glass windows and lovely arches, is a work of art.

Paolo notices me admiring it and comes over. "This is la Chiesa di Sant'Ambrogio. It's the oldest church in Milan."

"It's beautiful," I whisper.

"I'm glad you like it. Italians make the most beautiful things."

"Well, thank you, Paolo, for making this beautiful church. I love it."

"Not a problem, *bionda*. Just let me know if there's anything else you'd like, I'll have my people make it for you in a moment." His smile is so charming I'm momentarily stunned.

Carmen waves her arms for us to come into the church before the program starts and we enter through heavy metal doors. My gaze is drawn to the vaulted ceilings covered in cherubs and trimmed in gold. *Wow.*

Carmen leads us to our seats as a large woman in a tight dress the color of sapphires comes to the front. We must have missed her introduction. She launches right into "Nessun Dorma," and I'm secretly pleased it's a piece I've heard before.

Take that, ignorant American stereotypes!

Her voice fills up the whole chapel and makes the candles flicker. The crowd yells and claps dramatically.

"Brava! Brava! Ancora! Ancora!"

As more people yell *"Ancora!"* she actually comes back to the front and gives us an encore, singing the whole song again. *Hmm...if each person sings his or her song twice, this is going to be a long night.*

It's a long night. I don't know any other songs that are performed. *Curse you, accurate American stereotypes!* After two hours, I'm doubting how well I'm going to fit in with these new opera-going friends. *I know I was willing to give up a kidney, but this feels more excruciating.*

As though reading my mind, Paolo gives me a nudge and whispers, "We're getting out of here."

We quietly exit the church, and Paolo lets out an exaggerated sigh of relief, like we've escaped a prison camp instead of an evening of music.

"Well, I think we got what we paid for," he says as we head down the steps.

"It was free," Carmen says.

"Exactly."

"I liked it," Valentina says. "The last tenor was very talented."

"But so long!" Paolo says. "A little goes a long way when it comes to opera."

"The same could be said about Paolo," Carmen chimes in from behind and I laugh.

"Wait. Where's Jake?" Valentina says.

"He was sitting right next to me," Carmen says.

I was so distracted plotting my escape I'd forgotten about the American meeting us at the church. He must have been sitting on the other side of Carmen.

"Oh no! He didn't make it out!" Diego says. He turns back to the church like he's rescuing a friend from a burning building. Just as he starts to climb the stairs, the doors open. A young man with shaggy brown hair and medium build slips out. His cheeks are flushed, and he's humming.

"There you are! I was just coming back to rescue you," Diego tells him.

"Yeah, sorry," he replies. "I was following Carmen and then they started this piece from *La Boehme* that I love, and I stayed to hear the rest." His Italian is good. Better than mine in fact. He's wearing a dress shirt and dark pants.

He sees me and stops. "Oh, you must be Juliet. Carmen said she invited you. Glad you made it tonight." His face is unremarkable until he smiles. Then his eyes sparkle and dimples pop out in each cheek and it's harder to pretend he isn't attractive.

"I'm Jake Fields," he says. He leans in and kisses me on my cheeks. It should be weird since we're both American, but it isn't. I get a whiff of his aftershave, something fresh that makes me think of a lake surrounded by pine trees.

"It's nice to meet you, Jake," I say. "I'm Juliet Evans." I suddenly feel self-conscious. Of my Italian, of my clothes, of everything.

Before I can stop myself I blurt out, "There was a misunderstanding. I thought we were going to a rock concert. I would have dressed up if I'd known it was opera. In a church."

"Oh, that explains it," Paolo whispers loudly to Diego. "I just assumed dressing up was against the American religion."

My cheeks heat up, and I open my mouth to respond but Paolo takes my hand, places it on his arm and gives it a squeeze. "No, no, don't respond. I'm just being awful. You get used to it after a while. You look lovely this evening, Julieta. You needn't change a thing. You will be my *Julieta Dolcetta*."

My heart flutters. *Handsome Italian men calling me their little sweet? Yes please!*

"And if you wish to acquire some Italian fashion staples," Paolo says, "Carmen and I are going shopping tomorrow. We'd be honored to have the pleasure of your company."

"I'd love to come," I say immediately. Turns out Isa was right, I am the only one at school drop-off and pickup wearing jeans.

"Can I invite myself along as well?" Jake asks. "Milan's colder than Arizona, and I could use a few things."

"Well, there you have it, Carmen," Paolo says. "You and I will show these Americans all the secrets of the Milan fashion world."

Jake shoots me a raised eyebrow look that says, 'What have we gotten ourselves into?' and I reply with a smile and a shrug of 'I'm not sure, but it could be fun.'

We head to a pizzeria near the church and my mind is blown at how something so simple can taste so amazing. The crust is thin and chewy. The sauce tastes like fresh tomatoes from someone's garden. There are large circles of fresh mozzarella. It makes me want to go back in time to the Juliet who ate Dominos and grab her by the shoulders and shake her. 'That stuff is garbage,' I would tell her. 'No one should call that pizza!'

"I have never had pizza this good in my life," I say to the group when I pause eating to breathe.

"The pizza here is fine," Paolo says. "But if you want the best, you have to go down south. Sicilia has the greatest food you will ever eat."

"Oh really? What is the best dish?" I ask.

Paolo waves his hands around as if that's a supremely stupid question because there are so many delicious dishes it would be impossible to decide.

"My grandmother's lasagna," he finally says. "It's a recipe handed down for five generations. When my great-grandparents had to leave their village during World War II, they saved a family photo album and that recipe."

When I ask him to describe it, there are less words and more hand movements. And facial expressions that border on indecent.

I want to wrap Paolo up and send him to California so Maggie can see him.

The way he dresses, the way he talks, the way he moves his hands and eyebrows and shoulders, it's like the country of Italy perfectly embodied in one person.

"How did all of you meet?" I ask.

"Oh, it's been so long, who can say?" Paolo says.

"I can," Diego says. "The first time you met me you told me that my scarf was tied incorrectly."

"Indeed it was," Paolo says. "No thanks needed for helping you out with that issue."

"What you call help, I call public ridicule," Diego says, and I can see that it's still a tender point.

"But look how much better you wear scarves now!" Paolo retorts. "It's what a true friend does."

"It's a true friend when you've known them for more than an hour. It's a pretentious snob when you've known them for less than an hour."

"Hmm, that hour makes a big difference. What if your scarf had been bothering me for more than an hour, but I only mentioned it less than an hour after introducing myself?"

"We met at church," Carmen interjects before Diego's head can explode. "This little church started a program to get young adults into community service. It only lasted two years, but we all kept hanging out together on Mondays and Wednesdays. Before Christie went back home—that was the nanny before you—she made us promise that we would call the new nanny and invite her to hang out with us."

"Did Christie ever mention Isabella, the little girl I'm nannying?" I ask.

Carmen's eyebrows go up, and she flashes Valentina a look. There's an awkward pause.

"Christie said she could be challenging sometimes," Valentina says.

"That child is a monster," Paolo says matter-of-factly. "The last two nannies made that crystal clear."

Well. That is unfortunate news.

"Jake, how did you meet up with this group?" I ask. He looks at me and shakes his head.

"We watched him get robbed," Diego says.

My mouth falls open.

"Our whole group was hanging out on the steps," Carmen says, "and we saw these two little girls distract Jake while a little boy grabbed his wallet from his back pocket."

"Oh no! They took all your money?"

Jake opens his mouth to respond, but Paolo doesn't give him the chance.

"That's the best part!" Paolo says. "Apparently, our man Jake had seen the little hooligans at the edge of the piazza, figured he'd be the most likely target, and stashed his money, ID and credit cards in his backpack before he ever crossed the piazza."

"So, they didn't take your money?" I ask.

Paolo jumps in before Jake can respond. "This guy *left money in his wallet* for those thieving hooligans!"

Jake shrugs. "Kids gotta eat."

"And that is how we met Jake," Diego says.

"That's a great story," I say laughing. "You're a good guy, Jake."

Jake shrugs and smiles at me. I smile back.

It's a little past midnight as we head back to il Duomo and say our goodbyes. The piazza is nearly empty and feels even bigger without all the people.

"I will see you tomorrow, *la mia Dolcetta*," Paolo says before kissing my cheeks. I hold my new nickname tightly in my heart like a happy child who's just been given a balloon.

"Do you know which tram to take home?" Jake asks me.

"The 27."

"Perfect, I'll walk you to your stop."

"You don't have to."

"It's on my way. This way, I can walk you there like a gentleman instead of walking slightly behind you like a stalker."

He offers me his arm and I take it, feeling like a character in a Jane Austen novel. *Or a regular Italian, I guess.*

"So, Carmen says you're a doctor," I say as we traverse the piazza, the cobblestones uneven under our feet.

"I'm not a doctor yet," Jake says. "I just finished my undergrad. I'm doing an internship right now, and I'll start med school next year." We wait for a lone car to pass, then cross the street to my bus stop.

"What kind of work are you doing?" I ask, brushing one of my chunky braids out of my face.

"Almost all research," he says. "And lucky for you, your tram is arriving, and you've just been spared a boring conversation about cancer cells in mice."

"How do you know I would find it boring?" I ask, ignoring the squealing sound of the tram stopping next to us.

"Medical research is boring to pretty much everybody except the people researching it," he says. "And you've already sat through two hours of opera tonight."

"Fair enough," I say. Jake leans in for two quick cheek kisses. Up close, I can see that he has three little freckles just below his bottom lip.

"Good night, Juliet," he says. "Welcome to Italy."

I climb onto the tram feeling all glowy from my first night with my new friends. My brain is trying to remind me of the crucial detail that will spoil tomorrow's shopping trip, but I refuse to let it. *Don't ruin this for me,* I tell my brain. *I'll figure something out tomorrow.* Tonight, I just want to bask in the happiness of delicious pizza and new friends.

The next morning, I wake up, throw some clothes on, and zip to the kitchen. I've discovered that having Isa's bowl, spoon, and cereal ready for her before she comes to the table puts her in a good mood. I think it makes her feel like she has a personal servant. I'm willing to let her think whatever she wants if it decreases the incidents of verbal assault and airborne cutlery.

The Rossis are still sleeping so I eat breakfast as quietly as possible, then sneak out the door. The sun is shining, the cobblestones are cobbling, it's a perfect day to be in Italy.

Now, how to address the glaring obstacle to today's shopping trip? I'm broke. I mean, I have my first week of nanny wages, but based on the three stores I walked through this week, that will buy me half of one sweater.

I start brainstorming plausible excuses for not buying any clothes. None of them are that believable since I'm wearing jeans again today. *Stupid last-night Juliet. Why did she even make these plans?*

When I arrive at il Duomo, Jake is waiting on the piazza steps.

"Buon giorno!" he says.

"Buon giorno!" I say back. "How is your Italian so good?" I've been wondering since last night. Not that I was thinking about Jake much. Just wondering about his Italian.

"We spent a lot of summers in Italy when I was a kid," Jake says. "How about you? Your Italian is great, but you mentioned that this is your first time in Italy."

"My grandparents were Italian. I grew up hearing it. And I took classes in high school and college." I cover my eyes with my hands. "But apparently, it's still not good enough to distinguish an invitation to a rock concert from an invitation to the opera."

"Easy mistake to make," Jake says with an easy smile. "Tell me about the girl you nanny."

"She's six," I say. "She's smart. And she has thirty-seven Barbie dolls. I know because I helped dig each of them out of the bushes after she threw them off the balcony."

"Yikes. Sounds like you've got your hands full."

"Agreed. Tell me about your internship," I say, ready for a new topic.

"I work at the European Institute of Oncology."

"If you're trying to impress me, you'll have to do better than that," I say. "Last year, I worked at Jamba Juice."

It takes Jake a minute to realize I'm joking, and then a smile breaks across his face, transforming it. "Well, I tried to get a sweet Jamba Juice gig, but it was too competitive. I couldn't cut it."

I nod knowingly. "Not everyone is born to blend. Tell me about your second-choice job."

His face lights up as he describes a new way of treating brain tumors, focusing on the genetics of the individual. Cutting edge stuff, led by a brilliant boss.

"That was probably way more than you wanted to know," he says after a few minutes. "I tend to go on and on when it's something I'm excited about. Are you going to school? Tell me about your studies."

"Business," I say.

He waits for me to say more but I don't.

"Sooo...What do you plan to do with that?"

"Run a dry cleaner," I respond.

"Is, um, dry cleaning a passion of yours?" he asks, rubbing the back of his neck.

"Not particularly. But it's the family business."

He opens his mouth, then closes it and nods. It feels like a judgy nod.

"Not everyone has to feel passionate about their work," I say. "Sometimes you just need a good job that pays the bills."

"Sure," he says. But the furrow in his brow makes it clear he doesn't get it. Sure enough, after a second, he says, "But what about—"

"If you tell me to follow my dreams, I will poke you in the eye."

"I wasn't going to say that," he says. It's not convincing.

"Dreams don't pay the rent, Jake. Jobs do. I've already got a job lined up after graduation, and that's more than a lot of people can say."

I'm spared having to explain more by the arrival of Paolo, Carmen and Valentina. We catch a bus and walk a few blocks, then Carmen says, "Welcome to the Saturday market at Sant'Ambrogio."

White tents stretch as far as the eye can see, and under them sit rows of tables piled with shoes, purses, coats, pants, and more. The market is brimming with people and the chatter of vendors hawking their goods.

Carmen spreads her arms wide. "When I die, I imagine heaven will look like this."

At the first table, I pick up a pair of black ankle boots with a pointed toe and a skinny heel. I immediately feel more Italian just holding them. A hand-lettered sign says "Scarpe, 15 Euro." *Can that be right?*

"How much are the shoes?" I ask the man sitting behind the table.

"Americana!" he answers in a loud voice. "For you, only 15 euro!"

Relief and excitement rush through me. I turn and look at Carmen with big eyes.

"It's so cheap!"

"I know!" she squeals. "This is why we come here!"

Today is going to be a good day.

Two hours later, I've collected a pair of black pants, a black skirt, a black shirt that says Dolce and Gabbana (that is definitely *not* Dolce and Gabbana) and black stiletto ankle boots. I've blown through all my money, but I'm on my way to dressing like a real Italian. Isa is going to be thrilled.

Carmen and Paolo offer their fashion opinions, sometimes subtly and sometimes not-so-subtly. Paolo has found a dark gray peacoat and is doing everything in his power to convince Jake to buy one too, but Jake won't budge.

"But it is such a nice coat," Paolo pleads.

"It is," Jake agrees. "And it looks great on you. When you wear that coat, you look like a handsome Italian man. When I wear that coat, I look like a goofy American trying to look like a handsome Italian man."

"It is true, you cannot look as handsome as me, my friend. But you could look a bit better..." Paolo gestures vaguely at Jake's clothes. Valentina gives Paolo a poke in the ribs.

"I love the pants you found," Carmen tells me. "They'll be perfect for dancing on Wednesday."

"Dancing?" I ask.

"Yeah, there's a club that lets foreigners in for free on Wednesdays. We go almost every week. You'll love it."

"Nonsense," Paolo says. "Juliet is way too sophisticated to enjoy a terrible club like Calypso."

Carmen smirks. "Paolo doesn't like going there because he's the only one who has to pay."

"And because the music is awful and the decor tacky. Juliet's going to loathe it."

But Paolo is wrong because when we walk into Calypso five days later, I absolutely love it. A chandelier filled with lights of every color showers the dancers in shimmering rainbows. Black velvet booths and couches line the perimeter. Everyone is good-looking and dances like they're in a music video. It's hands down the coolest place I've ever been. I try to look nonchalant, like I go to places like this all the time, but I can tell I'm not pulling it off.

The air is humid and smells like warm bodies and cologne. I can feel the bass pulsing through me. It's too loud for anyone to talk so we all just dance. Jake dances like a dorky American, but I think he's doing it on purpose, which makes it kind of adorable. Paolo barely moves, he simply sways enough to look elegant and not awkward. Carmen and Valentina and Diego move like they've got the rhythm flowing through their veins. I feel self-conscious for a moment, then the music takes over and I relax.

A salsa song comes on and Diego offers me his hand. I take it and he spins me dramatically. By the third twirl, I'm giggling like a goose. A few songs later, I attempt to teach Paolo, but I keep getting the steps wrong. Paolo pretends to be exasperated, but I don't think he actually minds.

Toward the end of the night, Cotton Eye Joe comes on and Jake and I teach the others the line dance.

"Juliet, look at me," Diego says. "I'm a real American cowboy."

Diego pretends to lasso Paolo, who's sitting this one out. Paolo brushes the imaginary lasso away like it's a piece of lint on his clothing. I'm laughing while trying to keep up with Carmen and Valentina who have added their own twirls, dips, and stomps to the line dance. By the time the song ends, I'm exhausted.

"*That* was a good time," I say, flopping into the chair next to Paolo.

"I especially liked when Diego took off on his own, riding a horse only he could see," Paolo comments.

"Perhaps next time you'll join us," I say.

"Ah, Juliet, you do not know me very well yet."

We watch the others dancing, and I marvel at my good luck falling in with this group.

"Tell me, Dolcetta, what are you doing this Friday evening?" Paolo asks.

I scramble to think up something clever or flirtatious, but nothing comes to mind, so I just answer truthfully. "I have no plans."

"Perfect," he replies. "My boss gave me tickets to the theater. Would you like to accompany me?"

A simple yes would have worked, but like a total dork I blurt, "That sounds fantastic! I'd love to go! What a great idea!"

Paolo's lips quirk in amusement.

We leave Calypso shortly afterward and walk back to il Duomo to catch our buses home. Diego checks his phone and says, "They're showing the new Mission Impossible at Cine Centrale on Friday night. Should we go?"

"Ooh, I love Tom Cruise," Carmen says.

"Those movies are so confusing," Valentina says. "But yeah, I'll go."

"Ethan Hunt is the best!" Jake says. "Count me in."

Diego looks at me, and I realize I should've been thinking up something to say. I hesitate and Paolo says, "Juliet and I have plans that evening." His smile is smug.

There's an awkward pause, and then Jake says, "So what time does it start? Should we meet at Duomo first?"

They get into the details of purchasing tickets, and I studiously refuse to make eye contact with anyone. My cheeks heat, and I feel embarrassed for feeling embarrassed. *Is that even a thing?*

The boys get into a heated discussion over who would win in a fight, Ethan Hunt or Jason Bourne.

Carmen slows down, waits until they're out of hearing range, and then says, "So, you're going out with Paolo?" She raises an eyebrow. Valentina drops back to join our conversation.

"I am," I say with an attempt at a casual shoulder shrug.

"So do you *liiiike* him?" Carmen asks in a sing-song voice.

"I'm not answering that because we're not in the seventh grade," I reply. I clear my throat. "I will say that Paolo is funny and good-looking, and I'm looking forward to Friday."

"As well you should," Valentina says. "You're in Italy. You should definitely go on dates with good-looking Italian men."

"Paolo, you are good looking," Carmen says in English with a terrible American accent.

"You have a terrible American accent," I tell her, smiling.

"But am I good looking?" she asks in English again. She is giggling now so it sounds like "Ama goot looky?"

"You are," I tell her, giggling myself. "Very goot looky."

"You are both loonies," Valentina says, shaking her head.

On the tram home, I text Maggie.

> Guess who just spent a night dancing at the coolest club in the world and has a hot date with a gorgeous Italian guy on Friday? Me! I am that person!

Her reply comes as I'm climbing into bed:

> You are living a dream life!

She's not wrong.

Chapter Three

"I would not do that ridiculous handshake if they begged me!" Isa declares Friday afternoon. She stomps her feet on the crowded sidewalk outside her school.

I nod as though I have any idea what she's talking about.

"They do it ALL THE TIME," she continues. "It's not even that cool!"

I don't know who "they" are, but I get the feeling that's irrelevant. I take her hand and lead her through the crowded sidewalk toward home.

"Handshakes are supposed to be cool," I confirm.

Isa scowls at me. "What would you know about it?"

"I happen to know the greatest secret handshake ever created."

She stops and folds her arms across her chest. "Prove it."

We step off the sidewalk into the grass, so we don't hold up traffic, and I teach her the handshake I learned at gymnastics camp when I was thirteen. It has hand slapping, elbow bumps, toe taps and finger links. It's legitimately awesome, and we practice it all the way home. By the time we take the elevator up, she's actually smiling.

"Why do you keep tapping your hands like that?" she asks.

I look down and see my fingers beating against my thighs. I clasp them together to make them stop. "Sorry. I've got a date tonight, and I'm nervous. What do people wear to the theater?"

"Evening gowns."

"Hmm," I start tapping again. "I don't have an evening gown."

"Don't worry. I'll help you find the perfect outfit," Isa promises.

Once inside she heads straight to my closet, dropping her backpack on my unmade bed.

"Show me your dresses," she demands.

On the one hand, Isa recently learned to tie her shoes, and it feels ridiculous to take fashion advice from her, no matter who her father is. On the other hand, I've never been great with clothes, and Isa does seem like she knows a lot.

I pull out a yellow sundress with navy polka dots.

"Nope. What else do you have?" she asks with an imperious tilt of her chin.

I shake my head. "I have one other dress that I wore to my Aunt Marla's funeral, but it's terrible. My mom made me bring it in case I went somewhere fancy."

Isa giggles, apparently delighted that I have a mom who bosses me around. Her smiling stops when I pull out a plum dress with a high neckline and a pleated skirt.

We both stare at it for a moment of tragic silence.

"Do you have a fancy skirt?" Isa asks hopefully. "That you could wear with a fancy top?"

I shake my head. "I have neither of those things. I have a denim mini skirt."

"Is that the only skirt you have?" Isa asks.

"Yes," I mumble.

Isa starts rummaging through my closet muttering something about "looking like a farmer at the theater."

A farmer? Really?

I hear a muffled "Hey!" and then she comes out waving something on a hanger.

It's a full-length romper made from silky black material.

"What about this?" she demands, like I've been holding out on her.

"You asked about dresses!" I say. "And also, I forgot about it."

"It still has the tags on."

"Yeah, my friend Maggie bought it for my birthday last year, but I never had anywhere to wear it. I threw it in just in case. I haven't even tried it on. "

It takes me and Isa a minute to figure out how to actually get into this thing. Isa spots a tiny zipper up one side, and I wiggle in and zip it up. The length is perfect, just skimming my feet, and it's snug but not too tight in the bum and thighs.

"I think everything fits okay except the straps," I say to Isa who is leaping from foot to foot with excitement.

"It looks really nice on you!" She doesn't try to hide the shock in her voice, and I choose not to be offended by it.

"Also, the straps are like my mom's blue pantsuit. They go like this."

She adjusts them so they're sitting off my shoulders.

Wow. I am an idiot.

I check myself out in the mirror. The cut is flattering, and the style makes me look older than twenty, which I appreciate.

Isa hands me my black heels.

I slip them on and do my best runway model walk. Isa giggles.

"Is that what you think runway models walk like?"

"Yes," I say with a serious face. I add in some dramatic hip shimmies, and Isa falls over laughing.

"*Mama*! Come look at Juliet!" Isa hollers, still giggling.

There's a timid knock on my door and Sofia peaks her head in. "Wow, you look very nice," she says.

"Thank you," Isa and I say at the same time.

"*I* chose her outfit," Isa tells Sofia. "She's going on a date tonight. To the theater. With an attractive man."

She pauses and looks at me. "He *is* attractive, right?"

"Very," I confirm.

"Now let's put on all your jewelry!" Isa says, already rummaging through my closet.

"Oh. I don't really have any jewelry," I tell her.

Her face looks like I've just told her I don't really have fingers.

"I think I have just the thing," Sofia says.

I start to protest, but she's already gone. She comes back a minute later carrying a diamond necklace. Each stone is the size of a plump blueberry and I take two steps back.

Sofia sees my expression and laughs. "It's not real. It's just costume jewelry. Inexpensive."

She puts it around my neck and fastens it.

I looked good before, but now I look stunning.

"Wow," I say. "Thank you, Sofia. I'll take good care of it."

"I'm sure you will," Sofia says with a smile. "But it's not anything to worry about. Marco used it for a runway show last year and it's been sitting in a drawer ever since."

My jaw drops. "This was in a runway show? Worn by a real supermodel?"

Sofia smiles. "We just call them models over here. But yeah, one of the girls wore it with a swimsuit I think. That show had some eclectic combinations."

Sofia heads back to the kitchen, and Isa starts pulling at my hair.

"You should definitely wear it down," she says.

"I thought up might look fancier," I say.

"Your hair is the prettiest thing you have," she says, like she's explaining it to a toddler. "Keep it down all flowy, so he'll want to touch it."

This child is brilliant. I wonder how much time she's spent chatting with Marco's models.

"Isa, I'm terrified for when you start dating. Those boys don't stand a chance."

Isa nods in agreement.

The buzzer rings at 6:58 p.m., and I take the elevator down. I wipe my sweaty hands on my thighs and take a breath.

Paolo sees me through the glass door, and his mouth falls open. By the time I make it over to him, he's rearranged his expression into something more casual. But I know what I saw.

"*Buona sera*," he says. "Don't you look like a tempting treat."

I give him a big smile. "*Buona sera*, Paolo," I say. "You look very handsome yourself."

He's wearing a sharply tailored charcoal suit and a crimson tie. Will it be weird if I take a selfie with him to send to Maggie? He is hands down the best-looking guy I've ever gone out with.

His car is clean and smells like expensive cologne.

"So, is Italy living up to your expectations so far?" Paolo asks as he pulls out of the tiny parking lot.

"It's exceeding all my expectations," I reply. "My grandparents told me stories, but I was not prepared for how amazing this country is."

"Shame you didn't come last month," Paolo says. "We took a group trip to Florence. Now *that* is a beautiful city."

"That's in Tuscany, right?"

"Correct. We rented some of those bikes for tourists because Diego wanted to 'ride through the hills of Tuscany,'" Paolo says this like he's reading from a travel brochure. "Valentina didn't know how to ride a bike, but didn't tell us, because she didn't want to feel stupid and just pretended she knew what she was doing. She fell over a lot."

It's hard to imagine someone as lovely and graceful as Valentina falling off a bike. As Paolo talks, I keep my eyes on his face so I don't watch his driving.

"So, what's your story, Juliet?" he asks. "What brings you to Italy?"

"I'm a nanny."

He smiles. "I know that. I'm asking *why* you came to Italy as a nanny."

"To escape," I say accidentally.

Paolo raises an eyebrow. "What terrible things are you escaping?"

I sigh. "Business classes. And my future."

Paolo nods like he knows just what I'm talking about. "I've found that the best way to stop worrying about the future is to distract yourself with all the pleasure you can get in the present."

He gives me a smile, and I smile back. *That sounds like a very good plan.*

He parks his car in a spot barely big enough for a scooter, then opens my door and we cross the street to the theater.

Lanterns on tall hooks line the perimeter, making the stone building glow. We walk toward a line of elegantly dressed people, and I bring a hand to my giant necklace and stand up straighter. Once inside, Paolo leads me up three flights of stairs to a balcony suite with a center view of the stage. The theater is small, but a soaring ceiling makes the space feel grandiose. A large chandelier hangs above rows of red velvet seats.

"We have this whole space to ourselves?" I whisper. It comes out more suggestive than I mean.

"We do," Paolo says smiling. "It's a company suite. We take clients out sometimes, if we're trying to close a big deal."

The whole thing is so fancy and elegant, I give up on playing it cool and just gush.

"This is dazzling. I'm dazzled."

Paolo smiles, pleased. "Then my mission is accomplished."

The lights go out, and we settle into our seats. The pit orchestra starts a rousing opening song, and the curtain lifts to reveal a lovely setting in the park. We see a beautiful young woman sitting on a bench reading a book. She turns the pages, oblivious to the man staring at her from three benches over. Finally, he gets up and walks toward her on a cobblestone path. The music swells as he bursts into song. He says he thinks she's pretty, and he wonders what she ate for lunch. *Wait, I don't think that's right...*

"Paolo," I whisper, leaning toward him. "What did he say?"

"He said he thinks she's pretty and wonders if she is free for lunch," he whispers back.

"Thanks," I lean back in my seat.

The man and the woman are standing now, and she starts singing. Her voice is high and loud. She says she would love to go to lunch with him, but first she has to get her teeth checked. *Hmm. That seems weird.*

The two walk down the cobblestone path, singing a lovely duet. The song finishes and they climb into the gondola of a Ferris wheel.

The young man leans in and brushes some hair away from her face. Then he starts to sing about how all his life he's dreamed of finding the right cheese. She's nodding her head like she's had the same problem. I think I've missed something.

"Paolo," I whisper again. "Why has he been searching for cheese his whole life?"

Paolo, who has just taken a sip of water, snorts half of it out of his nose. There's a lot of coughing and sniffing mixed with laughter.

"Not *formaggio*," he says. "*Por algo*. He hasn't been searching for cheese his whole life, he's been searching for something his whole life." He narrows his eyes. "You're not understanding much of this are you?"

I think about faking it, but instead say, "Nope."

"Okay," he says, smiling and leaning in. "Let me tell you what is happening so far."

We spend the rest of the play this way, leaning close and whispering back and forth. It should feel romantic, but instead, it feels like girls camp when the counselors turned the lights off and me and Maggie stay up talking. It feels like friendship, in the best way. By the time the lights come up, something easy and wonderful has settled into place between us.

Paolo takes me by the arm and escorts me to his car. A September moon hangs low and bright in the sky and the air is just starting to smell like fall. The trip home goes by too quickly and when Paolo turns the car off, instead of getting out, I say, "Tell me about all the great things to do in Milan."

"Well, there's some good shopping, as you've seen," Paolo says. "Eating is a favorite pastime in this city. There are art museums and lovely parks. Two weekends ago, Carmen dragged us to some hiking trails outside the city."

I can't picture Paolo hiking. "How was that?"

"Not my favorite," he says. "But sometimes you just go along with the group. They love hiking. Valentina had on these big old hiking boots and a truly terrible hat."

I think about when Paolo mentioned Valentina on her bike. I try to remember Paolo interacting with her at the opera and Calypso. My gut is filling in some gaps.

"So you're in love with Valentina, huh?"

Paolo's eyes go wide, and his body goes still. "What? No, I'm not. That's crazy."

"How long?" I ask.

There's a pause. "A year." He sighs. "But it feels like a lifetime."

"Did you ask me on this date to make her jealous?" I ask, turning to face him squarely.

"No, I truly wanted to get to know you," he says.

I give him a look.

"I *announced* we were going on a date to make Valentina jealous. That's just taking advantage of the good timing."

I groan and elbow him in the ribs. "Paolo!"

"I've been in love with the same girl for a year, to no avail! When a lovely American distraction comes strolling into my life, of course I'm going to ask her out."

I make a harrumph sound.

"Are you saying you wish I hadn't asked you out?" he asks.

"No," I concede. "I had a wonderful time."

"Like a great time with your best pal?" he asks. His eyes lock on mine like he already knows the answer.

I pause. "Yes," I finally admit.

Now it's Paolo's turn to groan. "I knew it."

"Sorry," I tell him. "You remind me of my best friend Maggie from home."

"Oh, does she pick you up in an Armani suit and take you to a private suite at the theater?" he asks, waving his arms a bit.

"No," I say. "She does not. But she makes me laugh, and she's easy to talk to, and she makes me feel like I can be myself."

"Fine," Paolo says with a huff. "You and I will be friends, and I will remain hopelessly in love with Valentina."

"Maybe things with Valentina aren't hopeless," I say. "Does she have any idea how you feel?"

"No. Probably. I don't know! She's an enigma wrapped in a puzzle surrounded by mystery." He sighs again. "My attempts at wooing her have been wildly unsuccessful."

"What have you tried?" I ask.

"Okay, so far, I've tried nothing. Because I'm a coward."

"You're a very good-looking coward, if that helps," I say.

Paolo's hand goes to his hair. "It does. Thank you."

"Well, I can't make you do anything you don't want to. But as your new *best friend*, I advise you to ask her out."

"I think I may regret becoming best friends with you," he grumbles.

"Too late!" I say, "It's already done, no take backs."

Paolo walks me to my door and kisses me on the cheek.

"Thank you for a lovely evening, Juliet," he says.

"Right back at you, Bestie," I say.

Paolo shakes his head and turns around. "You are definitely not calling me that."

"Too much?" I ask.

"Way too much," he says.

I ride the elevator up to my apartment, humming the whole time. This date did not go the way I thought it would. It went even better.

Chapter Four

Carmen's text message has more smoochy face emojis than actual words.

> How was the big date?! I'm dying to hear all the details!!! 😘😘😘😘😘😘😘😘

It's Sunday afternoon, and I'm painting Isa toes while she sits perched on the coffee table.

"Don't move," I tell Isa. "They're still wet." The last thing I need is blue nail polish on the gorgeous red couch.

I reply to Carmen.

> Amazing. Probably the best date I've ever been on. I'll tell you more in person.

I'll make it clear to Carmen and Valentina that Paolo and I are just friends. And see if Valentina might be interested.

I switch to Isa's other foot and my phone chimes again. This time it's Jake. He must have gotten my number from Carmen.

BETTER THAN GELATO 35

> Ciao Juliet, it's Jake. I just found out that tomorrow is a holiday, and I have the day off. I was planning on visiting Castello Sforzesco. Would you like to join me?

A castle! That could be fun. I remember Jake's smile when he line danced on Wednesday night. *Hmm, this could be really fun.* I text him back.

> Hey Jake! I would be delighted to join you! Where should I meet you and what time?

I debate deleting the second exclamation point, but decide it looks too formal without it.

> Great! Does Duomo at 10:00 a.m. work for you?

I reply and let him know that works just fine. No exclamation points.

"Who are you texting?" Isa asks. Because of course my business is her business.

"Just a friend," I say. "We're going to explore a castle."

"Oooooh," Isa says. "Is it the boy you went out with last night? I knew that was a great outfit."

"Um, no," I say, and I feel my neck get warm. "This is a different guy."

"Wow. The last nanny never went on dates," she says. She thinks a minute. "Probably because she never let me choose her clothes."

That night, Sofia teaches me how to make chicken marsala.

"Marco is the cook in the family," Sofia says. "But he travels so much for work, I've had to learn a few meals."

Isa doesn't offer to help in any way, but she stays in the kitchen, and she doesn't throw anything, so that's nice.

We sit at the tiny kitchen table and dig into mushroom-filled heaven. Sofia's phone rings as we're finishing, and she takes the call in her bedroom. I savor my last delicious bite, then make a sink of hot soapy water and load the dishes in. Isa is rearranging magnets on the fridge, and I toss her a dish towel.

"Here, you can dry," I say.

"What? Why?" she responds, but I pretend I don't hear her and hand her a clean wet plate.

"Just dry it off with the towel and put it back in the cupboard. That way, your mom won't have to do it."

Isa has the puzzled look of someone who has never considered doing something for her mom. I keep washing the dishes and stacking the clean wet ones on the counter in front of her. Eventually, she picks up a plate and starts to dry it.

"So," I say. "If you could fly or be invisible, which would you choose?"

She puts the plate in the cupboard and starts on a glass. "Hmm. Could I choose when I got to be invisible?"

"Yes."

"I choose that one," she says.

"What would you do with that power?" I ask.

"Play pranks on people."

I nod, unsurprised. I finish the dishes and start on the pots and pans. "Okay, if you could only eat one food every day for a month, what would it be?"

"Pizza," she answers right away.

"Solid choice."

By the time Sofia comes into the kitchen, we've answered three more questions and put away all the dishes.

"*Tesoro*, Daddy is on the phone and wants to talk to you. Do you want to talk to him?"

Isa pretends she doesn't hear her mom.

"He misses you so much, *Topino*. I know he'd love to talk to you."

I pretend I'm not overhearing this conversation, which is comical because the kitchen is about eight square feet. I get a washcloth and wipe the table. I don't look at Isa, but out of the corner of my eye, I see her look over at me.

"Okay," she says with a martyred sigh. "I'll talk to him."

Sofia hands Isa the phone and leads her into the living room.

I head to my room and see a text from Maggie.

> Great friends?! Are you kidding me?! I had such high hopes for Paolo! Well, I suppose you know best. But sheesh! What a letdown.

BETTER THAN GELATO

37

I show up twenty minutes early for my date with Jake. We're meeting at Piazza Duomo, and I've been dying to take some pictures of this place. It's an overcast day, which makes photographing much easier. But still, it's hard to capture the scale of everything. I take shots of the main square, but you can't tell it's the size of a football field. I do close-ups of some of the ornate stonework and statues on the cathedral itself, but I can't manage to get the whole building. I take a step back. Then another. Then another, and I bump into someone behind me. I shriek and jump a foot in the air.

"Hey, Juliet, it's just me. Sorry." Jake puts a hand on my arm and smiles.

"No, not your fault," I say. "It's me, I just lost track of...other people. When did you get here?"

"Few minutes ago," he says. "I didn't want to interrupt. It looked like you were in the zone." He wipes his hands on his jeans, and I wonder if he gets sweaty hands too.

He holds out a white pastry bag. "I discovered this bakery by my apartment, and I can't get enough of their croissants. I thought you might like one."

Starting a date with a gift of food. That's a solid move.

"Thank you," I say, and take a bite. It's warm and flaky and melts in my mouth. "Wow. I need the name of this bakery and their hours of operation please."

Jake smiles at my enthusiasm and his dimples come out. I have the irrational impulse to touch one.

"That's a serious camera you have there." He points at the camera in my hand.

"Yeah, I'm having trouble capturing how awesome everything is. But also I can't stop trying. It's just so beautiful."

"Well, if you like beautiful old buildings, you're going to love this castle."

"Oh yeah?"

"Absolutely. For a while, it was the largest castle in Europe. It's more than 600 years old, but it's in really good shape. The walls are twenty feet thick. And its turrets are almost completely intact."

Jake's eyes sparkle and his words come out faster.

This guy is kind of adorable.

The castle is a short walk from the Piazza Duomo, and even with Jake's description, I'm blown away by how big it is. It looks medieval, but so well preserved I imagine a whole royal family still living there, oblivious to the crazy city built up around them. I leave the path and go right up to the castle wall and put my hands on the cold stone blocks. It feels 600 years old. I can tell this is going to be one of my favorite places in Milan.

I take my camera out and adjust the settings. I take closeups of the fresh green ivy crawling up the old brown walls. I zoom out and get some shots of the turrets, with the Milan skyline barely visible in the background.

We go back to the path and stroll around the outside of the castle. There's a silence between us, but it's a nice one.

"Do you want to hear some great news?" Jake asks after a minute.

"Yes, I love good news." I turn toward him, but he's looking down at the path.

"Even if it's a little bit braggy?" he asks.

"Especially if it's braggy," I encourage.

"Okay. I'm heading back to the US in a few weeks to do med school interviews, and I found out last night I got an interview with Harvard." He finally glances over to me, his smile both embarrassed and proud.

"Harvard?" I yell. "That's amazing!" I give a smack on his shoulder.

"Thanks. I mean, it's still a long shot. They only accept a small fraction of the people they interview." He jams his hands in his pockets.

"Well, no reason you can't be part of that fraction," I say.

I try to sound casual, like a lot of my friends interview at Harvard, but they don't. And despite Jake's boy-next-door vibes, I can't help but feel intimidated.

We make it to the entrance of the castle where a large sign blocks the door. *Chiuso.*

"It's closed?" I say.

"Oh man," Jake says. "Probably for the holiday. I should have thought of that. I'm so sorry."

"It's no big deal," I say. "And I'm sure Harvard accepts people who make those kinds of mistakes all the time."

Jake's eyes go big. "Whoa. You really went there, huh?"

BETTER THAN GELATO

"Sorry, couldn't help it," I smile. His eyes look legitimately worried, like Harvard might hear about this, and I laugh. "I'm just teasing, Jake."

"Well, I'm sorry all the same. Can I buy you lunch to make up for it?" I hear what he's really asking. *Would you like to keep spending time together?*

"Sure," I say. "Do you mind if I take a couple more photos first?"

There's a small pond snuggled next to the castle on one side lined by willow trees. I can see part of the reflection in the pond, and I want to see more, but there's a tree branch ruining the shot. I try different angles, but I can't quite get it. I'm too low, and the branch blocking it is too big. I'd have to wade out into the water to clear it, and it's way too cold for that. I look up at the branches above me. *They look pretty sturdy.*

"Hey Jake, could you do me a favor?"

"Sure, what do you need?"

"It's actually three favors. I need you to boost me up, hand me the camera, and then stand guard."

Jake opens his mouth, pauses and closes it again. "Okay," he finally says.

I lay the camera on a bench nearby. Then Jake boosts me up to the lowest branch. When I'm good and secure he hands me the camera, and I loop the strap around my neck. He stands guard, but there's really no one around. I make my way toward the end of the branch until I'm hanging over the water. I look through the lens, and my shot is perfect. I can see the old stone tower reflected in the still surface of the pond, framed nicely by tree branches. I take picture after picture and when I'm satisfied I've got it, I climb back to the trunk and drop down.

"How'd you do?" Jake asks. He picks a couple of leaves from my hair and pulls a piece of bark from my sweater.

"I got it!" I say proudly, and even on the tiny screen we can see what a cool photo it is.

We find a seafood restaurant with a view of Castello Sforzesco, and I devour a risotto filled with shrimp, clams, and scallops cooked in a white wine sauce. It tastes like summer at the beach. I don't realize I'm making little noises until I see Jake smiling.

"It's really good," I say defensively.

"I'm sure it is." His eyes are still smiling at me.

I keep eating but try to do it more quietly.

"On a scale of 1-10," I say, when I've finished, "how nervous are you about med school interviews?"

"13," he says. "Especially Harvard. They're known for their tricky interview questions."

"Really? Like what?"

"Here's one I read online last night. 'If you were given the task of moving Mount Fuji to Texas, how would you do it?'"

"Wait, how would you relocate a gigantic volcano? What possible answer could they want?"

"That's why it's been haunting me," Jake says. "But I think I've settled on my answer. Ask me the question like you're a Harvard interviewer."

I sit up tall in my seat and straighten my shoulders. "Good afternoon Mr. Fields," I say in my best snobby accent. "We have some urgent questions to ask you so we can determine if you are brilliant enough to come to our school. The health of the entire planet depends on you relocating Mount Fuji from Japan to Texas. How will you accomplish this task?"

"Well, that's a great question," Jake begins. "I'm glad you asked. For a challenge like this, I would rely on relationships I've cultivated with the extra-terrestrial community. I believe that coordinating efforts with this group will allow us to take advantage of their superior technology and accomplish this task. A joint project such as this would not only help us achieve our goal but also strengthen ties with this often-overlooked population."

I burst out laughing. "Aliens? Working with aliens is your answer?"

Jake breaks character and smiles triumphantly. "Yeah, I thought it was pretty good."

"It's the best answer they will get all day," I tell him.

After lunch we find a little lake that rents paddle boats. Jake pays the man in the booth, and we paddle to the middle of the lake and float. The trees block the sounds of the city, and it feels like we're in the countryside. I stretch my arms out and take a deep breath. There's a strong smell of wet dirt and moss. It sounds terrible, I know. It isn't.

The morning clouds have disappeared, and a hot sun beats down on our arms and necks. After a few minutes we move to the bench in the back under the umbrella. The bench is narrower than the seats, definitely designed for children. Jake's leg is pressed against mine from hip to knee. It sounds harmless, I know. It isn't.

My heart rate speeds up and my hands start to sweat. Jake's looking out at the water, and his head is turned so I can't see his mouth, but I can tell from the dimple in his cheek that he's smiling.

"So did you always want to be a doctor?" I ask, mostly to break the tension.

"Yep. Both my parents are doctors. It was always just a question of what kind of medicine I wanted to practice." He swirls his hand in the water, and I watch the ripples fan out. He turns and looks at me. "Did you always want to run a dry cleaner?" he asks.

"My family has run that place for twenty years," I say, tapping my feet on the back of the boat. "Some of my earliest memories are sitting on the counter by my dad, watching the suits and dresses slide by, smelling the starch and warm plastic."

"That was a really good job of not answering the question," Jake replies. "What do you actually want to do after college?"

I give my shoulders a little shrug, but he's not buying it. His eyes lock onto mine with an intensity at odds with his whole 'boy scout' vibe.

"I don't know you well," he says, "but you strike me as someone who knows what she wants. So let's hear it."

I pause a beat. "Photography."

"There we go." He shifts on the bench so he's facing me. "I'm not a photography expert, and I've seen exactly one photo you've taken. But I just watched you lose all track of time and space as you photographed Piazza Duomo and climb a tree in the middle of a public park to get the perfect picture. So I'd say it's something that's a big deal to you. Why not be a photographer?"

"There are just some other things to consider." I dip my hand into the water. It's cold, but it feels good with the sun. "So, how many siblings do you have?" I ask.

"One sister, two years younger," he says. "*What* other things to consider?"

I pull my hand out of the water and sprinkle little droplets onto my leg. Clearly he's not going to let this go. "Financial things. Family things."

His face still looks puzzled, so I lay it all out for him.

"Do I want to spend the rest of my life running a dry-cleaning business in the small town I spent a decade dreaming of escaping? No. Would I rather explore the world and photograph every inch of it? Yes, very much. Can I crush my dad's hope of having one of his kids take over the family business? No, I cannot. If you knew my dad, you'd understand. This year is a 'last hurrah' before I embrace my fate and become a real grown up."

"I see." His eyebrows are creased, and his dimples have gone dormant. "Why not have one of your siblings take over? Why does it have to be you?"

I shrug. "My two older brothers are both in the military. My two older sisters have kids. I'm the youngest, but I'm the first one in my family to go to college. I'm not going to waste that by studying something impractical like photography. Not when I can graduate with a business degree and run the business that supports my family."

Jake shakes his head. "It doesn't seem fair, that you don't get to follow your dreams."

I sigh. "I know it seems that way from the outside. But it *is* fair. My parents have sacrificed everything for our family. This is the least I can do. For me to graduate from college and then not come back and help, now *that* would be unfair. And it would break my dad's heart."

To my complete mortification, my voice breaks on the last word. This is more than I normally share on a first date. It's more than I share on any date. *Pull it together, Evans.*

I clear my throat. "So yeah, that's the plan."

"Well, my sister's plan is to scrap college and marry rich," Jake says. I can tell he's trying to lighten the mood, and I appreciate it. "You could always give that a try."

I smile. "Marriage isn't part of my plans for the near future."

"No?"

"No."

I think he's going push for more info, but instead he says, "Tell me about that tiny thug you nanny. Did she throw any more barbies off the balcony?"

"This week seemed better," I respond. "But she may be lulling me into a false sense of security before the real shenanigans start. It seems like something she would do."

We spend a long time in that little boat in the middle of the lake. We talk

BETTER THAN GELATO 43

about books. He likes detective mysteries with logical clues you can piece together to crack the case. I like fantasy novels where anything can happen, and I never see the ending coming. We talk about music. We both like the old stuff our parents listened to. We ask each other serious questions and silly questions. I feel myself liking him more with each answer he shares.

"What a delightful lake," I say after we've returned our boat.

"The chef at the restaurant recommended it," Jake says.

"Really? That seems funny."

"While you were in the bathroom, I told him I was trying to woo a lovely young woman and asked where I should take her next."

I stop walking. "You did not!"

"I did," Jake says with an open and honest smile. "He was very helpful. Told me about the lake and gave me some advice about mothers-in-law."

We walk a little while in silence.

"So, you're wooing me?" I ask and glance over at him. His eyes seem to catch the last rays of the setting sun. The medium brown of early morning has turned into warm honey.

"Yes, I am," he says. "How am I doing?"

"Terrible," I say, trying to scowl. But my mouth curls into a smile giving me away, and Jake sees and smiles too.

Honestly, the whole day has been lovely. I haven't felt this kind of chemistry and connection with a guy in a long time. Maybe ever. And I like his whole approach, it's straightforward, but not aggressive or uncomfortable.

"Are you ready for some dinner?" Jake asks.

"Honestly, I'm still full from lunch. But I am kind of chilly." The temperature's dropped considerably since the sun set. "Should we grab some hot chocolate? I've heard it's pretty good here."

Jake stops walking. "You haven't tried the hot chocolate yet?" The horror on his face is comical.

We walk ten blocks to Jake's favorite cafe, and he orders for both of us while I grab a table by the window.

"Prepare yourself," he says, dramatically placing my cup in front of me. "One sip will make you want to sell all your earthly possessions and spend the money on hot chocolate."

I pick up my glass. It's the size of a shot glass and filled with a thick liquid sprinkled with shaved chocolate bits. I take a sip. It's thick and warm and dark, but not bitter with a touch of vanilla and maybe cinnamon. I can feel the sweet warmth all the way down my throat.

I put my glass down and Jake is watching me like I'm a movie.

"It's okay," I say. "I mean, it's no Swiss Miss, but it's fine."

He shakes his head before I even finish talking.

"Nope. I don't buy it. You are amazed right now. I know you are."

I break into a smile. "I am amazed. This is incredibly good." I take another sip and feel the heat and sweetness spread through my whole body.

"I knew it. I knew you would be." His smile is so big and...genuine. Like it really makes him happy that I'm enjoying this hot cocoa.

It's dark when he walks me to the bus stop and the streetlamps cast shadows on the deserted cobblestone street. The city lights are too bright to see stars, but a bright moon shines, full and content.

"You're humming," Jake says.

"Am I?" I ask.

He nods. "I know that song. That's Moondance."

He sings the opening line and then softly takes my hand and pulls me in for a slow dance. I forget to breathe as his arm wraps around my lower back. My heart is hammering, and I'm sure he can feel it. I force myself to take a deep inhale and let it out slowly. His scent, cold lake in a pine forest, makes me lean closer, until I can feel the heat of his skin through his shirt. My body relaxes into his.

His voice is sweet and low, and his breath grazes my neck as he sings. Slow dancing in the middle of the street is not something I do back home. But everything feels different here. Jake sings until the very last line and then hums the last notes. When he lets me go, my body feels cold all the places it was touching his.

"Thanks for the dance," he says softly.

"You're welcome," I say softly.

Behind him, the 27 tram pulls up to the curb.

"*Buonanotte,* Juliet," Jake says. He leans in and gives me the softest kisses on both cheeks, sending tingles down my skin like the ripples on the lake.

I climb onto the bus and look at him out the window. *Oh man. I am in trouble.*

"Mags!" I practically yell into the phone. "It's me! Your bestie!" I'm snuggled into my bed on Tuesday afternoon bursting with excitement to talk to Maggie.

"Juls?" There are some muffled shuffling sounds, then she comes back on the line louder.

"It's me! What are you doing?" I ask.

"Well, it's 1:30 a.m. So I was, you know, sleeping." *Oh yep, that is definitely her middle-of-the-night voice.*

"Oh geez. I'm so sorry. On a scale of one to ten, how much do you need sleep right now?"

"Zero," she says immediately. "I need zero sleep. Tell me how you're doing."

"I went on the most amazing date yesterday, and I need to tell you all about it," I say.

"Yes! Fill me in. How is Paolo?"

"Oh. Um, it wasn't a date with Paolo." I climb out of bed, suddenly feeling too amped to lay there.

"Not with Paolo. Okay, fill me in a lot."

"Paolo and I are just friends, remember?" I start hanging the pile of clean clothes that have been sitting on my bed for a day. "This date was with Jake." Just saying his name makes me smile.

"Jake. Wait. Isn't he the American one?"

"Yes, he is but—"

"You turned down the sexy Italian, and you're dating the American?" The incredulity in her voice comes across all the way from California.

"I'm not dating him," I clarify. "This was our first date. And he is American, but also, he's kind of great."

"So is McDonald's. But you don't eat there when you're in Rome."

I make a growling noise I think she can't hear, but she does because she says, "Alright, I'll reserve judgment until I hear the whole story."

I tell her everything starting with his text on Sunday night and ending with his soft cheek kisses on Monday evening.

"Well, I'm really excited for you," she says. But it sounds more dutiful than genuine.

"Thanks," I say. "I mean, I'm not like planning on dating him seriously or making this a big thing..."

"Of course you won't date him seriously. It's you." Maggie laughs. "I just think it's funny that you move to an exotic country filled with gorgeous men and then find the only American within a hundred miles to date."

Well, it sounds real stupid when you put it like that. I make an angry noise.

"You're making your mad beaver sound again," Maggie says. "I can hear it. Look, I'm sorry. I'm being lame. It's the middle of the night, I don't even have my head on straight. You meet a great guy, you have fun together, that's great news. Maybe this one will even make it past the three-month mark."

"Maybe," I say. But just thinking about it makes me anxious.

Maggie tells me about all our friends back in Cali, and I crawl back into bed and let waves of homesickness wash over me. "I better let you get some sleep," I finally say.

"Yeah, I do have a chem exam today," she says.

"Good luck."

"And hey, I'm sorry about before. Do whatever you want with your last hurrah. I just want you to be happy."

"Thanks," I say. "Love you for life."

"Love you for life," she repeats.

I shower to wash off the homesickness and think about what Maggie said. She's right, dating Jake is ridiculous. Sure, he's sweet and smart and smells amazing, but I'm not going to seriously date him. Yesterday was a fluke, a combination of a romantic setting and delicious food. This is my hurrah year, I'm not going to waste it on Jake. I'll make it clear tomorrow night at Calypso that I'm only interested in being friends.

Chapter Five

Isa is on the rampage again.

"I want that toy!" she yells, stomping around the living room and pointing at the TV where a neon-clad girl plays with a flying unicorn.

"Of course my sweet cabbage," Sofia says. "You have that toy. I bought it for you."

"Well, where is it?" Isa demands.

"I'll go get it from your room," Sofia says and scurries down the hall.

Isa picks up the remote and turns up the volume on the TV until the frenetic sounds of Fiona the Magic Unicorn fill the living room. Marco is home tonight and looks like he wishes he wasn't.

"Isa, why don't we turn the volume down just a little?" he asks. He takes a step toward Isa, but she gives him a look of such rage that he takes two steps back.

I watch the whole scene from the kitchen, out of Isa's view. Does hiding in the kitchen make me a coward? Maybe. Would I rather be a coward than a victim of that child's death glare? Definitely.

Sofia comes back to the living room empty-handed. I can't hear what she says because the commercial is too loud, but Isa shrieks "You can't find it?!"

Probably because your room looks like a hurricane hit every toy store in the country and dumped the debris on your floor, I silently tell Isa.

The shrieking continues so I devise a plan and sneak out of the kitchen to my room. It's too early to leave for Calypso, but I put on a pair of sweatpants, my sneakers, and my favorite 49ers T-shirt. It has a bluish stain on one shoulder, but it's so comfortable I'll never get rid of it. I grab my purse and head out to the living room where Isa has pulled all the cushions off the couch. But she didn't throw them off the balcony, so that's something to feel good about.

"Have a good night guys," I call, breezing past them to the door. "I'm heading out."

Isa stops screaming and looks at me. "Where are you going?" she demands.

"I'm going dancing with some friends."

She gives my outfit a once-over. "You've got to be kidding me."

She looks so appalled I nearly start giggling, but I keep a straight face and shake my head.

"You can't wear that," she says.

I shrug like it doesn't matter to me either way. "Okay, what should I wear?"

With some exasperation, Isa stomps back to my closet and puts together an outfit for me. Black stiletto boots, slim black pants and a deep blue fitted blouse.

She grumbles about grown-ups so stupid they need a child to dress them, but her rage has lessened, and she seems to have forgotten about the unicorn toy, so I'll call that a win. As I walk back into the living room, Marco gives me a smile and taps his finger to the side of his nose, the Italian gesture for *clever*. I smile back at him and slip out the door to Calypso.

I arrive at the club just as Carmen gets there and we claim a big round booth near the door. Paolo and Valentina arrive shortly after. Paolo whispers in my ear, "She smells so good I hate myself," then wanders off to buy a drink.

"So!" Carmen says excitedly once he leaves. The rainbow chandelier showers her dark hair in blue and green and pink. "You had an amazing time with Paolo on Saturday? Tell me everything!" A slow song is playing and Carmen's voice feels especially loud. "I saw him whispering in your ear just now. There's definitely a spark. I'm dying to know what made it the best date you've ever been on!"

BETTER THAN GELATO

"Well, there is a lot to tell," I say, looking at Valentina. I need to gauge her interest in Paolo. And do I tell them about my date with Jake? Probably not. I don't want to give them the wrong idea. We're just friends. "Why don't we get together later, just the three of us, and I promise I'll tell you all about it."

"Okay, but I want every detail," Carmen says.

"Hey, there's Jake," Valentina says.

My heart speeds up at the mention of his name and I turn to see him standing near the door. His hair looks freshly cut and he's wearing a blue button-down shirt that fits him just right. I remind myself that my goal for tonight is to make it clear that we're just friends.

I give him a smile and he waves then heads toward Paolo at the bar. I was hoping he would come over here, but that's okay. I'll get plenty of chances to talk with him tonight.

I don't. I'm not sure what it is, but once the dancing gets underway, Jake never comes over to me. And when I try to make my way over to him, he disappears.

I know it's not in my head. When Jake comes back from the bathroom —yes, I am tracking his movements—we're all sitting in the booth. Instead of sitting next to me, where there is plenty of room, he goes to the other side and sits on half of Diego's left thigh. I pretend not to notice, but it hurts. We're just friends anyway, I remind myself.

After a few hours, my feet are killing me. My new market boots are gorgeous but seem to be cursed by an angry witch who I wronged in some former life. I can think of no other explanation for the excruciating pain spreading through my feet. The pinky toes on each foot have gone numb. They're the lucky ones.

I'm ready to call it a night. I don't know what I expected from Jake, but I feel disappointed. Okay, I do know what I expected. I expected talking and dancing and laughing and Jake looking at me like he did on Monday.

When the bus drops us off at Piazza Duomo Jake calls out *"Ciao ragazzi!"* and leaps off like he can't get away fast enough. And suddenly I feel angry. *You don't want to go out again, fine! But why ignore me?* I say quick goodbyes to the others, then sprint to catch up with Jake. It's the same direction as my bus stop, after all.

I'm walking so fast to catch him I accidentally bump into him. I would feel embarrassed if I wasn't so irritated.

"What's up?" I say.

"Nothing," he says. "Heading home." He doesn't meet my eyes.

I shake my head. "I'm not asking 'what are you up to?' I'm asking what is up with you?"

My voice is calm, but I can tell my eyes are fiery. "Why haven't you said two words to me tonight?"

It comes out more aggressive than I meant it to. Or maybe exactly as aggressive as I meant it to. Because now that I've said it out loud, I'm even more mad.

"Sorry, it was pretty crowded in there," he says. And for some reason, this is what hurts the most. Not that he's ignored me for the last three hours but that he thinks I'm stupid enough to buy that lame excuse.

"Nope," I say, my voice like steel. "Try again."

He looks me in the eyes this time. I see embarrassment and disappointment and a sliver of anger.

"I heard Carmen when I came into the club tonight," he says. "I wasn't trying to eavesdrop, but I heard her. If you have something going on with Paolo, I'm not trying to get in the way of that."

My stomach drops.

"There's nothing going on with me and Paolo."

He runs a hand through his hair. "Then why did you tell Carmen it was the best date you'd ever been on? And that you had an amazing night?"

I let out a tiny growl of frustration. "Because—"

He cuts me off before I can finish. "It's fine. You don't owe me any explanations. I shouldn't have asked."

His voice is kind, but tired. "Look, I had a great time with you on Monday. I thought it was a mutual thing. I get ahead of myself sometimes. It's not your fault."

"It *is* a mutual thing," I nearly growl. "I told Carmen it was the best date of my life because I went to the theater! And it was super fancy! But then two days later, I spent the day with you. And my date with Paolo got bumped down to second place. I just haven't updated Carmen."

Jake lifts his eyes to meet mine. "Really?"

"Really," I confirm. "But I will be spending a lot of time with Paolo, because we found out we're best friends."

"You're best friends?" His brows crinkle slightly.

"Yep. I'm working on an official secret handshake for us. Don't ask Paolo about it. He's embarrassed by his platonic relationship with a girl."

I see my bus coming and Jake sees it too.

"Thanks for setting me straight tonight," he says. "And sorry for ignoring you. I was just embarrassed. And disappointed. After Monday, I was already making plans for our next date, and then I heard Carmen, and I felt really stupid."

"I get it," I say. I think about my 'just friends with Jake' plan, decide it's inherently stupid, and say, "I can't wait for our next date."

"Are you free Friday?" Jake asks. His smile is nervous, and his eyes are hopeful.

"I am."

"Okay," he says, his smile growing. "There's something I think you'll love." He kisses my cheek and squeezes my hand and leaves me standing by the bus a little bit breathless.

Chapter Six

"*Ciao, bellissima!*" Jake calls when he sees me on Friday night. Piazza Duomo is packed, but Jake is standing on top of the steps and hopping from foot to foot, so he's easy to spot.

"Are you hungry?" he asks me first off.

"Starving," I reply. "Your text was clear. I ate no dinner and only the tiniest afternoon snack."

"Perfect," he says. "I promise it'll be worth it."

We grab a bus and head out of downtown. Ten minutes later, we get off at a convention center with a giant sign that says Fiero di Sapori.

"Fair of tastes?" I say looking at Jake.

"More like 'Festival of Flavors,' but you get the idea."

He grabs my hand and pulls me inside, nearly skipping with excitement. The space is huge and smells of garlic, bread, and wine.

"The first weekend in October, Milan hosts a showcase of different culinary specialties from all over Italy," Jake says. "My colleague told me about it, and I remembered that first night when you ate the pizza. And also how much you loved that seafood risotto. And basically every time I've seen you eat something you've been so happy about it."

I see signs for Sicilia, Emilia Romagna, Toscana, and Calabria. A nearby table is filled with samples of salami, cheese, and olives. Another table in this section has jam and honey. People are wandering between tables and sections sampling the different foods, comparing this region's bread with that region's bread.

I look at all the tables. I look at Jake. "I am never leaving this place," I say.

His smile grows even bigger. "I knew it. I knew you would love it here."

He leads me to a table with squares of fresh focaccia bread, still warm from the oven. There are shallow bowls of shimmering olive oil, some of it dark and opaque, others nearly transparent. We dip our focaccia into the bowls and eat it. It's more flavorful than such a simple thing has any right to be.

After we try all the samples from the Calabria region, Jake says, "We should take a trip to Calabria."

In the Emilia Romagna section, a large man with a beard offers us tiny cups of wine. I politely decline.

"You don't drink," Jake says to me. It's not a question, but he does seem to be asking for an explanation.

"Nope, not for me."

Jake nods his head, and we leave it at that.

We sample gelato, nuts, and honey, devour olives and cheeses of every kind and try pesto sauces, alfredo sauces and marinara sauces. And after every region, Jake says, "We should definitely visit this place." And every time, it makes me laugh more, and after two hours, we're food drunk and giggly.

"I didn't plan anything else for this evening," Jake says after we've taken the tram back to il Duomo. "But it seems early to call it a night. Are you up for a walk?"

Yes, I want to keep hanging out with you too.

Out loud I say, "A walk sounds wonderful."

It's dark and the night air is cold, but my body warms up as we go. We stroll through a neighborhood filled with restaurants and lit by strands of lights strung between balconies. We wander into the art district where the streets are lined with galleries and the stone walls of the buildings are painted with murals.

We walk for hours through wide avenues filled with stores and lined with Vespas. We stroll down winding cobblestone streets that end in piazzas and through narrow alleys that lead to nothing but a dead end.

And while we walk we talk. We've already had the main conversations about school and family and friends. So we tell each other the small things that don't matter at all. Like why Jake doesn't like coleslaw—soggy cabbage is gross—or how crickets creep me out.

He tells me about the time in fifth grade when a bully punched him in the face, and he went home and cried. And how the next day, he went back to school and punched the bully in the face and then went home and cried.

"Since then, I've tried to avoid getting punched in the face or punching anyone in the face."

I tell him about a camping trip my family took when I was twelve, and how proud I felt catching a fish that my dad cooked for dinner that night.

It's easy to talk when your body is in motion. You can share things in the dark while you're moving that you wouldn't say in the light as you're looking someone in the eyes. You can let there be silences in the conversation as you look at the city. With every street and every step and every word, we share another detail of who we are. All those small things, hundreds of them, take the shape of a young woman and a young man.

In a narrow alley, Jake takes my hand and doesn't let go. His skin is warm and smooth. I can feel the warmth spread through me, to my fingers and toes and ear lobes.

We make it to my bus stop just as the 27 is pulling away, and I'm not disappointed I missed it. We sit on a low stone wall and wait for the next tram.

"You know how some people don't like putting labels on things?" Jake says. He's running his thumb along the inside of my wrist. Who knew that could be such a lovely place to be touched? It takes some effort to focus on what he's saying.

"I'm not that way," he continues. "I like to have labels. Like if there's a box with an eggplant in it, and the box has a label that says eggplant. I know what it is, and the person next to me knows. And we are on the same page." He turns to me. "All this is to say, will you be my girlfriend?"

My body freezes.

Don't do it! my mind yells. *It's a trap!*

I take a breath. I'm not really girlfriend material. And I definitely didn't expect to be in a relationship with an American boy two weeks into my big year in Italy. But Jake is wonderful. If I ignore my panicked brain and just go by my feelings, I'm 70% delighted to be Jake's girlfriend and 30% reluctant. Or is that reversed?

You're out of time! Just say something!

"Yes," I say. "I'd be delighted to be your girlfriend." Which is 70 percent true. *Or is it 30 percent?*

Jake's whole body physically relaxes. "I'm so glad." He gives my hand a squeeze. "Also, are you part Irish?"

I shake my head and try to will my nerves away.

"I have another question," Jake says, looking at me with shy eyes. "Can I kiss you?"

There's something sweet and old-fashioned about him asking first instead of just going for it. I can't help but smile.

I manage to reply in a normal American accent, "I would like that very much."

He leans in and slides a soft hand to the base of my neck and gently pulls me closer. I can feel his breath on my lips and all the nerves in my body start singing. His lips meet mine, softly and tenderly, and I'm done for. He puts a hand on my lower back, pulling me closer, and I'm lost in his woodsy scent and the sound of blood pulsing in my ears. When he pulls away, I feel tipsy.

Whoa.

And apparently I say that out loud, because Jake smiles and says, "Yeah, me too."

My seventy percent just got bumped up to one hundred percent.

All the way home and as I take the elevator up to the Rossi's apartment I relive the feel of his lips on mine and his hand pulling me closer.

I text Maggie just before I crawl into bed.

> Jake and I are officially dating, and he kisses like a freaking rock star. Okay, I haven't actually kissed a rock star, so that may be inaccurate. But man can that guy kiss!

We're celebrating Diego's birthday tonight with a dinner party at Paolo's house. Jake picked up a gift from the two of us. I guess that's something we do now that we're a couple.

As we knock on Paolo's door, I'm hyper aware of the fact that I'm holding Jake's hand. In front of everyone. Because I'm his girlfriend.

How did I end up here?

I feel like a salamander wearing shoes, conspicuous and unnatural.

"*Benvenuti, Americani*," Paolo says, opening the door wide. He gives me a kiss on the cheek and takes our gift from Jake. He sees Jake holding my hand and gives me a raised eyebrow but makes no comment.

Paolo's apartment is just like Paolo—good looking and rich. The couches are leather, the rug looks expensive, and there's a mahogany bookcase filled with intimidating volumes. My brain pulls up the apartment Mags and I shared last year, furnished with thrift store finds. It's a stark contrast. My Italian bestie is an actual grown up. And I am...something else.

Jake gives my hand a squeeze, then heads over to talk to Diego who's sitting on the couch. I go help Carmen and Valentina set the table.

"So you and Jake!" Carmen whispers to me while she places plates around the table. "Wow! I did not expect that. Although I guess I should have. What happened with you and Paolo?"

"Me and Paolo are just friends," I whisper back.

"I think you and Jake look really nice together," Valentina whispers, setting a napkin at each place.

"Thanks," I say. "I feel weird."

"Why?"

I shrug lamely.

We finish setting the table, and I go looking for Paolo. I find him in a spotless kitchen filled with gleaming appliances.

"How can I help?" I ask.

"Sit on that barstool and tell me charming stories while I mix up this salad. The lasagna should be ready in a few more minutes."

"Ooh, I love lasagna."

"Well, you're in luck. This is my grandmother's recipe. Upon eating your first bite, you will immediately fall in love with me. But don't do anything rash. I promise you, it's just the lasagna influencing you."

"Thanks for that warning."

"Wouldn't want Jake throwing a punch in the middle of Diego's birthday party." Paolo drizzles olive oil over dark romaine lettuce.

"Sure wouldn't. Though he doesn't seem the type does he?"

"No, he does not."

I want to ask Paolo what he thinks of us dating, but I'm not sure I want to pull that thread right now. So instead I say, "How's work going?"

"It brings me no pleasure but pays me enough to pursue pleasure elsewhere."

What a Paolo thing to say. "What is it you do again?"

"Investments, banks transfers. It's much too tedious to talk about."

And you probably aren't allowed to because you're in the mafia. "Okay, well I'm all out of charming conversation."

"Perfect, you can bring the salad to the table and let people know dinner is ready."

I usher people into their seats and a moment later, Paolo sets the lasagna in the middle of the table.

"Are you ready for the best lasagna in Italy?" he asks.

"I've been waiting for this moment my whole life." Jake says.

"Perhaps you are teasing, my American friend," Paolo says. "But I promise you, I do not exaggerate. After this meal, you will never be able to go back to your bland, overcooked American pasta. It will be ruined for you. Forever."

"I'm ready for all other lasagna to be ruined for me, Paolo." Jake says.

"Very well."

Paolo serves a slice of lasagna to each of us and notices he's left with the seat at the end next to Valentina. He looks at me. He knows this is my doing. I flash him a smile, and he flashes me a look that says 'You're the worst!' But I think he really means 'Thank you.'

He takes his seat, fills his glass and says, "To Diego, may the best of your past be the worst of your future. *Compleanno felice.*"

We clink our glasses and then dig into the food.

Holy monkeys this is good. Paolo was right. My whole body fills with love for whoever made this delectable combination of cheese and meat and sauce and pasta. We tell him how delicious it is, and what a great cook he is and how wise his grandparents were to save that recipe from destruction during World War II.

Diego unwraps his gifts and we all ooh and ah. Paolo and Carmen both got him sweaters. They look more like something Paolo would wear than something Diego would wear, but Diego looks happy. Jake got him a fancy watch from the two of us. And Valentina got him a new cologne.

"Thank you, *ragazzi*, for the wonderful gifts. And thank you Paolo for hosting this delicious dinner." He pauses and an emotion I can't decipher flashes across his face. "It's been a wonderful birthday celebration."

"Well, it's not over yet," Valentina says. "I have one last surprise." She goes into the kitchen and returns with a huge cake lit with candles. Everyone starts singing, and when Diego blows out the candles, we clap and cheer.

Valentina cuts a large piece of cake and sets it in front of him. Then she starts cutting pieces for the rest of us.

If I hadn't been watching Diego's face when he took his first bite, I might have missed it. But as luck would have it, I was watching, and I didn't miss it.

He winces. Noticeably. He shoots a look at Valentina, but she's busy placing more slices of cake on plates. I watch him try to take another bite, then give up halfway through and discreetly cough into a napkin.

This could be a problem. I'm terrible at eating things I don't like. I stand up. "Valentina, let me help," I say.

"*Grazie*," she says and takes plates to Carmen and Jake.

I cut two tiny pieces and bring them to Paolo and myself. Paolo sees his tiny piece and opens his mouth to complain, but I give him a kick under the table. He looks at me, then takes a tentative bite. Actual tears well up in his eyes. He coughs and takes a big drink of water.

With dread I pick up my fork and take a bite. My gag reflex kicks in almost immediately. It has a sour, rancid taste. Like maybe this used to be a delicious cake, but it was left in a smelly gym locker for three weeks. I swallow hard and follow it quickly with a drink of water.

"Tell us about your dessert, Valentina," Paolo says.

"Of course," she says, settling herself into the seat next to Paolo. "This is called Prleška Gibanica. It comes from Slovenia, where my grandmother grew up. It's prepared with curd cheese and sour cream. You roll the dough into thin sheets and then top it with curd, eggs, and sour cream. We always do it for birthdays back home, so I wanted to make it for Diego." She gestures to the giant cake sitting in the middle of the table. "What do you think? Do you like it?"

Valentina is the sweetest one in our whole group. Every one of us would rather swallow glass than hurt her feelings.

"You were so kind to make this!"

"Wow! So many layers!"

"What a thoughtful idea!"

"I had no idea your grandmother was Slovenian!"

Valentina beams with pride.

"Do you mind if I have another piece?" Jake asks. His plate is empty.

What in the actual blazes?

"Of course, of course!" Valentina says. "I made a double batch, so there would be plenty."

She serves Jake an extra-large piece, grinning the whole time.

"How are you doing this?" I whisper to him when Valentina goes back over to Diego. "This tastes like decomposing socks."

Jake leans back a little, and I can see that he has a coffee mug on his lap, wedged between his legs. It's half full of cake. I watch him watch Valentina, and every time she's looking away, he scoops another forkful into the cup. In no time he's down to the last bite, which he leaves there. I'm too impressed for words. Jake gives me his nearly empty plate and takes my full one. He gets half of it in, but the mug is filled to the brim now.

"I need another mug," he whispers.

"Paolo, I'm going to try your cappuccino machine," I say like a bad actor in a low budget show.

I sneak two mugs back to the table. I hand one under the table to Jake, and he makes quick work of the rest of my cake. I hand the other mug to Paolo who catches on fast and whispers to Carmen. Before I know it, both their cakes are gone. But Diego still looks miserable. Valentina hovers nearby, making it impossible for him to ditch his disgusting dessert. He attempts another bite and there's actual sweat beading along his hairline.

Nobody should have to eat sock cake on their birthday!

"Hey Diego, have you seen the trailer for the new Indiana Jones movie?" I call from the other side of the table.

He drops the fork, and his face lights up. "They're coming out with another one? Harrison Ford is ancient!"

"Eighty-one," I say, "but he's still got the moves. Check this out."

I pull up the trailer on my phone, and Diego leaves his chair and comes over to watch.

"He's pretty sexy for an old guy," I say.

Jake looks at me alarmed, but I waggle my eyebrows in the direction of Diego's plate.

"Valentina, come look," I say. "Don't you think Harrison Ford is sexy?"

Valentina comes over to have a look, and I angle my phone to get her to face away from Jake near Diego's plate.

"I don't know, Julieta, I think he looks pretty old."

Valentina and Diego watch the whole trailer and out of the corner of my eye I watch Jake scoop the cake off Diego's plate into a coffee mug.

"We should definitely go see that," Diego says when the preview ends. He pauses and glances at me. "Do you know when it's coming out?"

"It says this summer."

Diego nods. He sees his empty plate and looks back at me. I give him a wink and a smile. He lets out a relieved sigh and smiles back. Jake and Carmen whisked all the mugs into the kitchen, and Valentina and I clear the rest of the table.

"Wow, everyone really liked the cake," she says, stacking the empty plates.

"It would appear so," I say.

"I'm glad I have a little left-over to share with my roommates," Valentina says. "They had so many questions watching me make it."

"I bet," Paolo says, joining us.

"So, it's getting pretty late," Carmen says looking at Paolo. "I don't know if we'll make it to il Duomo before the last tram leaves."

"Carmen, Carmen, Carmen," Paolo says, and I have a feeling this is a conversation they have often. He gives a sigh. "I'd be delighted to drive everyone home. Would you like me to tuck you in as well?"

"No, that won't be necessary." Carmen smiles triumphantly and goes to get her purse.

"Thanks, Paolo," Jake says. "We appreciate the ride."

BETTER THAN GELATO   61

Paolo waves away his thanks. "I'll get my keys and round up the others," he says.

"We'll meet you at the car," Jake replies.

Jake and I slip out the door and walk down the hall to the elevator. As soon as the door closes, Jake reaches for me. His lips are on mine, and it feels like I've been waiting for this moment all night. I trace my fingers over his three freckles. I run my hand through his hair. There's a dizzying feeling of electricity and adrenaline and then the doors open and we spill out into the lobby. The doorman averts his eyes, and Jake and I exit the building into the chilly fall air.

It's too dark to find Paolo's car, so we stand next to a tree to wait for the others to arrive.

"You look really lovely tonight," Jake tells me.

"*Grazie.*" Part of me wants to tell him how funny Isa was choosing my outfit, but a bigger part wants to kiss him some more, so that's what I do. His cheeks are cold, but his lips are warm. He wraps his arms around me and pulls me in extra close. I swear I've never been kissed like this in my entire life.

"Kissing you is my new favorite thing to do," he whispers in my ear.

I hear Carmen's voice as the crew comes outside. Reluctantly, I pull away from Jake.

He takes my hand, and we walk over to Valentina, Carmen, Diego, and Paolo.

"We couldn't find your car," I say. Because I feel like I need to say something.

"Ah, well, I usually keep it in the dark under that tree, but just for tonight I parked it right here." He's smirking at us, and I want to throw something at him.

He climbs into the driver's seat and Diego climbs into the passenger seat. Jake and I squeeze into the back with Carmen and Valentina. Valentina is mostly sitting on my lap, and her elbow is right in Carmen's face, but no one seems to mind. I get the feeling they all squish in here a lot.

We drop Jake off first since he doesn't live far from Piazza Duomo. I use all my self-restraint to give him a short kiss, acutely aware of the four other people in the car. Diego and Carmen go next. They live just two blocks apart. I fake a big yawn and mention how tired I am in the hopes that Paolo will take me home next and have some one-on-one time with Valentina. It doesn't work. Valentina's apartment is a five-minute drive from Carmen's, while I live another twenty minutes away in the suburbs.

"Sorry you have to drive me all the way out here," I tell Paolo.

"*Di diente,*" he says. It's nothing. "As the only one in the group with a car, Carmen sometimes mistakes me for the group's taxi driver."

"Well, you're a wonderful host. And it was a great party."

"Indeed it was. Until we got to dessert. I have no idea how a woman so lovely could create something so foul. I feel like I can still smell it in the car with us."

"I want to defend her and say it wasn't that bad, but it was."

"I'm going to remember that coffee mug trick."

"Jake is a pretty smart guy." I run my fingers over the leather armrest of my seat.

"Smart enough to snatch up a good thing when he sees it."

Do I like being snatched up?

We pull into the Rossis' parking lot and Paolo kills the engine.

"So, as a best friend, what do you think about it?" I ask.

Paolo looks at me innocently and stays silent.

"I know you have an opinion you're dying to share. Let's hear it."

"*Julieta Dolcetta.*" Paolo turns and faces me. "As your 'best friend,' I want you to be happy. If this makes you happy, I think that's great."

"You don't have to use air quotes for best friends. The sooner you admit that's what we are, the better off you'll be." Paolo smirks.

"So, you don't think it's too fast?" I ask. "Or lame that I'm dating an American? Or that we'll break up and bring a bunch of drama to the group? Or that we look like Barbie and Ken when we stand next to each other?" I rub a smudge on my window.

"I do not think any of those things." He pauses. "Do you?"

I sigh dramatically. "I don't know. Maybe. Isa told me I look like Barbie. And Jake does have some classic Ken features...But that's not my biggest worry. There are just a dozen ways this could go badly. What if I change my mind in two weeks and break his heart? And lose all my new friends in the process?"

"Julieta, you are worrying about problems that do not exist," Paolo says.

"That may never exist. You like him, he likes you. Take your ridiculously good fortune and enjoy it. Not all of us are that lucky."

I'm quiet a minute.

"You might be right," I finally say.

"I'm Paolo. I'm always right." And he looks at me with such confidence I believe him.

Chapter Seven

One minute Isa is fine sitting on the couch, digging through her backpack, looking for markers. The next minute her face is a thunder cloud, and I know we're seconds away from a category five storm. I've survived the last three weeks with this child by looking for the signs. So as soon as I see her expression, I lunge for my phone and play the first song I find.

"What are you doing?" she asks. Her body language is tense, like she's ready to spring, but there's confusion there too, and I'm hoping to capitalize on her bewilderment to buy me some time.

"Music," I blurt.

Isa narrows her eyes.

"It's Thursday." I shrug like I'm easygoing and chill, and not desperately trying to avoid whatever new hell she's about to unleash. "I'm ready for a Thursday dance party."

I turn the volume up as loud as it'll go. The living room fills with Justin Timberlake's voice singing "Can't Stop the Feeling."

"I know this song," she says. "It's from *Trolls*."

"Yeah, it's great for dancing."

I stand up and start dancing and after a second, Isa joins me. The living room is about ten square feet, but the limited space doesn't curb Isa's enthusiasm. Her long skinny limbs look like they're ready to fly off her body as she flings them about with abandon. *Is this what six-year-olds look like when they dance? It's amazing and terrifying.*

The next song is Pharell's "Happy." I clap my hands, and Isa's arm flailing gets even crazier.

"Can we do a dance party every Thursday?" she asks when the song ends.

"Absolutely," I say. Then I continue in my most casual, doesn't-even-matter voice, "So, do you have any homework or anything to do for school?"

The thundercloud returns. "A stupid worksheet about stupid numbers that my stupid teacher is making us do."

"Cool. How about you pick the next song to listen to while you do it? I bet you can finish before the song's over."

The grumpy expression stays, but Isa chooses a song on my phone and then fishes her homework sheet out of her backpack. She finishes well before the song ends.

As a reward, I pull up Neil Diamond's "Sweet Caroline" and scoop Isa into my arms. She's way too big to carry, but that's what makes it fun. I spin her and dip her and replace the chorus with "Sweet Isabella." I bang my shins on the coffee table twice, but it makes Isa giggle even more, so I decide it's worth it. We're mid-dip when Sofia walks in.

Isa leaps out of my arms and gives Sofia a hug. "We're having a dance party!"

"Well, that sounds lovely," she says. She's smiling, and I realize how rarely I see her smile. She always looks tense.

After dinner, Isa and I do the dishes and Sofia wipes the table.

"Isa," she says, then stops. "Tomorrow is Friday." She stops again, her lips pinched in dread. She swallows. "Do you have any homework to do?"

"Oh, I already did that earlier," Isa says.

Sofia's eyes widen in surprise, then her whole body relaxes. She looks at me with an expression of relief and mouths *"Grazie."*

After I put Isa to bed, I call my mama. I feel like I haven't talked to her in ages.

"Buon giorno my glamorous daughter!" my mom says as soon as she picks up. My mom hardly ever speaks Italian, even though she grew up

hearing my grandparents speak it. "Tell me everything about your Italian life!"

I fill her in on Isa and the food and my new friends. I leave Jake out of it.

My mom gives me updates on the fam.

"Brad gets his next assignment any day now," she says. "They're hoping for something overseas."

"That would be cool," I say.

"Brianna is coming to visit next week."

My older sister Brianna married Tyler five years ago and has been unhappily married for five years. She lives in Arizona and visits my parents a lot.

"Have you registered for your classes for next year?" my mom asks.

"Yep. I emailed my schedule to Sharon this week."

"Did you pick some classes you're excited about?"

A Venn diagram of my schedule for next year and the ten classes that put college students to sleep would be a perfect circle.

"Yes," I say. "It's going to be great."

And that is how you lie to your mother.

"I miss you," my mom says.

"I miss you too."

"But I'm so happy you get this special year," she says.

"Me too."

The last happy year of my life.

"Marco! Your hair!" I say and hold up the photo. Marco's tuxedo is perfectly cut, and his wild curls have been slicked into submission for the day.

"It was a one-time feat," Marco calls from the kitchen, "and it required more gel than you could possibly imagine."

Isa helped me choose a great outfit to go out dancing tonight, but then we got distracted by the Rossis' wedding album. The photographer did an amazing job. Each shot is perfectly framed, and the lighting makes them glow. There are some cool shots of the two of them in perfect focus and the wedding party behind them softly blurry.

I wonder what setting you use to do that.

BETTER THAN GELATO

My phone vibrates, but I ignore it. Marco and Sofia are preparing dinner but come out occasionally to provide commentary.

"Your dress is beautiful," Isa tells Sofia.

"A friend of Daddy's designed it for me. You like it?"

"So much," Isa says and Sofia's face lights up.

My phone vibrates again, and I finally take a look. It's from Jake. So was the last one.

> Hey, how is your day going? Are you coming to Calypso tonight?

That was fifteen minutes ago. Just now he sent:

> Just leaving my house. I can meet you at the bus stop if you want.

Ugh.

I feel a stab of irritation. Yes, I was planning on going to Calypso tonight. But we're enjoying a rare and wonderful peace in the Rossi house. I don't want to rush off.

I text him back.

> I'll be there, but I'm coming late, so go in without me.

I spend fifteen more minutes hanging out in the Rossi living room, then I say goodbye and head downtown. By the time I arrive at the club, I'm forty-five minutes late.

Calypso is thirty degrees hotter than outside, and I start sweating as soon as I walk in. I try to take my coat off, but it gets stuck on one arm, and I twist awkwardly for a moment before someone says, "Here let me help."

I feel the coat slide the rest of the way off, and I'm free.

"Whew. Thanks," I say.

"You're welcome. I'm Nicola." Nicola is a good-looking man in a fitted blue shirt and expensive jeans. He gives me a dazzling smile.

"I'm Juliet," I say.

"*Piacere,*" he says. Nice to meet you. He leans in for a quick kiss on the cheek.

When he leans back out, Jake is somehow standing right next to me.

"I'm Jake," Jake says. "Thanks for helping my girlfriend with her coat."

Wow, I thought flailing around with my arm stuck was awkward. This is worse.

"Happy to help," Nicola says.

We stand in a weird triangle for a beat longer and then Nicola turns and walks away. I try to breathe deeply in a way that Jake won't notice. *It's fine. That was a totally normal interaction.*

"You made it!" Jake says.

"Yeah. I was right in the middle of something with Isa," I say. *And why do I have to account for my time to you?* The feeling in my chest reminds me of the time I got locked in my grandma's closet. *Can you be claustrophobic in tight relationships?*

I do my best to shake the feeling off. I dance and let the music work its way into my brain and drown out my thoughts. Diego is extra goofy and makes me laugh, and Paolo seems to be talking to Valentina more. Carmen teaches me a new dance, and I'm so bad at it we're nearly falling over from laughing so hard.

After two hours of dancing, all my irritation has faded away. My body is tired, and my heart is happy.

"Hey, how did that lab test go?" I ask Jake as we wait for my tram. "Didn't you get the results back today?"

"Well, I could update you on my research. Or..."

He leans in and kisses me and my whole body responds. He was right. I don't care about his lab results. I don't care about anything. Only the softness of his lips and the gentle pressure of his hands on my hips. His smell, woodsy and fresh, is intoxicating. I never want to stop kissing him.

There's a horn honking and the 27 tram pulls in. Jake breaks away for the tiniest moment to wave the bus on and then he kisses me again.

I feel lightheaded, but somehow manage to say, "What about my bus?"

"We'll catch the next one."

And it's such a great answer because I don't want to move from this spot. I don't want to stop kissing this boy with the warm hands and snowy woods smell. At the same moment, I realize we're standing on a public street corner.

I pull back to catch my breath. I look up at him, and wow. He's staring down at me with brown eyes like glowing embers.

And that mouth. I can't help it. I kiss him again and it feels like fireworks going off everywhere. I break away when I hear another bus approaching.

"I've got to go," I say.

"Okay," he says.

Neither one of us moves. The bus driver gives a beep-beep that makes me jump.

"Good night," I say and climb on the bus.

"Good night," Jake calls behind me.

I make my way to a seat and catch a glimpse of my reflection in the dirty bus window. My lips are swollen, and my eyes are glazed. My messy bun is more mess than bun. I've never looked happier.

Chapter Eight

Jake leaves for med school interviews in America tomorrow. Am I going to miss him like crazy? Yes. We've spent every free moment together for the past two weeks. Am I also a little relieved he's going away for two weeks? Yes. We've spent Every. Free. Moment. Together. For a girl that doesn't love being in a relationship, it's been a lot.

Tonight he planned a special date for us, a nighttime tour of the Navigli Canals. The evening is cold, and the air smells like winter has arrived. We snuggle together in a little wooden boat while a guide tells us how Leonardo di Vinci built the canals to bring goods into the city. I listen to the water lap against the stone walls of the canal and watch the bare branches sway in the breeze.

"This is spectacular," I whisper to Jake.

"I'm so happy you like it," he whispers back.

And I can see that he means it. He keeps darting glances at me, like he wants to make sure I'm having a good time. So much of his pleasure is derived from my enjoyment. I think of how happy he was introducing me to Italian hot chocolate and the way he always watches me eat. Me being happy makes him happy, which I appreciate. It also makes me deeply uncomfortable to be responsible for someone else's happiness.

The boat tour ends, but it's still early, so we meander through the neighborhood. This area has a different feeling than other parts of Milan. Older maybe, or slower.

We come to a park with tall iron gates with a sign saying the park closes at sunset. A firm shake of the gate confirms that they're locked.

"Too bad, it looks like a cool park," Jake says.

"It does," I murmur. There are giant trees with branches that hang down almost to the ground. I look up to the top of the gate.

Jake says, "Uh oh," before I've even taken the first step. I look down the road. There's no one out. There aren't even that many lights on in this area. I give Jake my most persuasive look. And then without waiting for a response, I stick the toe of my shoe into the iron gate and start climbing. It's not that tall, and the gate is all horizontal bars, very easy to climb. I'm on the other side in less than a minute. I wander down the path, and it gets even darker in the densely wooded park.

Behind me I hear a light thump, and I know Jake has made it over. I don't look back, but seconds later, I feel his arms wrap around me.

"We've snuck into a park," he murmurs. "What other mischievous things should we do?"

I don't say anything, but I take his hand and lead him to a bench nearly obscured by long branches. I sit down and pull him down next to me. It's so dark I can just see his outline. I touch his face. Feel his full mouth, run my hand across his cheek and then into his hair. I pull his face to mine and kiss him gently.

He tastes like mint. His arms wrap around me, pulling me closer to him. His lips leave mine and go to my neck just below my ear. My breath catches, and Jake's arms tighten in response. He softly kisses all the way down to my collarbone. He scoops me onto his lap and we're a tangle of limbs on a park bench. I want to stay here until the end of the world.

Then I see a blinking light coming through the darkness.

"Jake," I whisper. "Don't make a sound."

Jake goes still. I can't see his face clearly, but his posture looks so nervous and guilty I start giggling. The light gets closer, and I make out a guy in a uniform. I jump off the bench and head in his direction. We're caught. No sense making him duck under all the branches.

"*Buonasera*," I say. Good evening.

"*Buenasera, signorina,*" he says, sizing me up. "The park is closed for the night."

"I know. I just wanted to take a closer look. I've never seen such wonderful trees."

"*Grazie,*" he says, as though he planted each tree himself. "Perhaps you'll come back and enjoy our lovely park during the day."

"We absolutely will," I tell him.

And without another word, he leads us back to the gate, unlocks it and ushers us through.

"*Grazie. Buonanotte,*" I say, wishing him a good night.

"*Buonanotte,*" he tells me, and he's smiling now. "Visit again soon." He gives me a wink.

I think the incidences of winking in Italy is substantially higher than in the US.

"Wow." Jake says, visibly relieved. "You totally charmed that old guy. He didn't even yell at us."

"Italians are romantics," I say. "I guarantee you, thirty years ago, that guy was doing the same thing."

We grab some hot chocolate to warm up, and I'm feeling content and cozy.

And then the night takes a disastrous turn.

"You look beautiful tonight," Jake says.

"I think it's the chocolate. Everything seems more beautiful when you're sipping this stuff."

"Maybe. But you also looked beautiful an hour ago on the boat. How do you explain that?"

I shake my head and smile. "I have no explanation for that."

"Ah hah!" he says, like he's caught me. It makes me laugh.

"You know how hot chocolate makes everything better?" he says. "You do the same thing. Everything is better when you're around. Even when you're not around. I remember the funny things you say while I'm working in the lab. I think about getting to see you again when I'm off work. You make me really happy."

I'm about to respond, but Jake continues.

"I think I might be falling in love with you."

It's like someone dropped a gallon of ice water on me.

BETTER THAN GELATO

"No. That's a terrible idea," I blurt before I can stop myself.

Jake tilts his head to the side. He waits a second before asking, "Why is that a terrible idea?"

My mind races for an appropriate response. *Because I might not fall in love with you back? Because it feels like too much pressure? Because I don't want to be trapped in a serious relationship?*

I can't say any of those things. My brain searches for a different explanation. *I'm a spy, working for the CIA, and I can't get involved with anyone.* It seems far-fetched, even for me. *Maybe I'm a vampire. Wasn't that the hip thing a few years back?* Jake sits there patiently puzzled. I opt for part of the truth.

"It just feels really fast."

"Yeah, I guess it is. It's just, the more I get to know you...You're smart, you're funny, you're beautiful. I like every new thing I learn about you."

Oh man, he's making it worse. How can I stop this conversation immediately?

"Look, I know you might not be where I am right now," he says, "and I get that. I'm not trying to scare you." He must see the panic in my eyes. "But I wanted you to know where I'm at. I'm really enjoying my time with you. And I see a lot of potential in this relationship. For the future."

Did he just say future? We've been dating for three weeks, and we're having a future talk?! Out. I've got to get out.

I take a drink of my hot chocolate to buy myself some time. We're not on the same page. This is clear. I need to end this relationship immediately before things get worse.

But then another thought hits me. *What kind of heartless jerk breaks up with her boyfriend the night before he interviews at Harvard?*

"Hey, I see that I freaked you out," Jake says. "I'm sorry. That wasn't my intention." He's rubbing the back of his neck, and his cheeks have gone pink. Probably because I haven't said anything in five minutes. "I was trying to be honest. But you know what they say about honesty in a relationship. Totally overrated."

I smile. *He really is adorable.*

"Jake, I also really like spending time with you. You're one of the coolest people I've met. I'm sorry if I seem freaked out. I appreciate your honesty. It just threw me off a little."

The date ends pretty quickly after that. As we walk to the bus stop, I can tell he wants to say more, and I pray to the gods of freaked-out girlfriends that he won't. It works. We settle onto the stone wall by the bus stop bench, and he tentatively takes my hand.

I lean over and kiss him and it's so much better than talking that I just keep kissing him until my bus comes.

"Good luck," I tell him just before I get on. "You're going to punch those interviews right in the face."

His brow creases in confusion, so I add, "It's a good thing."

And then I hop on the bus and it's moving away from him and a wave of relief washes over me.

"That looks like diarrhea," Isa says. "I'm not eating that."

It's a mean thing to say. Unfortunately, it's also accurate. I tried to cook chicken marsala, like Sofia showed me, but my head is a mess from how I left things with Jake last night. I clearly missed some crucial steps because the mushrooms shriveled up and the wine sauce turned into brown sludge.

"I have a new plan for dinner," I tell Isa, and she looks relieved. Marco is in Barcelona and Sofia had a late meeting, so it's just the two of us this evening.

I whip up some toasted PB&J and present it with a flourish. She's skeptical at first but gives it a try and eats most of it.

After dinner, I suggest seventeen different things we could do, and each one gets shot down with a "No."

"Well, I'm going to go read a book," I say. I hop up and head to my room.

Isa looks alarmed that nobody is going to entertain her, but I pretend I don't notice. I grab *Harry Potter and the Sorcerer's Stone* from under my bed and bring it out to the living room. My grandma ordered me a copy in Italian a few years back, but I never made it very far through it. I open it to chapter one.

I can hear Isa moping around the kitchen, and eventually she sulks into the living room.

"Your book looks boring," she says.

"Yeah, it probably does look that way to a Muggle."

"What's a Muggle?"

"A non-magical person. This book is about magical people. Witches, wizards, that sort. There are potions and spells. And flying broomsticks. You probably wouldn't like it."

"Fine, you can read it to me if you want," she says, flopping onto the couch next to me.

By the end of the first chapter, she's hooked. After I help her get on her PJs and brush her teeth, I read chapter two to her and the forty-seven stuffed animals that live on her bed.

Once I'm sure she's down, I head to my room and call Maggie.

"Mags! It's me! I'm in dire need of romantic advice."

I can hear her laughing. We've been using that phrase since we were twelve. We read it in a book somewhere and thought it was wildly funny.

"I'm so glad you're calling me!" she says. "I've been missing you like crazy. I have a thousand things to tell you, but none of it's important. Tell me about your love life. Is this about the American?"

"Yes," I say with a sigh. "He said he's falling in love with me."

"Whoa. It's been, what, three weeks? What did you say?"

"I gave him a perfectly reasonable response. Like any normal girl would." I climb under the covers.

"I want your exact words, please."

"No. That's a terrible idea."

"It can't be that bad," Maggie says. "Spill it."

I cough. "Um. That's what I said to him. 'No. That's a terrible idea.'"

Maggie gasps. "You didn't!"

"Oh geez. It sounds worse now that I'm repeating it to you."

"Well..." I can tell she's trying to put a positive spin on this but coming up empty.

"I will point out that I didn't tell him I worked for the CIA," I say. "Or that I was a vampire."

"Why would you tell him those things?" She sounds truly puzzled.

"You know, as good reasons for him not to fall in love with me."

"I see," Maggie says. But she says it slowly, in a way that makes it clear she does not see.

"Maaaargh! This is the worst," I say.

"Why is this the worst?" she asks.

"Because! He's always taking me to cool places and feeding me delicious food."

"That monster," she says drily.

"I'm serious. He's wonderful, and I like him, and now I have to break up with him." I can tell I'm slipping into a whiny voice, and I hate it.

"I know you're scared of the 'L' word," Maggie says, "but you don't always have to do this."

"Do what?"

"Freak out and bail when things get serious."

"I don't *always* do that," I protest.

"You broke up with Adam Jensen the day after he told you he loved you," she points out.

"He showed up at my house drunk and was only saying that to get me to sleep with him. Gross."

"How about Curly-Haired Tom that you dated for three months last year and refused to call your boyfriend. You referred to him as 'That guy I hang out with sometimes.'"

"Things with Tom were not that serious," I explain.

"Because you wouldn't let them get serious."

"Because serious is the worst!"

"Juls, you're overthinking this. Which is a thing you do."

"It's not a thing I do," I start to say as she interrupts me by saying loudly, "It's totally a thing you do!"

"Listen," she continues, "maybe this feels uncomfortable at first, but give it a chance. You're trying a lot of new things over there. Try out being a girlfriend. You might like it."

I make a grumbling sound, but Maggie can tell I'm agreeing and lets out a tiny whoop of triumph.

"Fine," I say. "I'll give this a try. Maybe it'll be great. Maybe I'll be the best girlfriend ever."

Twenty-four hours later it's clear I am not the best girlfriend ever.

Chapter Nine

The night is dark and moonless, but I'm safely tucked into the brightly lit 27 tram. Paolo and I met up for dinner, and I spent most of the evening trying to convince him to ask Valentina out. He spent most of the evening listing things he'd rather do than ask out Valentina: shave his head, swim in shark-infested waters, eat her cake, etcetera.

I watch billboards and buildings whiz by my window. Suddenly, a black car pulls even with the tram, and I find myself looking into the eyes of a dark-haired man in a black coat. We're separated by two windows and twelve inches.

He smiles in surprise and calls out, "*Ciao, bella!*"

I smile back and say, "*Ciao!*"

The car pulls ahead, and I see him tap the driver. Then the car slows down until our windows are matched up again.

"Where are you going?" he calls to me.

"Home," I call back.

"Come out with us instead!" he says. There are three other guys in the car.

I laugh. *Yeah, right.*

"Tell me your name, *bella*," he shouts. Although now that we're stopped at a red light, I can hear him perfectly fine.

"Juliet," I say, and his whole face lights up like I've just told him he's won the lottery.

The light turns green, and the tram lumbers off with the black car driving alongside, like a momma whale and her calf.

The man calls, "You are very beautiful!"

"*Grazie*," I call back. I'm tempted to add "you too," because he is, in fact, very good looking. But I don't want to encourage him. The tram veers away from the car lane again, and I lose them.

I don't quite register when the tram stops to pick someone up. And I'm absolutely shocked when that person comes and sits down next to me.

He holds out a hand and says, "*Ciao, Julieta*, I'm Lorenzo." I'm too surprised to speak, but I shake his hand.

He's even better looking up close. All sharp angles and dark eyes. He's grinning victoriously.

The black car makes another appearance with all his friends yelling and cheering out the windows. He waves them away and turns to me.

"Can I get your phone number?" he asks. He looks me right in the eyes. And maybe it's not wanting him to look bad in front of his friends, or maybe it's because I feel like he's earned it. Or maybe it's because he is *really* good looking, but I give in.

He pushes a couple of buttons, and I get a text with a smiley face.

"There. Now you have my number."

The tram has stopped at a bus stop, and I can see the black car idling nearby.

"I better get off here," he says. "It was a pleasure meeting you, Julieta. I look forward to seeing you again."

And then he takes my hand and kisses it. I sit there slightly stunned as he walks off the tram and gets into the car. I can hear more yelling and cheering. I look around to see if anyone else saw the crazy thing that just happened, but there's only one old man on the tram with me and he's asleep.

I get Lorenzo's text during breakfast the next morning.

BETTER THAN GELATO

> Buon giorno bella! This is Lorenzo. Can I take you out tonight?

Wow. Less than twelve hours, and he's already texting me. Now, how do I tell him no? I can't actually go on a date with some random guy who got on my tram. I'm dating Jake. That's that.

Or is it? I think, two hours later, folding laundry. *I mean, what harm would it do if I go on one date? Jake isn't even in the country!*

By two o'clock, I still haven't texted Lorenzo back. I think about calling Maggie again. Or even running it by Paolo. *He can be discreet. He's mafia.* But then I remember I'm twenty years old. I can make my own decisions.

Which is how I end up at a cozy table in the back of a restaurant with Lorenzo that night. There's a large fireplace in one corner and oversized photographs of trees and mountains on the walls.

"This place is really cool," I tell Lorenzo. He looks gorgeous in a leather jacket and dark pants.

"Thanks," he says. "It's one of my favorites."

"So Lorenzo, what do you do?"

"I design restaurants actually." He gives me a smile. "This was my first."

My mouth falls open a little. "You designed this?"

"Yes."

Lorenzo tells me about the company he started a few years out of college and how he's hustled to build a name for himself.

"How about you?" he says. "Are you working? In school?"

I did the math while he was talking, and it's clear that he's much older than me. Admitting that I've completed two years of college and have resigned myself to running a dry-cleaning business my whole life seems pathetic.

"I work as a nanny," I say. "And I'll go back to school in the fall. But in the meantime, I'm enjoying every second in your amazing country."

Our first plate arrives, fresh tomatoes topped with mozzarella and basil. I cut myself a small triangle, balancing the red, white, and green in a little stack on my fork. The first bite is juicy and savory and zingy. I take two more bites, then breathe and say, "This is really good."

"The food in America is terrible, yes?"

"It's not that bad."

"I heard that they have cans of cooked pasta already mixed with the sauce and you just heat it in the microwave."

"Okay, it's pretty terrible."

The next course is a wild mushroom risotto with a strong, earthy flavor. Then the main course arrives, some kind of herb-crusted white fish. It's flaky and flavorful. I eat until there's not a crumb left on my plate.

"You liked the cod?" Lorenzo asks with a smile, and I nod.

I feel embarrassed, but if people don't want me to eat every last bite, they shouldn't serve me such delicious food.

Lorenzo tells me a story about one of his restaurant clients, and I have a hard time concentrating on his words while looking at his face. *What is wrong with me?*

The waiter brings out two small dishes of crème brûlée. I pick up my spoon and gently crack the golden-brown sugar crust on top. The crème underneath is smooth and thick and sweet. When I've eaten the last bite, I'm sorely tempted to lick my bowl but manage to resist.

"I thought we could check out a pub nearby," Lorenzo says. "It's just a short walk from here."

As we leave the restaurant, Lorenzo takes my hand in his. He does it easily, like we're... hand holders. I remember how uncomfortable I felt showing up to Diego's party holding Jake's hand.

As though reading my mind, Lorenzo asks, "Does it bother you if I hold your hand?"

"Not at all," I say honestly.

What does it say about me that I'm uneasy walking into a room full of friends holding my boyfriend's hand, but fine walking into a pub full of strangers, holding a stranger's hand?

I don't know what pubs in America smell like. I've never been to one since I'm under the drinking age. But in my head, they smell like beer, bad pickup lines, and vomit. This place smells like an Italian grandmother's house; fresh bread and sauteed garlic.

Lorenzo introduces me to the bartender, and it sounds like they're old friends.

"We're going to head to the back and see what the boys are up to," Lorenzo says.

"Hogging the pool table," the bartender offers.

BETTER THAN GELATO

Before we even make it to the back room, the three guys who were playing pool drop their sticks and walk toward us.

"She showed? I don't believe it!" says one guy with a neatly trimmed beard.

"He has all the luck," says another, shorter guy.

"It's not luck," says the third. "Lorenzo has the gift."

Pretending he didn't hear any of this, Lorenzo closes the gap and introduces us.

"Julieta, these are my friends. Nico, Luca, and Giorgio. *Ragazzi*, this is Julieta."

There are *piaceres* and cheek kisses, and then Luca says, "Are you up for some pool?"

I try to play well. I really do. But my first shot jumps off the table, and my second shot sinks two of their balls. Lorenzo does that thing no man can resist where they stand behind you and show you how to hold the stick. It doesn't help. We lose badly.

"Do you feel like dancing?" he asks afterward.

"Yes," I say. I'm much better on a dance floor than a pool table.

"Perfect, I know a great spot near here."

In the month I've been here, I've only ever been to Calypso. This club's a lot flashier. A neon sign out front says *DIAMANTE*. Diamond. French doors open onto a double staircase that leads down to the dance floor. Each step is embedded with glittering stones that catch the light from the chandelier. It feels like walking on stars.

The dance floor is a dense forest of moving bodies, and the pounding music stops my brain from working, in the best way.

Lorenzo is a good dancer. His hips sway to the beat of the music, and occasionally he takes my hand and twirls me around. When a bachata song comes on, he pulls me close, and I can feel the skin on the back of his neck, hot and slick with sweat. His heart is beating fast. Or maybe it's just the bass.

The chemistry between us has been building all night and by the time Lorenzo walks me to the Rossis' apartment, I'm dangerously close to kissing him. Everything in me is geared up for that moment. One look in his eyes tells me I'm not the only one.

And that's when the guilt comes crushing in with brutal clarity.

What am I doing? I'm dating Jake. Whatever mental trick let me ignore that fact all night has abandoned me now. *I can't do this. I shouldn't even be here.* I stand on tiptoes and kiss Lorenzo on his cheek.

"Thank you for a lovely evening," I say. "I really enjoyed it."

The disappointment in his eyes is clear.

"Thank you for joining me."

I still want to kiss him. I know that if I make eye contact right now and go up on my tiptoes again, we'll be kissing in less than two seconds. Instead, I keep my feet firmly planted, look at his chin and say:

"Goodnight, Lorenzo."

"Goodnight, Julieta" he says.

He's holding my hand. I still have a chance to lean in and kiss him. But I don't. I give his hand a squeeze and then let go. I turn and walk toward my apartment, relief and disappointment flooding through me.

I spend the next day moping around the Rossi house grumpy and confused. Lorenzo texts me in the morning, asking when we can go out again, but I don't respond. My brain is firing questions at me: *Am I going to keep dating Jake? Am I going to go out with Lorenzo again? Am I going to convince Paolo to let me join him in the mafia?*

Isa notices my mood and makes me a cup of tea. It's the nicest thing I've seen her do. We read three more chapters of *Harry Potter and the Sorcerer's Stone*.

I go to Calypso with the crew on Wednesday night and bring my camera for some photo therapy. I've gotten two more texts from Lorenzo. I hate that I've turned into the kind of girl that ghosts a nice guy, but I don't know what else to do. And I have no idea what to tell Jake when he gets home.

So I take pictures of the colorful chandeliers, and a profile shot of the bartender mixing drinks. I take photos over the balcony of the dancing crowd below. I take candids of Carmen and Paolo arguing and Diego and Valentina salsa-ing.

"Alright, *ragazzi*! Time for a group shot," I holler. I set the timer, then squish with everyone else onto a tiny sofa. There's a blinking light and a flash, and I know that this moment is recorded forever.

Then the light starts blinking again.

"Smile some more," I call, just before it flashes. We're trying to untangle ourselves from the couch when the camera blinks again. It flashes a third time capturing our tangle of limbs and confused faces. It flashes a fourth time capturing waving hands and everyone looking at me. It flashes a fifth time just as Carmen falls off Diego's lap, which makes Paolo spill the drink he was holding, and accidentally elbow Valentina in the head.

As I edit the photos the next morning, I laugh so hard I have tears in my eyes.

Chapter Ten

The muscles in my shoulders are as tight as guitar strings and there is so much sweat pouring out of my body I feel like I'm part slug. Jake got in from the states this morning, and I'm heading downtown to see him. And break up with him. Or not? I was up all night worrying and now I'm about to see him, and I still have no idea what to do.

On the one hand, I hate serious relationships and it's clear I suck at being a girlfriend. On the other hand, I think about sitting on a boat with him in the middle of a lake. Holding his hand down cobblestone streets. Eating with him. Dancing with him. Kissing him. I think about the way he looks at me and the way he listens to me. The way my heart speeds up when I think about him. I've missed him these last two weeks. But I'm also anxious.

I know once I see him, everything I'm feeling is going to be written all over my face. And I'm terrified to find out what that is.

He's waiting on the steps of the piazza when I get there, but the place is packed, and he doesn't see me yet. I close the distance between us. Twenty feet, then fifteen. I see the exact moment he spots me and it's like the sun rising over his face. He jumps off the steps and comes running toward me, and I guess at some point I start running toward him, because I jump into his arms with a fair amount of force. We collide in an explosion of happiness.

And we're kissing and smiling and laughing and kissing more. I can feel his stubble against my cheek and his hand on the back of my neck. I can feel electricity zinging from the soles of my feet to the top of my head. It's shocking how good it feels to be in his arms. It's fireworks and wonder. His arms encircle my waist and pull me closer to him. *Why was I so scared of this?* I wonder blurrily. This is magic and excitement and every good thing.

I melt into him and feel the tension drain out of my body. He kisses me, and it's *Hello* and *I've missed you* and *How are you doing?* I kiss him back and try to tell him that I'm so glad he's here, and I'm so glad I'm with him. When we finally break apart, I'm breathless and smiling and giddy.

"Hello," Jake says.

"Hello," I say back.

"I missed you."

I nod. "Me too."

We stand there holding each other for a long time, unwilling to let go. Finally, I remember my manners.

"How were the interviews? How was your trip? How are you doing?"

"I'm doing amazing. I can't think of a time I've ever felt this good." His eyes are bright, and he's grinning at me and ohmygosh, I want to start kissing him again. I take a step back.

"Tell me about the interviews," I say.

"I think they went well. I'll know more in a couple of weeks. For now, I'm relieved it's over."

"What do you feel like doing?" I look at him closely, and he looks exhausted. "Do you want to take a nap?" I know his flight was a red eye.

"I do," Jake says nodding. "But I'm not ready to leave you yet."

"I'm a pretty good nap buddy..."

His eyes go wide, and his mouth opens a little. "Are you?"

I nod my head. "I don't snore. I share covers. And I'm an accomplished spooner."

"I'm sold."

I reach up and kiss him again. I've missed this. I've missed him.

My phone vibrates, and I ignore it. Then I get three more texts. Reluctantly, I pull it out and see a message from Carmen.

86 LIBBY TANNER

"No mangiare il pane davanti ai poveri."

Then she texted three separate messages full of kissy faces. I crane my head looking for her in the crowd, but I can't spot her. I show the text to Jake.

"'Don't eat bread in front of the poor.'" he translates. He laughs and rubs his head in this adorable way he has. "I haven't heard that saying before. That's...very descriptive."

"But what if I want to keep eating bread?" I say with a smile. "What if I'm hungry?"

"So hungry," Jake says, already leaning in. "Starving."

A while later, we head back to Jake's house, and he leads me to the bedroom he shares with Giancarlo. It's a disaster except for one neatly organized desk and perfectly made bed. I don't have to ask which side is his.

Jake takes a quick shower and comes back wearing navy blue sweatpants and a white T-shirt. His hair is wet and tousled. Sweat collects in the palms of my hands.

I climb into his bed, and he snuggles in next to me, and I hold my breath. His arms wrap around me, and his fingers gently stroke the curve of my waist. He kisses the back of my neck and lingers there for a moment sending chills down my spine.

"You're right," he says. "You are a very good spooner."

"The secret is being little spoon," I say. "Big spoon is too much responsibility."

He chuckles into my ear, and I close my eyes. His skin smells warm and soapy. His chest rises and falls with each breath. He runs a hand down my waist, over my hip and down my thigh. All my senses are awake and tingling.

He turns me until I'm facing him and then kisses me long and slow. My body melts into his, and my head gets fuzzy. I feel like I'm falling into a deep lake, but in the best way. When we pull away we're both breathing hard.

"I have never felt less sleepy." Jake says. He puts some space between us.

"Me either."

"So, tell me what I missed while I was gone." His voice is ragged.

"Hmm, well you definitely didn't miss anyone bending over and ripping a hole in her jeans and everyone in the pizzeria seeing her blue underwear."

Jake bursts out laughing. "That is quite specific. It makes me think that maybe I *did* miss it. What happened?"

"I moved to Italy and ate all the food I could get my hands on, that's what happened! And then I bent over to get something from Isa's backpack and my pants split."

"I'm so sorry," he says, his eyes filled with laughter. "I mean, it's hilarious. But I'm sorry it happened to you."

"Me too. Isa was cackling with glee. You should have heard the things she said about my bum."

Jake gives my hip a squeeze.

"I happen to really like you bum. In fact, I adore every inch of you."

"Even my elbows?"

"Especially your elbows. They beguile me. When I first saw you I thought, 'Oh no, those elbows of hers are going to be my undoing.' And I was right."

We lay together, laughing, snuggling, soaking each other up. Eventually I hear Jake's breathing slow, and his arms get heavier. I lay next to him and listen to him sleep. I think about being here with him when I could be somewhere else with someone else. I decide this is the only place I want to be.

Isa and I have just finished another Thursday dance party when I see the text from Paolo.

> I did it. I asked her out and she said yes. I'm elated and terrified. What do I do? Desperately need your help.

I don't know what's more surprising, that he actually asked Valentina out, or that he's openly admitting he needs help. I text him back.

> Woohoo! You did it! I knew you could! Give me all the details.

My phone rings immediately and it's Paolo.

"Julieta."

"Paolo." I say back and wait for more.

"What have I done?" His voice is panicked. I get a drink of water for Isa, who is flopped on the couch, covered in sweat, and then sneak down to my room.

"You went for it!" I say. "And she said yes!"

"I thought her saying no was the worst thing that could happen. But this is worse. What if everything goes terribly? What if I make a complete fool of myself?"

I've never heard Paolo like this. He's literally the most self-assured person I know.

"Paolo," I say. "You can do this. You're going to have an amazing time, and at our Monday lunch, you're going to tell me every detail in giddy excitement."

Four days later, I meet Paolo for lunch. He looks neither giddy nor excited. I wait until we've ordered our food and finally ask, "How was your date on Saturday?"

Paolo's shoulders drop. "Wonderful. A disaster. A wonderful disaster."

"Start from the beginning."

"I took her to a work party. Everyone there loves me, and she could see how successful and respected I am."

I snort but make no comment.

"Then, when things were winding down, I asked if she wanted to get some dessert. We went to this little cafe with the best *torta al cioccolato*. We talked. She told me about her family. We were really connecting, you know?"

His face looks earnest and hopeful. It's not an expression I've seen on him before.

"So, what happened next?"

"Well, I ruined it, that's what happened next."

I raise an eyebrow. "Elaborate."

"I couldn't keep my dumb mouth shut. I told her everything."

Paolo seems to think he's explained himself, but I press for more information.

"You told her everything about what, Paolo?"

"How she smells like my grandmother's garden. How her hair shines like warm olive oil. How the sound of her laughter makes me want to learn how to juggle."

"Oh."

"I know."

"In those exact words?"

Paolo hangs his head and mumbles, "Even the part about juggling."

Yeesh.

"How did she respond?" I ask in what I hope is a neutral tone.

"Well, she didn't run screaming from the cafe."

"That's good."

"She walked silently from the cafe."

"That's not good."

I make Paolo promise he'll come to Calypso Wednesday night to do some damage control. He says if he hasn't left the country by then, he'll think about it.

"Has Paolo said anything to you about me?"

The question comes from Valentina while we're washing our hands in the bathroom at Calypso. "I know you guys are pals, and I just...wondered."

I'm not sure how to answer. I don't want to betray Paolo's trust, but he's already told her how he feels, so it's not like I could spill the beans.

"He told me the two of you went out on a date and that he had a really nice time with you," I say. I grab a paper towel and dry my hands.

"If he had such a nice time with me, why hasn't he asked me out again?" Valentina asks.

"Do you want him to ask you out again?" I ask, careful to keep the surprise out of my voice.

"Yes!" Valentina says. She turns the water off. "Our last date ended...kinda weird. But I thought he'd at least ask me out again."

"What do you mean weird?" I pry shamelessly. I need to know her side of things.

Valentina shakes her head. "He started rambling and said I smelled like a grandma and my hair looked oily. Even though I showered just before our date. And then there was something about him becoming a juggler. He was mumbling a lot and looked really embarrassed. Maybe he was embarrassed to be seen with me when my hair looked so oily? Anyway, I left as quick as I could."

Wow. This has gotten out of hand.

I don't want to meddle, but...I'm going to meddle. I check the stalls, make sure they're empty and then grab Valentina by the shoulders.

"Do you like Paolo?" I ask her.

"I do," she says with eyes filled with longing. "I have for a long time. I know he can come off kind of cynical, and a little vain, but deep down he's a good guy. And I was so excited when he asked me out..."

"Here's the deal," I say. "Paolo is crazy about you. He has been for ages. He thinks you smell like his grandma's garden and that your hair shines like olive oil. At the end of your date, he was trying to tell you how he felt. And then he was embarrassed for coming on too strong."

"Coming on too strong? I had no idea what he was even talking about! I went home and washed my hair again!" She shakes her head. "Men are such idiots sometimes!"

I can see the meaning of my words sink in and a slow smile spreads across her face. "You think he really likes me?"

"I know he does."

We head back to the dance floor, and I think about her liking Paolo all this time. Watching him ask me out on a date and still being sweet and supportive must have sucked for her. I watch her dance with Carmen and Diego. She is beaming.

Paolo better not screw this up.

I spy him at the bar, watching Valentina from a distance. I march up to him and say, "You need to ask Valentina out again."

"What? Really? Right now?"

"Sometime tonight. Do it before you leave."

"You think she wants me to?"

"Yes. And I'm officially done meddling. The rest is up to you two."

The club seems extra full tonight, and after an hour of being jostled I need a break. I'm sitting next to Diego and Carmen, and Jake has just gone to get us some bottles of water, when Britney Spears' "Hit Me Baby One More Time" comes on. It's a weird techno version, but still, it's Britney.

"We've got to dance to this one," Carmen says.

"But my feet," I protest.

Either she doesn't hear me, or she plain ignores me, because she grabs my hand and pulls me up. I grab Diego and Valentina, who are nearby, and we head back to the dance floor. Valentina and I are shaking our hips and giggling when someone puts a hand on my waist from behind. I can tell right away it's not Jake. I push the hand off and twist away without bothering to look behind me. Valentina sees and gives me a sympathetic look. I shrug my shoulders. This happens sometimes. It's fine.

Until it isn't. Two seconds later, the hands are back on my hips. I whirl around to see a tall Italian guy with a smirky grin and beady eyes.

"*Basta*," I say loudly so he can hear. Enough.

I push his hands off my hips and turn back to Valentina. I'm about to suggest we sit down when I feel his hand grab my butt and squeeze hard.

And just like that I'm filled with rage. I don't even think. My right hand clenches into a fist, and I turn and punch him in the stomach as hard as I can.

The force of my anger catches him solidly in the solar plexus and knocks the wind out of him. He doubles over, stumbling, and a couple of girls nearby yelp. I grab Valentina's hand, and we head to our table in the back. Adrenaline is pumping through my body and my hand is throbbing.

"How did you do that?" Valentina asks as we sit down next to Paolo.

"I have no idea," I answer honestly.

"Do what?" Paolo asks.

Before either of us can answer, Diego and Carmen come running over.

"OhmygoshIcan'tbelievethatjusthappened," Carmen says in a rush.

"That was amazing!" Diego says. "You were like Trinity from the *Matrix*."

"Are you okay?" Valentina asks. She's staring at my hands trembling in my lap.

"What just happened?" Paolo demands.

"This guy was getting handsy with Julieta on the dance floor and she took him out. Solid punch to the stomach. He was at least six inches taller than her, but she took him *down*. You don't mess with Julieta." Diego puts his hand up to high five me, and I high five him as gently as I can.

"Is this loon speaking the truth, *Dolcetta*?" Paolo asks me. His tone is light, but his eyes are filled with concern.

"More or less that's how it went down."

Paolo whistles. "I would have loved to see that."

"I bet he has a broken rib," Diego says.

"Who has a broken rib?" Jake asks. He's just arrived at the table carrying two bottles of water.

"The Italian man your girlfriend just knocked to the floor with one punch," Paolo says.

Jake's mouth drops open. Carmen and Valentina and Diego share their eyewitness accounts and it's comical to watch the expression on Jake's face as he listens. He goes from surprise to disbelief to anger to concern while I open a bottle of water and take a long drink.

"That slimeball does not have a broken rib," I say. "He got the wind knocked out of him, that's all."

"Are you okay?" Jake asks. He puts his arm around my shoulders, and I let myself relax into him.

"I'm okay," I say.

"Where'd you learn to punch like that?" Carmen asks.

"My brothers. But that's the first time I've ever punched anyone. He only went down because he wasn't expecting it. I'm not actually that strong and impressive."

"I think you are incredibly strong," Valentina says. "I was very impressed."

For some reason, her words make tears pop up in my eyes. I think the adrenaline is still messing with me.

"Hey, do you realize what song we were dancing to?" Diego says.

"Yeah, it was Britney Spears," Carmen says.

"It was 'Hit Me Baby One More Time,'" Diego says.

The table loses it. Diego starts singing the chorus and throwing air punches, Paolo is snorting and wiping away tears and Carmen and Valentina are shaking with laughter. My hand's still throbbing, but apart from that I feel pretty dang good.

Chapter Eleven

I'm wearing a sweater, my special thermal pants and my long coat, but I'm still cold. There is a *sciopero* for the fourth straight day and all the public transportation in the city is shut down.

I haven't seen Jake in five days. Which may not seem like a long time, but we've seen each other every day for the last month, so five days apart seems like a lot. Plus he's sick. So I've got my comfy sneakers and an audiobook to get me the 5.3 kilometers to his apartment. Isa helped me make a tasty soup this afternoon and it sloshes in its Tupperware in my backpack.

I'm nearly halfway through my book, right when the fairies are plotting a revolution, when I make it to Jake's. I knock on his door and one of his roommates answers it. I should know his name by now, but I don't, and I'm too afraid to guess.

"*Ciao*, I'm here to see Jake."

"Sorry, he's sick." He doesn't look particularly sorry.

I smile as nicely as I can. "I know. That's why I came."

He shrugs his shoulders and moves out of the way, which I take as an invitation to zip to Jake's room.

"Juliet!" Jake says. His voice is low and croaky, and his face is pale. He does not look good.

"I brought you soup!" I say in my most cheerful voice. I place my backpack on his desk and carefully take out the Tupperware.

"Soup?" he asks. He struggles to sit up in bed, and I help him prop an extra pillow behind his back.

"Yes, soup. And a pomegranate from that fruit vendor I told you about."

"Is the strike over?" Jake asks, grabbing a box of tissues and blowing his nose. He sounds like my Uncle Melvin.

I shake my head. "I walked."

"From your apartment?" His croaky voice rises in surprise.

"I'm a fast walker. And you're sick."

"You're the greatest girlfriend in the world," he says.

I flinch a little at the word girlfriend, then jump up to grab a bowl and a spoon from the kitchen. When I get back, Jake has scooted to one side to make room for me on the bed.

"I must look terrible," he says, as I snuggle in next to him. He's probably contagious, but I don't care.

"I've missed your face," I say.

He takes a bite of his soup. "This tastes amazing."

"Thanks, Isa helped me make it."

"How is she doing?" he asks, taking another bite.

"Not great. Sofia put her hair in pigtails and then Isa cut one off because she only likes ponytails. Then she yelled at Sofia, like an angry asymmetrical pixie, because clearly this was Sofia's fault." I shake my head and smile. "Now they're trying to find a salon that's open during the strike."

"Oh man." He's nearly finished his soup, and I swear he looks a little bit healthier. "What have you photographed lately?" he asks.

I tell him about the pictures I took this week around the Rossis' neighborhood. All the ordinary things I don't want to forget. The cobblestone path to the park with a big crack through the third stone. The front door of the Rossis' apartment. The bus stop where Isa and I catch the bus every morning.

"Do you remember when you threatened to poke me in the eye if I encouraged you to follow your dreams?" Jake asks.

"That doesn't sound like me."

Jake smiles. "I'm counting on the fact that I look too pathetic for you to poke right now. What's so terrible about following your dreams and becoming a photographer?"

"We've had this conversation before," I say.

"Yeah, and I didn't get it then either."

"Have I told you about my grandpa?" I ask. Jake's eyebrows knit together at the abrupt change in topic.

"I don't believe you have," he says.

"My grandpa was a painter. He pursued his dream of painting even when it didn't pay the bills." I look around Jake's room. At his desk, at a poster on the wall, anywhere but him. "My dad grew up with nothing. He's the oldest of seven, and he got a job at fourteen to support the family. All while my grandpa painted." I try to say it lightly, but it doesn't quite work.

"That must have been hard for your dad," Jake offers. His voice is full of sympathy.

"It was. So, when he became a dad, he worked eighty hours a week to make sure we always had food on the table. We barely saw him when we were kids. And somehow we were still poor."

I smile to show that I'm over it, and it's not a big deal.

I clear my throat. "Anyway. I think sometimes you need to be realistic about your dreams. There are other people to think of. My dad's already been hurt by one dream chaser. I can't do that to him again."

I don't wait for Jake to respond.

"Can I get you some more meds?" I ask.

Jake looks at me like he wants to say more, then shakes his head and says, "Sure, the meds are on my dresser. I don't think they make much difference, to be honest."

I bring him the bottle and his water. Within minutes, his eyelids start drooping and his voice gets floaty.

"Thank you for taking such good care of me. I feel like I'm a hundred years old."

"I'm so sorry you feel so bad. I'm going to let you get some rest."

His eyes fly open. "No, I don't need rest! Stay."

"Okay, I'll stay," I say. His eyelids flutter back closed.

"Good. Stay forever."

I smile but say nothing. When his breathing has gotten nice and even, I collect my things and let myself out. I zip up my coat, put in my headphones, and start the long walk home.

Chapter Twelve

Today is an obscure Italian holiday and the whole gang is going to Switzerland for the weekend. Switzerland! Paolo managed to book us two rooms at a bed and breakfast at the base of the Alps. The rates are super cheap. He says it's because we're sleeping three to a room, but I suspect it's because it's a mafia safe house.

We arrive to a world of white. I've never seen so much snow in my life. I didn't even know that much snow could exist in one place. Paolo shivers and mutters something about missing Sicily.

We drop off our bags at the lodge and go exploring. Pine branches bow under the weight of the snow and all the shops look like they're made of gingerbread. It's idyllic, but this California girl starts losing feeling in her toes quickly. I'm relieved when we head back to the lodge.

A snowball fight breaks out just as we near the entrance, and after narrowly avoiding a snowball to the face, I zip up to the girl's room to grab my camera, then settle onto the front porch to record the battle. Jake and Diego are crouched behind a wheelbarrow filled with snow. Diego lands a snowball in the center of Paolo's back and then drops down before Paolo can see him. Carmen is darting behind trees getting close to Jake and Diego, but they haven't seen her yet.

I snap and snap and snap. I've been watching tutorials on action shots, and I think I've gotten better. It's hard to zoom in when everyone is moving so fast, but I love capturing their expressions best of all. Carmen is steps away from Jake and Diego's position, and I focus on Diego's face and wait. I know Carmen will go for him first.

Sure enough, just as he's about to launch a shot at Valentina, he takes a snowball to the back of the neck at close range. His mouth drops open in surprise, and his eyes squinch shut in cold, and I capture it perfectly. I swivel to capture Carmen's triumphant face. Her hair is in disarray, and she's laughing.

Eventually we head to our rooms, wet and cold and promising vengeance.

"We've been here three hours, and I've gone through all my clothes for the weekend," I tell Valentina and Carmen as I lay my wet socks on the radiator.

"Just buy some new ones," Carmen says.

"This is a Swiss resort town. I don't think pants cost the same here as they do at the Sant'Ambrogio market."

"So have Jake buy some for you," Carmen says. "He's loaded." She's changing out of her sweater and laying it out to dry.

"He's not loaded," I say reflexively.

"Okay, his family is, same thing." She says it like everyone knows this.

I look at Valentina for a second, but I'm not quite sure what to ask.

Carmen slips a dry sweater over her head and then looks at me curiously. "You didn't know he was rich?"

"I never thought about it. He doesn't seem..."

Now Carmen is smirking at me. "What, because he doesn't dress like Paolo? And he always needs a haircut? Both of his parents are *doctors*. And his house is gigantic."

My face heats. *How could I have been so oblivious?*

"When did you see pictures of Jake's house?" I ask.

It comes out more accusatory than I meant, and Carmen does not respond well. Her hands go to her hips, and her eyes narrow.

"I saw pictures of his house when we were all sharing photos of our homes," she says defiantly. "It was before you got here. And if I know more about him than you, it's because I'm paying attention."

I need to leave this room.

For a moment, I try to think of some polite excuse, but when I can't, I simply open the door and walk out. I head down to the first floor and find a tiny library tucked into a hallway near the lobby.

I'd just assumed that Jake's family was like mine. *Only why would they be when my parents run a dry cleaner, and his parents are both doctors?*

I plunk into a big red armchair and replay conversations I've had with Jake. Talking about going camping as a family, because we were too broke to go on a real vacation. Worrying about how I'll pay off my student loans when I get back. How stupid I must have sounded. I'm scuffing my shoe on the carpet and feeling like a moron when there's a knock on the door frame.

"Come on in," I mumble.

Jake sits in the chair next to mine. "Cool library."

"Yeah." A thought pops into my head. "Do you have a library in your house?"

"A small one, yeah. It's filled with my parents' books from med school. Why?"

"Are you super rich?" I ask bluntly.

He gives me a weird look. "We do okay."

I suck in a breath. "You're so rich you have to downplay how rich you are."

Jake holds his hands out and raises his shoulders in the universal gesture for, 'I'm not sure what to tell you.'

My shoulders slump. I don't know what I want from him.

"You seem surprised," Jake says, taking my hand. "And upset. Is it a big deal if my family has money?"

"I just feel weird around you now." I fiddle with the trim on the arm of my chair. "All my stressing about paying off student loans, I thought it was something you would get. But you don't."

I take a deep breath and look at him. "And there's probably a bunch of stuff I don't get about you. Does your family own a yacht? Do you have a personal chef? Do you swim in a pool filled with caviar?"

"We don't own a yacht," Jake says. "We had a housekeeper who cooked dinner a couple times a week because my parents worked crazy hours. I have never once swam in a pool filled with caviar. We fill ours with champagne. Better for swimming."

He smiles at me and when I smile back, he pulls me into his chair and wraps his arms around me. "I'm sorry if this makes things weird. Maybe now you can stop feeling bad when I pay for dinner."

"I know that should make it better," I say "but now it feels like I'm a spoiled girlfriend whose rich boyfriend buys her everything. Nobody wants to be that girl."

Jake coughs. "Actually, lots of people want to be that girl. I've had the misfortune of dating that girl a time or two."

"Well, I don't want to be that girl," I say firmly.

"Wait, what are you saying?" His eyes fill with hurt.

I backtrack immediately. "I'm sorry, I didn't mean it that way. I love being with you. I just got freaked out about the money thing, which is something that happens when you don't grow up with it. But I'll adjust."

I take another deep breath. "And I probably need to apologize to Carmen. Otherwise, sharing a bed tonight is going to be super awkward."

"You could apologize...or you could sneak into my bed." He gives me dramatic eyebrow raises like a cartoon character.

I laugh and give him a kiss. I expect to see him smiling, but his face suddenly looks serious.

"There's actually something I wanted to talk to you about," he says.

My hands start sweating. *What does he want to talk to me about? About sneaking into his bed? Was he serious about that?* I climb off his lap and move back to my own chair.

"I never know when to have this conversation," he starts. "And this is probably too early, but ..."

What's early? What's he talking about??

Jake runs a hand through his hair. "Remember when we were walking, and you told me about your first kiss?"

"Yes..." *Spin the bottle, seventh grade, Andy Bowers.*

"And I told you about my first kiss?" *Michelle Terry. Mistletoe. Eighth grade.*

I nod my head, still unsure where this is going.

"Well, that was my only first. There haven't been any other firsts."

"You haven't kissed anyone since eighth grade?"

That's weird, right?

"No, there have been other kisses," he says. He looks up at the ceiling.

BETTER THAN GELATO

"But no, um, other first times." He tries to meet my gaze but doesn't quite make it there. His cheeks are pink.

"So you've never...?"

He shakes his head. "No." He risks a quick glance in my direction. "It's not a big deal. I don't have any judgments toward people who do things differently. I just have my own plan. One that involves a really great wedding night."

Oh.

"This is probably more information than you needed at this point," Jake says, running his hands down his thighs to his knees. "I just wanted to get on the same page."

I debate a second and then say, "I don't think it will be an issue. I'm not necessarily waiting until marriage, but I do have certain expectations for who and when, etcetera, and so far they haven't been met. So...I'm in your same boat."

"You're in my same boat?" Jake finally makes eye contact with me.

"I am."

"Well, that's a relief." He rubs one hand down his face.

I laugh. "Have you been afraid of me trying to seduce you?"

He smiles. "Half-hoping, half-dreading, I suppose."

I don't love conversations like these, but I'm glad Jake brought it up. I also like being on the same page.

"Well, I guess that means I'm sharing a bed with Carmen tonight," I say dramatically.

"Yeah, better go work that out," Jake says.

"I've been pretty insensitive," I say standing up. "You and I became a thing, and if it works out with Valentina and Paolo, Carmen will be the only single girl in our group. That can't feel good."

"You're probably right." He takes my hand and starts tracing the veins at my wrist. "Do you feel like finding the rest of the gang and playing pool? Or would you rather hang out here a bit more?" His tone is casual, but the look in his eyes is not.

"I'm terrible at pool," I say, and let him pull me onto his lap.

A long time later, we leave the library holding hands.

We find the rest of the group in the rec room finishing their game.

"*Benvenuti ragazzi,*" Paolo says. "You missed a great game."

"If by great you mean completely demoralizing," Carmen says.

"Yes, that's exactly what I mean," Paolo says.

"The boys beat us pretty good," Valentina admits. "How about a new game? And maybe we switch up the teams."

"What's the matter, Valentina?" Diego asks. "Tired of being on the losing team?" Valentina nods her head unabashedly.

The game room has a pool table, a foosball table, and a ping pong table. And on one wall, waiting for me like an old friend, hangs a dart board. A tingle of excitement fizzes in my veins. I suck at pool, but I'm great at darts. We played for hours growing up. In college, I discovered I could make an easy twenty bucks off the jocks in the common room if I played things right.

"Let's try one more boys against girls," I say. It's been a few months, but I think I've still got it.

I don't suggest darts, but I try to get us there.

"How about ping pong?" Diego suggests.

"Doesn't work for six people," I say.

"Plus, we would demolish the girls," Paolo says.

"How about foosball?" Diego asks.

"That's four people at most," Carmen says.

"And also, we would demolish you," Paolo says again.

Finally Jake says, "How about darts?"

I hold my breath and keep quiet until everyone else agrees.

"Prepare to be demolished," Paolo tells us.

"Actually," I say, "I think me and my girls can take you three pretty easily."

"Care to place money on it?" Paolo says. He grins at me, and I grin right back.

"I couldn't take your money, Paolo. We're besties." I take a step closer. "But I *could* allow you to treat the girls to dinner tonight. To thank us for teaching you a lesson in humility."

"Ooooohh," Diego and Jake say, and it sounds like the beginning of a junior high fight.

"Losers pay for dinner? We absolutely accept those terms," Paolo says. "I think I'll order the lobster."

I look at the girls. "What do you ladies say?"

Valentina is shaking her head, but Carmen says, "We absolutely accept those terms." There's a fire blazing in her eyes.

"All right, let's get started," Diego says like the announcer at a sporting event.

"Three oh one," Paolo says. Then he turns to me. "Each team starts with three hundred and one points. You throw three darts per turn. The first team to get to exactly zero wins." I nod and pretend I don't know the rules by heart.

The boys grab some darts, and my hands start to sweat. I take a breath. *I've got this.*

Diego goes first, and his dart misses the board completely. "Just warming up," he says. He rubs his right wrist. I saw him rubbing it earlier. I think he must have hurt it in the snowball fight. He throws two more and earns a total of fourteen points for his team. My brain pulls up their score, 287.

Valentina goes next, and her first two darts bounce off the board. Her third manages to hang on in the 20 spot.

"Pulling out to an early lead," Carmen says to Paolo and gives me a high five.

Paolo goes next, easily beating Valentina's score.

"Hope you enjoyed your lead while it lasted," Paolo says.

Carmen goes next, then Jake. They both throw just fine, but clearly they're not dart players. When it's my turn, the score is Girls 255, Boy 247. Carmen hands me some darts. She looks nervous, but I feel calm. I take a breath and throw. Triple 20. Another breath and throw. Triple 20. Last breath, last throw. Triple 20. 180. It's a perfect turn. I only pulled that off twice last year. I just dropped our score to 75.

I can't help smiling a little. Then I turn to look at the gang and smile a lot. Paolo, Diego, Jake, and Valentina wear identical expressions of shock. Eyes wide, mouths open, like a surprised barbershop quartet. Carmen is pumping her fists in victory and looking happier than I've seen her in a while.

Jake comes over and gives me a kiss. "Have you played this game before?" he asks with a smile.

"Maybe once or twice," I say.

Diego has a bad first shot, but his next two are decent. Valentina, apparently inspired by our tremendous lead, earns us 30. We're at 56. Paolo and Jake take their second turns, and they're better than their firsts, but nowhere close to overtaking us. After Carmen takes a turn and hands me the darts and we're down to 26.

I pick up a dart and look at the board. I try for the double 12, but I'm off just a hair and land on single 12. *It's okay. I've got two more.* I take a deep breath and aim in the exact same spot. My second dart lands just a sliver away from my first dart. Alright, 2 points left. Paolo starts to say something, to psych me out I'm sure, but I pay him no attention. My last dart lands in the black of the 2 with a satisfying thunk. It's the sound of victory.

"Well, it looks like that's the game," Jake says with a laugh.

"That's the fastest game of darts I've ever played," Diego says.

"Can you really call what you were doing, playing?" Carmen asks.

"Do they serve lobster *and* steak at this restaurant?" I ask Paolo. "Something about crushing victory makes me crave seafood and red meat."

Jake comes over and gives me a big kiss, and Diego mumbles something about kissing the enemy. He's taking the loss pretty hard. Paolo actually gives him a hug, and Paolo never hugs anyone.

"You were incredible," Jake says. "I had no idea you could play like that."

"I can," I say simply.

The girls do some more celebrating and gloating and then we head upstairs to get ready for dinner.

On the way, I stop Carmen and apologize.

"I'm sorry about earlier. I didn't mean to be so accusing."

"No, it was my fault," she says. "I was angry about some other stuff. Anyway, after handing us that win, you are forgiven of all things."

"Carmen, if you ever want to talk about other stuff, I'm here," I say.

"Maybe. For now, let's go celebrate."

We take showers and change into nice dresses.

I curl Valentina's hair, then Carmen does my eye makeup. By the time we meet the boys in the lobby, we look pretty amazing. It feels like a double victory to look this good after beating them so bad.

"The lovely champions have arrived," Jake says, and I give him a big smile. Diego still looks sad about losing, but Paolo is looking at Valentina, and he is definitely not thinking about darts.

The restaurant has soaring ceilings, full-length windows, and at least three large fireplaces that I can see. The food is excellent. Instead of steak and lobster, I get a Swiss dish I can't pronounce that involves a lot of potatoes and cheese and a very tender meat. Jake and Paolo pick up the bill, which makes everything taste even better.

———

The next morning, I wake up to the sun reflecting off the frozen lake outside our lodge, lighting up our whole room. Carmen and Valentina are still asleep, and I tiptoe to the bathroom. I pause when I see a slip of paper on the floor by the door.

Juliet,

Not sure if you're an early riser, but if you're awake meet me in the library.

-J

A thrill of excitement zings through me. I brush my teeth and put on a bra. Then I slip out the door and head to the library. The wood floor is chilly on my bare feet, and I shiver. Jake is waiting in the big chair. He's wearing faded jeans and a dark blue sweater. I don't say a word, just fall into his lap and start kissing him. This is better than sleeping in. This is better than anything, actually.

"I got your note," I whisper.

"I see that," he whispers back. He smells clean and fresh, like the snow outside. But he's all warmth, his arms and his lips. I feel my muscles warming up and relaxing, my whole body melting into his.

"This is a very good way to start the day," he says. His voice is low and rough.

I imagine waking up this morning next to Jake instead of Carmen. The picture in my head is so clear it makes my cheeks flush. Jake's eyes look into mine, two shades darker than normal, and I wonder if the same thought has popped into his head.

He leans in and kisses a trail from my collarbone to my jawline, then to my mouth. The world outside the two of us is distant and irrelevant as we kiss in the early morning light. As usual, it's Jake who breaks away first. His breathing is fast and shallow. He runs a shaky hand through his hair.

"So, libraries, huh?"

"Pretty hot," I agree.

"I think kissing you is pretty hot wherever we happen to be."

"Sure. But isn't there something about the two of us tucked away in a tiny library in a rustic lodge in the Alps?"

He shakes his head and gives me one more slow kiss. "You aren't making this easy for me."

I climb off his lap and give him a big smile. Then I start dancing the Floss.

"What are you doing?" he says with a bemused smile.

"I'm making it easier for you."

He bursts out laughing. "By doing the Floss dance?"

"Yes. The least sexy dance in the world. Is it helping?"

He laughs. "You do look much less seductive than you did one minute ago."

"Not fair. You can't leave me a note to meet you in the library in the early morning hours and then call me seductive. This one's on you."

"Okay, you're right. I take full credit for the brilliant idea of luring you here."

"As long as we're straight on who's luring who."

Jake stands up and starts doing the Floss next to me. We look ridiculous, I know, but I have not ripped all his clothes off, so I'll call that a win.

And that's when the other four members of our group walk into the lobby and see us in the library.

Diego trips into Valentina. Carmen bursts out laughing. And Paolo says, "I was under an entirely different impression of your activities when the two of you sneak away together."

They're all dressed and ready for the day.

"We were just coming down for some breakfast," Valentina says. I can tell she's trying hard not to laugh.

"Yes, well, so were we. We just thought we should get some morning exercise to really work up an appetite. But we're ready now. Let's eat."

"Aren't you wearing pajamas?" Diego asks me.

I am, in fact, wearing pajamas. They're purple flannel. With stripes. But instead of doing the smart thing and admitting it, I dig in.

"To the untrained eye, I can see how these might *look* like pajamas. But they're very much day clothes. They just match a lot. It's called color blocking. Very trendy right now."

I shoot a glance at Carmen, who manages to keep a straight face and say, "Color blocking. Yes. Trendy."

And so we all go to the dining room, and I eat a delicious Swiss breakfast in my pajamas in a room full of fully clothed guests.

After breakfast, we choose sleds from a pile behind the lodge. We hike to a nearby hill, and Jake is the first one to go down, whooping and hollering the whole way. Carmen and I follow him. The hill starts off steep and then turns into a gentle slope at the end. A perfect sledding hill. I rush down, barely passing Jake at the end, and we both end up in a snowbank. I haven't been sledding since a family reunion in Idaho a decade ago. I forgot how exhilarating it is.

The other three come sledding down right after us and two of them land in the same snowbank we did. Diego somehow lands in a bush ten feet away.

"How do you steer these things?" he asks, tromping through the snow towards us.

"You can't," Jake says cheerfully. "You just point them and go."

We hike to the top of the hill for another go. Diego ends up in the bushes again, and Jake offers to switch sleds. Which begins the game, 'Will Diego End Up in the Bushes No Matter Which Sled He's On?' The short answer is yes. We swap our various sleds, some hard plastic saucers, some wooden with rails. It doesn't seem to matter. Diego ends up in the bushes every time, but he's unhurt and seems to be having just as much fun as the rest of us.

The sun is near blinding, reflected off the white snow, and the sky is a bright blue. I don't know how many times we go down that hill, but we're wet and exhausted by the time lunch rolls around. And too tired to do much else for the rest of the day.

We watch a movie on the giant screen in the game room. Valentina sits next to Paolo, and the romantic vibes from those two are bouncing off the walls. I think again about Carmen being the odd girl out. I make a note to talk to her about it.

That night, Paolo convinces the proprietors of our lodge to start a fire in the outdoor fire pit for our little group. I zip upstairs to change my socks, which have gotten wet yet again.

I'm slipping on some dry ones when Carmen comes in. She doesn't see me at first because she's looking at her phone. Her face is twisted in anger and worry and when she finally notices me she startles.

"Sorry," I say. "Just getting some dry socks."

"No problem."

She doesn't say anything else, and neither do I. I slip into some boots and head to the door.

"Are you coming down?" I ask.

"I'm going to call it a night."

"It's only 9:30."

"Yeah, I just don't feel like hanging out with everyone right now."

She's tired of hanging out with a bunch of couples. I knew it.

"Hey, it seems like this weekend has been hard for you," I say.

She narrows her eyes but doesn't say anything, so I continue.

"With the group splitting into couples it can be easy to think, 'Why aren't I dating anyone?' I just want to remind you that you're smart and beautiful and funny. You're going to find someone wonderful."

Carmen looks at me a moment, then bursts out laughing. There's a note of bitterness to her laughter.

"You think I feel bad because everyone in the group is dating someone and I'm not?"

"I did...until exactly this moment."

"Julieta, I'm married."

There's no sound except my jaw hitting the floor.

"I'm married to a lunatic. That's why I left Peru."

I can't make any words come out of my mouth.

Carmen flops onto the bed. "Our divorce was supposed to be final this weekend, but apparently some of the paperwork was filed incorrectly."

"I had no idea."

"Yeah, no one does. It's a part of my past I'd like to keep in the past."

"I'm sorry."

"Me too." She smiles a little. "It's sweet of you to be concerned, but I've spent the last two years trying to undo the last romantic mistake I made. I'm not trying to make new ones."

"Can I...are you...is there anything I can do?"

Another faintly bitter smile. "Nope."

She reaches out and squeezes my hand. "But thanks for asking."

"Sure," I reply lamely. "Enjoy your night in."

I head to the back patio, still trying to process this news. *Carmen married? Boy did I misread that one!*

We spend a couple of hours by the fire. Diego tells ghost stories, and in the firelight, his face looks eerily pale. But the stories aren't scary because he keeps mixing up the endings and forgetting parts. Paolo plays the guitar, and he's very good at it.

Sometime after midnight we call it a night. Instead of following me upstairs to the rooms Jake takes my hand and leads me back to the library.

He pulls me onto his lap. His lips meet mine and everything around us disappears.

Chapter Thirteen

Christmas hits hard in Milan. There are lights strung up across every narrow street. Wreaths on every signpost. There's cutthroat competition among the shops around il Duomo to see who can create the most over-the-top Christmas display. Gorgeous evening gowns for holiday parties compete against festive place settings for family gatherings and elaborate gingerbread houses with candy reindeer and Babbo Natale, the Italian Santa Claus.

I take pictures of everything. I've been watching YouTube tutorials and trying out some new settings. Jake is incredibly patient as I stop every few feet to take "one more shot."

"You're really talented," he says one night as I edit some photos on my laptop.

We're curled up on the couch in the Rossis' living room. The Rossis are spending two weeks in Egypt at a spa with special dead sea mud. Isa is the only six-year-old I know who gets spa treatments.

"Thanks," I tell Jake.

I close my laptop and snuggle into his lap.

"I've been thinking about your grandpa," Jake says.

"Weird way to set the mood, but okay."

"I've been thinking about him as an artist," Jake continues. He rubs a hand down my arm. "Just because he neglected his family to pursue his own dream doesn't mean that following your dream is selfish or bad."

"I know that," I say.

"Do you? Because you seem set against doing something you love, and determined to do something that will make you miserable."

"I'm determined to do something that makes sense," I say. "My dad didn't have the luxury of going to college. I do. I'm not going to waste it earning a degree in something frivolous that won't pay off my loans or help my family's finances."

Jake makes a frustrated sound. "It's not about the money."

"For you it's not because you've always had it. For my family, it's always about the money." I sit up, out of his reach. "But it will be different for my kids. If I earn a degree in business and work hard, I can make that dry cleaners profitable. I can make the kind of money my dad always tried to and never quite could.

"My kids won't eat free lunch in the cafeteria. They won't dig through the bins at the Salvation Army for their school clothes. They won't endure the teasing that followed because Catrina Bradshaw was dropping off a couch with her parents and saw and told everyone at school."

"Juliet, I'm sorry. I didn't—"

"You didn't know. I get it. And the truth is, you'll never know. But you don't have to feel sorry for me either. I'm not that poor little girl anymore. I'm a grown-up who gets to make her own choices. And I'm choosing a life of financial security over dream chasing."

Jake doesn't say anything.

"We'd better go, or we'll be late," I say. I grab my coat, and Jake follows me to the door.

Every December, they set up an ice-skating rink in the middle of the piazza. By the time me and Jake get there, our whole gang is already on the ice. They are all terrible skaters. Valentina and Paolo keep falling, and Diego is hanging on the side of the rink out of breath. We spend an hour skating, falling and laughing.

Afterward, Jake and I grab some hot chocolate. It hasn't snowed yet, but it feels like it could any moment.

"Are you feeling homesick?" Jake asks.

I shake my head. "I was just thinking how if we were back home, I'd be the cliche college girl who brings home a boy at Christmas."

"You'd bring me to meet your family?" he asks. His tone is the kind you use with a skittish horse you don't want to spook.

"I mean technically, if we were back home, we would have never met. So when I invited you, you'd be like, 'I don't know you. Seems weird to meet your family.'"

He ignores my joking and says, "That's a big deal."

"Maybe I'm ready for a big deal," I say.

He doesn't say anything, just smiles and kisses me.

"I didn't know it was possible to smile and kiss at the same time," I say.

"I'm a very good multi-tasker," he says, still smiling.

The holidays do funny things to you. Like make you wear outlandish sweaters with tinsel, and drink gross beverages like eggnog, and think ridiculous things like *I'm in love with Jake.*

"Merry Christmas!" Jake says. He sets a large bag of groceries on the Rossis' table and slips a backpack off his shoulder. We're hosting Christmas Eve dinner for the whole gang at my place tonight, and I'm super excited.

"I got everything we need," Jake says.

He nudges his backpack with his foot and looks at me, then looks away.

"I also brought some, um, pajamas. And a toothbrush. I thought, since it'll probably be a late night and we talked about spending Christmas morning together, maybe I could spend the night here, in Isa's room. Unless that feels weird to you. It's totally up to you." He's wiggling his left foot like he has a kink in it. "I'm fine either way."

"You're adorable either way. I'd love it if you spent the night. I definitely don't want to do all the dishes myself."

Jake's posture loosens in relief. He brings his backpack to Isa's room and then comes back into the kitchen and says, "What should I make us for lunch?"

"This. This right here is why I—" I stop just in time. "Why I'm glad you're here."

Jake looks at me funny.

BETTER THAN GELATO

"Because lunch is great," I clarify. "And I'm very hungry."

Jake opens the fridge to see what we have, which is not much because I've procrastinated grocery shopping.

"How about frittata?" he says. He pulls out eggs and cheese and half a bell pepper and four mushrooms and some greens that could be spinach.

I watch in wonder as he turns these things into a tasty lunch.

In the afternoon, we jump into making fried chicken. It seemed like a weird choice for Christmas Eve, but Jake was excited about it. Apparently, it's a Fields family tradition.

Paolo and Valentina show up together, which I take as a good sign. Carmen and Diego arrive a few minutes later and everyone looks happy to be out of the cold. I've moved the kitchen table into the living room so we can all be together.

"Okay *ragazzi*, we've got a *lot* of fried chicken," I say. "We also have salad, biscuits, and mashed potatoes. Before we dig in, I just want to thank you guys for coming tonight and tell you how grateful I am to have stumbled into this wonderful group." I was going to say more but suddenly find that my throat is tight, and my eyes feel itchy.

"*Buon appetito*," I say.

"*Buon appetito*," the group echoes.

Then we dig into the food. I haven't had fried chicken in ages, and this tastes delicious.

"Wow, Julieta, this is even better than Paolo's lasagna," Diego says.

"Diego, I know you're saying that to hurt me," Paolo says, "so I will disregard it as the lie that it is. No offense, *Dolcetta*. The chicken is very good."

"That was all Jake. It's a family recipe."

Paolo raises an eyebrow, and Jake says, "Yes, I know how to cook, and yes, Americans can have family recipes too."

After we eat, I make everyone go around the table and share something they're grateful for. Just like my dad makes us do on Christmas Eve.

Diego starts. "I'm thankful for all of you. I don't have my family here in Milan, but I do have a family here in Milan." He turns his head and rubs his left eye. I think Christmas time makes everyone more emotional.

"I am also grateful for good friends," Carmen says. "Christmas is a time to spend with people you care about. And I care about all of you. Even you, Paolo."

"When I left Argentina to come to Italy," Valentina says, "I had no idea I would meet people that would make this new country feel like home. I am truly grateful for each of you."

There's such a feeling of love and friendship in the room. This is what the holidays are all about.

"I'm grateful for the S&P 500," Paolo says. "It's had a great year."

Jake bursts out laughing and sprays cranberry punch all over his plate. I jump up to fetch some paper towels.

"Julieta, come back," Paolo says. "I'm only kidding. Believe it or not, I also have a heart. And like the rest of you, I'm grateful for the amazing people in my life. They make the bad moments good and the good moments better."

Jake mops up his plate and brings it into the kitchen. When he comes back, we're staring at him expectantly.

"At this point, it's not going to sound very original, but I was wandering alone in the piazza, getting pickpocketed by children, and you guys took me in. That means a lot."

There are "awws" around the table and some misty eyes.

"This is a terrible tradition," Paolo mutters.

"You're a terrible tradition," I mutter back.

"That doesn't even make sense."

"You don't even make sense."

It's well after midnight when everyone leaves, and I take one look at the kitchen and decide to leave the cleanup for tomorrow.

I'm tired but excited for my first sleepover with Jake. He's gone into Isa's room to change. I zip into my bedroom and put on my fanciest pink and black silky pajamas and then make us some hot chocolate. It's just the powdered kind, but it's still yummy and hot.

"Juliet in pajamas with hot cocoa," Jake says, coming into the kitchen. "This is just like that dream I had." Jake's wearing black sweatpants and a Johns Hopkins T-shirt. His huge smile matches my own.

"Merry Christmas," I say.

The hot cocoa is too hot to drink so we snuggle on the couch, which turns into kissing on the couch. When we pull apart, our chocolate has gone cold. I want to stay on the couch kissing Jake for the next three hours.

Instead, I move the mountain of stuffed animals off Isa's bed and tuck him in. He gives me a long, lingering kiss.

"Good night, Jake," I say.

"Good night, Juliet."

And then I crawl into my own bed and try to forget that Jake is sleeping on the other side of my wall.

The sound of my phone ringing wakes me up, and I know without looking it's my parents. As soon as I answer, they launch into "We wish you a Merry Christmas." My parents, like me, are not natural singers, but it's good to hear their voices. I can tell from the echoey sound that they have me on speakerphone.

I tell them all about Milan.

"The city is huge!"

"My new friends are awesome!"

"Isa made it a whole week without screaming obscenities at anyone!"

"I've gained 15 pounds but I'm fine with it."

And they tell me about home.

"We saw Maggie, and she misses you."

"We hung up your stocking, even though you're not here."

"The main steamer at the shop broke, but we got the repairman to fix it in exchange for free dry cleaning."

My stomach clenches at the mention of the shop that has captured my future.

I tell them about the party last night.

"Fried chicken?" my mom says. "For Christmas Eve?"

"It was Jake's idea" I say. "It turned out great."

"Jake is your American friend, right?"

"Right. And we're, um, kind of dating."

"What is kind of dating?" my dad asks.

"Well, not kind of dating. Actually dating."

"Oh! That's a big deal," my mom says.

116   LIBBY TANNER

"It's not a big deal," I say. "More like a small deal. Medium at most. Anyway, it's getting late there. You probably have more presents to wrap. I'll let you go."

"Sounds like someone doesn't want to tell us about her boyfriend." My dad draws out the last word in a sing-song voice.

"I love you. I'll email you some more photos soon."

"We love you too," my mom says. "Dad put a little money in your bank account so you can buy something special from that fancy market you told me about."

"Thanks, Mom. You guys are the greatest."

For just a beat after I hang up I feel a wave of homesickness. I shake it off and head to the bathroom. When I come out, I hear Jake in the kitchen humming and doing the dishes.

"Merry Christmas!" I yell and jump into his arms.

"Merry Christmas!" he yells back and hugs me tight. Then his mouth meets mine and my eyes close. There is nothing like this feeling. Chemistry and comfort. Safety and excitement. All mixed in one.

"So what would you like to do today?" I ask him between kisses.

"I'm already doing it."

I grin like an idiot. I feel the same way.

We finish cleaning up from last night, then make pancakes and eggs for breakfast. Afterward, we snuggle on the couch and take turns telling each other about our best and worst Christmases.

"All I wanted was my own mummy," Jake says. "I was sure I could use magic to bring it back to life. But no. I got roller blades."

I tell him about the Christmas I got my first camera, a used one my dad got from one of our dry-cleaning customers.

"I took approximately three thousand pictures the first week. Most of them were terrible and out of focus. But I still loved it."

"I can see how happy it makes you. I was so anxious the whole time you were dangling from that tree branch, but you had a huge smile on your face."

I'd forgotten about climbing that tree on our first date. *I'm such a dork.*

"How about your worst Christmas?" Jake asks.

My mind flashes to Christmas Eve when I was nine. My parents standing in their bedroom. My dad's arms covered in bandages.

"Hey, you okay?" Jake asks.

"Yeah, fine. Roller blades. The year I got roller blades. That was the worst."

Jake looks at me funny. "That's the thing I just said."

"Oh." *Dang.* "I mean a music box. It broke. Hey, are you ready for your Christmas gift?"

I can tell that Jake wants to ask me some follow-up questions, but I don't let him. I jump up and head to my room. I take a deep breath and then another one until my heart slows.

I pull his gift from the top shelf of my closet and fix the bow because it's gotten all squashed. When I hand it to him, Jake carefully unpeels the wrapping paper. I watch his face light up, and my heart lights up too.

It's a picture of us. One I took on the paddle boat. I'm looking slightly left and laughing, and Jake is looking right at me, smiling. I made it black and white because everything looks cooler in black and white. The photograph is the back wall of a shadow box, with a little glass door you can unlatch. Inside are things from our time together.

"We make a good-looking couple," Jake says. "Tell me about these things inside." He opens the latch and starts pulling things out.

"That's a pebble from the shore of that lake with the boats. This is my ticket stub from the Fiero di Sapori. This is a coaster from Calypso. Here's a leaf from that park we broke into."

"What's this?" Jake asks, picking up a tiny glass bottle with liquid inside.

"That was the hardest one to get. I went back to the Navigli Canals and got some water from the canal."

"Wow. That was a lot of effort for my Christmas gift."

I don't really know what to say so I just shrug.

"Thank you," he says. "What a great way to remember all the things we've done together. I love that it has a door to add more. By the end of this year, it's going to be filled."

"Maybe so," I say.

"Now it's time for your gift." He hands me a small box wrapped in shiny blue paper. My heart starts beating faster.

"Go on. It's nothing scary," Jake says.

I open the box, fold back the tissue and find...a flash drive.

"You got me a flash drive," I say.

"You can never have too many," he replies.

I'm truly puzzled at this random gift but then I see the edge of Jake's mouth turn.

"There's something on here," I say, almost sure.

"I don't know, put it into your computer and check it out."

I do and it's a video file. Behind the giant play triangle I can see Jake's face grinning at me. I hit play.

"Merry Christmas!" video-Jake says. "For your Christmas gift, I wanted to make you a video of all your favorite things in Milan."

The scene changes, and I see the white tents of the market. Neal Diamond's "Forever in Blue Jeans" starts playing.

"The song choice here is supposed to be ironic," Jake-on-the-couch says. "Because you don't actually wear jeans anymore."

The video shows all the tables at the market filled with shoes and purses and clothes. I've been there three more times since my first visit and have collected a decent Italian wardrobe. It really is one of my favorite places.

Then the music changes to "Cotton Eye Joe," and I'm looking at the outside of Calypso.

The video goes on to showcase the steps at Duomo, Castello Sforzesco, some of our favorite restaurants. Each new scene has its own song to go with it. They're all upbeat and happy, but it's making me weirdly emotional.

And then suddenly, Valentina, Carmen, Diego and Paolo are on screen, sitting on the steps at il Duomo.

"Merry Christmas Julieta," Valentina says. "Jake asked us to help him make this video for you and of course we said yes because we love you!" My eyes start to get all prickly.

"Merry Christmas Julieta," Carmen says. "I'm so glad the new nanny turned out to be you."

"Julieta, you are the coolest American I know," Diego says. "Wait, sorry Jake. I forgot about you. Should I do mine over?"

"Okay, fine I'll say it," Paolo says. "But only because Jake is bribing me. Merry Christmas, Bestie."

I burst out laughing. "How did you—" But I don't finish because video Jake has come back on, and I don't want to miss a word he says.

"*Ciao, bella!* I had such a great time filming your favorite people and places in Milan. Now I want to show you my favorite thing about Milan."

The opening notes of Ed Sheeran's "Perfect" start to play and the screen fills up with a picture of me. I'm sitting in a restaurant, looking down at my plate of pasta, and grinning like it's a plate full of diamonds.

Then there's a picture of me in the tree trying to get that shot at Castello Sforzesco. I didn't even know Jake took that picture. There's me dancing at Calypso. Me at the Fieri di Sapori. Me on the steps at Duomo. Waiting for the tram. Eating gelato.

I've never seen any of these pictures. I've never seen myself like this. I look happy. No, more than that. I look...transformed.

"I'm your favorite part about Milan?" I ask couch-Jake.

"You're my favorite part about everything," he says.

The song ends on a picture of me laughing at something off camera, as Ed Sheeran tells me I look perfect tonight. I feel perfect tonight. Or this morning. Whatever. I feel complete and whole and filled with something strange and wonderful. Filled like I might burst.

I look up, and Jake is watching me, gauging my reaction.

"What do you think?" he asks.

"I love it."

"You do?"

"And I love you."

"*You do?*"

I lean in and kiss him and try to put all the love I feel for him into that kiss. All the love that has been trying to come out for weeks, but I kept pushing it back in. Because I was too scared, and I didn't feel ready. I'm still scared. But I can't keep it in anymore. I let it all go, and I swear I can feel it flowing from my body to his.

Jake pulls back. His eyes are shiny, which suddenly makes my eyes tear up. *Why is Christmas so emotional!?*

"You already know I love you, don't you?" Jake says.

I do. It's in everything he does for me. Every time he looks at me. The way he touches me. I nod and kiss him again.

We spend most of Christmas Day kissing and telling each other "I love you." Later, as we're eating giant slices of Panettone cake, Jake says, "You know, I think even if I had gotten a mummy when I was seven, today would top that Christmas."

"Whoa, I beat out the mummy huh?"

"You did. Hard earned victory. Oh! And I got you another gift."

"What? Your first gift was perfect. There's no topping it. I wouldn't even try. You'll only feel silly."

Jake smiles and kisses me again. "This is a gift for both of us."

He jumps off the couch and dashes to Isa's room. He comes back holding a white envelope, which he hands to me.

I open it, and there are tickets inside. They have a symbol of a train. I check the date and the destination. December 30 to January 1, Firenze.

"What do you think?" Jake says. "Celebrate New Year's in Florence?"

I give a squeal. "That's the best idea anyone has ever had. In the whole history of ideas."

"I don't know, penicillin was a big deal. The Internet was kind of a game changer."

I wave those things away with my hand. "This is the best. And you are the best. And this week is going to be the best."

Chapter Fourteen

If six-months-ago-me saw current-me, she would puke. Or punch me. Or punch me while puking on me. Jake spends the rest of the week at the Rossis', and we tell each other "I love you" so much you'd think we'd get sick of it. We don't. We snuggle, nap, eat, read books. We go out to eat a few times and invite the gang over to watch Jake's favorite Christmas movie, *Home Alone*. They have a lot of questions.

"How did they forget one of their kids?"

"Why didn't the mom just have a neighbor come over and look in on Kevin until the family could get back from France?"

"Does he have grandparents? Where were the grandparents?"

"How did Kevin know how to do all those terrible things to those burglars?"

"Do all American kids know how to do that?"

"Is this something they teach in the schools?"

Two days after movie night, Jake and I catch a train south to Florence. We travel through rolling hills dusted with snow and dotted with quaint towns.

As we pull into the city of Florence, I take in the piazzas, buildings, and cathedrals. The Arno River catches every ray of sunlight and sends it sparkling back.

We grab a taxi at the train station, and our driver hurtles us toward our hostel. It's a little far from central Florence, but it's spectacular. A magnificent villa perched on a hill. There's a huge fountain in front and big marble columns.

Jake checks us in while I stare at a ceiling that looks like a Renaissance masterpiece.

"I've got a key for you," Jake says. "The good news is you have your own private room. The bad news is, from the map she showed me, it looks like a closet that they turned into a room."

The women's dorms are in the west wing and the men's dorms are in the east wing. And Jake is right. My room definitely used to be a closet. It has a bed, a shelf, and two hooks on the wall for clothes. I put my stuff away and meet Jake by the fountain out front.

We go straight to the Galleria Dell'Accademia to see the David. The wait to get inside is long, but when I finally lay eyes on him, he's even more incredible than I imagined. The sculpture is fifteen feet high, and it's standing on a tall pedestal so the feet are above eye height. The ripples of the ribs and abdominal muscles look so real it's hard to believe it's stone. The veins under the marble skin look like there could be blood running through them.

I have limited experience with naked men, and I get uncomfortable easily. But I don't feel uncomfortable staring at this work of art that seems more living man than stone. It's the kind of beauty that dazzles you so much you don't feel awkward.

Next, we make our way toward the Uffizi Museum. It's an impressive building with a large courtyard and a thousand ornate columns. We opt for an audio tour, and I swear the low Italian voice coming through my headphones is trying to inform me and seduce me at the same time. We emerge two hours later with our heads full of beautiful things.

"My mom would love this," I say.

"Yeah?"

"Yeah. My dad is a homebody, but my mom is more like me. She loves traveling. I mean, she would if she ever got to travel. And I know she's always wanted to see Italy, where her parents grew up."

We head to the botanical gardens of Bardini Villa and stroll along stone paths under canopies of purple wisteria. We explore the hedge mazes, sculptures, and fountains. We stay so long I almost believe we live here together in this palatial villa.

We walk across Ponte Vecchio, the oldest bridge in Florence. It's lined with shops selling souvenirs, jewelry, and trinkets. Jake buys necklaces for his mom and sister. I pick up some bangle bracelets for Maggie.

By the time we get to the other side, the sun is thinking about setting. The hour before sunset is called the "golden hour" because the light makes everything vivid and vibrant. It's my favorite time to take pictures, and Florence is the most photogenic city I've ever visited. I get shots of the bridge, the river, and an old couple walking hand in hand. I'm so engrossed in my picture taking I startle when Jake wraps his arms around me.

"You should take pictures, Juliet," he says into my ear.

"I am taking pictures," I whisper back.

Jake shakes his head and gives me a kiss. "As your job," he clarifies.

I shake my head. *Not this again.*

"If you could see your face right now," Jake says. "You look so happy. It's the same look you have when the server brings out your food at a restaurant."

I smile and give him a kiss. "Who's to say my face doesn't look like this when I'm working on spreadsheets? Now tell me about those lab mice of yours. Cured any of them yet?"

Jake tells me about his research as we watch the sun drop behind the Florence skyline, turning the sky a rosy pink, then a soft purple, then a dark violet.

We take a bus up to Fiesole, a hilltop town overlooking the valley of Florence and find a cozy steakhouse for dinner. We're instructed to order the *bistecca fiorentina*, which is the specialty here. Our waiter doesn't explicitly say our descendants for three generations will be cursed if we don't try it, but he does imply it.

It's a gigantic cut of meat cooked rarer than any steak I've ever had. The red puddle growing in the middle of my plate would be off-putting if the meat itself didn't taste so delicious. My plate is still half full, and I can't take another bite. I look longingly at my bread.

Jake reaches across the table and takes my hand. "You're feeling sad because you want to keep eating, but you're too full?"

My cheeks heat up, and Jake smiles. I love and hate that he knows that about me.

Just as we're about to go, we hear a loud boom followed by crackling and a thousand white lights appear in the sky.

"Fireworks!"

They're coming from somewhere down in Florence, and we have the perfect view. Jake comes around and sits by me, and we watch the show. They explode across the sky in brilliant colors. They whistle and shriek and split into droplets of fire. When it's over, we clap and cheer and yell great things about Florence.

It's nearly 11 p.m. when we get back to the main piazza of Florence. It's only half full when we get there, but it's packed forty-five minutes later. They've set up large speakers and a local station gives highlights and lowlights of the last year. Each piece of news is greeted with wild cheering or vehement booing. By the time we're closing in on the last minutes of the year, the crowd is whipped into a frenzy. The air is electric with anticipation. Finally, the DJ starts the countdown.

"30, 29, 28, 27, 26..."

The crowd yells along with him.

"...25, 24, 23, 22, 21..."

Jake is telling me something, but I can't make it out over the yelling.

"...20, 19, 18, 17, 16..."

He leans in close. "Thanks for making this the best year of my life."

"...15, 14, 13, 12, 11..."

"Just wait until next year," I tell him with a smile.

And then the volume level goes up to an impossible pitch as we all count down together.

"...10, 9, 8, 7, 6, 5, 4, 3, 2..."

Before we make it to one, Jake has me in his arms. I can hear shouting and yelling and people popping champagne, but all of it is background noise as Jake's lips find mine. People bump into us, but I hardly register it. Happiness is zipping through my body like an electric current. If I live a thousand years, there will never be a moment as perfect as this one right now.

There are fireworks and cheering, and we kiss. There's yelling and singing, and we kiss. Someone nearby is spraying champagne everywhere, and we continue to kiss. When we break apart, I can see that the piazza is a sea of chaos and celebration. I'm soaked head to toe in beer, wine, and champagne. Jake's face is flushed, and his hair is wet. His smile could light a city block.

"Happy New Year!" he yells.

"Happy New Year!" I yell back.

We stay in the piazza a few minutes longer, soaking up the intoxicating energy from the crowd.

"Are you as covered in beer as I am?" I ask Jake.

"Yes. I can't wait to shower once we get back to the hostel. Are you ready to call it a night?"

"Ready."

Jake consults the map and leads us to a bus stop a few blocks away. We've been waiting five minutes when a group of teenagers walks by and one of them yells in English, "No buses."

"Hmm." Jake looks at the schedule posted at the bus stop. Sure enough, the buses stop running at 11 p.m. on New Year's Eve.

"What about taxis?" Jake yells to the group of teens. The same kid turns around and smirks. "No taxis."

"Well. That's not great news," Jake says.

"Who doesn't love a three-mile stroll at midnight?" I reply.

Jake takes my sticky hand, and we start walking. I'm exhausted, but I also feel like I could walk next to Jake, holding his hand, for miles. The last stretch is the hardest because the villa is at the top of a hill, but finally we make it back.

The smell of my own sweat is mixing with the beer and wine soaking my clothes. I've never been more ready for a shower. One of the staff unlocks the door for us and crushes all my hopes.

"The amenities are closed for the evening, and all guests are asked to go directly to their sleeping quarters."

"But the showers are still open, right?" Jake asks.

"All the amenities are closed for the evening," he repeats in a maddening monotone.

"But we're covered in beer!" I say. He says nothing, but his expression makes it clear he feels that's a problem of our own making. I think about trying to explain that it's not our beer, but I give up before I start. It's obvious he's not changing his mind.

Jake walks me to the women's wing, and we share a very pungent kiss. Once in my tiny closet room, I strip down to my underwear and fall into bed.

The next morning I shower, a glorious ten minutes that makes me feel like singing. The trip home goes by fast. The train's not crowded, and we're able to stretch out and sleep. When we get back to Milan, we head to Jake's apartment so he can drop off all his dirty clothes and grab some new ones. Then we head back to the Rossis'. We only have a few more days of break left, and we want to spend it together.

On the tram home, I text Maggie a picture of the bracelets I got her.

> Merry Christmas! You'll get your gift when I see you in 7 months.

I add a picture of me and Jake in Florence.

Her text comes a few minutes later.

> Oh my gosh you are in love with this boy! Don't even try to deny it, it's all over your face. Wow. Juliet Evans in love. This is huge. Call me ASAP. Also, thank you for the bracelets, they look lovely.

I laugh and promise her I'll call her in three days when the love of my life has gone back to his apartment.

Her reply is a string of exclamation points and question marks.

"So, what are your New Year's resolutions?" I ask Jake when we get back to the Rossis' apartment.

"I want to learn to play the guitar," Jake says.

"Ooh, I'm picturing you with a guitar," I say. "You look very sexy."

"How about you?"

"Yes, I would also look sexy playing the guitar," I say.

Jake laughs. "Agreed. But what about your New Year's resolution?"

"To learn the fascinating secrets of running a small business."

Jake sighs. "Do your parents even know you want to study photography?" he asks.

I wait a moment then ask, "Do you want to hear about my worst Christmas?"

He nods and doesn't say anything.

"I was nine. It was Christmas Eve. I got up to get a drink of water, and my parents' door was open. I watched my dad hand my mom a stack of cash. I watched him slip off his jacket and saw two big bandages on each arm. I listened to him tell my mom about driving to four different places to sell plasma, removing the bandage from the last place so they'd accept him at the next place. He looked exhausted.

"The dry cleaners wasn't bringing in much, and there were four kids looking forward to Christmas." I can feel Jake's eyes on me, but I focus on the Rossis' yellow curtains. "I ran back to my room and never told them what I'd seen. And I cried on Christmas morning when I got the Barbie doll I'd asked for."

I take a second to compose myself. "And now I'm supposed to tell the man who sacrificed everything for his kids that I'm too good to run his company? That I'd rather do my own thing? That's not going to happen."

Jake looks a bit stunned. I don't know why I even told him. I've never told anyone about that, not even my siblings.

"I love you, Jake," I say. "And I know you love me and want me to be happy, but I won't be happy at my dad's expense."

Chapter Fifteen

When I pick up Isa from school on the first day after Christmas break, she looks like she's been in a bar fight. Half of her hair is coming out of her ponytail, there's dirt all over her uniform, and her eyes are daggers looking for something to slash. She shoves her backpack at me and walks past without a word.

We walk home in silence. When we step into the elevator I say, "I can see that you've had a rough day. Would you rather I ask you a lot of questions about it or pretend I don't notice?"

She narrows her eyes, like maybe this is a trick question. Finally she says, "Pretend."

"Very well," I say as the elevator stops at our floor.

"Your parents are going out to dinner, so it's just you and me tonight. I thought we could do a spa night. I'm ready to reveal all the secrets of how us California girls look so *gorgeous*." I make an exaggerated smoochy face and flip my hair out.

The barest sliver of a smile shows up on Isa's face.

"Right this way, madame." I say, leading her to a chair in the kitchen. I'm trying for a French accent, but it's hard in Italian.

"Do I have to?" she asks in a whiny voice.

"Yes." I wrap a towel around her shoulders and roll up her pant legs.

When I move her feet into a pot of hot water she yelps, "That's our spaghetti pot!"

"Well, tonight the spaghetti pot is the feet pot." Another tiny smile graces her face. I squirt some body wash in so it's bubbly and smells nice.

"Now, tell me, Madame Isa, would you rather have smashed avocado on your face or mayonnaise in your hair?"

She lets out a surprised sound. "Avocado on my face?" she asks.

"Excellent choice." Before she can argue, I start spreading on a thick layer of mashed up avocado. I make a big show of licking my fingers, which makes her giggle.

"You look gorgeously green. Now it's time for mayonnaise." She looks like she's about to resist, so I move fast, spooning out generous globs of mayonnaise and slathering it into her hair. I work from the roots all the way down to the tips.

"Now, Madame Isa, which color would you like for your fingers and toes?" I hold up a bottle of red nail polish and a bottle of pink.

"Pink," she says quickly. And then adds in a pouting tone, "I guess."

I paint her tiny fingernails bubblegum pink.

"Now for this next part it's very important that you close your eyes," I say.

"Why?"

"So you can relax. Relaxing is very important."

Isa closes her eyes. I dash into my room and get my camera then dash back.

"Now if you hear a clicking sound, that's just the sound of your foot bath bubbling. Not the sound of a camera. Your sweet nanny would never take a picture of you with a green face like an exotic lizard."

Her eyes fly open just as I snap the picture. "No," she yells, reaching for the camera. I snap two more.

Her mortified face suddenly turns calm.

"You should take a picture of both of us, so we can remember this special night."

"Great idea," I set the timer and place the camera on the counter across from us. Then I squeeze in next to Isa and crouch so our faces are level.

On the second beep, Isa darts in fast as lightning and smushes her messy face all over mine. The camera flashes and captures my open mouth and surprised eyes and green face.

"You tricked me!" I holler.

Isa cackles with delight.

I turn her chair around so her back is to the kitchen sink. I use a washcloth to clean the avocado from her face and then tip her head back and pour cups of warm water over her hair. It feels thick and slimy, but as I rinse, it gets softer and softer. By the time it's all clean, it runs over my fingers like silk.

While Isa watches a TV show about kids who can travel through space, I whip us up a delicious pasta with fresh tomatoes and mozzarella.

"I'm not that hungry," she says when we're seated at the table.

"That's okay," I reply. "Just eat what you feel like. It's not as good as your dad's, but I did my best."

Isa's eyes fill with tears and I know I've said the wrong thing.

"Hey. Am I still pretending nothing is wrong?" I ask. "That I don't notice those tears?"

She nods. "You definitely don't notice those."

"Okay," I say, nodding back.

We eat in mostly silence, then I help her get ready for bed. We spend an extra long time reading *Harry Potter*, and it's way past her bedtime when I give her a kiss on the forehead and tell her goodnight.

"I love you," I say.

"Do you also like me?" she asks, looking right in my eyes.

It makes me smile. "Yes, I also really like you."

I don't know when it happened. It wasn't that long ago that living with Isa felt like being trapped in a cage with a sarcastic tiger. But now... the tiger has faded into a brilliant little girl who makes me laugh every day.

To my surprise, Isa's eyes fill with tears again. She squinches them closed and says, "Federica said my dad doesn't like me, that's why he's gone so much. She said he probably loves me, because he's my dad and he has to, but if he really liked me, he wouldn't always be in a different country."

I'm momentarily shocked at the meanness of children.

"What do you think?" I ask.

"I don't know. He's gone all the time. I thought it was mostly for his job...but maybe it's a little bit because of me."

I tilt my head from side to side like I'm considering this possibility. "Can I tell you what I see?"

She nods.

"I see the way your dad looks at you when you walk into the kitchen each morning, like the sun has risen now that Isa is awake. I see how he laughs when you tell him funny stories from school. I see him standing in your doorway, watching you sleep. I see how sad he looks when he hugs you goodbye before his trips. I see a dad who loves his little girl, not because he has to, but because she's so wonderful he can't help it."

Isa doesn't say anything to this, but she nods, and I'm hoping it's a nod of agreement.

"Julieta," she says, turning her big eyes on me. "I have something important to tell you."

"Go ahead," I say encouragingly.

She leans in and says in a very quiet voice, "You still have avocado all over your face."

I laugh and Isa looks pleased at her surprise joke. I touch my cheek and feel dry, gritty avocado gunk.

"I'm going to hop in the shower," I say. And kiss her goodnight one more time.

The next morning, I discreetly evaluate Isa for signs of sadness. She looks a lot better than she did yesterday. She's wearing a shirt with a silhouette of the Paris skyline where all the windows are sparkling gemstones

"Isa, I love your shirt," I say.

"Thanks," she says. "My dad brought it back for me on his trip to Paris. Because he likes me so much he brings me gifts from the cool places he visits. I thought my best friend Federica would like to see it. She never gets gifts from cool places. And she loves Paris. And gemstones."

Her eyes are wide and innocent, but she's smiling wickedly.

Wow. I've got to hand it to her. That's a total power move.

I give her an extra tight hug as I drop her off. That fierce little hooligan is going to be just fine.

132   LIBBY TANNER

It takes Isa a while to warm up to Jake. She was appalled that I chose to date the American who wears a bright green Adidas jacket instead of the Italian she saw picking me up for the theater in an Armani suit. But Jake slowly wins her over, along with Marco and Sofia. Throughout the cold months of January and February, he's a near-constant presence in the Rossis' living room, playing Uno with me and Isa, and reading *Harry Potter* in funny voices.

February turns into March, and I wake up early one Saturday morning and lay in bed staring at the texture of my off-white ceiling. I'm officially twenty-one years old today.

There's a text from Maggie waiting for me on my phone.

> Chow Juls! Happy Birthday! Do you realize this is the first time in a DECADE I have not been there on your birthday?! I don't like the precedent we're setting, but I'll allow it based on how cool your life is at the moment. Which is why I supported this nanny idea from the beginning.

I snort. Maggie complained long and loud about me abandoning her this year.

> I just want to tell you that I am so happy you were born, and my life would suck without you. Hope you are well celebrated today.

I miss that girl.

While I'm still holding my phone it rings, and I know it's my mom.

"How are you doing? How do you feel?"

I give her all my updates, and she makes encouraging noises. "What a wonderful life you have created for yourself!" she says. Then my dad gets on the phone. He tells me he's proud of the young woman I've become. He gets teary, and it makes me laugh.

"I love you, Dad," I say.

"I love you too, Juls," he says. "I hope your day is as amazing as you are."

It is a spectacular day. I go shopping with Valentina and Carmen at the Sant'Ambrogio market, then Jake takes me to lunch and a soccer game, and

BETTER THAN GELATO

in the evening, we head to a restaurant downtown to meet the gang for dinner.

"*Benvenuti, tanti auguri!*" they yell when they see us.

"Happy birthday," Paolo says to me in English.

"Your English is as impeccable as your shirt," I say.

"You are too kind," he says with a charming smile, switching back to Italian. "How does it feel to be twenty-one years old? You look so elegant and sophisticated, no one would ever guess you're American."

I give him an elbow to the ribs and a "thank you."

We spend the next hour eating and talking. A giant tiramisu lit with candles arrives at our table and everyone starts singing "*tanti auguri.*" When the singing stops and it's time for me to make a wish, I can't think of anything I could want that I don't already have.

Let this last, I think as I blow out the candles. *Let this good thing I've found continue.*

Jake starts dishing out cake, and Paolo leans in and whispers, "Valentina wanted to make her special Slovakian dessert for you tonight, but I let her know it was against the restaurant's policy to bring in outside food."

"Paolo, you are a true friend," I say. "And I mean that from the bottom of my stomach."

I've barely finished my last bite of tiramisu when Diego starts chanting, "*Regali! Regali!*" and suddenly the table is filled with presents.

"Wow. Thanks, *ragazzi,*" I say. Suddenly my throat feels a little tight. Six months ago, I didn't know any of these people, and now, they're my people.

Jake hands me a gift.

"That's mine," Diego calls from the end of the table. I carefully unwrap it and find a silver antique-looking brush.

"Diego, this is beautiful!" I tell him.

"Well, I noticed that you have a lot of hair," he says. "Then when I was thinking about what to get you for your birthday, I saw this cool brush and remembered all the hair you had, and I thought you'd like it."

"I love it," I tell him. When I give him a big hug, I notice that he's put on some weight. I guess I'm not the only one.

The next gift is from Paolo. It's a large glossy white box with an elaborate pink bow on top. I carefully lift off the lid to reveal six giant pomegranates nestled in tissue paper. A smile slowly spreads across my face, and I lift one up to show the group.

"You got her a box of *melograno*?" Carmen asks. She looks appalled.

"Pomegranates are my favorite," I say. "It's a fantastic gift!"

"Julieta happened to mention Angelo, who she buys pomegranates from near her apartment," Paolo says. "And I thought, when you know your pomegranate vendor by name, you really love pomegranates."

I lean over and give Paolo a hug, and he whispers in my ear, "I didn't want to upset Jake by giving you diamonds."

He says it lightly, but it makes me think how doubly thoughtful his gift was.

"Okay, mine's next," Carmen says. She pushes a gift bag toward me.

I pull out a full-length dress in a dark slinky material.

"This is just what I needed!" I say delighted.

"I know," she says. "It's a wardrobe staple. It's a mid-weight material, so you can wear it casually, or dress it up and wear it formally. I think the cut will be very flattering on you."

"It looks perfect," I say. "Thank you, Carmen."

There's one more gift left on the table wrapped in paper with a daisy print.

I unwrap it and discover a large canvas with a black and white photo of Milan. In the bottom right corner it says, Milano 1910. It's stunning.

"I know you like photography," Valentina says. "And I thought this would be a great way to remember your special year in this city."

I feel tears pricking in my eyes. I give Valentina a hug.

"I love it," I whisper to her.

"I'm so glad," she whispers back.

"Thank you for the incredibly thoughtful gifts," I say. "You guys are the best."

"Hey, Jake, where's your gift?" Diego asks. Carmen gives him an elbow.

Jake slips a white envelope from his jacket pocket and hands it to me. I pull out a sheet of paper and read through it.

It's an email confirmation. For a plane ticket from Sacramento to Milan. For my mom.

I stare at Jake in shock. "How did you even do this?"

"Marco let me know the dates they're going out of town for spring

BETTER THAN GELATO

break. Your mom was reluctant to let me buy her ticket, but she came around when I told her what a great gift it would be for you."

"What is it?" Diego hollers.

I hold up the ticket and wave it above my head like a maniac. "My mom is coming to Italy!" I let out a squeal and throw my arms around Jake. "You are the greatest human alive," I tell him and then kiss him good. There are some whoops and hollers from the table, but I ignore them.

After dinner, we load all the gifts into Paolo's trunk and then squish into his car. Me and Jake are wedged into the back seat with Carmen and Diego, and I start tickling Carmen just to make things worse. I feel silly with happiness. I'm twenty-one, and my mom is coming to Italy!

Paolo drives us to a new club that just opened. It's a little tacky, decorated with more geometric shapes than is healthy for the eyes, but it plays very danceable 90s music. We spend the next two hours enjoying Britney Spears, the Spice Girls, and Backstreet Boys. Jake and I try and fail to teach the group the "Bye Bye Bye" dance.

At the end of the night, Paolo drives us to Jake's apartment so we can pick up my shopping bags from the market. Jake loads them into Paolo's trunk as Paolo counts each bag. "Good heavens, woman! What will you buy next week if you bought up the whole market today?"

I ignore his question and pull Jake in for a kiss. "Thank you for your amazing birthday gift. I can't believe you did that for me."

He kisses me and whispers in my ear, "There's not much I wouldn't do to make you happy."

We drop off Diego, Carmen, and Valentina, and by the time we make it back to the Rossis', the clock on Paolo's dashboard says 1:05 a.m.

"Let's get you and your ridiculous pile of birthday treasure up to your apartment," Paolo says.

"I do have a lot of things, don't I?"

"Yes, my Dolcetta, you have a lot of things."

I load up my birthday treasures and my bags from the market and we head to the apartment. I hit the elevator button with my elbow and when it arrives, I let Paolo go in first. I squeeze in next to him and one of the bags lands on Paolo's pile of stuff and two more land at my feet.

Paolo looks at me and says, "Excuse me, *bella donna*, your bag has landed on my foot."

I can barely see the floor, but I make out a pink and gold blouse spilling over Paolo's shoe. I start giggling.

"Oh, I'm so sorry," I say with feigned horror. "Let me get that."

I dramatically drop all the bags I'm carrying and bend over to retrieve the bag on his foot. My jostling must have upended the pomegranate box because I feel two slip out and land on my back before rolling to the floor. I'm giggling so hard I'm hiccupping now.

"Madam, are you well?" Paolo asks in a polished tone, but I can tell he's moments away from losing it.

"Oh yes, quite well," I say. "Just collecting my things."

"Well, if there's anything I can do to be of assistance," Paolo says, "please keep it to yourself."

I give him the grade school hit to the back of the knees, and it sends him crumbling to the elevator floor with his pile of boxes and bags.

"Oh, you've come to help!" I say between hiccups. "How kind of you!"

"Yes, I'm very kind," Paolo says. "Everyone who knows me talks of Paolo's kindness."

The elevator dings and the doors slide open to find us in a heap on the floor. For some reason, the ding makes me laugh even harder. "Ding!" I repeat. "Ding!"

"Dolcetta, did you have some birthday drinks?" Paolo asks suspiciously.

That makes me laugh some more. "No, I don't drink," I say.

"Yes, I'd heard that," Paolo says. "And yet what am I to make of the hiccupping girl on the floor of the elevator?"

"You're on the floor too," I point out.

"That's true. Let's get ourselves sorted." The doors to the elevator have started to close.

Paolo scrambles over a box and punches the open-door button just in time. We manage to collect our things and get them back where they go. I crawl out and give Paolo a hand up.

"We did it!" I yell and throw my hands up victoriously. The bags swing wildly, and Paolo has to duck to avoid getting hit in the face.

"We made it from the car to the apartment," he says. "It's quite the achievement."

"It's not as easy as it sounds."

"Yes, I think we have a gift for making the simplest things a challenge. Would you like some help carrying your things to your room?"

"Yes. But we must be quiet like ninjas. Can you be quiet like a ninja, Paolo?"

"I am stealth personified," he says.

I open the door and scoop up my bags and then motion for Paolo to follow me as I tiptoe down the hall to my bedroom. He carefully unloads his packages onto a chair in the corner and then we tiptoe back down the hall to the front door.

"Thank you for everything," I whisper.

"Happy birthday," he whispers back.

I snuggle into bed and let all the wonderful things about my life fill my mind and lull me off to sleep.

Chapter Sixteen

The train platform at Stazione Centrale smells like urine and cigarettes, and an overweight Italian man is telling me things I pretend not to understand. I've watched three airport shuttles come and go and my mom still hasn't arrived. I'm so amped with excitement that when she finally steps off the train, I nearly trample a group of tourists to get to her.

"You made it!" I say, throwing my arms around her.

"I can't believe I'm here!" she says.

"Me either!"

She hugs me for a long time, and when she lets go she says, "When am I meeting Jake?"

"We're meeting him for lunch right now."

"I could not believe it when he emailed me about this trip," she says. "I mean, what a birthday gift! And I wanted to tell you I was coming so bad when I talked to you on your birthday, but of course I didn't want to spoil his surprise."

When we get to the restaurant, Jake's waiting out front with a bouquet of flowers.

"Mom, this is Jake. Jake, this is my mom."

My mom shoots me an amused look. She's noticed that my words are tinged with an Australian accent.

"It's a pleasure to meet you in person," Jake tells my mom. "You've raised an amazing daughter." He hands her the bouquet of flowers. And that is how Jake wins over my mom in less than thirty seconds.

"Wow," she says. "Thank you for the flowers. They're exquisite. And thank you again for flying me out here. This is a real treat." She looks dazzled by Jake, and dazzled by Italy, and I wonder if this is how I looked when I first showed up.

We find a table by the window and spend a long time choosing the perfect entree for my mom's first meal in Italy. After we order, my mom asks Jake about his work at the lab and his plans for the fall. His answers are charming and impressive, and I feel a weird pride at how awesome he is.

"Thank you for looking after Juliet," my mom says to Jake.

It's a total mom thing to say. She makes me sound like a sad orphan Jake took in.

To make it worse she adds, "I've never seen her this happy. I'm glad you were able to win her over."

"I think I'm nearly there," Jake says. "She's a hard girl to pin down."

"What's that supposed to mean?" I say.

"Well, there was that time you tried to break up with me when I told you I loved you."

My mom bursts out laughing and nods her head like she's not surprised.

"I did not try to break up with you," I say mortified.

"Oh, but you wanted to," Jake says, delighted to put me on the spot. "I could see it all over your face. The only reason you didn't was because I was flying home to interview at Harvard the next morning. Tell me I'm wrong."

Wow, I did not hide that well, apparently.

"Okay, well, we got past that."

"We did," Jake agrees. "A month after I got back, you stopped flinching every time I called you my girlfriend."

"It wasn't that bad," I protest, but Jake is making a face like 'yeah it was.' I'm saved from this terrible conversation by the arrival of our food.

We devour tortellini and lasagna and gnocchi. Jake asks my mom about raising five kids. My mom asks Jake about his family in Arizona. By the time Jake walks us to the bus stop, they are laughing like old friends.

"There's a boy who will love you forever," my mom says on the way home. And I think she might be right.

"Are you really the mom of Julieta?" Isa asks when we get back to the apartment.

It takes me a second to realize my mom doesn't understand.

"She's asking if you're really my mom," I translate.

"Ask her if she's really the little girl you nanny."

I translate for Isa. She narrows her eyes, then shows my mom our special handshake to prove that yes, she is the girl I nanny.

Marco makes us chicken marsala and tells my mom kind things about me. "She's a wonderful nanny. A very happy presence in our home. We're lucky to have her."

My cheeks heat, but it makes me feel good.

"Are you excited to see *i nonni* tomorrow?" I ask Isa. The Rossis are using Isa's spring break to visit Marco's parents.

Isa makes a face. "It's going to be so boring! There's nothing to do in the country!"

"There's plenty to do," Marco says. "You can ride bikes. And..." He pauses and looks at Sofia for help.

"Climb trees," she contributes.

"Trees are the worst," Isa says.

She's still whining when we put her to bed a few hours later.

"She's not so bad," my mom says when we head back to my room.

"We've come a long way," I say. "Six months ago, she would have lit something on fire."

The next morning, after the Rossis have left, my mom and I take the train down to Rome and spend four days exploring. We visit St. Peter's and Michelangelo's Pieta, admiring the exquisitely sculpted folds of Mary's gown and the protruding ribs of Jesus as he lays across her lap. We take a tour of the Vatican and lay on our backs gazing up at the Sistine Chapel, getting lost in its beauty and complexity.

We walk through the Castel Sant'Angelo. If we hadn't just gone through

St. Peters and the Vatican, the castle would be a lot more impressive. But we did, and it isn't.

We spend a long time at the Colosseum. The thick walls muffle the sounds of traffic and vendors, making it feel like ancient Rome. I take a million pictures, but none of them quite capture how it feels to be here. We visit the Pantheon, Trevi Fountain, Le Boca de la Verita, and the Circus Maximus, which we rename the Suckus Maximus, because it kind of sucks.

Trevi Fountain is my favorite. I have no idea what's happening or what all the different pieces are meant to represent. But the feel of it, all that water tumbling and cascading down the white rocks and statues, is captivating. I take a dozen pictures of its chaotic beauty.

"This trip has been perfect," my mom says on the train ride home. "The photos you've sent us are incredible, but there's something about seeing it yourself, isn't there?"

"Yes," I agree.

"I know you've been taking pictures since you were a kid, but seeing you here with your camera, it's clear how much you love it. Have you ever thought about majoring in photography?"

I look at her, surprised and guilty. "Who would take over the store from Dad?" I say, hoping she can't hear my heart pounding.

"We'd figure out something," she says.

"How?" I press. "You were barely able to get away to come on this trip."

"That's true," she says.

"Besides, I already registered for all my business classes."

She looks at me for a moment. "You're a good daughter," she says.

"You can say favorite. I won't tell the others."

"I think they already know," my mom says, and her expression looks so guilty I laugh.

Chapter Seventeen

A week after my mom leaves, Jake shows up at the Rossis' apartment in the middle of the night. Okay, it's only 10:30 p.m., but I was reading in bed and drifted off, so when I get his text it *feels* like the middle of the night.

He sent me a picture of him in the lobby, and I don't ask questions, I just throw on my coat over my pajamas and tiptoe out the door. It's March but the night air makes it feel like winter.

He scoops me into his arms and kisses me, and it feels so perfect I wonder what selfless deeds I performed in a previous life that earned me this reward. *I probably saved an orphanage from a fire. Or told a young Taylor Swift that she should consider a career in music.*

I kiss him for a long time and when he starts to tell me something, I shake my head and keep kissing him. He laughs, and I finally pull away.

"Are you interested in a night picnic?" he asks.

He's got a backpack, and his eyes are sparkling as bright as the moon.

"Yes, I am," I say.

We walk to a little park nearby, holding hands, not talking much. My brain is still trying to wake up. Tall pine trees surround an open, grassy space and Jake leads us right to the center. He pulls a blanket, two bottles of orange-flavored San Pellegrino, and a pastry box full of sweets from his backpack. He's humming the whole time.

"Are we celebrating something I don't know about?" I scramble to think of the date. *Oh no. We're not a cheesy couple that celebrates our sixth month anniversary are we?*

"Do you want to hear some good news?" he asks.

"Always," I say.

"Even if it's braggy?"

I gasp. "You got into medical school!"

"I got into medical school!" His smile goes wide, and his dimples deepen.

I crawl into his lap and wrap my arms around his neck.

"Of course you did. Because you are the smartest and best-looking guy they've ever seen." I give him a good long kiss. "Tell me everything!"

"I got waitlisted at Harvard and accepted at Columbia and Johns Hopkins."

"That's amazing! How do you feel?"

"Relieved! Harvard is flattering, but in the end useless. Unless a bunch of people who got into Harvard decided they *don't* want to go- which feels unlikely- I'm not getting off that waitlist. So it's Columbia or Johns Hopkins."

"Which direction are you leaning?"

"I'm not sure. I loved doing my undergrad at Johns Hopkins. I definitely wouldn't mind going back there. But the research they're doing at Columbia is super interesting."

We spend another hour weighing the pros and cons of each school and talking about what Jake's life will be like as a med student. His face is glowing with happiness. We eat yummy pastries and make ridiculous and long-winded toasts with our San Pellegrino. We giggle and kiss. We try to point out the constellations, but we don't know any of them and instead we make up funny names and stories for the glittering dots in the sky. Everything seems funnier when it's dark and you're outside on a blanket.

"You're going to be exhausted tomorrow," I tell Jake as we kiss by the elevator.

"Worth it," he says. And kisses me again.

I think about Jake while I take Isa to school the next day. He looked so happy last night. And I feel happy for him. But there's something slinking around my belly that feels a lot like envy.

I shake it off. Jake's worked hard for this. He deserves it.

When I get back from school drop off, I call my mom. It's late there, but I know she'll be excited to hear Jake's news.

"Oh! Juls! How are you?" Her voice sounds funny.

"Jake got into medical school! He's going to Columbia or Johns Hopkins!"

"Wow!" she says. "That's very exciting for him."

"Yep. He's super happy."

I take out some nail polish and start painting my toes. A nice bright pink for spring.

"Hey is Dad there? Isa 'accidentally' spilled red wine all over Sofia's silk blouse. I'm hoping he has some ideas for getting it out."

There's a pause.

"Dad's not here," my mom says.

"Where is he?" The shop closed hours ago, and my dad has no life outside of work.

Another pause.

"He's actually in the hospital."

My mom does this terrible thing where she shares bad news in her most cheerful voice. She thinks it makes it better, but it doesn't. All the muscles in my stomach clench, and I carefully screw the lid back on the nail polish bottle.

"Juliet, are you there?"

"What happened?" *Was it a heart attack? My grandpa died of a heart attack. Of course he weighed 300 pounds, and my dad barely tops 175.* My mind is racing as fast as my heart.

"He's okay. He fell off the ladder cleaning out the gutters and broke his hip. They're keeping him overnight, and he has hip replacement surgery scheduled for tomorrow morning."

"He's spending the night at the hospital?" The thought of him lying in a hospital bed is absurd.

BETTER THAN GELATO

"It's just for tonight, he should be able to come home tomorrow evening."

"How long is the recovery?" I ask.

"Dr. Bartlett says he should be walking around in a couple of weeks."

"That's not so bad." My mind tries to process everything.

"But he'll need four months of physical therapy before he can go back to work."

My stomach sinks again. "What about the shop?"

"We haven't figured that out yet. But Dr. Bartlett said Dad can't stand for that many hours. Or lift anything over thirty pounds."

I ask my mom a dozen more questions and she does her best to answer. She promises to call me after Dad's surgery tomorrow.

Over the next twenty-four hours, I research hip replacements online, watch a video on YouTube that makes me want to puke, and call Jake three times with questions.

When my mom finally calls, around 3 a.m. my time, I snatch up my phone on the first ring.

"Mom! What's the news? How is Dad?"

"Juls, I'm doing great!" My dad's voice is strong and clear and just hearing it makes me feel a zillion times better.

"Dad! What happened?"

"Everyone thinks this old man lost his balance and fell, but I'm telling you there was a rusty rung on that ladder, and it dropped me like a trapdoor. I'm going to inspect it tomorrow and prove it. If your mom lets me out of bed."

"How did your surgery go?" I ask.

"Hurt like the dickens. Woke up with a pain in my hip like someone stabbed me with a hot poker dipped in tabasco sauce. I had a private room, but a semi-private gown, if you know what I mean. And they kicked me out of the hospital before the spinal wore off. I peed all over the car seat on the way home."

"Oh, Dad!" Tears of laughter mix with tears of relief.

"It's good to be home. Your mom's taking good care of me. And of course running the shop. I don't think she's slept more than a few hours in the last few days."

"I wish I was there! What can I do to help?"

"Oh, we'll get things squared away. You just worry about taking care of that girl of yours. She sounds like a real hooligan."

"She's not so bad," I say.

It takes thirty more minutes for my dad to convince me he's going to be okay. Listening to his description of the hospital food and the mean nurse who took care of him has me laughing so hard I'm afraid I'll wake Isa. I hang up the phone feeling better about everything. My dad is okay. Everything's going to be alright.

And then Brianna calls early the next morning.

"Hey Juls, have you talked to Mom and Dad?" Brianna's the oldest, and even when she asks you a question, it feels like she's bossing you around.

"Yes. I'm so relieved!"

"Did Mom talk to you about Dad's recovery plan?"

"She said four months before he can go back to work."

"At least. Brad's taking a month leave to come down and help Mom run the shop. I know you can't come home right now, so we'll take care of everything until you get back. Were you planning on heading back to school in the fall, or could you stay in town a little longer? I just think they'll really need the help. Mom can't care for Dad and the shop at the same time."

"What about Kayla?" I ask, speaking past the horrible tightness that has seized my throat. "Maybe she could help out for a while."

"She's...not very reliable these days." I'm not surprised, but the words still hit like a punch to the gut.

"How about selling the business?" I say. "I know it means a lot to Dad, but maybe it's time."

"They can't," Brianna says. "They tried a few years ago but the offer was so low they couldn't accept it. They need something for retirement. It's up to us to keep it afloat. I would go down myself if the twins weren't such a handful right now."

"Sure."

"Nothing's set in stone, but maybe plan on sticking around for a while after you get home, okay? You could head back to school in the spring. Or catch a summer term or something."

"Of course. Yeah. Whatever the family needs."

"You're the best, Juls. We're lucky to have you in our family."

"Thanks, yeah, you too, Bree."

I hang up the phone and pull my knees up to my chest. I stare at my half-painted toes. Getting the school to hold my scholarship this year was a miracle. There's no way they'll hold it until next spring. And there's no way I can afford tuition. If I don't go back to school this fall, I won't be going back.

Chapter Eighteen

I watch the rolling hills glide by my window, green and glowing in the early morning light, as I try to forget my conversation with Brianna. Spring is making a tentative entrance, and we're heading to Cinque Terre for a day of hiking. It's barely past dawn and the train is quiet. Jake sits next to me, holding my hand. Paolo and Valentina are snuggling in the seat in front of us. Carmen is reading a book, and Diego has fallen asleep next to her.

"You doing okay?" Jake asks. He tucks a piece of my hair behind my ear. "Are you still feeling anxious about your dad?"

I nod vaguely. I haven't told him that I'm not going back to school in the fall. That I'll be spending the rest of my life in my hometown. Seeing the same twenty people pick up and drop off their dry cleaning. Going to the grocery store and the movies and bumping into all the other kids from high school who never managed to get out of that place.

"What do you think about Greece?" he asks, breaking my depressing train of thought.

"If you're talking about Greece the country, I love it," I say. "If you're talking about Grease the musical, not a fan."

"Greece the country. I found some crazy cheap tickets from Milan to

Athens. What do you think about going for a week before we head back home?"

My mouth drops open. A week in Greece. With Jake.

"A MILLION times yes!"

I kiss him to let him know how brilliant he is, but he breaks away mid-kiss.

"What do you have against Grease the musical?" he demands. "It's John Travolta at his finest."

I wave the question away, already jumping into planning mode. "We've got two months left. I'm going to save up all my nanny money. Plus I still have some birthday money I didn't spend at the market."

Jake smiles. "Juls, we've talked about this. I love treating you."

"I know. And you're exceptional at it. But you can't pay for the whole trip."

He tilts his head a little. "Why not?"

"Well...because...it wouldn't be fair."

Jake is smiling at me and to his credit, it's not a patronizing smile, just a sweet one.

"I know you have piles of money." I wave my hands to indicate piles of money, "but I can't be a freeloader the whole time."

"You are not a freeloader, but I appreciate where you're coming from. What if I cover the costs, and you take care of the planning? Research the best places to visit and find the coolest things to do?"

I think about this. "I *am* a great planner. Okay, deal. But I get to pay for our first dinner out. I'm going to find someplace incredible and treat you."

"Deal."

Our train drops us off at Riomaggiore, and I snap a picture of Paolo, Valentina, Jake, Carmen, and Diego. We stretch our legs, tie our sneakers, then find the trail to Manarola and start walking.

The air is chilly and smells like wildflowers. This part of the trail is less like a hike and more like an easy stroll, paved and flat. We're flanked by grape vineyards on the left and the shimmering Mediterranean on the right.

Paolo leads with Valentina next to him, holding his hand. It makes my bestie heart happy watching them. I've definitely noticed a change for the better in Paolo. He smiles more. And he's a lot nicer to Diego.

Carmen strolls along with me and Jake, and Diego brings up the rear.

He keeps stopping to look at things—a cool rock, a butterfly, a tree that looks like a tree by his house—and then catching up with the group.

While we walk, Jake tells us about the mouse he named Felix in his lab. Valentina tells us her cousin is getting married. Diego gives us a play by play of the soccer match he watched on TV the night before. Before long, we arrive at the charming town of Manarola.

"Should we get some gelato?" I say. "I feel like we deserve it."

"It's 9 a.m.," Paolo says.

I stare at him unblinking.

"Which is a great time for gelato," he finishes.

Jake laughs and takes my hand. "Meet back at this fountain in twenty minutes?"

The group agrees, and Jake and I head off to find a gelateria. Jake gets cantaloupe, and I get raspberry, and we take our tiny cups of heaven to a bench overlooking the ocean.

"So, pretty exciting for Valentina's cousin," Jake says.

I have no idea what he's talking about.

"Getting married?" he prompts.

"Right."

"So..." he looks out at the ocean, then at a tree nearby, then finally at me. "You mentioned a long time ago that marriage wasn't part of your plans for the near future."

I nod. When I don't add anything to that he says, "I guess I was just, you know, wondering why."

Fair enough.

"My two older sisters got married when they were twenty. One is unhappily married. The other is unhappily divorced and drowning her pain in alcohol with reckless abandon. I'm not interested in either of those paths."

"Those aren't the only options, you know," Jake says.

"I know. Which is why I've always planned on doing things differently. Finishing college. Growing up. Taking the time to create a life for myself before I attach it to someone else's."

Jake nods. "That makes sense." Pause. "I'm sorry about your sisters."

I shrug. "I can't do anything for them but learn from their mistakes."

We meet up with the group and find the next part of the trail toward

Corniglia. This section is twice as long as the last part, but the trail is still easy, and the time goes by fast. There are more vineyards here, and no matter how long I look out at the ocean, the view never stops dazzling me.

The town of Corniglia is filled with little shops and cobblestone streets. Jake looks at me. "Gelato?" he says.

"Yep," I say back.

"We're going to find gelato," he tells the group. "See you back here in twenty."

We enjoy our gelato at a table in the shade. There are a few boats sailing off the shore, and we watch them quietly.

"You know how you don't want to talk about what we're going to do in June?" Jake says as we settle onto a bench.

He keeps trying to have terrible conversations about the future but so far, I've managed to avoid most of them.

"Yeah..."

"What if we talk about after-June?"

"After-June?" I ask.

"Yeah. Instead of working out all the logistics, if we do long distance, if one of us will relocate, let's assume we'll find some way to make this work. We're smart people, we'll figure things out. So let's jump to five years from now. What should we name our sailboat?"

I can't help smiling. "We have a sailboat five years from now?"

"I think we should. Don't you?" His dimples are dimpling, and I lean over and kiss his cheek.

"I do," I say. "And we could name it Straciatella."

"Straciatella?" He looks unconvinced.

I hold up my straciatella flavored ice cream. "It's a great name for a boat."

"I think we should keep brainstorming," he says.

We talk about pets, and by the time we meet up with the group we've agreed on two dogs and a cat, with the possibility of a python as long as Jake doesn't have to feed it.

The next section of the trail is closed due to a mudslide, so we go by train to the next village. We rest our legs and enjoy the view. We eat lunch in Vernazza and afterward, Paolo and Valentina offer to check at the tourist booth to see if the last section of the trail is open. Diego and Carmen rest in the shade.

"We're going to find some gelato," Jake says. "We'll meet everyone at the main piazza."

Paolo narrows his eyes. "Is gelato code for something else?" he asks.

"We wouldn't tell if it was," I say.

But really, we just love gelato. And the stuff they make here is especially delicious. I choose hazelnut and Jake goes with lemon cream.

The last stretch of the trail, Vernazza to Monterosso, is harder than the first two. There are steep stairs and twisting switch backs. It takes us about an hour and a half, and we're all drenched in sweat by the time we finish. Diego flops down on a bench as soon as we make it into town.

The town of Monterosso is the biggest of the five towns and has the nicest beach. We find a public restroom and change out of our sweaty hiking clothes and into our swimsuits.

Even though Jake and I have been dating for seven months, we've never been swimming together. I look at my reflection in the scratched mirror of the beach restroom, and I'm very aware that Jake has never seen me in so little.

I've worn this turquoise bikini a dozen times, but it felt different in Southern California. I adjust the bottoms and the top, but it doesn't help.

"*Ragazze*, can you help me?" Valentina calls from her stall. I go in and see her struggling with the ties around her neck.

"It keeps coming undone," she says.

Probably because your boobs are so big.

That seems like the sort of thing you're only allowed to tease about if you also have big boobs, which I don't. So I keep my mouth shut. I tie a double knot at the nape of her neck and then we both look at her in the mirror. She's wearing one of those vintage one-piece swimsuits with the boy cut legs and the sweetheart neckline. She looks like a 1950s pin-up model.

"Do I really have to go out there like this?" she asks.

"Valentina," I say, "if I had a body like yours, I would only wear that swimsuit. To go to the beach, to run errands, to pick up Isa from school."

She laughs. "Of course, you have gorgeous long legs."

"Valentina, you are a total smokeshow. I can't wait to see Paolo's face when he sees you."

BETTER THAN GELATO 153

Valentina smiles at this. "Yeah, I don't think men are as critical as we are."

"They aren't," I confirm.

"Are you guys ready?" Carmen asks, coming out of her stall. She's wearing a coral one piece that's ruched on both sides, with a colorful sarong wrapped around her waist.

"*Si, siamo pronte,*" Valentina says. We are ready.

We leave the shelter of the bathroom and walk the sandy path down to the beach. The boys are already there, and they've managed to commandeer a couple of lounge chairs and umbrellas. Diego and Jake are trying to make the umbrellas stay up in the sand, so they don't see us right away. But Paolo, who studiously avoids manual labor, has noticed us and his reaction is priceless.

I wish I had my camera to capture the look on his face. Valentina pretends she doesn't see him ogling her, but I can tell from her tiny smile that she really does. She walks over to him and says, "*Ciao bello.*"

And Paolo says nothing because he's incapable of stringing words together at this moment. It's hilarious. I wander away from the two of them and head to Jake and Diego. Jake is trying to twist the umbrella into the sand while Diego pounds on it from the top.

"Need some help?" I ask.

"Sure that'd be—whoa." Jake looks up and sees me. I try to look less awkward than I feel, but I'm not sure I'm pulling it off. I swear I was not this awkward in California.

"You look...You're wearing...I've never seen you...wow."

"Thanks," I say and give him a kiss on the cheek. "Nice job getting these umbrellas and chairs. Can I help you get them in?"

"Nope, that umbrella is dead to me now. Sorry Diego, you're on your own."

Then he scoops me up honeymoon style and carries me to the water's edge. I think he's going to toss me in, but he doesn't. He wades in waist deep and then gently sets me in the water. It's cold and my skin breaks out in goosebumps, but it feels good.

We're only ten yards from the beach, but suddenly it feels like we're alone. Jake pulls me closer to him, and his chest is warm from the sun. His arms wrap around my waist, and I lean into him. My hands are in his hair and then running across his shoulders, and it feels so good to touch his bare skin, that I don't even notice when he's scooped me up again and I've wrapped my legs around him like a koala. Suddenly we're kissing in a way that is not appropriate for public consumption.

Italy has a way of making you feel like you're in a private bubble, but it's a trick. You are, in fact, making out at the beach where anyone can see. I muster all my self-discipline and common courtesy and untangle myself from Jake.

Jake lets out a shaky breath. "So that escalated quickly." He's slowly moving away from me.

I nod my head.

"So," Jake says. He's still breathing heavily.

"So," I reply.

I stand there waist-deep, checking Jake out, and it doesn't do anything to slow my heart rate. For a scientist, Jake has the muscles of an athlete, and I remember that he played soccer at Johns Hopkins. A bead of water drips down his sculpted shoulder, over his chest and through the gauntlet of abdominals as I watch, mesmerized. This image of him, naked from the waist up, standing in the Mediterranean and glistening in the sun, is one I'll have with me for a long time.

Jake coughs, and I snap out of my ogling. I spot a buoy thirty yards out.

"How about a race?" I say, pointing.

"You're on," Jake says. "On your mark, get set, g—"

I'm under the water before he can finish. I take long strokes with my arms and hard kicks with my legs, and it feels good to get this energy out. It's been ages since I've swam, and I didn't realize how much I missed it. I come up for air, then keep pushing myself as hard and as fast as I can. When I smack my hand against the buoy, Jake is a half a body length behind me.

"You smoked me!" he says when he reaches me.

"I really did." I can't help gloating a little.

"I had no idea you were such a good swimmer."

"What can I say? I'm a California girl."

"Stupid Arizona desert with its stupid cactuses," Jake grumbles. "So, darts, swimming, any other secret talents I should know about?"

I shake my head. "Not really. Although I do play the bagpipes."

Jake's eyebrows shoot up. "The bagpipes? Really?"

BETTER THAN GELATO

"Learned from my paternal grandmother. She also taught me Swedish. My accent isn't great, but I can carry on a conversation."

"Wow. I had no idea."

"I'm also a two-time regional chess champion. And last year, I published a book of limericks."

"Is that so?" His eyes narrow, and he's smiling.

"Did I go too far with the chess champion?"

"I believed all of it right up until the limericks."

"I knew that one was too much. I could sense it." I wipe a strand of wet hair out of my face.

"So how much of that is real?"

"The darts," I say with a smile. "And the swimming."

He shakes his head. "What should I do with you?"

"I have some ideas," I say, and then we're kissing again.

We slowly make our way back to the beach. We do more races, a handstand contest, and Diego and Jake build a decent-looking sandcastle with a moat and everything. We stay until the sun is almost setting, then we grab dinner and catch the last train back home.

"I think I'm going to go with Columbia," Jake says as I snuggle in next to him.

"Yeah?"

"Yeah. It's an amazing school. Their research is cutting edge. And I've always thought it would be cool to live in New York City."

"They're lucky to get you," I say, pushing down the rising sadness I feel about my own thwarted college plans.

Jake asks what kind of house I want to live in and after some discussion, we agree on a beach house with a secret passageway. This game of make-believe is addicting. It's easy to picture a wonderful life with Jake if I look at us ten years down the road and not two. The odds for long distance relationships aren't good. And one of us relocating really means me following him to New York.

But I don't think of those things. I stubbornly and defiantly block them out. Instead, I think about Jake in the ocean, smiling at me with saltwater dripping off his shoulders.

Chapter Nineteen

"Hey Juls, do you have a minute?"

My brother's voice doesn't sound panicked, but I can't help but hold the phone tighter, anticipating bad news.

"Yeah, I've got a minute." I put down the shirt I was folding and sit on my bed. "Is everything okay? How's Dad?"

"He's fine. I just wanted to talk to you about the plans for this fall."

I let out a relieved breath, but my stomach tightens thinking of running the shop in a few short months.

"I already talked to Brianna," I say. "I told her I'd do it." I pick up my shirt and start folding again.

"Well, I may have found a way you don't have to."

"What?" I sit up straighter. "Really?"

"It's still early, and I can't tell you details, but I wanted to make sure you enroll in your classes. Just in case this works out."

Brad has always been especially sweet about me going to school. I think because he would have liked to himself, but didn't get the chance.

"Okay," I say, the tiniest shred of hope springing up in me. "I will."

BETTER THAN GELATO 157

I've never seen a flamingo try to line dance, but I'm nearly certain it would look like this. It's our Thursday Dance Party, and I'm teaching Isa the "Cotton Eye Joe" dance. She's hopping around the living room on her little stick legs, and I'm trying my best not to laugh.

My phone rings, and I turn the music down a notch and move into the kitchen. Isa keeps dancing with a look of concentration on her face and the grace of a skinny pink bird.

"Dad! How are you? How's the hip?" I've talked to my parents more in the last three weeks than I have in the whole seven months I've been here.

"Juls, I'm doing great. And my hip's doing great. I'm going to put you on speakerphone, we've got some big news to share!"

I hear my mom's voice. "Juliet! How are you?"

"I'm doing great. Dad says you have news."

"We sure do," my mom says. "Go ahead and tell her, hon."

"Well, it started a couple weeks ago," my dad begins. My dad is a good storyteller, but not a fast storyteller. I make myself comfortable.

"Do you know that bike shop that burned down a few years back?" my dad asks.

"Yes..." I'm trying to figure out where this is going when my mom exclaims, "We're selling the business!" Her voice is filled with glee.

I hear the words, but it doesn't compute.

"What? Really? Why?" I ask.

"Because life is short," my dad says. "We're ready for less working and more living."

This does not sound like my dad. This sounds like a motivational poster.

"Are you sure you didn't bump your head during that fall?" I ask.

My dad laughs. "My head feels great. But my fall did put some things in perspective."

"Dad's been spending three days a week at physical therapy," my mom says. "I think all the old retirees there talked him into it."

"But how? Brianna said you guys tried a few years ago, and the business wasn't...um, it wasn't worth much."

"Well, Brianna's right," my dad says. "But when Brad came down a few weeks ago to help out, he commented on how much this area has changed. That sad old mechanic shop got bought up and turned into a salon. And they rebuilt the bike shop that burned down a few years back, and it sells these fancy electric bikes now. So Brad started talking to some real estate people..."

I listen as he lays out the whole thing. The equipment and customer list are not worth much, but the building, which my dad bought twenty years ago, has skyrocketed in value. The location is going through something of a renaissance and investors are coming in and buying everything they can. High-end restaurants and spas are popping up all along the block.

"We've gotten a very generous offer from a gentleman who's going to turn it into a luxury coffee house," my dad says. "He says Mom and I can have free coffee anytime we want!"

"I think he's more excited about the free coffee than the buyout!" my mom says.

My brain can hardly believe what it's hearing, but my heart is leaping with excitement.

"We're getting more than we ever imagined!" my mom says.

My mom's always seemed happy with her life, but there's a lightness in her voice that's new. The lightness of freedom.

"We're signing all the papers next week, but we wanted to talk to you first," my dad says. "I know we've always said we'd turn the business over to you after graduation. As you know, I didn't start out with much. And I always wanted to be able to pass something on to my kids, so they wouldn't have to start from scratch." My dad's voice cracks with emotion.

"We've had some rough years, but I've tried to hang on, tried to keep things running until we could pass it on to you. I knew you could turn this place into more than I ever did." There's a little sniffle before he continues. "And then Mom talked to me after she got back from Italy."

"I saw how much you loved taking pictures," my mom says. "I'm sure you always have, but with the kids and the chaos, we missed it. When it was just the two of us, it was obvious. You light up when you take pictures, Juls. And the way you talk about photography, well, you don't talk about business that way. I feel like an idiot for being so slow to see it, but is photography what you really want to do with your life?"

I'm laughing and crying and barely know how to respond. "Yes," I finally blurt. "I didn't want to let you guys down. But yes."

"Oh, Juls, you could never let us down," my mom says. "We are so proud of you. We never meant to make you feel like you had to take over the shop or carry that burden."

"Absolutely not," my dad says. "We want you to be free to follow your own path. And we know you'll do great."

"Thank you, Dad," I say, still in disbelief.

"So we have your permission to sell?" he asks. I can tell from his voice he's smiling.

"You don't need my permission, Dad. But yes, you have it."

Can this really be happening?

"What are you guys going to do?" I ask.

"Whatever we want!" my mom says, and she sounds like a little kid on the first day of summer.

"Dr. Bartlett has invited me fishing next week," my dad says. "So I may have a new hobby."

"And I think I might visit Brianna and her kiddos in Washington," my mom says. "I think she could use a hand."

"I'm so excited for you guys!" I say.

"We're excited for you, Juls," my dad says.

When I hang up the phone I can't move. I stare at the wall replaying the conversation in my head.

For the first time everything I've ever wanted is right there for the taking.

Chapter Twenty

I go into the living room, scoop Isa up and turn on "Best Day of My Life" by American Authors. We dance, and I belt out the lyrics at the top of my lungs. I feel like I'm at Disneyland on Christmas, and I've just downed a case of Red Bull. When the song's over, we lay in a heap on the couch, and I plan my next steps.

I turn my phone over to Isa to take command of the playlist. Then I go onto the UC San Diego Visual Arts College website and pull up the application for the photography program.

It's intense. I don't have any of the prerequisite classes the other applicants will probably have. But the application says those are encouraged but not required. There's an essay, letters of recommendation, and a long list of photography samples they need. My brain is fizzing with excitement and then I see the deadline and my stomach drops like a broken elevator.

The deadline to apply is tomorrow.

My heart starts pounding, and within seconds, my whole body is covered in sweat. *I can't pull this off. I need more time.* Isa notices me hyperventilating on the couch and comes over.

"*Cosa c'e che no va?*" Isa asks. What's wrong?

"I've got a big project due, and I'm not sure I'll get it all done in time."

Isa says, "You can do anything."

BETTER THAN GELATO 161

That's all she says, but the look in her eyes is so sincere and confident, I take a deep breath and channel my thoughts into an action plan.

I reach out to my two favorite professors from last year and ask for a letter of recommendation adding that I need it by tomorrow and promising all kinds of Italian treats in return.

Then I jump into the photo section. The application asks for six different photo samples: portrait, landscape, action, still life, architectural, and photojournalism. I don't even know what the last one means.

I pull up the folder of all the photos I've taken since I've been here. I feel frantic, but Isa's surprisingly calm presence next to me grounds me. I quiet my mind and take my time sorting through. I find my action shot right away. It's the snowball fight in Switzerland. Paolo is running from Diego, and Carmen is sneaking up behind Jake.

"Just looking at that makes me feel cold," Isa says, and I take it as a good sign.

I move on to landscapes and pull up three I took in Florence. With Isa's help, I choose the best one and then go looking for a portrait.

I stumble onto a photo I don't even remember taking. It's Isa at the park. She's holding a frog, and her eyes are wide, and her mouth is a little 'O' of surprise. Her delight and wonder jump off the page.

"That's me!" Isa says pleased.

"It is," I say. "Do you mind if I use it?"

"I think you'd better. It's the best one."

For the still life, I choose a photo of a caprese salad I ordered at a restaurant near Parco Sempione with Jake. Bright red slices of tomato topped with creamy white chunks of mozzarella and dark green basil leaves. The whole thing is drizzled with a violet vinaigrette glaze. It makes my mouth water.

I'm feeling good. Four down, two to go. I check the time. We've got another hour and a half until Marco and Sofia come home. They're laid back people, but I know they feel like they don't get enough time with Isa, and I want to be there when they get home from work.

"Okay, Isa, we've got two more photos we need. Should we head downtown and find them?"

"Yes!" she says and leaps off the couch. Her enthusiasm pumps me up, and by the time we walk out the front door, we're skipping and leaping and bounding to the bus stop. I'm doing the math in my head. Thirty minutes to get downtown, thirty minutes to take two amazing photos and then thirty minutes home. It'll be tight, but we can do it.

Until we can't. The bus makes it less than three blocks before dying in the middle of traffic. We wait thirty minutes for a mechanic to come and twenty more while he tries to fix it. At this point, Isa and I are the only ones still on the bus. Everyone else figured out a long time ago that this bus isn't making it downtown today.

My shoulders slump with frustration and anxiety.

Maybe there are some amazing photos I missed when Isa and I looked through them?

But deep down, I know we would've spotted them if they were that good. And I can't submit photos that aren't good. I've got one shot at this.

"It will be okay," Isa says.

"Of course it will," I say. But I'm lying to make her feel good. Inside, I'm filled with doubt.

After dinner I call Jake. I'm euphoric at being so close to my dream and panicked I won't get my application in on time. My words come out fast and crazy like a squirrel who's had an espresso and is trying to explain quantum physics.

"Hold on, I want to make sure I have this right," Jake says. "Your parents are selling the dry-cleaning business?"

"Yes!"

"And you get to be a photographer?"

"Yes!"

"But the deadline for your application is tomorrow?"

"Yes!"

"Was there something in there about coffee? Have you had some coffee tonight?"

"The guy who's buying the place is turning it into a coffee shop. I haven't had any coffee tonight."

"Really? Nothing?"

"I think it's adrenaline. My heart has been pounding for the last five hours. That's normal, right?"

"Maybe take some deep breaths."

"Ooh, that's a good idea."

We breathe together on the phone, and it sounds silly, but just hearing Jake's deep breaths calms some of the panic rising in me.

"You can do this," Jake says. "You deserve this. You deserve every good thing."

By the next day, my nerves are shot. My application is due in less than twelve hours, and I'm missing two photos. I stayed up crazy late writing an essay on What Photography Means to Me and filling out all the questions on the application.

I drag myself out of bed and bring Isa to school, then call Maggie and fill her in on everything. She's known about my secret dream of being a photographer for years, but we never talked about it openly. She knew, like I did, that it wasn't really an option for me. When I give her the news, she whoops and hollers like she's just won the lottery. Then she listens while I read her my essay and go over every application question.

By the time I get off the phone, Maggie's hyped me up so much I feel like I could conquer a small island nation. Or at the very least take two photographs. I hold onto that feeling as I take the tram downtown, fighting valiantly to keep the doubt from crashing in. When we reach the piazza and I step off the tram onto the worn cobblestones, Il Duomo is waiting for me like a gothic fantasy.

I can't imagine a better subject for an architectural photo. The tension in my neck starts to ease.

I can do this.

It takes a while to capture il Duomo in all its colossal glory. I remember the frustration I felt the first time I tried to photograph it. Eventually, I find an angle that allows me to get the whole thing from the steps filled with people to the spires filled with gargoyles. It involves lying on my belly in the middle of the piazza, but it turns out so well it's worth it.

One down, one to go.

From what I learned, photojournalism is about telling a story. All the examples of photojournalism I could find online were about war or natural disasters. I sit on the steps and wait for an earthquake to hit. Nothing.

I watch the people in the piazza go about their mornings to the

164 LIBBY TANNER

soundtrack of downtown traffic. There's some honking and commotion at the corner of the piazza. I watch an old Italian man climb out of his car and wave his arms at a young man on a Vespa who cut him off. It's the kind of scene you see at least twice a week. I remember telling my mom the story of an especially funny incident my first week here. I thought it was going to come to blows, but in the end, the two men drove off.

The thought of storytelling triggers my brain. I grab my camera as fast as I can. I'm not sure if I'm close enough. I focus the shot as close as it will go and then zoom out a little to capture a wide view of the scene. I take shot after shot of the old man yelling and the young man looking away. I snap until both men drive off. I'm not sure if it's what the photography department has in mind, but I think it tells a pretty good story of Italian road rage.

I ride a wave of triumph all the way to Isa's school. I got my shots. I can feel it. I'll need a few hours to make my final decision on the photos I took today, plus edit all the photos I chose yesterday and review the rest of my application and essay. But I should be able to get it all done in time.

I'm feeling so good it takes me a minute to register Isa's sour face.

"Failed your calculus exam?" I guess.

She shoots me a dark look. "I forgot my caterpillar project."

"Tell me about your caterpillar project."

"It's a big project that shows the life cycle of a caterpillar, from tiny egg to big butterfly. They were due today, and I didn't have mine."

"Because you forgot it at home?" *I don't remember seeing this thing.*

"Because I forgot to do it."

"Oh."

"Yeah."

Her lip quivers like she's trying not to cry and barely making it.

"Can you bring it tomorrow?" I ask.

"I don't think so."

"Well, let's ask."

We go inside, and I talk to Signora Zonta. She's sweet as can be and says it's no problem if we bring it in tomorrow. We might have given her the impression we already had it done and had simply forgotten to bring it.

"Well, it looks like we've got some work to do," I tell Isa as we walk out.

Isa throws her hands up in despair. "It's no use! All the other kids

BETTER THAN GELATO

worked on their projects for weeks. They are *really* good. We'll never get ours done in one day."

I question how really good a first-grade project can be, but I don't argue. Instead, we sit on a bench and come up with a plan and a list of supplies. We make it back to the Rossis' with a large poster board, colored tissue paper, and approximately thirteen kilos of glitter. Isa said it was essential.

We finish just before bedtime. We would have finished sooner, but halfway through our first attempt, Isa declared the whole thing garbage and tried to throw it off the balcony. It took half an hour to talk her down, then we flipped the poster board over and started on the other side. Our second attempt went better.

Marco and Sofia ooh and ahh and Isa flushes with pleasure. The caterpillar eggs are bedazzled, and the butterfly wings are so weighed down with glitter, there's no chance this guy could fly. But it's done.

The kitchen table is a disaster. Dripping glue runs down sand dunes of glitter, but I'll worry about that tomorrow. Tonight I've got work to do.

The deadline for my application said 5 p.m. But that's California time. Since Italy is nine hours ahead, I actually have until 2 a.m., and I'm going to need every minute.

My computer takes an extra-long time to turn on, and the mean part of my brain tells me not to bother, that my photos are horrible. *They are not,* I tell the mean part of my brain. But then even the nice part of my brain starts having doubts. *They may not be garbage, but let's be realistic. You've never taken a single photography class. How good can they be?*

I put on some music to tune out all the voices in my head and get to work. I sort, edit, and re-edit until I'm satisfied I have the very best version of the very best photograph for each category. I double check all my answers to the application questions and answer the ones I didn't get to last night. I read through my essay again and make a couple small tweaks. Both of the professors I contacted came through with glowing letters and reading them builds my confidence.

By 1:30 a.m., my application looks good. And at this point, my brain has turned to mush, and I can't make any improvements anyway. I take a breath, say a prayer, and hit submit.

Chapter Twenty-One

The world is my oyster!

Although when I actually tried fresh oysters with Jake a few weeks ago, I was appalled that people would deliberately eat something that looks, tastes, and feels like your waiter just coughed up a pile of phlegm onto your plate.

Nonetheless, for the last week, I've had the blissful feeling that the world is full of opportunities, and that doors that have always been closed to me have suddenly opened.

It's early Saturday morning, and Piazza Duomo is full of people.

I find Jake sitting on the steps looking especially attractive.

"*Buon giorno!*" he says. "You look wonderful this morning."

"Thank you," I say. "I feel wonderful this morning."

Jake and I spend the whole day together, walking nowhere in particular, eating a delicious lunch, finding charming park benches to snuggle and kiss on.

Jake listens patiently as I ramble nonstop about the photography program, my application, and each of the photos I submitted.

"The career placement percentage for UC San Diego's photography program is really high," I say. "There's a huge range of jobs—weddings, journalism, advertising, sports. And the pay is actually way more than I thought."

The sun is nearly setting as we walk from Castello Sforzesco back to il Duomo. Jake's hand in mine makes me feel happy to be alive. And it appears Jake sees my good mood as an opportunity to have another one of those horrible conversations I try my best to avoid.

"Maybe we should discuss how we're going to do long distance when we go home next month," he says.

I groan dramatically. "How many ways are there not to see someone?"

"I just mean we could come up with a schedule for visiting each other. I get my exam lineup in a few weeks, and we can plan out some dates."

"Okay."

"And then between visits, we can call each other in the evenings or text when we get a chance."

I nod my head. *What else can we do?*

"And I'd hope that if you ever wanted to go on a date with someone else, you would let me know beforehand."

"Jake, I love you. Why in the world would I go on a date with some random guy?"

And then before I can stop it, my brain pulls up an image of me and Lorenzo holding hands, eating dinner together, dancing.

But that was different. A million years ago. Before I fell in love with Jake.

We walk quietly with only the cars breaking the silence. My hands start sweating.

Do I tell Jake about Lorenzo? Does it even matter anymore? That was ages ago. What good would come of telling him?

I keep walking and try to put it out of my mind. But my thoughts keep hounding me.

Do I really want to have some big secret between us? No, I do not. I'll just tell him and that will be that.

"I can't wait for you to visit me at Columbia," he says.

"Mm-hmm." *Okay. How to start?*

"You're going to love New York City."

"Yep." *This is harder than I thought.*

My face squinches up as I search for the right words.

168   LIBBY TANNER

Jake sees my expression and gives me a smile. "I know it's not fun talking about this stuff. I just don't want anyone getting hurt."

I have to tell him now. I can't think of a good way to say it, so I just say it the regular bad way, all in a rush.

"I went out on a date with someone while you were in America."

Jake stops and looks at me. He drops my hand. "What?" The hurt in his eyes tells me he heard and understood.

I take a deep breath. "I'm sorry. I thought I was breaking up with you when you got back. I didn't think it would matter."

He takes a step back. "Why didn't you tell me?"

"You were interviewing at med schools! I didn't want to get in your head and wreck things."

Jake nods once, like he concedes the point. "Who was it?" He's not looking at me anymore. It's better, I can't stand to see the pain on his face.

"Just some Italian guy who asked me out." He flinches. Would he have been happier if it was someone in our group? If I'd gone out with Diego and we'd never told him?

"What happened?"

I shrug my shoulders. "We went out to dinner and then we went dancing."

"Did you kiss him?" His voice is cold. Not cruel, just devoid of warmth. Tears spring up in my eyes.

"No. I never even saw him again after that night. I never returned any of his calls or texts."

This is not making things better. I just sound like a jerk.

"Why?" he asks, finally looking me in the eyes.

"I felt trapped," I say truthfully. "I had fallen into a relationship with someone I barely knew. It was moving way too fast for me. I wanted out, but I didn't want to hurt you or mess up your interviews. An opportunity came that looked like a way out, just for a night, and I took it."

"I see," he says. He turns and starts walking. Unsure what to do, I follow him.

"I'm sorry," I say again.

He shrugs like my apology makes little difference.

I know I messed up, but a fierce little voice in my head is pointing out that I wasn't the only one who made mistakes.

Jake is walking faster than me, and I jog to keep up with him.

"I understand this is hard to hear. And I know this is a tough conversation to have. But I think we should have it so we can work through it and move on."

"I wasn't here, and you went out with someone else at the first opportunity," Jake says with brutal simplicity. "Doesn't make me all that confident in your ability to handle a long-distance relationship."

He gives me a look like he gravely misjudged me. "What more is there to say?"

My heart fills up with anger and pumps it to the rest of my body until I can feel it in my fingertips. "There's a lot more to say. I'm not the only one who messed up."

"Oh, this is my fault now?" His arms cross and his eyebrows go up.

"I take full responsibility for my actions. But you're not blameless."

Jake stops again and looks at me.

"We'd been dating for three weeks when you told me you loved me, Jake. And we'd known each other for barely four." Jake has the decency to look embarrassed. "Can you blame me for feeling freaked out and claustrophobic? I didn't want to have a boyfriend in the first place. And then everything got so serious, so fast."

He coughs uncomfortably. "I was just trying to be honest."

"It was way too much, way too soon." I squeeze my hands into fists and release them.

"Secondly, it's unfair to hold me to the mistakes I made at the beginning of our relationship. You and I both know I'm not that girl anymore. And things between us are completely different than they were back then. I love you."

"I love you too," he says. "That's why this hurts so much."

He turns and starts walking again. I try to follow, but he stops me. "I need some time, Juliet."

So I stand there and watch the back of his head disappear into the crowd until my vision blurs with tears.

The next few days are rough. I bring Isa to school. I pick her up from school. In between, I hide my phone under my bed so I won't text Jake.

I skip dancing Wednesday night. If Jake doesn't show up, I'll know it's because he can't stand to be around me. And if he does, I'll have to look at his hurt face all night.

Instead, I play Uno with Isa, read her two more chapters of *Harry Potter and the Sorcerer's Stone*, and then put her to bed. I change into my pajamas and check my email. There's a message from UC San Diego Photography Department.

I open it with a rush of excitement. It takes reading it twice for the words to sink in.

Dear Juliet Evans,

Thank you for submitting your application to the UC San Diego Photography Department. Admission is highly competitive, and we regret to inform you that you have not been accepted at this time. We encourage you to apply again for next year's program beginning in the spring.

Sincerely,
Walter O'Brien
Department Chair

I stare at the screen for a long time, then slowly close my laptop. It's the sound of all my dreams dying.

Chapter Twenty-Two

I wake up the next morning exhausted. My mind kept churning over my rejection all night. Trying to come up with a new plan for my life. But there is no new plan. *This* is what I want to do. What I've always wanted to do. And for one brief, shining moment I thought I might get to have it.

I can't transfer to another college to study photography because I need my scholarship money. I can't apply next year because I barely have enough funds to get through four years of college. I definitely can't afford five. I have no answers, no solutions, and no will to get out of bed.

If there was a time I've felt this low, I can't remember it. The soul-crushing disappointment is a stark contrast to how excited I've felt since I applied. Already imagining the next two years immersed in something I love. Already imagining a life for myself, out of Lakeport, exploring the world, having adventures. I got ahead of myself. And now I feel like an idiot.

I put on clothes. I bring Isa to school. Then I come home and sleep all day.

By the time night rolls around, I've almost made my peace with it. I knew it was a competitive program. I knew most other applicants would have classes and experience that I didn't have. It was always a longshot. Just because I had the chance to chase my dream didn't mean I would catch it.

I pull up the photos I sent and look at them objectively. I like them. They're good photos. It's a small victory, but it means something that I worked hard and did the best I could. Sometimes your best isn't good enough and there's nothing you can do about it. And that sucks.

And sometimes, you didn't give something your best, and you know you could do better if you had another chance.

I send Jake a text and ask him to meet me at il Duomo tomorrow night.

I have a speech in my head and a bag of pastries in my hand. *I can do this.* Jake's reply took forever last night, but he said he'd be here.

The piazza is nearly empty, and I see Jake right away. My heart starts beating double time. He gives me a little wave, and I wave back. The fact that he showed up is a good sign, I tell myself. And he waved at me. That's two good signs.

My hands clench and unclench as I wait for the light to turn green so I can cross the street into the piazza. Suddenly there's a firm tug on my arm.

"*Scusi, ragazza*! Can you help an old woman bring her groceries home?" There's a tiny old woman standing at my elbow. She looks to be 102, and she's carrying a large bag with *supermercato* written across it. It takes me a minute to grasp what she's saying.

"*Disculpe, che*?" I'm sorry what?

"Do you speak Italian, child? I need your help. Let's use that young body of yours for more than looking pretty. My apartment is two blocks this way." She passes the bag of groceries to me, links her arm through mine and leads me away from the piazza, presumably toward her apartment.

Is this really happening right now?

I look over at Jake, who's watching us. I try to motion for him to wait just a minute, but one arm has a heavy bag and the other a tough old Italian woman. The best I can manage is a bewildered headshake.

We walk three blocks, not two, and I bring her groceries up three flights of stairs to her apartment. She thanks me and offers me a slice of cake, but I decline and hustle back to the piazza. Jake is still there. He's sitting on the steps now.

BETTER THAN GELATO 173

"What just happened?" he asks when I jog over. "Did that old lady make you carry all of her groceries home?"

"Yes! That's exactly what happened! And it was a third-floor walkup!"

Jake laughs, his dimple popping out, and for a split-second, things are normal between us.

He looks at me, and I take a seat next to him and launch into my speech. I want to get it all out before he walks away again.

"I love you," I start.

And then my speech dissolves. All the points I outlined in my head blur like wet ink. "I'm sorry for hurting you. I'm sorry I didn't value our relationship before. I didn't know how amazing it was going to be. But I do now. And knowing that changes everything. I won't ever make a mistake like that again."

I risk a glance at Jake, but I can't read his face.

"If you still need some time, I understand. I can be patient. If you need me to be a better girlfriend, I promise I can do that. I'm ready to give this my very best."

He still hasn't said anything, so I lift up the bakery bag. "And if you need a croissant, I brought some." I hand him the bag, and he takes it from me and sets it on the step beside him.

Then, excruciatingly slowly, he takes my face in his hands and kisses me. This is not a make-up kiss like in the movies, exciting and passionate. This is soft and sad. This is trying to find our way forward again, and hoping it works. This is 'I love you, but I'm hurting.' Finally, we draw apart.

"I love you," I whisper.

Jake nods his head. "I love you too," he says.

I want to say sorry again, but I resist the urge. "Do you want to take a walk?" I say. I feel like we're the most us when we're walking.

We hold hands and eat croissants and cross the street toward Parco Sempione. We don't talk for a while. He keeps looking at me, and I try to guess what he sees.

I ask how things are going in the lab, and he tells me about some of their research results. Still inconclusive, but promising.

"When do you hear back from the photography department?" he asks. For a little while, I'd forgotten about the program. Now it comes rushing back.

"I heard back already."

"You did? That's amazing!"

He scoops me into his arms and squeezes me tight. It feels good being in his arms again, but he lets go when I shake my head.

"I uh, I didn't get in." It sucks saying the words out loud. And I feel even more pathetic when my eyes fill up with tears. They run down my cheeks in fat droplets.

"Oh, Juliet."

When Jake got accepted to med school I felt so proud of him. I wonder if he wishes his girlfriend wasn't such a loser.

"Did they...say why? Or explain anything?"

I shake my head again. "It's very competitive," I mumble.

"I'm so sorry," he says. "I know how long you've wanted this."

"I'm glad I know. I submitted my best work, and I don't have what it takes. That's good information to have, so I don't waste any more time on this dream."

I'm going for mature and gracious, but the last word comes out as a sob, ruining everything.

Jake doesn't say anything, just pulls me into his arms and holds me for a long time.

Chapter Twenty-Three

I've been trying my best not to mope, I know I should be grateful I get to go back to college at all. My brain keeps making lists of possible career options, and my heart keeps pointing out how terrible all those options are. It's exhausting. An action movie is exactly what I need to forget about real life.

I meet up with Jake, Paolo, and Diego at a movie theater downtown. Carmen and Valentina are busy tonight, so it's just me and the boys. We watch the latest Marvel movie, and it feels like all the other Marvel movies, but it's funny and full of action and takes my mind off of things.

Afterward, we walk toward a pizza place we like, and I drop back to walk with Diego. He's usually leaping around throwing punches after these movies, but tonight he's especially quiet.

"When you're a famous movie star," I say, "do you want to be more like Star-Lord or Thor?"

Diego doesn't respond. I look over at him, and his medium-brown skin looks as pale as mine.

"Diego, are you okay?"

He nods his head but then stumbles on a cobblestone. I reach out to grab his arm, and it's slick with sweat.

"Diego—"

Before I can say anything else, he collapses at my feet, his head hitting the sidewalk with a stomach-dropping thwack.

The hospital is cold and smells like disinfectant. Paolo was listed as Diego's emergency contact, so he got to go back with him. But Jake and I remain in the lobby, shocked and confused.

I'm frustrated that Jake, who's practically a doctor, doesn't know what's wrong with Diego.

"I only saw him for a few minutes before the ambulance came," Jake explains for the third time. "His pulse was faint but steady. That's all I know."

After an eternity, Paolo comes back and pulls a chair in front of us. He sits but takes a minute before speaking.

"Diego is sick. Leukemia. Stage 4."

The words sink in slowly.

I ask stupidly, "How many stages are there?"

Jake takes my hand and squeezes. "Just four," he whispers.

We both look at Paolo. He opens his mouth to say more, but then his whole face crumples like melting plastic. He bows his head, and I watch his shoulders shake as he cries silently. I put my hand on his shoulder, but I don't think he notices. After a minute, he collects himself, takes a breath, and tells us everything.

"Diego found out about a year ago. He's been getting treatments at your hospital, Jake."

"I saw him there," Jake says now, and it's hard to decipher the emotions on his face. Realization? Regret? "It was months ago. He said he was visiting a friend. I-I didn't have any reason not to believe him."

"He didn't want anyone to know," Paolo says. "For a while, the treatment was working so well, he thought he could just keep the whole thing a secret and get through it on his own."

I think of goofy, smiling Diego trying to get through something like this on his own, and my heart breaks.

"Then five months ago, the treatment stopped working," Paolo continues. "His body just stopped responding. The doctors don't know

BETTER THAN GELATO 177

why. That's when I found out about it. I heard him throwing up early in the morning in Switzerland."

Early in the morning. When Jake and I were kissing in the library. When the group came down and saw me and Jake doing the Floss dance and Diego laughed so hard.

"I made him tell me everything, and he made me promise not to tell anyone. He didn't want the pity."

Paolo sighs and rubs his eyes. I notice for the first time the bags under his eyes, the wrinkles crossing his brow. He's been carrying this secret on his own and it's taken a toll.

"They tried different treatment options, none of them worked," Paolo says. "He...he made the choice to discontinue treatment."

None worked. Discontinue treatment.

Jake clears his throat and asks, "How long?" His voice is hoarse.

"They said a month or two," Paolo says. "That was a month ago."

My brain refuses to understand what it's hearing. "He was great on our Cinque Terre hike. He was smiling and laughing the whole time."

Jake nods slowly. "A lot of patients do better after stopping treatment. Without the side effects, their body feels good for the first time in months." He pauses. "But then the cancer progresses unchecked."

I feel a sudden rush of anger. For the unfairness of cancer. For Diego's decision to stop treatments.

"Well, then we check it. We fight this. We find some better treatments." I pin Jake with an accusing look. "Isn't this what you do with your mice? You cure cancer. That's what you told me. So cure Diego, give him whatever you're giving those mice."

Jake shakes his head. "We're years away from clinical trials. Our research is promising, but it's still in the early stages."

I feel like we're wasting time. We need to be doing something about this. I stand up suddenly and my chair falls over, clattering loudly, breaking the oppressive silence of the lobby. The noise feels so good I stalk over and kick another chair. And then another, each one crashing to the ground with a satisfying clang. I want to hurl a chair through the window, light the ugly gray sofa on fire, burn this whole building to the ground.

I feel arms wrap around me. I hear Paolo's low voice.

"I know how you're feeling right now," he says.

I look in his eyes and see pain, anger, and defeat shimmering behind a veil of tears.

"We can fight this," I say again, but with less conviction.

"Diego's been fighting this a long time," Paolo says gently. "He's ready to stop fighting."

With those words, all the fire in me dies out, replaced with a hopeless sadness I've never known before.

The next two weeks go by in a blur. Jake flies Diego's mom out and pays for a hotel by the hospital. Paolo and Jake take turns visiting Diego every day and give me updates.

Carmen and Valentina and I go to visit him on Sunday afternoon. His mom is there, a tiny woman with dark hair and bags under her eyes. Did Diego keep this from her too? I don't know. We tell her we'll stay with Diego for a few hours if she wants to go back to the hotel for a nap. She gratefully accepts.

Diego is asleep. He doesn't look peaceful, like people do in movies. He looks exhausted, broken, small. It's hard to reconcile the boy in the bed with the yappy puppy Carmen described the first night we met. We stay for two hours, but he doesn't wake up.

A week later, I go back and visit him on my own. I sit in an aggressively uncomfortable chair holding Diego's hand and sort through all the things I've learned about Diego in the last two weeks. His dad died three years ago, and he came to Milan to work and support his mom and two younger siblings. He worked at a hotel, which I knew about, and picked up extra shifts at a bar, which I didn't know about.

The pain of losing him is combined with the regret of not being a better friend. Why didn't I ask Diego about his home? His family? His work? Because I was too caught up in my own drama, fretting about my own dreams. What about Diego's dream? I know making it in Hollywood was always a longshot, but doesn't he at least get to try?

He squeezes my hand, and I nearly jump out of my seat.

"Diego!"

He gives me a weak smile, and I can see how much he hates this. Being here. People seeing him this way. So I shove down all the words of sorrow that are fighting to spill out. I give him a smile and shake a finger at him.

"If you didn't want to get pizza, you could have just told us, instead of collapsing." I shake my head and try to sound annoyed instead of anguished. "Diego, Diego, so dramatic. You actor types are all the same."

His smile goes from weak to grateful. He gives my hand another light squeeze, and I prattle on about nothing. About Isa and her latest shenanigans. About my twin nephews who escaped my sister's house and ran around the neighborhood naked. We ignore the fact that we're sitting in a hospital room. We ignore the fact that he's dying.

"How's the food?" I ask.

Diego makes a face.

"It could be worse. They could make you eat Valentina's cake."

Diego laughs, which turns into a cough that wracks his whole body and contorts his face in pain. When he's through it, he says, "You distracted her with that video, and saved me from her cake." His voice is soft and raspy.

"I did," I say.

I want to tell him that I'd sing and dance and juggle and tightrope walk if it would save him from this. Instead, I squeeze his hand and tell him a joke that Isa told me about a goose and a fox.

Two days later, he's gone.

The funeral service is being held in Chile. Diego's mom flew home yesterday with his body. We have our own memorial service of sorts at Paolo's house. There's a lot of crying, but there's laughter too.

We share our favorite memories of Diego. Line dancing at Calypso. Sledding into the bushes in Switzerland. Telling our gang the plot of every single Spiderman movie over pizza one night. Building that huge sandcastle at the beach at Monterosso. His terrible ghost stories. By the end of the night, there's a feeling of gratitude for Diego and the time we had with him. We didn't know it would be this short. But looking back, I see we filled it well.

Chapter Twenty-Four

The first time I take my camera out it hurts a little. I haven't taken a single photo since my rejection from the photography program. And after Diego's passing, I didn't really see the point.

But Isa has made a castle out of a set of blocks I found under her bed and demands that it be recorded. She's been a good sport over the last three weeks. Not asking too many questions. Even giving me a hug when I started crying during *Harry Potter* one night.

Isa stands next to her castle, like a game show hostess displaying the grand prize. She changes poses and facial expressions, each one more dramatic than the last. I turn on the camera, screw on the lens and adjust the settings. Then I start snapping. The first one turns out great, and I smile. I'd forgotten this feeling.

"When you're a famous photographer, I'll be your model," Isa says.

"That's a very generous offer," I say. "But actually, I'm not going to be a photographer."

"What are you going to be?"

"I don't really know," I say. I know I should be looking into other majors, but I just can't muster the energy. Switching from photography to teaching or nursing feels like going from a delicious lasagna to a limp stick of celery.

BETTER THAN GELATO 181

"Well, I think you should be a photographer," Isa says.

"That's what I thought too, but it didn't work out."

"Why not?"

I don't want to talk about it. I told Maggie and my parents about Diego, but Jake's the only one who knows about getting rejected from the photography program. At the time, it seemed unimportant compared to Diego. Now it feels too depressing to talk about.

But Isa's face says she doesn't care about my feelings. She wants answers.

"I didn't get into the photography program," I say, not meeting her eyes.

"What? After all our hard work? *Porca Miseria*! Why not?" Her hands go to her hips.

"I don't know," I reply with a shoulder shrug.

"Ask them."

"I can't just ask them," I say.

"Why not?" Her eyes are narrowed and focused on me like laser beams.

The only thing more pathetic than getting rejected is asking why you were rejected.

"It just doesn't work like that," I say. "They already made their decision."

"But why did they decide that?"

"I don't know!" I say, irritated.

"Then ask!" Isa says, with even more irritation.

Her eyes are full of fire, and her shoulders are back in the posture of a person who demands things and gets them.

"When I forgot my butterfly project, you talked to Signora Zonta and asked her if I could turn it in the next day. And she said yes!"

I don't know how to tell her that college isn't like first grade. She can tell I'm not convinced because she says, "It can't make it worse. They already didn't let you in."

She's right. Maybe I just don't want to hear how bad I was. Maybe nothing seems to matter that much after Diego's passing. Which I know would piss him off. He's not here to live his dream, so I'm giving up on mine?

I tried! I tell Diego and Isa and every other critic in my head.

"Fine," I tell Isa. "Maybe I'll give them a call."

Isa looks at me expectantly.

"What, right now? I can't call them right now. It's 7:00 p.m. our time, which means it's..." I do the math. "10:00 a.m. in San Diego."

"And is your college open at 10 a.m.?" Isa asks, eyebrows raised.

Dang. I guess I'm making this call right now.

I grab my computer and pull up the number. I'm hoping Isa will give me a little bit of privacy, but when I see her expression, I know there is zero chance of that happening. I dial the number and listen as it rings. It's only when someone answers that I realize I have no plan. No idea what to say. I should have thought this out beforehand.

Dang Isa and her peer pressure!

"UC San Diego College of Visual Arts, this is Lottie." The voice on the other end of the phone reminds me of sweet tea.

"Hi, Lottie, this is Juliet Evans." I'm so nervous it's coming out Scottish. I take a deep breath before continuing. "I recently applied to the photography program, and I wasn't accepted. And I was wondering if you could tell me...um...or give me any information about...why not?"

I can almost but not quite hear a sigh.

"I'm sorry, I'm not the one who makes those decisions."

Yeah, Lottie, I was under no illusions that the lady answering the phones was the one making those decisions.

I channel the most professional version of myself I can find.

"Of course, I understand. I was just wondering if there was any information you could give me. Any notes anyone left on my application."

"Well, it is a very competitive program to get into," she says. But she asks for my name again and says she'll look through the stack. "Are you sure you made the deadline? Because we only look at the applications and photo samples that made the deadline."

"I made the deadline," I say.

By the time Lottie comes back, my shirt is soaked through with sweat.

"Okay, your application did make the deadline," she says, in her honey-sweet voice. "But it did not have any photo samples."

My heart plummets.

"There's a Post-It note on it saying that there are no photo samples to go with this application," Lottie continues. "You were supposed to submit six different photo samples. Did you know about the photo samples?"

BETTER THAN GELATO 183

"I know about the photo samples, Lottie!" I bark. I take a deep breath. "I submitted the photo samples."

"Well, they're not here."

"Well, maybe whoever was supposed to print them, forgot to print them," I say.

"*I* am the one who prints out the photo samples. And I didn't forget. We didn't have any to print this year. All our applicants dropped them off in person."

"Well, at least *one* of your applicants is living in Italy at the moment and couldn't make it to your office to drop off her samples."

Isa looks delighted by my rude tone, and I take a long, deep breath.

"I emailed my photos to the address listed on the application page," I tell Lottie.

I pull up my email and look through my sent messages. Panic courses through me. Did I somehow forget to attach them? But no, there it is. The email with six photos attached.

"I have it right here," I say. "I emailed the photos to collegeofvisualart@ucsd.edu."

"That's not the right email address," Lottie says immediately. "It's college of visual *arts*. With an "s" after art."

My heart folds in on itself like a dying flower. How could I have made that mistake?

I pull up the application page. I stare at the email instructions. *Please submit all photo samples via email to collegeofvisualart@ucsd.edu.*

I gasp. "You have it wrong on your application page."

Lottie doesn't respond, but I can hear fast typing on the other end. "Oh!" she says in a surprised voice.

I want to yell "Aha! It's *your* fault, not mine!" But I don't. I just wait.

"It looks like Kyle the intern put the wrong email address on the application page," she says, nearly under her breath.

"Yeah." I say. And then wait some more.

"Well, that was clearly our fault," she says. "I am sorry about that."

"So what can we do?"

"I'm afraid at this point, there's not much to be done. The deadline has passed, and all the spots have been filled."

Are you kidding me? This is how this ends?

184   LIBBY TANNER

"I followed the instructions and submitted my application by the deadline," I say. I keep my voice calm, but rage is building in my chest and racing toward my mouth. "This is not fair."

There's a sympathetic noise from the other end of the phone then Lottie says, "Well, you can apply next year. And I'll make sure we update the application page with the correct email."

Oh, would you? How helpful.

I bite back a sarcastic reply and say, "Thank you, Lottie. I appreciate the additional information."

I hang up. Then I walk into the kitchen, close the door, and yell every Italian swear word I know. A whole string of beautiful profanity gives voice to my fury. I see Isa's head peek around the door. Her eyes are wide and I take a deep breath. I'd feel worse about swearing in front of a child, but I learned most of those words from her.

I slump onto the kitchen floor and fill Isa in on what I learned. Tears of frustration leak out of my eyes, and I brush them away, annoyed.

"But that's not fair!" she says. "It was their mistake not yours."

"I know. But Lottie says they already filled all the spots in the program."

"Who's Lottie?" Isa asks, and I realize I never told her the receptionist's name.

Then I think, *Who's Lottie?* I sit up straighter. *Is she the one calling the shots in that place? Probably not. Is she the person that's going to keep me from something I have dreamed about for years? Definitely not.*

"You're right, Isa," I say. "We need to talk to the person in charge. And that is not Lottie."

I get off the floor and march over to my laptop on the couch. I pull up my rejection email and look at the signature. Walter O'Brien, Department Chair. With Isa hovering over my shoulder I pull up the photography department faculty page and find him at the top. I copy his email address, paste it into a new email and start typing.

I explain everything. I tell him that I have dreamed of studying photography for years. I tell him I will accept not getting into their program if my application does not merit it, but I will not accept rejection because of an administrative error. I ask him, kindly but firmly, to please look at my photos and consider my application.

I attach all six of my photos and a link to my saved application. I read through it twice, translate it for Isa, and reject all of Isa's suggestions of clever insults to include. Finally, I hit send.

I call Jake that night and tell him everything.

"I can't believe it," he says. As I'm retelling it, it does seem unbelievable.

"I guess they didn't notice because all the other applicants dropped off their photos in person."

"I'm really proud of you for fighting for this," he says. His words feel like a hug.

"Thanks," I say. "It was only because I was bullied into it by a six-year-old."

"She is a wise and fierce six-year-old," he says.

"Agreed."

"So now you just have to wait for a response from the chair," he says.

"And hope that he responds at all," I add.

Chapter Twenty-Five

Against my wishes, June arrives. I wake up early and watch the sun settle on the world outside my window. Today is Isa's last day of school. I can't help thinking about that morning, a million years ago, when I brought her to school on her first day.

Isa has behaved like an angry racoon all week. Yesterday was especially rough. Sofia said she always gets this way when she has to say goodbye. I get it, but I also don't want to waste our last day together. I can think of zero good ideas for breaking through her funk. So I come up with a terrible idea and decide to go with that.

I slip out of my pajamas and into the dark blue slinky dress Carmen got me for my birthday. I brush my hair and leave it down, rippling over my shoulders in waves. I head to the kitchen and get Isa's cereal all ready. Angry stomps alert me to her presence in the hall. She stands in the doorway to the kitchen and scowls.

"What are you wearing?" she demands.

"An evening gown," I say, like it's obvious.

"Why?"

"It's the last day of school. I thought I should celebrate."

"It's not a big deal," she says, crossing her arms. "It's just the stupid first grade."

BETTER THAN GELATO   187

"Oh, I'm not celebrating you, I'm celebrating me."

Isa's face turns even stormier. "Why are you celebrating yourself and not me?"

"For the last nine months, I did a great job of bringing you to school. We didn't get lost. We didn't get hit by a car. We were on time. That's worth celebrating."

"So you're actually going to wear that on the bus and everything?"

"Sure. And I thought as we were walking into school, I could do a little celebration dance like this." I wiggle my shoulders back and forth and then my hips side to side and then my shoulders again. I look ridiculous, I can feel it, but it's worth it when I see Isa's lip curve slightly.

"What do you think?" I ask.

"I think it's a terrible idea," she says.

"I agree," I say. "But I didn't have any good ideas for making you smile, so I had to go with this one."

At the mention of her smile, the scowl returns. Then she looks me over again. I give another shimmy. She doesn't smile, but her eyes are twinkling.

I get her some breakfast and when Marco and Sofia come in, Isa announces that I'm taking her to school wearing an evening gown.

"It's to celebrate neither of us getting hit by a car," she clarifies horribly.

Marco and Sofia look at each other, as if the other one might know how to appropriately handle this, and then quickly drink their coffees and head off to work.

Isa is smiling all the way now and even starts giggling when we get on the bus and everyone stares at us. It feels so good to hear her laugh, it makes my heart ache. When we get close to the entrance of her school, she stops and looks at me.

"What about the dancing?" she asks. I give a hip shake, a shoulder shimmy and a pretty good twirl.

"My nanny is crazy," she says, but she's laughing, and I eat it up.

The last night with the Rossis is busy. They'll be gone for six weeks, staying with Sofia's parents down south, and the pile of things they're taking looks twice as big as their car.

I help where I can, and when I can no longer be useful, I pull Isa into my room, and we snuggle into my bed and read *Harry Potter*. We read three chapters and get all our protagonists safely out of harm's way. There's only one chapter left, where they wrap it all up, but Isa wants to save that for the morning.

I wake up at 6:30 a.m., and I tiptoe quietly into the kitchen. I make pancakes and put some on a tray with silverware and orange juice and bring it into Isa's room. At first, I think she's still sleeping, but when I look closer, I can see that she's awake and staring at the ceiling. She turns when she hears me come in.

"Good morning," I whisper.

Isa sighs. "Bad morning."

I nod. "That's what I thought at first too. But then I made pancakes and turned it into a good morning."

"That doesn't work," Isa says.

"You doubt the power of pancakes?" I say in astonishment. "I thought I could finish reading *Harry Potter* while you eat your pancakes and Polyjuice —I mean orange juice."

Isa doesn't say anything but takes the tray from me and starts eating. I read the last chapter. Harry and the gang make plans to keep in touch over the summer and go to the Quidditch World Cup. Ron says he's even learned how to use a phone so he can call Harry at the Dursleys.

"Can I call you?" Isa asks suddenly. "In America?"

"Any day you like," I say. "And in the meantime, I got something for you."

I run to grab her gift from my bedroom.

"You got me a going away present?"

"It's really more of a celebration present," I say.

She carefully pulls off the wrapping paper. It's a photo album, a big thick one, filled to the brim with pictures we've taken together. It's the kind of album that has room to write things next to each picture, and I had a great time adding my comments to the memories.

"Hey, I remember this one!" Isa says pointing. "You covered my face in avocado!"

"That was for our spa night. And turn the page. I included the picture of you smearing your avocado cheek all over me."

"Oh yeah, that was funny."

We look through some more. One that Sofia took of us coloring. A selfie

BETTER THAN GELATO

I snapped during a Thursday dance party. A photo Marco took of us doing our secret handshake.

"We haven't done our handshake in ages," Isa says.

"We better do it now so we don't forget."

We do our handshake and then I scoop Isa into a hug.

"Do you know how much I've loved being your nanny?" I whisper.

"I think I do."

"Good."

Sofia knocks on the door and says it's time to go.

Tears pop into my eyes. I want to scoop Isa onto my lap and beg Sofia for just one more hour with this amazing little girl. But of course I don't. I help Isa get some clothes on and get her unicorn suitcase. I help her find her coloring book and crayons for the drive. We take the elevator down with Marco and Sofia and I walk them to their car.

"How long is your drive?" I ask.

"Five hours." Marco says.

"That's not too bad," I say. And then all four of us have run out of things to say.

"Thank you for hiring me," I blurt. "It has been an incredible year. And none of it would have happened if you hadn't chosen me to be your nanny."

Marco smiles. "Thank you for all you have done for Isa and for our family."

"*Di niente,*" I say, which seems funny because it wasn't nothing, it was actually everything.

I bend over and give Isa one more hug. I don't say anything to her, and she doesn't say anything to me, but we hug for a long time.

When I stand back up, Sofia turns to Marco and says, "Don't they usually have a fashion expo in Las Vegas in December?"

Marco nods. "We've never gone before, but Bianca is always saying we need to branch out to the American circuit. Is Las Vegas close to you?" he asks me.

My heart leaps with hope. "Super close! I could come and see you so easily!"

He turns to Isa. "Would you like that, *tesoro*? To go to America like I promised you, and visit Julieta?"

Isa makes a big show of thinking about it. "I mean, if we're already going...and Julieta's nearby...I guess we could visit her..."

I snatch her up and dance her around on my hip like she's a baby monkey. She giggles and holds on tight as I swing and dip her. "Whew. This is such a good plan. For a moment, I was worried I wouldn't see you again and it was terrible! But now I know we'll get to hang out in December, and it's so much better."

"It is better," Isa says with authority. "Because you're really going to miss me."

"I really am," I say. And then I put her back down by the car and watch them all climb in and drive away. Isa rolls down the window and waves to me. I wave back until they're out of sight. I'm missing that sweet hooligan already.

Sunday afternoon, Jake and I snuggle on the couch and watch a movie. Okay, there's a movie playing in the background while we make out.

His hands are tangled in my hair, and his lips are moving down my neck. There's a delicious buzzing in my brain. Everything feels soft and blurry.

I'm vaguely aware that our kisses have gotten hungrier, his hand on my back stronger as he pulls me to him. I can feel my heart speeding up, my nerves leaping in excitement.

We're past the point where we usually stop and take a break.

Does he not want to stop? But if he wanted us to take that step in our relationship, we would talk about it, right? Isn't that what people do?

Jakes slides his hands up my back under my shirt, his fingers cool against my hot skin.

Or maybe people don't do that. Maybe one thing just leads to another and there's not much talking at all. I don't know how this works!

I pull away. "Hey."

My breath comes out fast, and I can't look him in the eye. "I um...I need to..." and I can't think of a single thing I need to do. I just know that I can't stay here with him like this. "Shower," I finally say. "I'm going to go take a shower. Get ready for dinner."

"Okay," Jake says. I can't tell if he's oblivious to the sexual tension, or just better at hiding it than I am.

I stand under the hot water, letting it run through my hair and down my back. I take some deep breaths and shake the haziness from my brain.

Fifteen minutes later, my hair is washed, my legs are shaved, and my head is on straight. Jake sits on the couch. Not reading, not looking out the window. Just sitting.

"Can we talk?" I ask.

"Of course."

"About our sex life." My cheeks flush with heat, but there's nothing I can do about that.

Jake's eyes go wide. "Do we um, have a sex life?"

"You were up front with me at the beginning, but now I feel like I'm getting mixed signals from you. I don't know when to stop or keep going. I don't know what you want."

I breathe out.

"But I know what I want. I thought I was waiting until I fell in love, but that's not enough for me. I want to feel like I have a future with someone. We're going to schools on opposite sides of the country. All of this might be over in a few months and that's not something I want to worry about when I have sex for the first time.

"So from now on, I'm not just trying to make things easier for you, so I don't mess up your plans. I'm trying to make things easier for myself. And I'd like your help with that."

Jake doesn't say anything for a minute. He looks a little shocked honestly.

"I'm sorry," he finally says. "I'm sorry for giving you mixed signals and making things harder on you. I can do a better job."

"Thanks," I say.

He pulls me into his arms and hugs me for a long time. I feel a little silly after my big speech, but I'm still glad I said it.

"I love you," he says.

"I love you back," I say.

"Should we grab dinner at Il Tavolo Grande tonight?" he asks.

"Yes! I've been craving their risotto!" I say. "Let me grab my jacket."

I grab my jacket and cell phone from my room. And then, like I've done every hour for the last week, I check my email. And unlike every other time I've checked, I have a reply from Walter O'Brien. My whole body goes still as I read it.

I let out a yell of triumph and leap off my bed. I gallop around my room. I pump my arms. I dance like a lunatic. Then I run into the living room and throw my arms around Jake.

"Guess who has a spot in the highly competitive and world-renowned photography program at UC San Diego?" I ask.

"You."

"ME!" I shriek.

"The chair responded to your email?"

"Yes!" I pull it up and let him read every word. There's an apology and an invitation to join the program and at the end, he wrote, "Photography is not just about skill, but passion. It looks like you have both. Welcome to the program."

I call my parents to share the news, and they're ecstatic.

"I'm so proud of you," my dad says, his words wobbly with tears. He's always been a crier.

"Thanks," I say. "I'm proud of me too."

Chapter Twenty-Six

On Monday, I share my news with Paolo over lunch. He listens as I tell him all about UC San Diego's photography program and even manages to look interested for a moment or two. Then I mention Jake's sister is coming to visit next week, and he sits up straight.

"Are you worried she won't like you?" Paolo says immediately.

"What? No. I'm a delight."

"Love is war, Julieta. You can't always tell your enemies from your allies."

I take another bite of bruschetta. "I'm not worried."

"Then that's your first mistake." Paolo takes his napkin and folds it, then lays it next to his plate. It's his signature move when he's about to launch into a big speech.

I swallow and give him my full attention. "You clearly have some advice you want to dole out. Let's hear it."

"First, beware of traps."

"What tr—"

"Trap one, she asks probing questions, looking for anything you've kept hidden from Jake. Tell her nothing." Paolo holds up two fingers.

"Trap two, she interrogates you about your future with Jake. If your response is too enthusiastic, you're a gold digger, if it's not enthusiastic enough, you're wasting his time."

"How do I respond?"

"You don't. But make it seem like you did."

I take a long gulp of water, suddenly feeling out of my depth.

"Trap three, if she brings up any of Jake's ex-girlfriends, put on your most bored expression. Imagine Jake droning on about his research."

"I like hearing about his research."

Paolo raises a single eyebrow to show he doesn't believe me.

"And don't under any circumstances, tell Jake within hearing distance of his mom, that you thought her soup was too spicy."

"His mom? No, it's his sister. Wai—" My eyes narrow. "Paolo, where did you learn all this? What happened?"

"Nothing!"

"Paolo..." I give him my most menacing look and finally he sighs.

"I brought Valentina down to meet my family last weekend."

"Whoa! That's a big deal."

"It is. But after Diego..." he clears his throat and rubs his left eye. "You never know how much time you have. And the only thing that really matters is the people you love. I wanted Valentina to meet everyone."

I nod. I understand this new feeling of urgency. "How did it go?"

"Worse than I could have ever imagined." He takes a bite of his pasta.

"Oh no! Were they mean to her?" I ask.

"Yes, but in the Sicilian way."

"What's the Sicilian way?" I ask and drink the rest of my water.

"You make them think you like them and then use their false sense of security to find their weaknesses and go in for the kill."

"Ooh, I don't like the Sicilian way."

"No one does," he says, shaking his head. "My male cousins follow general rules of engagement. But my female cousins...they're wily and ruthless and follow no rules." Paolo stares into the distance like he's contemplating a pack of hyenas.

"How is Valentina?"

"She's speaking to me again, which only took five days and three dozen roses."

BETTER THAN GELATO 195

I can see from his face how awful he feels. "I should have prepared her."
He looks me dead in the eyes. "Which is why I'm preparing you."

On the bus to meet Jake's sister, I review everything Paolo taught me and
make a mental list of reasons this won't be as bad:

1. There's just one family member, not a coordinated attack like
   Valentina faced.
2. I'm on my home turf.
3. Jake is the nicest person I know, his sister can't be that different.
4. She's not Sicilian.

It's a good list, and I cling to it as I walk to the restaurant. I see them
before they see me. Naomi doesn't look like Jake. She has red hair and fair
skin. She's wearing expensive jeans and a silky green blouse.

They both spot me and smile. And then Naomi looks over at Jake, sees
his face lit up with happiness, and her expression changes.

I give Naomi my nicest smile as I settle into my chair. "You must be
Naomi. I'm so glad you're here. How was your flight?"

"Long. I sat next to a snorer on the second leg, and he slept the whole
flight, no matter how many times I elbowed him."

Elbows strangers on planes. Noted.

The waiter takes our orders, and I get the baked ziti while Jake orders the
spaghetti carbonara. Naomi chooses the ravioli. Then changes her mind and
asks for the lasagna. Then two minutes after our waiter leaves, she makes
Jake find him and switch her order to fish.

"It's hard for me to choose too," I say. "But everything here is so
delicious, you can't go wrong no matter what you order."

"So, you've been enjoying the food here?" Naomi looks me over.

"Yeah, it's amazing." *Wait, what did she mean by that?* My cheeks flush,
and I brush my hands over my thighs.

"So Naomi, tell me what you want to see while you're here," Jake says
when he comes back to the table.

"Do we have to stay in Italy?" she asks with a whine. "I've already seen everything here. My friend Roxy says Malta is cool. Is that close?"

How could she not want to hang out in Italy? This place is the best!

"Why don't we look online tonight and see what we can put together?" Jake asks.

We make conversation, which is mostly Naomi talking while Jake and I nod along.

"That job was toxic," she says. "I can't be surrounded by that for twenty hours every week. I had to quit. Like for my own wellness, you know?"

"Sure," Jake says, and I nod along.

"Juliet, what do you do?" This is the first time Naomi's asked me a question, and it catches me off guard.

"I'm a nanny."

Naomi furrows her brow. "I'm so sorry." She shoots Jake a look that clearly asks, *'Why are you dating the help?'*

I'm thrown off but try to rally. "Actually I love it. The girl I nanny is awesome, and the family I live with is wonderful."

Naomi's gaze drifts to the ceiling, obviously bored. In an attempt to impress her I say, "The dad is a fashion designer."

That snaps her attention back to me. "Ooh, really? Could he get us tickets to some shows?"

"Oh, well the show season is over in Milan."

"Bummer. So maybe just some free designer clothes?"

I give Jake a panicked look, and he jumps in. "Why don't I take you shopping tomorrow?"

"Okay, but we have to use your card, I'm already at my limit."

Our food comes, and I'm so happy for the distraction I eat faster than usual. I eye Jake's plate, and he's down to his last few bites, but Naomi's barely touched her fish. We'll be here for ages!

"How's your boyfriend?" Jake asks.

"You mean ex-boyfriend," she says.

"That's a bummer. I thought you really liked this one," Jake says.

"I know, I thought I did too," she says, picking at a perfectly manicured nail. "But sometimes, people just aren't who you think they are."

"Sorry," I say, aware that I haven't spoken in a while.

"Me too. The whole time we dated, I thought his family owned a beach house in Martha's Vineyard but turns out they actually just own a condo in," she wrinkles her nose, "Jersey City."

I must be making a judgy face because she looks at me and says defensively, "It's the honesty that bothers me. You have to have honesty in a relationship."

"Sure," I offer.

"Speaking of exes," Naomi says looking at Jake. "I bumped into Gwen the other day. She sends her love."

My senses go on high alert. I want to ask some benign questions about Gwen, something totally casual and subtle, like on a scale of one to ten, how beautiful is she? Then Paolo pops into my head. I fake a yawn, which turns into a real yawn because I'm suddenly pretty tired.

"How's her family doing?" Jake asks politely, and Naomi launches into how marvelous Gwen's family is.

Jake gets up to use the restroom, and Naomi leans across the table toward me.

"So, are things between you and Jake pretty serious?" Her tone is friendly, like we're co-conspirators, but I know it's a trap. I do my best to answer without answering.

When Jake comes back Naomi launches into her "brilliant" idea of starting a cosmetics line for pets. She has pictures, which I'm hoping she photoshopped, of a Pomeranian wearing a Taylor Swift shade of red lipstick.

It's only 9:00 p.m., but I'd rather rip my own ears off than listen to Naomi any longer. The next time the waiter walks by, I give him my desperate eyes, and he gets the message and brings the check.

Jake hands over his credit card, and Naomi smiles at me and says, "It's nice to have someone who pays for everything, right?"

"Um..." I don't know how I planned on finishing that sentence, but Jake saves me the trouble.

"It's nice to have someone like Juliet who always thanks me for treating," he says to Naomi. "You're welcome for your dinner, by the way." He gestures to Naomi's plate. She didn't take more than two bites.

"Thank you Jakey," she says in a sugary voice that makes me want to vomit.

198   LIBBY TANNER

Before anyone can suggest dessert, I stand and grab my purse. "I'm feeling pretty beat, I'm going to call it a night. Naomi, it was nice to meet you. Jake, thank you for the lovely dinner."

"It looks like this week is still up in the air," Jake says. "But we'll come up with a plan tonight, and I'll text you the details."

We both assumed I would go traveling with him and Naomi this week, but now I'm wondering if we can un-assume that.

"Sounds good," I say to Jake, giving him a quick kiss. "Good night, Naomi."

"Buh-bye," she says, not taking her eyes off her phone.

I head toward the door, but I'm still within earshot when Naomi says, "Gwen was way prettier."

I don't know how one person, in less than an hour, can make me feel insecure about my job, my looks, and my relationship. By the time I get home, all I want to do is crawl into bed.

I wake up late the next morning and see a text from Jake.

> I'm taking Naomi shopping this morning. Want to come?

He sent it two hours ago. I text him back.

> Just woke up. I'll meet you downtown after my lunch with Paolo.

I mentally high five myself for dodging a horrendous shopping experience with Naomi, then hop in the shower and brainstorm other ways to get out of spending time with her this week. Can I convince Jake that the Rossis came back and demanded I take care of Isa?

Paolo chose the restaurant this week and got us a table on the balcony with a view of il Duomo.

"How was the enemy combatant?" he asks as soon as I sit. "Did you follow my training?"

"She wasn't that bad," I say, trying to be diplomatic. "I think she might have been jet lagged."

He makes me recount the whole evening in excruciating detail and then draws his own conclusion.

"She's a terrible human being."

"There may be some evidence to support that theory," I say. I take another bite of my soup. Soup is the best. Then I ask the question that's been rattling in my brain all night.

"Paolo, do you think I'm good enough for Jake?"

Paolo stops eating and folds his napkin next to his plate. I think I'm getting another big speech, but he looks me in the eyes and says simply, "Dolcetta, you are the bestie of Paolo Zarantonella, you are good enough for any man on this earth."

I nod, embarrassed I asked. I hate feeling insecure.

"I really don't want to hang out with Naomi anymore." I moan and plop my chin into my hand. My head feels too heavy to stay up on its own.

"And she's here all week?" Paolo asks.

"Yes. And just thinking about being around her makes my head hurt."

"Julieta, is your head hurting right now?" Paolo asks.

"Yes."

"Hold on." He gets out of his chair and puts his hand on my forehead. "You're burning up."

I put my hand to my head.

"I don't feel hot at all," I say and earn a snort of derision from Paolo.

"Your head doesn't feel hot to you because your hand is also hot."

"Oh man. I never get sick."

Paolo has a scheming look in his eye.

"This is perfect," he says. "You're too sick to go traveling with Jake and his sister."

"Ooh, that is good. I really didn't want to do that."

Somehow realizing I'm sick makes it even worse, because suddenly, I want to lay my head down on the table. I'm slowly moving in that direction when Paolo says, "We've got to go find Jake. He's shopping downtown right?"

His thumbs fly over his phone as he texts Jake.

"Yeah, but I just want to go home and crawl into bed. I don't want to see Naomi."

Paolo shakes his head. "He's got to see you. That will seal the deal. Trust me, you look awful."

I think about hitting him, but it's too much effort.

"Hang in there for another fifteen minutes, and you'll get out of everything for the rest of the week, I promise."

"Okay," I say. "But I feel bad tricking him."

Paolo laughs. "Julieta, you're not tricking anyone. You really are sick. You're just taking advantage of the good timing." He checks his phone and grins. "Jake is on his way."

We walk over to the steps, and by the time Jake and Naomi arrive, my head is throbbing.

"Juls!" Jake sits next to me and puts a hand to my head. "Wow, you definitely have a fever."

"My head feels like a bowling ball being hit with a hammer. And my bones are cold."

"I'm so sorry, *amore*." He gives me a little kiss. Naomi doesn't understand Italian, but can see enough to keep her distance, which is nice.

"Paolo, can you stay with her while I run into the pharmacy and get some meds?"

The pharmacy is right off the piazza, and we watch Jake go in. Once he's inside, Naomi turns to Paolo and says, "So, Paolo, you're Italian?"

Paolo nods.

Naomi gives him a big smile showing off bright, even teeth. "I love Italy. It's so romantic. What are you doing later?"

"I have a girlfriend," he says.

It's funny hearing Paolo speak English. He sounds British.

Naomi is undeterred. "I don't see her around," she says. "Why don't I let you buy me dinner tonight?" She's literally batting her eyelashes.

"No thank you," Paolo says, and I want to cheer. But I also don't want to move.

Naomi darts a look at me, but I don't even have the energy to gloat at her rejection.

Jake comes back with some pills and a bottle of water.

"Here, take this," he says, handing me two pills. My throat feels tight and lumpy, but I get them down.

"Thanks," I say. Jake looks at me, and it's nice to see that he still has the sparkly love eyes, even when I must look terrible.

"We're not leaving for Malta until tomorrow," he says. "Maybe you'll be feeling better by then?"

"Maybe," I say.

Paolo shakes his head. "They won't even let her on a plane looking like that. Better she stays here and rests."

Jake nods his head. "I'm so sorry," he says again.

"S'okay." I say. "I'll rest and be good as new when you get back."

Jake squeezes my hand. "Okay. Let me get you home."

I don't hear what he says to Naomi, but her response is loud enough for all of us to hear.

"What? We haven't even made it to Prada!" I notice the pile of designer bags behind her.

"We'll be back in an hour, I promise," Jake says.

"I can get home on my own," I say. "It's just sitting on a bus."

"It's not safe," Jake says. "Those meds are going to kick in soon, they're pretty powerful."

"I'll take her home," Paolo says. "I have some errands to do out that way anyway." Paolo couldn't possibly have errands by my apartment, because there is nothing in that area that they don't have downtown. But his voice is so authoritative there's no arguing.

We say goodbye to Jake and Naomi, and then Paolo and I walk to the bus stop. By the time we get to the Rossis', I can barely stay on my feet.

"Paolo, remember that time after my birthday with all the pomegranates in the elevator?" I start to giggle, and I can't stop.

"I do remember, dear girl. What I don't know is what in the world Jake gave you."

"I'll be fine. He's a doctor."

Paolo helps me to my bed. I close my eyes. With supreme effort, I open my eyes and then take off my left boot. My right boot does not want to come off, but Paolo unzips it and takes it off for me. He's a good friend.

"I love you," I tell Paolo. "Not like that, not like that. But you know, friend love."

Paolo looks amused. I may be slurring a little. "I love you too, Dolcetta."
And that's the last thing I remember for the next twelve hours.

When I wake up it's dark outside. My head feels better, but my limbs feel like they're made of cement. I check my phone, and I have a bunch of texts and a voicemail from Jake. I text him to let him know I'm okay and then immediately fall back asleep.

Many hours later, there's a knock on the door. I'm sweaty and for some reason, I'm sleeping on the living room couch instead of my bed. I stumble my way to the door and manage to open it on the second try. It's Paolo and Valentina.

"Hello!" I croak. *Whoa. My voice does not sound good.*

"Oh, Julieta!" Valentina says. I can tell from her face I look dreadful.

"Come in," I say. My voice sounds better the second time.

"We brought dinner," Paolo says. I look at the clock on the wall, and I'm surprised it's 6:30 p.m.

"How are you feeling?" Valentina asks.

"Better than yesterday. Paolo helped me get home and into bed."

"He told me," Valentina says.

"He also turned down Jake's sister who was putting the moves on him," I add.

"Hmm, he didn't tell me about that," Valentina turns to look at Paolo.

"He said he had a girlfriend, but she still said he should buy her dinner. And Paolo said, 'No thank you.'"

"You remember all of that, but you don't remember how to take off your boot?" Paolo mutters under his breath.

They stay for the next hour and hearing about Valentina's experience with Paolo's family makes me feel a bit better about Naomi.

"Thank you," I tell them as they go, "for the soup and the visit."

"*Di niente,*" Paolo says. "If a best friend can't bring you dinner when you're sick and your boyfriend has gone off with his horrible sister, what are we even here for?"

I spend the next week resting so much, my body is forced to get better. Jake and Naomi get home this afternoon, and we're meeting up for dinner tonight.

Maybe it's what I overheard Naomi say to Jake about Gwen being prettier than me. Or maybe it's the fact that the last time they saw me, I looked a total mess. But I want to look stupendous for dinner tonight. I take a shower and wash my hair. I follow a makeup tutorial on YouTube. I wear one of the outfits Isa always chose for me: loose turquoise blouse, black fitted pants, ankle boots.

This time, I make it to the restaurant before them and stand outside the door to wait. And because the universe loves me, or because I'm a blonde woman in Italy, I'm being offered a ride on a Vespa by an attractive man named Giuseppe when Jake and Naomi arrive.

"Thanks for the invitation," I say. "But my boyfriend's here, and we're going out to dinner."

Giuseppe gives Jake a head nod and then rides off.

I turn and smile at Jake and Naomi. I don't say anything about Giuseppe to make the point that this kind of thing happens so often, it's not even worth mentioning.

"Welcome back!" I say. "How were your travels?"

I miss Naomi's reply because Jake has scooped me up and is whispering in my ear, "I missed you so much. I love you. You look gorgeous tonight." We hug for a long time.

We go inside the restaurant and dinner goes a lot better than last time. Not because Naomi's less obnoxious—she's somehow worse—but it doesn't bother me the same way.

She complains about how crowded the plane was, how much walking there was, and how terrible the food in Malta was. Out of nowhere she asks me, "Is your dad a lawyer?"

"Nope. Runs a dry-cleaning shop."

I enjoy the appalled look on her face. I could have said he's retired, but her question was obviously trying to make a point, and so was my answer. I give her a look that says, 'Your watch may cost more than my car, but you're not better than me.' At least I try to. It's not easy to get all that in a look.

"I'm so glad you're feeling better," Jake says for the third time as we leave the restaurant.

"Me too," I say. "I'm just glad it happened now and not next week."

"What's happening next week?" Naomi says.

"We're flying to Greece," Jake says. "I told you about it on the plane to Malta."

"I wasn't listening," she says, unapologetically. "Greece...That sounds interesting..." She has a calculating look in her eye.

"You know—" she starts, but I interrupt her.

"I better catch my bus. Safe trip home tomorrow!" I tell her cheerfully. Then I give Jake a kiss and book it out of there as fast as I can.

Chapter Twenty-Seven

Tonight's going to suck. And I don't know how to make it not suck. The last time our whole gang was together was a month ago, right after Diego passed. I know everyone's been busy. I also know that being together makes it glaringly obvious he's not with us anymore. I think we've avoided meeting up to lessen the pain of his absence.

On top of that, it's the night Jake and I say goodbye to everyone. We leave for Greece tomorrow, and after that, it's back home to America.

I stand next to my bed staring at the pictures I printed this week. They're from the night I brought my camera to Calypso. My heart aches to see Diego smiling goofily, knowing that he was already sick but keeping it from us. His face is so full of life, it's hard to look at.

I took my time choosing the perfect shot for each of my friends. The first one we took turned out great, and it goes to Carmen. For Paolo, I choose a shot where Carmen, Diego, and I are looking at the camera, but Valentina and Paolo are looking at each other. And Valentina gets the last picture in the series where we're laughing and confused and a tangle of limbs. We all look so happy.

There's a part of me that doesn't want to look at any of these pictures. That wants to remove all the reminders of Diego from my heart and my mind, because it's too painful. It's the part of myself that's a coward. I force myself to look at his face and remember his laugh, even if it hurts.

I slip each photo into a frame, then wrap them and tuck them into my purse. On the way downtown, my brain keeps throwing depressing thoughts at me. *This is the last time you'll zip past these stores. This is the last time you'll meet all your friends on the steps of the piazza.* By the time I get to il Duomo, I feel like a pile of limp spaghetti.

And then something amazing happens. Jake and Valentina and Carmen are all sitting on the steps waiting for me. But Paolo is standing. He's wearing jeans and a T-shirt and tennis shoes. He has a baseball cap on his head. He sees me and yells in a terrible American accent, "Hey dude! What's up?"

I burst out laughing. "What in the world are you wearing, Paolo?" I ask.

"Actually, it's Paul," he says.

"Paul?"

"*Si.* Paul the super cool American."

I look at Valentina, and she shakes her head.

"Paolo thought you might have a hard time saying goodbye. I think dressing up like an American is supposed to cheer you up. I told him it was a terrible idea."

He looks absurd. The jeans are baggy, and his T-shirt has a couple of holes in it. The baseball hat is covering his thick hair, which he is enormously proud of. It reminds me of wearing an evening gown so Isa wouldn't be sad on her last day. *This* is why Paolo and I are best friends.

"It's a brilliant idea," I say to Valentina and Paolo.

Jake takes my hand and the five of us make our way to a pizzeria nearby and get a large table in the back. I sit down and look at Jake, Carmen, Valentina, and Paolo. I look at the spot where Diego should be. I want to burst into tears.

Carmen sees my face and says, "We aren't moping or saying goodbye all night. Got it?"

"Got it." I forgot how forceful she can be. But she's effective. I don't mention leaving or missing people.

I do talk a lot about UC San Diego's photography program.

Is this how Jake feels when he talks about his research? Like the people you're talking to sure look bored, but how can they be when it's so interesting? Surely they want to hear more.

We talk about Diego some. Paolo's been keeping in touch with his mom. He sent her some of the photos he'd taken of Diego on their trips.

Carmen mentions she got some great news from a friend back home. She doesn't tell us what it is but says she's excited for a fresh start. I'm pretty sure her friend is a lawyer.

When it's time to go, I give Carmen and Paolo and Valentina their gifts. I wanted them to open them right now, so I could see their reactions, but I change my mind at the last minute.

"Open them when you get home," I say.

And then we're outside the restaurant and it's time to say goodbye. I think about the first time I met this crew, how glamorous and 'other' they all seemed. And now they feel like a part of me. In fact, the best parts of me.

I planned to bid my friends farewell with dignity and grace. Instead, I sob into Valentina's hair and blubber, "This has been the greatest year of my life," while Carmen pats my back. Then I hug Paolo and try to explain how much he means to me, while also trying to keep my snot off his tacky American T-shirt.

Turns out I'm not a gracious goodbye-er. Finally, after promising to write and visit, Jake leads me to my bus stop, and we sit on the bench.

"That was pretty awful, wasn't it?" I say, embarrassed about my tears.

"I thought you did great." He wraps his arms around me.

And then, for the last time, I take the 27 tram to the Rossis' apartment.

Chapter Twenty-Eight

The flight to Athens is less than two and a half hours. In that time, I say "I can't believe we're flying to Greece," at least seven times. As we descend, I see the Aegean Ocean sparkling beneath us, and Greece's most famous ruins waiting to be explored.

Jake gets us a cab at the airport, and I take in the city of Athens as we speed toward our hostel. It's loud. And indecently hot. And I can't understand anything. But my skin is tingling with the thrill of being in a new country.

We check in at our hostel then go straight to the restaurant next door. I get a Greek salad. The tomatoes are red and juicy. The cucumbers are fresh and crisp. The olives and purple onions add sharp bites of flavor.

"You're making your happy food sounds again," Jake says with a smile.

After we finish, I head back to the counter and thank the wonderful souls who made my food.

"Amazing work you guys. Truly incredible. There should be statues built of you." I'm not sure how much English they understand, but one of them gives me a thumbs up.

"Okay," I tell Jake once we're out on the sidewalk. "I've planned the perfect day for us. Are you ready to get punched in the face by Ancient Greece?"

"I think so?"

"Perfect. Follow me."

The hike to the top of the Acropolis is steep and the heat is sweltering. By the time we make it to the top, Jake and I are both covered in sweat and grinning like maniacs as we gaze at the ruins around us.

"This is incredible!" Jake says.

"I know!"

I take approximately one trillion photos. We stroll along the towering columns that make up the perimeter of the Parthenon. We visit the temple of Athena Nike and explore the Ancient Agora and Temple of Hephaestus. I tell Jake interesting facts about each site.

"Wow," Jake says. "Did you already know all this stuff, or did you learn it so you could be a sexy tour guide?"

"Not telling," I say. Then Jake wraps his arms around me and starts kissing me just below my ear. It gives me the shivers and makes me giggle.

"Okay, fine. I read a bunch of stuff on Wikipedia to impress you."

"It worked. I'm impressed." He kisses me until I've forgotten everything about the Acropolis and my first name.

"Should we blow off these ruins and go make out somewhere?" I whisper.

"And miss out on you as a sexy tour guide? No way!"

We keep exploring until our legs ache and our stomachs start growling.

"Are you ready for some dinner?" I ask Jake.

"If it means I can sit down, yes."

"You're in luck," I say. "I chose one of those fancy Greek restaurants with chairs."

I use the tourist map and lead us to our destination.

"We're having dinner at a hotel?" Jake asks.

"Just wait," I say, taking his hand and pulling him into the elevator.

The Athens Gate Hotel has a rooftop restaurant with a 360-degree view of Athens. A hostess leads us to our table, and I watch Jake's face as he looks around him. The whole city is laid out below us. Purple clouds have formed behind the Acropolis making it look especially dramatic. He turns to me with a huge grin.

"Wow," he says.

"I know!"

"How did you find this place?" he asks, turning to look at the view behind him.

"An old woman came to me in a dream and told me about it."

"Really?" His eyes are huge.

I laugh. "No. I found it on the Internet."

"Well, it's the coolest restaurant I've ever been to." He squeezes my hand, and I feel pretty proud of myself.

We devour pita with house-made hummus and flavorful tzatziki sauce, mushrooms stuffed with spinach and garlic, and grilled pork skewers so juicy I have to lick my fingers and hands. I eat so much it's physically painful, but I have no regrets.

We stay at our table and enjoy the view as the sun sets, the white marble of the Parthenon turning pink in the sunset's glow.

"Thank you for an awesome day today," Jake says. "I loved all the things we saw."

"I can't take all the credit," I say. "The people who actually built the monuments did their part too. But you're welcome."

The check comes and Jake takes it. I take it back. "It's my night to treat."

"Yeah, I was thinking about that," Jake says. "It seems so silly for you to pay."

"But we agreed." I say. "I worked hard and saved for this."

"I know you did. You're amazing. But what if you used that money toward a plane ticket to visit me in New York?"

"I'm going to get a job when I get home," I say. "I can save more money."

"Do you have a job lined up already?" he asks.

"Not exactly," I say, heat creeping up my neck. "But I was going to talk to the manager at Jamba Juice and see if I could get my old job back."

"I think it would just be easier this way," Jake says. "I would rather pay for stuff here so you can fly out to Columbia later and not put a strain on your finances."

I hand him the check just so we can be done with this conversation. I was excited to pay for dinner at this fancy restaurant tonight. I felt really cool and mature. Now I feel small and lame. I know Jake's trying to be kind, but for the first time, he seems like a rich guy paying for his girlfriend because she's too poor to pay for herself.

"I'm going to use the bathroom," I say. "I'll be right back."

I take my time. I admire the bright blue tiles around the mirror. I take some deep breaths. *It's not a big deal.* Jake is literally the nicest guy I've ever met. I head back to the table and resolve to get over it. And it's easy. Jake is sweet and the view is amazing and as we walk back to our hostel, I marvel at how lucky I am.

That feeling only grows over the next two days as we explore ancient and modern Greece and gorge ourselves on unbelievably yummy food. We bid farewell to the city of Athens from the deck of a ferry headed to the islands. The sun shines, the sea shimmers, and everything about the world is golden.

We disembark in Naxos and follow the other passengers down a long dock. I foolishly imagined the Greek islands would look like Hawaii. They don't. Naxos is an island of craggy cliffs and scrubby shrubs. Less palm trees and more pine trees, and the air smells like maple syrup. We stroll through a town square and up a hill, then Jake stops in front of a group of white condos.

"This is us," he says.

It's not big, but it's got everything we need. Two bedrooms. A bathroom with a shower and tub. A small living room and a kitchenette. From our balcony, we can see all the way out to the ocean.

"What if we stay here and never go home?" I ask. "Ooh! We could fake our own deaths! 'Young couple dies tragically in Greek volcano incident.'"

"Or..." Jake says, "We could just come back on our honeymoon." He gives me a hopeful look.

"That could work," I say. "But if we end up marrying other people, that would make for a very awkward trip."

I take a shower in our connecting bathroom, happy to rinse the sand and seawater out of my hair. The water pressure isn't great, and it only gets lukewarm, but it still feels divine.

Fifteen minutes later, Jake knocks on my door. I'm sitting on my bed trying to brush out my hair.

"It's me. Jake," he says, which makes me laugh. *Who else would it be?*

"Come on in."

I give my hair a vicious yank. The complimentary conditioner was pretty much worthless.

Jake looks fresh and clean from the shower, and his nose and forehead are kissed from the sun. He glances at the brush I'm holding in a death grip.

"Did I ever mention that Naomi taught me how to French braid?" he asks.

"You did not."

He climbs onto the bed and sits behind me. He takes the brush from my hand and gently works out the rest of the tangles, starting at the tips. He doesn't rush. His hands move slowly and tenderly, freeing each knot. Each brush of his fingers on my neck sends tingles down to my toes. Then he starts at the top and, strand by strand, works his way down, French-braiding my hair.

He doesn't say anything and neither do I, but the air in the room seems to buzz with a charged energy like the beach before a storm.

When he's done, he says, "There," very softly, and puts the hairband at the bottom.

"Thanks," I say. But I don't move. Jake's hands move from my neck to my shoulders and down my arms until he's enveloped me. We stay like that for a long time. Eventually, he gives me a sweet kiss good night, and I lay in bed with my heart pounding.

There is a lot to enjoy about Naxos, and we spend the next five days doing it all. We spend an afternoon at a secluded beach near an olive grove. We're the only ones there and the air is filled with the intoxicating scent of warm olive oil. We eat snacks and swim. And when the sky gets pink, we kiss and whisper sweet things to each other. It's one of those moments when the whole universe seems to exist solely for our pleasure.

We spend one morning riding bikes around the port town of Naxos. We stop to visit a beach and quickly discover it's clothing optional. I try to play it cool, but of course I turn bright red, because my body betrays me every chance it gets.

The low point of the week comes when we go to rent scooters. It's not fair to call it a fight, but a disagreement doesn't quite capture what transpires.

We wanted to check out more of the island and scooters seemed like a good time. I've never actually driven one, and I was excited to try. And then this happened:

"There's not much to it," the guy at the shop says. "Just take it easy on the turns. A crash could wreck your whole vacation."

And I think, *'Easy on the turns. Got it. Let's go.'*

And Jake says, "I don't think this is a good idea."

And I say, "Why not?"

And he says, "I don't want to crash and wreck the rest of our vacation."

And I say, "We're not going to crash."

And he says, "People crash. My parents put them back together every day."

And I say, "We'll be just fine."

And he says, "I don't think it's worth the risk." And his tone is so...conclusive. Like he is the decision maker, and he's made the decision.

I don't push or pout or complain. Even though I think it's really stupid to miss out on something so fun.

We get a boring car, and I try my best to have a good attitude as we drive, boringly, to the other side of the island. But Jake still seems bothered.

Finally, I say, "It looks like something's bothering you. Do you want to talk about it?"

And Jake sighs and says, "I'm just surprised that you weren't concerned about driving a scooter for the first time in a foreign country." The judgment in his voice is evident.

I don't know what to tell him. *You got your way. We're driving the lame car. What do you want from me?* I shrug my shoulders and say, "I wasn't."

And the deep disappointment in his eyes seems out of proportion to our situation. So I take a stab in the dark.

"You're not just concerned about us on scooters today. You're projecting things ten years down the road, the way you do, and you don't trust me to drive our kids to school in a minivan."

I know I'm correct by the look on his face. And then he says, staring straight ahead, "I just think you're pretty reckless sometimes. Like you don't understand or care about the consequences."

My hands squeeze into fists in my lap and all the muscles in my neck tighten. I understand how consequences work. I understand that as a consequence of being the youngest of five kids, I'm on my own for college.

So I worked hard to earn a scholarship to cover tuition. I understand that as a consequence of my parents paying for one sister's rehab and another sister's divorce, they don't have money to help me with rent or groceries. So I got a part-time job to cover my expenses. I carefully crafted a plan to leave my hometown and make something of myself. Recklessness had nothing to do with it.

For a while, I'm too angry to say anything. I stare out the window of our stupid car and look at the trees whizzing past.

After a few minutes, Jake puts his hand on my leg and says, "I just think you could be more responsible." I brush his hand off.

I'm a terrible singer. I don't understand film noir. But I am responsible. I set goals and achieve them. I am self-disciplined and levelheaded. Apparently, Jake doesn't know that about me, and that hurts. But I know that about myself.

I don't turn to look at him, but I speak loudly so I can be sure he hears.

"I actually like being just the way I am."

The rest of the drive is pretty awkward. We don't talk. When we make it to the other side of the island, we find a steep trail to hike. It gives us something to focus on and a reason for not speaking. By the time we drive back to our condo, most of the weirdness has disappeared. We never talk about it again.

On our last night in Naxos, we participate in a traditional Greek dinner. Jake made friends with the guy at the snorkel shop—because of course he did—and scored us an invitation to his daughter's engagement dinner. We eat home-cooked souvlaki, smash plates, and dance like hooligans under a bright moon. It's one of those nights I'll remember forever.

Then we're off to Santorini. I think this might be my favorite place yet. White houses cling to rocky cliffs above water the color of sapphires. I want to photograph every square inch.

We spend our first day hiking the trail connecting Thira, where we're staying, to Oia at the very tip of the island. It's hot, but there's a cool breeze blowing. The sea is a dark blue, like it contains all the mysteries of the world. As we hike, I think about Jake, and that feeling I had in the car that he didn't really know me. I wonder what I don't know about him.

"What's your most embarrassing moment?" I ask.

Jake scoffs, "I've never had a single embarrassing—eighth grade basketball tryouts."

I laugh. "You didn't make the team?"

"I did not. I took a shot, got hit in the face by the rebound, and broke my nose." He kicks a rock off the trail, and it goes tumbling down the hillside into the ocean. "All in front of Sarah Flemming, who I'd been trying to impress."

I burst out laughing. "I am so sorry."

"It's okay, that's when I got into soccer. Turns out I'm better with my feet."

"Once you were a star soccer star, did you ask Sarah out?"

"I did not." Jake takes a swig from his water bottle. "She dated Brad Meyer, a basketball player, on and off through high school. And when she wasn't dating Brad, I was dating other people, so it never worked out."

"Who did you date in high school?" I ask without thinking. I stop to take a drink from my water bottle.

"Different girls," he says. "I was in relationships through most of high school and college. What about you?"

"I was the opposite. I hung out with different boys. Maggie and I were both pretty boy-crazy in high school, but I never liked having a boyfriend. For the most part, I managed to avoid falling into that trap."

"Okay, the first month of our relationship is starting to make more sense," Jake says.

"So many girls at my school 'fell in love,' ditched all their friends and ended up heartbroken six months later," I explain. "No thanks. Besides, the guys at my high school were idiots."

"Okay, so what about college?" Jake asks.

"What about college?" A giant puffy cloud has moved over the sun, giving us some relief from the heat.

"Did you find someone to date and fall in love with in college?"

"I wasn't trying to find someone to fall in love with. I was trying to pass my classes while working five shifts a week. There were certainly better options in college than my small high school. But I never actually...wait, how many people have you fallen in love with?"

There is silence, and I wish I could take the question back. Because suddenly, I'm sure it's more than the one person I've ever fallen in love with. I feel like an idiot.

Of course Jake's fallen in love before. Probably a heap of times. Why did I assume I was his first just because he's mine?

Jake still hasn't answered. *Ohmygosh is he counting?! This is excruciating.*

"You don't have to answer that," I say. "It was a stupid question."

"I don't think it's a stupid question," Jake says. "But I don't think a lot of good will come from pulling at that thread. All those girls are in my past. You're my present. And hopefully my future."

It's a sweet thing to say. *But* all *those girls? How many are we talking here?* This time, I keep the question to myself. Instead, I tell him about my most embarrassing moment involving junior prom and self-tanning lotion.

The whole hike takes us less than three hours, and then we're in Oia, the iconic Greek town. There's a staircase carved into the side of the cliff and after descending approximately seven million steps, we get to the beach.

It's not crowded, and I'm so hot I don't feel embarrassed as I strip off my shorts and tank top and dive into the cool water in my bra and undies. It feels glorious. I don't come up for a long time. Long enough for my body to go through the shock of the cold and then acclimate. When I do break the surface, Jake is just a few feet away.

"Doesn't the water feel amazing?" I ask.

His hair is dripping, and his smile is big. "You know what else is amazing? That thing you did where you took all your clothes off and jumped into the sea in your underwear."

"What else was I supposed to do?" I say. "It's a million degrees, and I don't have my swimsuit. Besides, my bra and underwear cover just as much as my bikini."

Jake tips his head from side to side. "Maybe. But it feels different."

"Well, if I'm offending you with my indecency, feel free to look away."

"Oh, if only I could."

And then he's kissing me, and it's the kind of kiss that lets you know everything he's thinking and feeling and wanting.

We stay at the beach for a long time, swimming, and when our muscles are worn out, laying in the shallowest part of the shore where the waves wash over our legs. We're two of the last people on the beach, and I never want to leave.

BETTER THAN GELATO 217

Eventually, we put our clothes back on and tackle the giant staircase. My legs feel like Jell-O. The kind of Jell-O that complains when you make it walk up stairs.

Oia is famous for its sunsets, and it feels like the town was designed to appreciate them as much as possible. We choose one of a dozen restaurants with patio seating and stuff ourselves on a platter of the restaurant's specialties.

I fall in love with spanakopita, a light and flaky pastry stuffed with spinach and cheese. I also eat several little balls of herb rice wrapped in grape leaves. They're called dolmades, and they're my new favs.

We're just finishing our last bites when the sky show begins. The white clouds melt into a vibrant orangey pink that seems to grow until the whole sky looks like it's about to catch fire. It feels like everyone in the restaurant is holding their breath as we watch the red blazing orb finally drop below the horizon.

We stay on the terrace until the pink has melted away and the sky is indigo. Then we take a taxi back to our hostel and spend the rest of the evening playing cards with a group of travelers from Australia.

Just when I'm feeling ready to climb into bed, Jake says, "Well, guys, I think we're going to call it a night."

He gets up from the table and offers me his hand. And I know it's not a big deal, and I know I was just thinking about going to bed. *But why does he get to decide when we call it a night? What if I wanted to stay up and keep playing cards?*

I take his hand and get up from the table, but feeling suddenly stubborn I tell him, "I'm actually not ready for bed. I'm going to head down to the beach."

"See you later," I say to the Aussies and head to the door.

"It's pretty late," Jake says, following me.

I shrug my shoulders. "I'm not tired."

Which is silly because I am really and truly exhausted. But I've decided to dig in, so that's what I'm doing.

"Didn't you say we have something planned for tomorrow morning?" Jake asks.

"Yep."

"So shouldn't we get some rest?"

I can tell that he thinks he's being reasonable, and I'm being unreasonable. And that makes me unreasonably irritated.

"You can if you want to," I say. "I'll see you in the common room at nine."

I head out the door into the warm summer air. Jake follows me.

"You can't go out by yourself," Jake says.

"Of course I can."

I head in the direction of the beach. It's not far, I can hear the waves crashing.

"It's not safe," Jake says and reaches out a hand as though to take my arm, but at the last second changes his mind.

"Jake, I'm perfectly fine on my own," I say. "If you're feeling tired, go to bed. If you'd like to join me on the beach that's fine too. But come for my company, not as my chaperone."

Jake pauses and then softly takes my hand. "I always love your company," he says. He looks at his watch. "Even at one in the morning."

Most of my irritation melts away as we walk down to the beach. The area is not well lit, and I feel the cool water slide over my flip flops before I see it. I look out to the sea but can't make out the horizon.

"Look at the stars," Jake whispers.

I look up and suck in my breath. The sky is sparkling like a thousand diamonds spilled across black velvet. The moon is a tiny sliver, as though embarrassed to show up and get upstaged. We lay on our backs on the dry sand and gaze up at the sky.

"This is incredible," Jake says.

"It really is."

"So, what's the first thing you're going to do when you get home?" he asks.

The question catches me off guard. Laying on a beach in Santorini under a blanket of stars, home is far from my mind.

I shrug my shoulders, realize he can't see, and say. "Not sure."

"I'm going to get a bacon cheeseburger and chocolate milkshake from Shake Shack," Jake says. "I haven't had a shake in ages."

"Hmm."

"They're phenomenal. I'll take you there. Maybe you could come for Thanksgiving."

BETTER THAN GELATO 219

Suddenly my eyes fill with tears, and I don't even know why. I lay on my back and let them slide down my cheeks into my ears. Jake rambles on about all the things he's excited to do back home and how fun it'll be to show me everything. I stare up at the stars and cling to this moment in this little Greek village and refuse to think about leaving.

"What do you think?" Jake asks.

I have no idea what he's talking about. I clear my throat, which still feels tight with tears and then answer. "Sorry, I missed that last part."

"It doesn't matter. I think you're just tired. Should we head back to the hostel?"

"Sure," I say. And we leave the stars to watch over the beach without us.

Santorini is small, and after three days, we've seen most of it. We took a boat tour around the island and explored some underwater caves. We hiked a volcano and lounged on a beach with sand the color of obsidian.

When it's time, we walk down to the main dock and catch the last ferry of the day. After this, we'll catch our flight from Athens to Milan, and our trip will be over. The ferry slowly pulls away from the dock. We stay on the deck and watch the sun sink into the Aegean. The sky remains a stubborn pink long after the sun has gone, like it's clinging to something that's no longer there. I know the feeling.

Chapter Twenty-Nine

The airport smells like old carpet and crushed dreams.

"You okay?" Jake says. "Feeling bummed about going home?"

I'm curled up in a blue vinyl chair, picking at a hole in the fabric.

Bummed isn't the right word, but devastated seems dramatic. Jake gives me a smile and it's so tender my heart squeezes. I remember with gratitude that my favorite thing about Italy is coming back to America with me.

Jake managed to get a flight that leaves just an hour after mine. Now we're sitting at my gate waiting for my plane to arrive and break my heart.

"You know, America's a pretty good country," Jake says. "Some people even come from other countries just to live there."

"I'm sure I'll remember the good things about it once I'm there," I say.

"I know today sucks," Jake says, wrapping his arm around me. "I got you something to cheer you up."

He hands me a white envelope, and I remember some of the other white envelopes he's given me. Sure enough, I open it and pull out a roundtrip ticket from San Diego to NYC in September. I look at Jake.

"To make leaving each other easier," he says. I burst into tears. I'm not handling this well. I know I'm not. But I don't know how else to handle it.

"Thank you," I say, when I get my tears under control. *When did I become such a crier?*

Jake rubs my back and tells me about the cool things we'll do in New York City when I come visit. I listen and try to feel excited. Eventually my flight is called. When there are only three people in line, I stand up and collect my carry-on.

Jake stands with me and wraps his arm around me. "I love you," he whispers. I nod my head. I know this.

"I love you too," I say. But I can't bring myself to let go.

"I'll see you in six weeks," he says.

"Okay, six weeks," I repeat.

And then they're calling all passengers to board, and I finally let go. I give him a small kiss and walk over to the flight attendant. She scans my boarding pass, hands it back to me, and then gestures to the jetway. Casually. As though she isn't encouraging me to leave behind all the wonder and magic I've found this last year.

I walk two steps, then turn for one more look at Jake. I feel frozen to the spot. I can't do this. I can't leave him.

And then Jake sprints past the flight attendant, scoops me into his arms, and kisses me like I'm oxygen and he's drowning. My hands lock around his neck, and my toes aren't touching the floor. He kisses me, and I know he's feeling every single thing I'm feeling.

There's a loud cough which we ignore, and then a *"Ragazzi, per favore," kids, please,* which makes Jake return my feet to the ground and release me from his arms. He takes a step back.

The flight attendant gives us a smile and a head shake, like, "We've all been there."

Jake turns and goes back to the waiting area. He smiles at me with dimples in his cheeks and love in his eyes.

"Ciao, bella!" he calls.

"Ciao, bello!" I call back. And then I'm turning and walking down the jetway and the tears are rolling off my cheeks and dropping onto the floor before I even make it to my seat.

The trip home is long. I make a list of all the wonderful things that have happened in the last year.

1. My parents sold the business, and I got into the photography program.
2. I fell in love, for crying out loud!
3. I made friends I will have for the rest of my life.
4. I tamed a velociraptor child. Or at least befriended one.
5. I traveled to Florence, Switzerland, Rome, and Greece.

My head lists all these things, but my heart is crying too loud to listen.

As soon as I get off the plane, I find a bathroom and wash my tearstained face. I do my hair and put on makeup until I look like a human being again.

My parents see me before I see them, and I hear my dad yell, "There she is!"

I spot Maggie running toward me and when her hug lands, I'm nearly knocked off my feet. We hug and laugh and talk over each other.

"You're back!"

"Mags!"

"You look so Italian!"

"I missed you so much!"

My parents make it over to us, and Maggie lets go so my dad can give me a hug. His eyes are teary, and he doesn't speak. *This is where I got my crying from.* My mom squeezes in for a hug and there are no tears in her eyes, only happiness.

"I'm so glad you're home," she says. "Was it hard to leave?"

"Incredibly hard," I admit. "Right until this moment."

"Well, good job getting on that plane," she says. "I'm glad you did."

"And great job getting into your photography program," my dad says. "I knew you could do it."

"Thanks," I say.

I haven't told them the whole story yet, about getting rejected and then fighting to get in. But there's time for that later.

We go to dinner at the Olive Garden, which was my dad's idea. It was a terrible idea. The pasta is obnoxiously overcooked, and the server corrects my pronunciation of bruschetta.

BETTER THAN GELATO

The ride home is filled with storytelling and laughter and inside jokes and new jokes. My dad drops Maggie off at her house and then we pull into our driveway a few streets over. Our house feels smaller than I remember.

My parents follow me to my room, each dragging a suitcase. My dad reaches around me and switches on the light. My bed is all made up and on the walls are vintage posters of Rome, Florence, and Athens.

"Ta-da!" my dad says. "We thought you'd feel right at home."

"They're amazing!" I say.

"We're so glad you're home," my mom says.

My dad doesn't say anything. He's gone teary again.

I wake up before the sun rises the next morning, and I can't go back to sleep. I take a long shower. I give my heart a mental poke to see how it's feeling, and it's better than I expected. Yesterday's sadness of leaving mixes with today's happiness of being home.

I send Jake a selfie of me in front of the poster of Florence.

It's like I never left

He texts me a picture of him in front of a brand-new pickup truck.

I love you in Florence! Look what my dad got me as a welcome home gift!

I can't help but laugh. I give him a call and for a moment, it's so good to hear his voice that all of yesterday's sadness comes rushing back. But it gets easier the next day. And the day after that.

The summer goes by quickly. For as long as I've known them, my parents have worked incredibly long hours. It's fun to see them with free time on their hands. We paint the kitchen cabinets like my mom's been wanting to do for a decade. We play Scrabble together in the evenings. My dad cheats when he thinks we're not looking.

I take photos around my small town. The shops on Main Street. The crowds at the park on Friday night where local bands play. The sunrise on the lake, smooth and shiny and silver. I text the best ones to Paolo and Carmen and Valentina.

I spend hours with Maggie filling in the gaps from the last year. I show her all my photos.

"Your description of Paolo did not prepare me for how hot he is."

And she tries on all my new clothes.

"I want to go shopping in Milan!"

She listens as I talk about Diego and hugs me while I cry some. She laughs as I tell her about Isa and asks if she can come with me to Vegas to meet her.

I talk to Jake for hours every day and send him some of the photos I'm taking around town.

"I'd like to visit this Lakeport town," he says. "It sounds made up."

"I know, it kind of does. But it's real, I promise. And I would love to show you. We'd finish the tour in about ten minutes. And then we'd go skinny dipping in the lake. "

"Count me in."

He tells me about Arizona. He makes up funny songs about stuff we did in Italy. He sends me flowers for no reason.

Before I know it, Maggie and I are loading up her tiny car for the drive down to San Diego. My parents stand in the driveway and wave as we pull out. Then Maggie cranks up her road trip playlist, and I'm headed back to college.

Chapter Thirty

The first day of classes is rough. I'd forgotten how boring the minutiae of school is. We go over syllabi and office hours and exam schedules. I do my best not to let my mind wander to nights dancing at Calypso and kissing Jake in tree-filled parks.

My Italian class is wonderful and awful. Wonderful because it's taught by a young TA named Giovanni that reminds me so much of Paolo I want to hug him. Awful because it fills me with homesickness for a place that is not my home.

Then it's time for my photography class. My hands start sweating. I wore my black pants and a gold-splattered blouse Carmen found for me at the market. It makes me feel like a cool artist type. I find my classroom and take a seat in the middle row, center seat. I lay out my notebook and pencil and give the girl next to me a shy smile.

I've built this class up so much, I'm nervous it will fall short. Instead, it exceeds every one of my ridiculous expectations. Professor Melvin is brilliant and knowledgeable and talented. But also funny and down-to-earth and relatable. If I were a cartoon character, my eyes would turn into hearts right now. He gives us our first assignment, a photograph that is autobiographical, but is not a photo of ourselves. As I walk to my next class, my head is swirling with ideas, and my heart is pinging with happiness.

After English class and a chemistry lab, I head over to the Jamba Juice on campus. I don't know any of the people behind the counter, but the manager Mike is still there and remembers me as a hard worker. I ask for a job, and he gives it to me, just like that. Which is awesome, because student jobs on campus are crazy hard to get, and I did not have a Plan B.

I call Jake on the way home and tell him my great news. He tells me about his visit to the cadaver lab, which sounds disgusting but was clearly the highlight of his week. I'm just about to tell him about my photography class, but someone comes to his apartment, and he has to go.

I tell Maggie instead. She's sitting on our faded, lumpy couch eating canned peaches straight from the jar.

"Where are Petey and the Pirate?" I ask. Our two other roommates are both named Jessica. Petey's last name is Peterson and Pirate's last name is Roberts, like the Dread Pirate Roberts from *The Princess Bride*.

"Library," she says. "Pirate's studying, and Petey's trying to get a kid who works there to ask her out."

I grab one of her peach slices and head to our room to work on my photography assignment. I take a dozen photos of various things in various settings, but nothing feels right. An hour later, I'm muttering Italian swear words and questioning what autobiographical even means.

I take a break and finish unpacking. I hang up a photo of me and Isa from my first week in Milan. Then I hang up one of me and the gang at our last dinner together. Side by side, the difference is remarkable. In the second one, my shoulders are relaxed, my face is fuller, and my smile is huge. I think of all the ways this last year has changed me. I fell in love. I lost a friend. I learned a language. I gained twenty pounds. I escaped my fate and got to live my dream instead.

I pull out a pair of jeans and a UC San Diego T-shirt and my Nikes. I lay them down on the floor of my room. There's not a lot of space between our twin beds, but it's enough. Then I get out my black pants and one of my runway blouses and lay them out above my pointy-toed stiletto boots.

As a visual, it's not bad. A nice contrast. I'd like to show a transition from one to the other. I pull out the giant Italian flag from my suitcase and lay it between the two outfits. Then I fold the edges down in front so it forms an arrow, from the American outfit to the Italian one.

After it's all laid out, I start photographing. It takes a while. The first few have one of Maggie's socks in the corner. But I tweak and adjust and finally get there.

Two days later when I walk into my photography class, I'm greeted by glossy eight-by-tens hanging from each wall.

"I was delighted to see the creativity we have in this group," Professor Melvin says. "Since we're going to be working together for the next few months, I thought we'd better get to know each other. I find the best way to get to know someone is to understand the way they see themselves."

We go around, one by one, and talk about our photos. There are twenty of us, so it takes some time, but it's interesting. There's a superb photo of a guitar. One of a dog. Someone photographed their friends.

When it's my turn to explain my photo, I'm not sure what to say.

"Well," I start, and then stop. "I was trying to capture a transformation. I spent the last year in Italy. The people I met there and the experiences I had shaped me into who I am at this moment."

Professor Melvin nods, and we move on to the next person. After we've gone through everyone, we settle in for the lecture. It's so good I'm still scribbling notes when class ends, and I'm the last one to collect my photo.

"I really enjoyed your take on this assignment," Professor Melvin says. I jump a little. I didn't notice he'd come up behind me.

"Thank you."

"So many people choose to focus on one aspect of who they are, and you chose to capture the recent circumstances that shaped you into who you are."

"I wasn't sure I explained that very well," I say.

"Yes, well that's why we have photography, isn't it? So we can express those things we don't have words for."

When I leave the classroom, I look at the back of my photo. One hundred percent with a little handwritten note that says, "Looking forward to getting to know you and your work." I walk to my apartment grinning like an idiot.

Before I know it, I'm deep in the routine of things. Classes in the morning, studying in the afternoon, and serving the students of UC San Diego delicious smoothies in the evening. I make up nicknames for some of the regulars that come in every day and order the same thing. Caribbean Passion Polo, cause he's on the water polo team, Watermelon Breeze

228   LIBBY TANNER

Brunette, because she has shiny brown hair like a Disney princess, and Orange Dreamy Dream, an attractive preppy type.

Jake and I talk in the morning before my first class, and in the afternoon after his last class. Sometimes we talk for an hour, other times we barely squeeze in two minutes.

Considering how I bawled my eyes out all the way home from Italy, I feel surprisingly good in my life here. I'd forgotten how gorgeous the campus is. How fun it is living with roommates. How great it feels to work hard on an assignment and get an A. Even though I'm in the same apartment with the same job and roommates, it doesn't feel like I've fallen back into my old life. I feel like a new person, creating a new life for myself.

And the fact that I'm taking photography classes instead of business classes makes me feel like the luckiest girl alive. Professor Melvin has stolen my brain. It's like when someone steals your heart, but intellectual instead of romantic. I give my roomies summaries of every lecture. I can feel myself driving everyone crazy, like the time my Aunt Marla went vegan and worked it into every conversation, but I can't stop myself.

Last week, it occurred to me that the new nanny must have arrived at the Rossi house. I sent a welcome text to my old phone number and ordered the next *Harry Potter* book in Italian for them to read.

I'm excited for her and the year she has in front of her, and I'm also excited to be right where I am.

"And then I cut right through the chest cavity. It took longer than you'd think, even with the surgical saw. And then we pried up the breast bone and took out the heart. It was slippery. Lucas almost dropped it."

I put my PB&J back into its Ziploc bag and adjust my phone against my ear.

"Wow, that's really interesting."

I listen to Jake as I walk the hilly path home from campus. I'm exhausted. I worked a double shift at Jamba Juice yesterday because someone called in sick, then just as I was going to bed I remembered an English assignment that was due. It took me until nearly midnight to finish it. And then I woke up at 6 a.m. to talk to Jake.

"The surgical resident is super cool," Jake says. "He says he thinks I would be a good fit for surgery."

"That reminds me of my photography lecture today," I say as I push the door to my apartment open with my shoulder and throw my backpack on the couch. Maggie is eating cereal at the table and gives me a wave.

"It was about fitting your subject into the right frame." I'm about to launch into a description of the lecture, when I hear a thumping sound on Jake's end.

"I want to hear all about it," Jake says. "But can I call you back later? I told Gilbert I'd help him prep for clinicals tomorrow."

"Of course. No problem. I'll talk to you later."

"What's Jake up to?" Maggie asks.

"You're eating, so I'll spare you."

"Appreciate that." She swallows a big bite. "Do you ever tell him about your classes, or do you just play cheerleader to all his stuff?"

"I tell him about my stuff," I say.

She shakes her head. "Your last three conversations have just been you saying 'Wow, that's really interesting,' like a thousand times."

"Why don't you get your own life and stop hovering in mine?" I say.

I grab a snack and head to my room. Things with Jake are...fine. I mean, long distance is hard, right? Everyone knows that. And yes, Jake is a little different than he was in Italy. More stressed out. Doesn't joke like he used to but that's to be expected. Med school is hard. We just need some time together. Two more days, and I'm flying out to visit him. And then everything will feel better.

Chapter Thirty-One

"Jake's already seen you in these clothes," Maggie says, taking a blouse from my suitcase. "Bring some California clothes. Blow that kid's mind." She grabs a black mini skirt from my closet and a bikini top from my drawer. "Voila."

"Yeah, that's going to go over real well with his East Coast med school friends. I need to look smart."

"You are smart," she says matter-of-factly.

"Small town smart. Jake and his people are brain-surgeons-curing-cancer smart. I don't want to look like a dumb blonde from California. I want to fit in."

"Why do you care about fitting in?" Maggie asks. "Are you planning on transferring to Columbia?"

I give a sigh. "No. I'm not transferring to Columbia." Which isn't to say I haven't thought about it.

"Fine. No mini skirt. But at least some sexy underwear." I give her a look. She knows me and Jake aren't sleeping together. She starts rummaging through my underwear drawer anyway.

"What's this?" she asks. She has a flash drive in her hand.

"That's Jake's movie. I wanted to show you but forgot where I put it." I grab my computer and pull up the video.

"He made this for me for Christmas," I say. I want to say more, but I don't.

We watch Jake smile and wish me a Merry Christmas and tell me he's made me a video of my favorite things in Milan. Neil Diamond's "Forever in Blue Jeans" comes on as the video shows the white tents and tables of the market.

"This is the Saturday market at Sant'Ambrogio, where I bought all the beautiful clothes you borrow when you think I'm not looking."

Then the song switches to "Cotton Eye Joe" and a video of Calypso.

"This is where we went dancing on Wednesdays. You saw it in some of the photos."

The video plays, and I point out the steps at Duomo, Parco Sempione, and my bus stop.

And then the whole gang is wishing me Merry Christmas.

"What are they saying?" Maggie asks.

"Oh, they're wishing me a Merry Christmas and saying they're happy we're friends. That sort of thing." My voice comes out wobbly. The sight of Diego smiling and telling me I'm the coolest American he knows sends tears leaking out the corner of my eyes. Mags sees and squeezes me closer to her.

"Did Paolo just say 'bestie'?" she asks.

"Yes," I say, laughing. I'd forgotten about that. "Jake made him say "Merry Christmas bestie' cause he knew it would make me happy."

Then Jake is back on camera.

"*Ciao bella*. I had such a great time filming your favorite people and places in Milan. Now I want to show you my favorite thing about Milan."

Ed Sheeran sings "Perfect," and we look at photos of me with a bowl of pasta, me perched in a tree, me dancing and laughing and eating.

The song ends, and we stare at the last photo of me smiling like I'm the happiest girl in the world.

"Wow," Maggie says finally. "No wonder you fell in love with him."

"Thank you," I say. "I think you can see I had no choice."

I take the flash drive out and put it back in my underwear drawer. Watching the video has me feeling all the things. And questioning all my decisions.

My heart is pounding as I follow the signs toward curbside pickup at La Guardia. There's a crowd of people, and I scan the faces for his. Then I hear a yell from behind.

"Juliet!"

I turn and Jake is coming toward me. My brain registers that he has a bouquet of flowers while my body leaps into his arms. Then he's kissing me, and I'm kissing him, and my thoughts are slipping out of my head.

I'd forgotten how good this feels. Or maybe I was ignoring the memory until I could have it again. He smells just the way I remember, pine trees and cold water. I stay in his arms a long time, until all the muscles in my shoulders finally relax.

"It's so good to see you," Jake says, but it's more like a groan. "I've been dreaming about this moment for years."

I smile. "We saw each other last month."

He shakes his head. "It feels like ages."

It really does. But now that I'm back here, and he's holding me, it's like no time has passed at all.

I pick up the flowers that got dropped on the sidewalk.

"These are beautiful," I say.

"I got them for you."

"I assumed you got them for the bald guy I sat next to on my flight," I say. "Glad I was wrong. This is my first time getting picked up at the airport with flowers. I feel like one of those girls in one of those movies."

I see something flicker across Jake's face. I wonder if he's thinking of all the girls he's picked up at the airport with flowers. I squash that thought. *It doesn't matter.*

"I would really like to stand here and kiss you for a few more hours, but I'm going to try to be a good host. Would you like to get something to eat?"

"Always," I say, and it's like we're back in Italy.

We take a cab to a restaurant Jake likes. It's weird eating American food together. Afterward, we walk five blocks to his apartment. It's my first time in New York City, and I'm a little overwhelmed by the lights and the buildings and the smells. The number of people we see on our walk home is greater than the population of my hometown.

Jake's apartment is a third-floor walkup. I meet his roommate Gilbert, a first-year med student with flaming red hair. I say hello and he gives me a wave and disappears into his room.

"He's pretty shy," Jake says. "We're working on that."

He takes my hand and leads me down the hall to his room. There's a bed and a desk. There are no decorations except the framed picture I gave him for Christmas. I look at us, partly obscured by the mementos we collected. It seems like a long time ago.

"Come here," he says and pulls me onto the bed with him. And that's where we spend the next three hours. Kissing. Holding each other. Talking about stuff that doesn't matter. We speak in Italian some. He sings to me some. We reconnect second by second and minute by minute until it feels like we've erased all the time we spent apart.

I wake up the next morning, and my heart feels happy before I even remember why. I'm at Jake's house. I creep from his room and snuggle next to him on the couch. I don't even remember him leaving last night, but here he is, curled up with a blanket.

"*Buon giorno, bella*," he whispers, eyes still closed.

"*Buon giorno*," I say back. His hair is messy and there's a wrinkle from the pillowcase on his cheek. He looks gorgeous. I snuggle in next to him and close my eyes and listen to his heart beat.

"Do we have to do stuff today?" I ask. "Or can we stay here like this?"

"We can stay like this all day."

So we do. We lay on our backs staring at the ceiling. He tells me all the things he's nervous about in med school and all the things he's excited about. I tell him how amazing my photography class is and funny things that happened at work.

We eat lunch at a little Greek restaurant nearby and then Jake takes me on a tour of Columbia University.

Cobblestone paths cut through vibrant expanses of green grass leading to old buildings covered in ivy. Students mill around wearing cardigans—actual cardigans—like they're being filmed for a Columbia propaganda video.

"What do you think?" Jake asks.

"It's amazing. I think you chose well."

That night, we go to a mixer for new med students. Jake introduces himself to some people, and by the end of the night so do I.

"Juliet Evans, pediatric neurology," I say to the tenth group of people we've met.

"Pediatric neurology huh?" Jake says. "I had no idea."

"I am very interested in feet," I say with my most serious expression.

Jake laughs and kisses me and whispers, "I love you," in my ear.

We duck out after an hour and head back to Jake's place. We eat Chinese takeout on the roof and soak in the sights and sounds of the city and the magic of being together again.

The next day we tour NYC—visiting Times Square, taking a boat out to the Statue of Liberty, and watching Wicked on Broadway. Late afternoon finds us under a tree in Central Park, Jake's head in my lap. We look up at the clouds. We watch people pushing strollers and jogging. We lose track of time.

For dinner, Jake takes me to a Brazilian steakhouse. Tuxedoed servers roam the room with giant slabs of roasted meat. It's absurdly delicious and by the time we leave, I feel like I am 90% roasted meats.

The sun has set and the city glows with a million lights. Jake slides his hand into mine and leads us to the Brooklyn Bridge.

"What do you think of New York?" he asks.

"I feel like a traitor to the West Coast, but I love it."

"And you liked Columbia, right? I mean the campus and everything?"

"I did. It's easy for me to picture you happy here."

"And what about you?" He squeezes my hand.

"What about me?"

"Do you think you could be happy here?"

I take a deep breath and look at the traffic zipping past. I knew this conversation was coming, I was just hoping to put it off a while longer.

I'm trying to formulate the best response, but Jake continues.

"Just imagine how easy everything would be if you transferred here. We'd see each other every day. We could eat lunch together, study at the library together. Maybe next year we even get an apartment together."

He wraps his arms around me, and I look up at him.

" Jake..."

"If you're worried about getting in, the acceptance rate is a lot higher for transfer students. I think you'd have a good shot."

"I'm not worried about getting in," I say slowly. "I already got into a school I love. In fact, I got a scholarship. And I worked and fought to get into my photography program. And I love it."

"I know, but I'm sure they have photography here. I mean, I don't know what to do about your scholarship, but we could figure something out. Plus graduating from an Ivy League would give you a lot more career options."

I try to push down the defensive feelings rising in me. I'm not entirely successful.

"I have a life in California," I say. "It's not an Ivy League life, but it's a life I love. One I've spent time and effort building."

Jake blows out a long breath, clearly frustrated.

"I don't know why you won't at least consider it. It would make things so much easier for us. It's not like I can move to California."

I look him in the eyes. "And I would never ask you to. Because I know this is your dream, and you worked hard to get here."

He looks away.

"I know my school isn't as fancy as yours," I continue. "I know that being a doctor is a way bigger deal than being a photographer. But just because my dream is smaller than yours doesn't mean it's less important. I've worked hard to get where I am. I am not giving that up."

There's a long silence and then Jake says, "I don't think your dream is less important than mine. I just wish we didn't live on opposite ends of the country."

"I know. Me too."

"Look, you don't have to make a decision right now," Jake says, completely ignoring the fact that I've already made my decision. "Just think it over."

I nod. "Sure, Jake. I'll think it over."

He pulls me into a hug and then kisses me as the cars rumble past. It's a hopeless and desperate kiss. The kind that tries to convince you of the impossible.

I can't sleep that night. I made my decision, but what if it's the wrong one? It's clear Jake doesn't think we can last long distance. People say love conquers all, but this does not feel like love conquering. This feels like love getting its ass kicked.

Obviously, things would be easier if I lived here. Am I being selfish to want to finish college?

I sit up in bed and grab my phone. I'm about to text Maggie for some advice when I see a text from my mom.

> What do you think? Dad got it enlarged and professionally framed. He says once you're famous we'll sell it and pay for a new house!

There's a picture of my parents' living room and one of my photos, a landscape from Florence, is hanging proudly over the fireplace.

I keep staring, and my eyes fill with tears. I wipe them with the back of my hand and reply.

> Thanks, Mom. I love it there.

Of course my parents think I'm great. That's their job. But Professor Melvin also says I have real talent. His note on my last assignment was "Insightful and revelatory." I don't even know what that means, but it feels good. And maybe he doesn't say that to every student.

I think about how I felt when I got accepted into the program. And how I feel every time I go to a lecture. And how I've felt every time I've picked up a camera since I was a kid. I turn my phone off and crawl back into bed, finally able to sleep.

"I'm not moving here, Jake."

We're at the airport. I've waited as long as I can to say it, but I know this is a conversation we need to have in person.

I think he'll argue, but he just nods his head.

"I'm sorry about last night," he says. "I should have never asked that of you. I know how hard you've worked. And I'm so proud of you." He rubs the back of his head. "I don't tell you enough. I'm so proud of you for going after your dream. And I love seeing how happy it makes you. I just miss you. I just want to be with you."

"I think we can make this work," I tell him.

He nods again.

"I'll call you as soon as I get home."

"Okay."

"I love you," I tell him. And it feels like goodbye. He leans his forehead against mine, and I can tell he feels it too.

"I love you too," he says.

Chapter Thirty-Two

I'm exhausted. I've spent the last two weeks studying, making smoothies, and trying to make a long-distance relationship work. Two out of three are going well.

Today is a stormy day, dark skies and a wind that blows the leaves off the trees. All I want to do is curl up and nap. Instead, I finish my classes then put in two hours at the library and four hours at Jamba.

I call Jake on my way home. We don't talk for long. I tell him what my professor said about my latest photo, and he congratulates me. He tells me about only sleeping five hours last night, and I console him.

"I love you, and I'm sorry you're not getting any sleep," I say.

"Thanks," he says. "I'm sure it'll get better soon."

He doesn't say I love you back, which is not a big deal. It's not like we say that to each other all the time.

Still, I try to think back to the last time he told me he loved me. *In New York at the airport, for sure. But that was ages ago. Surely he's said it more recently.* I rack my brain. *Well, just because he doesn't say he loves me doesn't mean he's not thinking it. He's probably thinking it right now while he listens to my voice.*

"We sliced open a really large cadaver today," Jake says. "We had to get through a foot of greasy, yellow fat before we could get to the organs."

Okay, maybe not.

We keep things on the surface these days. We don't talk for long, and we don't dive too deep. And maybe that's weird, or maybe that's just fine. *Relationships adapt, right?*

When I get home, Maggie is trying on my blue dress from Carmen in the middle of the living room. It's the only place in the apartment that has decent lighting.

"And which unsuspecting gentleman are you planning to seduce?" I ask.

"His name is Ben. And I'm going for approachable, not seductive."

"Then that is not the dress for you."

Maggie digs through a pile of clothes on the coffee table, and I settle onto the couch and pull out my chemistry book and a fat stack of index cards.

"I'm definitely ready for him to ask me out," Maggie says.

"Who's asking you out?" Petey asks, plopping onto the couch next to me.

"Ben, if he knows what's good for him," I say.

Pirate comes out of her room, and we all take bets on when Maggie and Ben will have their first date. Based on the fact that this boy has never spoken to Maggie, Petey and Pirate choose dates three or four weeks from now. But I, who have seen Maggie's boy-bewitching magic firsthand, choose this Saturday.

By the time the evening is over, I've written out all the formulas for my exam on Friday, and Maggie has put together an outfit that is the perfect combination of seductive and approachable.

The next day, I end up working three extra hours at Jamba Juice. I was supposed to be out by 6 p.m., but someone called in sick, and Manager Mike asked if I could stay until close. He also mentioned six-week evaluations coming up and the prospect of a raise. I know it will only be fifty cents an hour more, but still, I could use it.

I text Jake to let him know.

> I have to close the store tonight. I can't do our 6 p.m. call. So sorry.

> It's okay. Just call me when you get off.

> It'll be after midnight your time.

> It's fine. I'll probably be up anyway.

My shift goes by fast, and I want to sprint out the door, but I make myself do a thorough job cleaning up. Manager Mike opens tomorrow, and I want him to see how pristine I left everything.

It's nearly 9:30 by the time I call Jake.

"Hi," I whisper when he picks up. "Are you awake?"

"Yeah. How was your shift?"

"Lost another finger to frostbite, but I still have a few left. How was your day? Didn't you have rounds with that resident you like?"

"Yeah, it was really great. I got to help intubate someone, which I've never done before."

"That sounds cool."

"It was."

And then silence. That's how it's been lately. I get so excited when it's time to talk to Jake and then we run out of things to say pretty quickly.

"Hey, maybe this is too early to start planning," I say. "But you talked about coming to Lakeport for Thanksgiving. Do you think that's still a possibility?"

"Thanksgiving? Oh yeah, no. That's not going to work." He sounds like he doesn't even remember suggesting it.

"Okay, no worries. I've got three weeks off at Christmas, and I was thinking maybe I could do two at home and then I could catch a flight to Phoenix and spend a week with you. Phoenix isn't that far from San Diego. I bet I could get Maggie to come pick me up and bring me back to school. Plus you could meet Maggie."

I realize slowly that Jake hasn't said anything the whole time I've been talking. Usually he chimes in encouragingly when I have great ideas for us.

"Jake?"

"Yeah, I'm still here."

"So...what do you think about Christmas?"

"I don't know..."

He doesn't know?

I hear the smallest sigh. "Look, um, I've got a pretty crazy semester. Why don't we just see how things play out?"

I don't know what this is, but this is not my Jake. He does not sound interested in seeing me over Christmas. Or ever.

I don't know how to respond, but it doesn't matter because before I can say anything Jake says, "Can I give you a call later? I've got to catch some shut eye before lecture tomorrow."

"Sure, of course."

And then before I can stop myself, I blurt it out, the thing that has been festering in my brain for too long:

"You never say I love you anymore."

It's not a question. But it's a statement that begs an answer. It's met with silence. The seconds stretch and I sit there, vulnerable and trembling, like a hermit crab out of its shell.

"Juls," Jake says. And his voice is so soft and tender, it sounds just like my Jake. Tears spring into my eyes because my body knows what's about to happen before my brain does.

"We've always been really intentional saying that to each other," he starts. "I only say that when I really feel that way."

The obvious hangs in the air between us. He doesn't feel that way.

My legs feel wobbly, and I sink onto the grass.

"So what...what does that mean?"

My brain is working at half speed, but one thing is getting through to me: *Jake doesn't love me anymore. He doesn't tell me he loves me because he doesn't love me anymore.*

Another tiny sigh. "Listen, let's not do this tonight."

My throat feels like it's closed up. With effort, I push the words out. "It's already done."

"Juliet," he says. "I care about you. It's just too much. If you were here, it would be different. But...you chose not to come. I'd still like to be friends."

It takes me a second to realize he's waiting for some kind of response. *What did he just say? He still wants to be friends?*

I finally find my voice. "Yeah, no. That's not going to work."

"Juliet." That tender voice again. The one that told me so many magical things. The one that is breaking my heart with each word. "I'll call you tomorrow. What time do you wake up? I'll call you first thing."

"No, Jake." My heart hurts so bad I can barely open my mouth. But I force myself to say the words. "Don't call me tomorrow. Or the next day. This is done between us. So let's be done."

A pause. Then a tired, "Okay."

I don't say "goodbye" because it hurts too bad. Or "talk to you later" because I won't. I simply hang up.

I take a breath. I take stock. I'm sitting in the grass on the other side of the parking lot from my apartment. Tears are flowing freely down my cheeks and my hands are shaking. Who knew the world could end on an ordinary Wednesday night?

I pick myself up and walk with trembling legs across the parking lot and up the stairs to my apartment. Petey and Pirate are watching a movie, but I angle my face away from them and make it to my bedroom undetected.

Maggie finds me there an hour later, curled up in the fetal position. My face and pillow are soaked with tears and snot.

"Juls, what happened?"

I shake my head. I can't talk. I can't say the words out loud.

"Are you okay?"

Another head shake. I'm not okay. I'm wrecked. I had no idea it would be like this. The physical pain in my chest. The feeling of complete annihilation.

She picks up my phone and punches in my password.

"You have three missed calls from Jake," she says. I don't respond.

She comes and sits on the bed next to me and strokes my hair.

"How bad is it?" she asks. "Do you think you can work it out?"

I shake my head again. It's all I seem capable of doing. Everything in me feels numb.

"What happened?" she asks.

I squeeze my eyes tight and then say it. "He doesn't love me anymore."

"Hey, that's not true," Maggie says in a soothing voice. "Long distance is just hard."

My shoulders crumble. "It is true," I say. "He told me. He told me he doesn't feel that way anymore."

BETTER THAN GELATO 243

And then my body is heaving with sobs. My shoulders are shaking so hard I feel like I'll shake apart. There will be nothing left of me but pieces.

Maggie rubs my back and says over and over, "I'm so sorry, Juls. I'm so so sorry."

The sun rises the next morning, and I don't even know why.

I don't get out of bed. I don't go to classes. Maggie calls Manager Mike and tells him I can't make my shift. She checks on me between her classes and brings me little plates of crackers that go untouched on the dresser.

Jake calls two more times, but I don't answer. I block his number. The hours pass slowly and at the same time, unreasonably fast. I'm surprised when I roll over in bed and the sun has set. I hear voices outside my door.

"Maggie said don't bother her," Petey says.

"She's been in there for hours," Pirate says. "We need to make sure she's alright."

They're debating if they should call Maggie for permission. I get up and open the door. The room sways a little, and I see black spots. I lean against the door frame. I should probably eat something. When the spots clear, I see Petey and Pirate staring at me. Their faces are filled with sympathy and horror. I'm guessing I don't look so hot.

I don't say anything but move past them to the bathroom to pee. When I come out, they're by my door, hovering.

"He-ey," Petey says, stretching the word into two syllables. Filling the last one with pity. Before I know it, my eyes have filled with tears again. *I can't do this.* I shake my head mutely and walk past them into my room and close the door.

I grab one of the plates of crackers and bring it to bed with me. I catch a whiff of myself as I settle in. I do not smell good. I sniff my sheets. They do not smell good. It's like my sadness has an odor that has oozed over everything. What I need is a shower, but the idea of showering is as nonsensical as the idea of flying. I can't move. All I can do is lie here, sad and unloved.

Maggie comes in without me noticing. I must have fallen asleep again.

"How are you doing?" she asks. Her voice is gentle. And it's the

244 LIBBY TANNER

gentleness that brings the tears again. Because I know I've become this fragile, wounded animal that must be treated gently.

I shrug my shoulders helplessly.

"Do you want some dinner?" she asks.

"I had some crackers," I tell her. I know she's trying her best to take care of me. I want her to know I'm trying too. But I can't do dinner. I already feel sick.

"On a scale of one to ten, how bad is the pain?" Maggie asks like a nurse.

"I'd like some morphine, please," I say.

She lets out a deep breath. "This sucks," she says. "And there's no way around that. But what we have to do now is damage control. I know you have a chemistry exam tomorrow. You left your flashcards all over the house. What time is your class?"

"It doesn't matter. I can't go."

"You can go," she says. "And you need to."

"Chemistry doesn't matter. Nothing matters." Maggie's eyes fill with concern as she realizes I mean it. And then her mouth tightens in determination. She's in problem solving mode.

"You're probably right. But on the off chance you want to keep your scholarship and finish college, you need to take exams and pass classes."

My eyebrows scrunch up at her words.

"I know you need time to fall to pieces and process everything. You can have that time. But not tomorrow. Tomorrow you need to pull it together for one hour. Then you can have the whole weekend to sleep or cry or yell or break things. Whatever you need. But tomorrow you need to take your exam. Now what time is it?"

"Nine," I mumble.

"Okay, perfect. I've got a nine o'clock class too. I'm going to get you up early. We're going to get ready. I suggest you shower. Then we're going to head to campus."

It's too exhausting to argue with her, so I just agree.

The next day she wakes me up, and I numbly eat some cereal. My stomach gurgles unhappily. I walk to campus on five-hundred-pound legs.

We make it to my chemistry building, and she gives me a hug.

"You can do this. As soon as you're done, you can go straight home and crawl into bed. Just one exam first. You've got this."

BETTER THAN GELATO

She's wrong. I don't got this. The professor hands out the exam and the words and diagrams on the page mean nothing to me. I vaguely remember studying something like this. But that was a lifetime ago. Back when the world made sense. Back when Jake still loved me.

I fill in some answers. I write in some words. Honestly, I'm barely aware of what I'm doing. When the professor says the time is up, I hand in my test and walk back home.

I wake up Saturday morning to Maggie bringing me an omelet. After two days, I suddenly feel ravenous. I eat until my plate is empty, and Maggie is visibly relieved.

Pirate sticks her head in the door. "Sorry to interrupt. There's a package for you."

She brings me a box wrapped in brown paper and for a moment the irrational part of my brain says, *It's from Jake! He's sent me a box of*—but even my irrational brain doesn't know how to finish that sentence. *What could he possibly send me? A box full of all the love he doesn't feel for me?*

"Thanks," I tell Pirate. "You didn't interrupt anything. I'm just lying here, smelly and unloved."

She nods and turns to leave but then stops at the doorway and clears her throat. "You're not unloved."

Anger flares up, and I want to tell her she doesn't know what she's talking about. She must see it in my eyes because she winces a little but doesn't back down. She points to Maggie.

"This girl's been taking care of you day and night."

And then she leaves. And I'm crying again, and I feel like a jerk, because of course she's right, and I've been wallowing and ungrateful and oblivious.

"I'm so sorry," I tell Maggie. "I'm so sorry that you've had to take care of me."

"It's okay," Maggie says. "That's what I'm here for. Really." She looks a little weepy, and Maggie never cries.

"I notice she didn't correct you on being smelly," she says after a minute, and I actually smile.

"I think I probably do need to shower."

246   LIBBY TANNER

"Open your box first," she says.

It's from my parents. A batch of my mom's homemade chocolate chip cookies and a note in my dad's careful handwriting that says, "We heard you were having a hard time. We love you."

"Look, more people who love you!" Maggie says, and I cry some more. *Sheesh, when will I run out of tears?*

We eat cookies for a while in silence.

"Do you feel like talking about things?" Maggie asks. "About what happened?"

Maybe it's the sugar, but all of a sudden, I do feel like talking about things.

"I'll tell you what happened. He tricked me into falling in love with him when I was really trying not to, and then a year later he broke my heart."

I suddenly feel like yelling about things.

"He's a heartless, elitist jerk who lives in a stupid mansion," I say loudly. "His family doesn't go camping on vacation. They go skiing in the Poconos."

It feels good to talk loudly, so I talk even louder.

"He's condescending, like 'I'm very rich and go to an Ivy league school, and I think it's adorable that you're going to UC San Diego on scholarship. Why don't you leave your tiny little dreams and come be a cheerleader for my big, impressive dreams on the East Coast?' Also, he's no fun."

Maggie raises an eyebrow at this.

"Okay, he's some fun. But he's also a scaredy pants. Not a risk taker. He's always like, 'Juliet, don't break into that locked park. Juliet, don't go to the beach in the dark. Juliet, don't ride that scooter, you'll crash the minivan on the way to dropping our kids off at school.'"

Maggie is noticeably alarmed, and some part of me recognizes that I've turned hysterical, but I'm on a roll.

"Well, you know what? I did all that stuff, not the minivan thing, but the other stuff, and I didn't get hurt at all. No scratches! Totally unscathed! But I dated him for a year, and kaboom, shattered. Absolutely shattered." I cross my arms over my chest, pleased with the case I have made.

Maggie nods. "I see." A pause. "I have some follow-up questions."

"I'll do my best, but I feel like that's mostly the gist of it right there."

"But why did you actually break up? Was he seeing someone else?"

"I don't think so."

"Then why break up?" Maggie asks. "What did he say?"

I try to recall his exact words, but it's hazy.

"He said it was too hard. That it would be different if I was there, but I chose not to move there."

"And he chose not to move here," she points out loyally.

"Anyway, that was after he admitted that he didn't love me anymore, which is a pretty good reason to break up."

"That must have been hard to hear," Maggie says.

"It didn't feel great." The anger drains out of me and the tears are back, and I don't even try to fight them. I just let them take over while Maggie holds me and makes soothing sounds.

At some point, Petey comes in and tells me she's made a nice hot bath for me, and doesn't that sound nice? She speaks to me like I'm an old lady, or a child, or mentally unstable. I suppose the last one isn't far off. And a hot bath does sound good.

I slip my grungy clothes off and slide into the water. I can hear them talking through the door.

"I've never seen her like this," Petey says.

"She's never been like this," Maggie says.

"Did you see her get into the bath?" Petey says. "She's skin and bones."

"Yeah, because she stopped eating," Maggie says. "And you *know* how she feels about eating."

"What do we do?" Petey asks.

"I can hear you, ya hooligans," I yell through the door.

There's a startled yelp and then Maggie's voice. "We're not talking about you," she says. "We're talking about someone else. Lynn. Just went through a breakup, the poor girl. She's not handling it well. Not like you. You're doing way better than Lynn."

This actually makes me smile. Pirate is right. I have good people who love me.

I stay in the bath a long time. When I dry off and get dressed, I avoid looking at myself in the mirror. I'm not ready to deal with whatever weird thing my body is doing.

When I come out, the girls are eating sandwiches in the kitchen.

"I made you one," Pirate says.

"Thanks, apparently I'm just skin and bones."

"I'm so sorry," Petey says. "I should not have said that."

"You weren't even talking about her," Maggie says. "You were talking about Lynn." She gives Petey a theatrical elbow nudge and earns another smile from me.

We watch a movie that afternoon. I couldn't say which one.

I try to make pasta in the evening. But as soon as the smell of warm olive oil fills the kitchen, I'm reminded of the beach we found by the olive grove in Greece. Where we kissed for hours and told each other "I love you."

I give up cooking, and Petey makes frozen burritos and sprinkles cheddar cheese on them to make them "fancy."

The next morning I wake up sad again. Each morning is an opportunity to remember all over again that this special thing I had is now lost. I gingerly climb out of bed. I feel like an old woman. Or how I assume an old woman feels. My limbs are creaky and my muscles ache. I don't know why my body feels like it's run a marathon when I've barely gotten out of bed in the last seventy-two hours. *Heartbreak is exhausting.*

I go into the kitchen where Petey is making pancakes and chatting with Maggie and Pirate. Conversation stops when they see me. Maggie starts cheering.

"You got out of bed! You came out of your room! And all by yourself! You're amazing! A marvel! Hurrah!"

It's over the top but very Maggie. I give an awkward wave.

"Morning." My throat hurts. From crying. Or yelling. Or maybe I caught strep throat at the same time my heart broke.

"Sorry for all this," I mumble and wave a hand to encompass all of me.

"It's fine," Petey says, and dishes me a pancake. I eat and let the carbs work their magic.

"So, did you think you were going to marry this boy?" Pirate asks after a while.

I give a shrug. "I definitely wasn't ready for marriage. I think he was. We picked out pets. And named our sailboat."

The tears are back so hard and fast I feel like I'm drowning. *When will this pain stop? Shouldn't the hurting diminish at some point?* It still feels fresh and raw and deep, like there are not enough days in eternity for this wound to heal.

"Thanks for the pancakes, Petey," I whisper. Then I put my plate and fork in the sink and head back to my room.

At some point, Maggie discreetly took down all the pictures of me and Jake and replaced them with pictures of Nicolas Cage being a weirdo. It makes me smile.

As night falls, I face the fact that I have to go to school and work tomorrow and somehow pretend my heart wasn't ripped from my chest and torn to shreds.

I unbury my computer from a pile of clothes and check my schedule. It's not going to be fun, but I don't have any assignments due, so that's a piece of good luck.

There's an email from my parents telling me how much they love me and how wonderful I am.

There's one from my Chemistry TA because I failed the exam on Friday. He's reaching out because I got an A on the last exam and all the quizzes so far. This is a drastic shift. *Why yes, TA Chad, this is a drastic shift, isn't it?*

The last email is from Jake. I didn't notice right away because it doesn't have his name as the sender, just a weird edu email address. I read the first line.

Juliet, I'm so sorry. I never meant to hurt you.

I close my laptop before I know I'm doing it. The way your hand reacts instinctively when you touch a hot stove. Because it's protecting you from pain before the pain gets worse.

I know that if I read that email, if I email him back, if I unblock his number and engage with him under the flimsy excuse of closure or civility, I will never get over him. I will be in love with him forever. And he will still not love me back. And it will be excruciating.

So I make a solemn vow to do none of those things. I will not indulge in "what ifs" or "should haves." I won't even dwell on fond memories. Maybe there will be a time and space for that later. For right now, it's got to be a total shutout, or I'll never survive this.

Chapter Thirty-Three

I master the art of disguise. I learn how to pass myself off as a walking, talking human when really, I'm a scarecrow.

I manage to cook dinner tonight. A delicious pasta primavera that floods my brain with memories and fills my eyes with tears.

I yell at a stranger today, for no other reason than he got in my way and looked vaguely Jake-like.

Michael Bublé's "Moondance" comes on at work. I have a flash of Jake's arms around me, slow dancing at the bus stop. I have to go into the back room until I get a hold of myself.

Photography assignment: What is Fall? My photo of moldering flowers hangs next to shots of pumpkin lattes and knit scarves.

Giovanni reads us a funny Italian poem. I burst into tears for absolutely no reason.

Professor Melvin assigns us a photo series due in two weeks. The theme is growth. He encourages us to start brainstorming what our subjects will be and how we'll best capture them. I have zero ideas.

After the initial devastation of the first week, I throw myself into my classes with complete and total focus. It's a relief to cram my head full of facts, they quiet the painful thoughts.

I did not completely derail my academic future, as Maggie feared I might. Turns out, we get to drop our worst exam in Chemistry, so I have some hope for that class after all. If I do well on my final English paper, which should be easy, and get at least a B+ on the final Chemistry exam, which will be harder, I think I can pull off straight A's. So I will graduate sad and alone, but at least I'll graduate.

I've lost contact with all my Italian friends. Jake was on the text thread, and I didn't want any part of it. When Paolo and Valentina and Carmen reached out to me individually, I ignored them.

Then one day, I get a text I can't ignore.

> We're coming to a show in Las Vegas in December. Can you meet us there?

I text back right away.

> Of course. I can't wait to see you guys.

As soon as I hit send, my phone rings and Marco's voice is in my ear a mile a minute.

"*Ciao Julieta*. I thought it was easier to call you and work out the details over the phone. I'm already committed to the show, which I'm having second thoughts about, but it's too late to back out now. I haven't bought tickets for Sofia and Isa yet. I wanted to make sure you're available. They'll be bored out of their mind with me in fittings all day."

"*Ciao*, Marco, how are you?"

"Sorry, *tesoro*. I am doing fine. A little stressed. But otherwise, fine. How are you?"

"I'm doing well," I lie. "Thank you."

"Isa got the *Harry Potter* book you sent. Very sweet of you. How's school?"

"It's going well," I say honestly.

"And how is Jake doing?"

My response takes a beat too long. "We broke up, actually."

"Oh, *topino*," Marco says. "I'm so sorry."

"Yeah me too," I say.

"Sometimes it works out that way," he says. "Some love is like gelato."

My brow dips in confusion. *I've had gelato. This is worse.*

He correctly interprets my silence as skepticism.

"Gelato is sweet and wonderful and fills you with happiness. And then it melts. It's gone. You no longer have it. That doesn't mean that what you enjoyed wasn't wonderful, just because it didn't last forever. That doesn't mean your relationship wasn't real just because it ended. You enjoyed it for a time. And now that time is over."

Huh.

"Thanks, Marco. I'm definitely available in December. Just send me the dates, and I'll be there."

"Perfect. I'll get those to you today. *Ciao ciao.*" And then he's gone, and I'm left thinking about love like gelato.

The first time I laugh, it startles me so much I jump a little. I'd forgotten what that sounded like. I'm in my Italian class and the kid next to me just said, "My greatest goal in life is to be an avocado." I'm pretty sure he meant lawyer, the words sound similar in Italian. I picture a ripe avocado wearing a little suit, and I can't help laughing.

I get a couple of weird looks. The girl who's been coming to class depressed for the last month just laughed out loud. I think word spread that I got my heart broken by an evil Italian man. The truth is even sadder, so I let that rumor go unchecked.

When I get to Jamba Juice, Manager Mike is waiting for me.

"Hey, Mike," I say.

"Hello, Juliet," he says. "Can I speak with you before your shift?"

"Sure."

Kevin by the blender mouths "you're in trouble." I follow Mike to the back room, which is ten degrees colder than the rest of the store. He's not much for chit chat, which I appreciate.

"This is your second year here," he says. "You're a hard worker. I was able to get you a seventy-five-cent hourly wage increase."

"Thanks, Mike." I say. "It's more than I expected."

"Well, I tried to get you the full one-dollar increase, but the franchise owner wouldn't go for it."

I'm touched. "Thank you," I say again.

He clears his throat. "I know you've been, uh, going through a rough time, and well, I appreciate your dedication to this place."

Mercifully, that's the end of his speech. He reminds me to check that the wheatgrass is fresh and then leaves for the day.

He's not wrong about my dedication. I've worked twice as many shifts as I signed up for. The hard work is good for me. So are the money and forced human interaction.

"So, you got a raise," Kevin says when I come back out.

"Yep."

"You deserve it. You work harder than anyone else here."

"That is true," I say.

"And for that you should be rewarded."

"Seventy-five cents isn't much of a reward, but I'll take it."

"I'm not talking about money," he says and gives a head nod to the door.

Orange Dreamy Dream is walking in. I check the clock: 3:30 p.m., right on time. Kevin gives me a big grin, which I pretend not to see. I don't know if Kevin is gay or not, but I think even a straight man would agree that Orange Dreamy Dream is attractive.

"Hey," he says, walking up to the counter.

"Hey," I say back.

"I'll take the Orange Dream," he says.

"Sure thing," I say and take his credit card.

I make him his smoothie, he says thank you and then leaves.

"Wow, that is some hot banter," Kevin says.

Kevin ends up leaving early due to a personal emergency, which I know is him being too bored to stay here another second. I do all the closing on my own and head home.

Petey and Pirate are at the movies, and Maggie's on a date with Ben. Her third!

I make a bubble bath for myself and enjoy it with a plate of apple slices and a new book. It's a young adult post-apocalyptic novel, and it's making me feel better about my life. *Yes my heart got smashed, but I didn't see my own mother get body snatched by aliens and have to put a bullet in her head, did I?* So there's that.

"Are you sure you don't want to come home for Thanksgiving?" my mom asks.

I've gotten into the habit of calling her on my walk home from campus. The time I always talked to Jake, now I talk to her.

"I'm doing good, Mom," I say, answering the question she's really asking. And I think she can tell it's true because she doesn't push it.

"How are your classes going?"

"Like grapes at a wine festival."

Confused silence.

"Because I'm crushing them," I clarify.

"Well, that's wonderful. I'm so proud of you. Not just for your classes, but for everything. You've done a great job getting through a hard time."

I make a snorting sound. "There are people battling cancer. I don't need an award for getting through a breakup. How's Dad's fishing?"

"It's coming along." She's using her diplomatic voice. "Dr. Bartlett is very patient."

We've lived on this lake my whole life, and my dad's never had an interest in fishing. He has no idea what he's doing or what any of the gear is, but he's decided it's his new hobby.

"Well, give him my love," I say. "And let me know when he catches his first fish."

I decide to get him one of those ugly fishing hats for Christmas. Picturing him wearing it makes me smile all the way home.

Thursday afternoon I set out to explore the campus with my camera. Not for an assignment, just for me. I used to wander around Milan, taking pictures of every cool thing I saw, and it feels like ages since I've taken pictures for fun. I photograph the green open space, the tree-lined walkways, the buildings with slivers of ocean behind them. I imagine I'm sending all these photos to the gang in Milan to show them my school. What would I want them to see?

After I've taken a dozen or so, I think maybe I should send them some

BETTER THAN GELATO

photos. And some American sweets as an apology for blowing them off when they were just being kind.

I sprawl on the grass and go back through my shots. They need some edits, but I got some good stuff. I stretch out and let my eyes close for a minute. I listen to the sounds of students chattering and seagulls squawking. I listen to the even sound of my own breath.

When I open my eyes, there's a heart-shaped cloud floating directly above me. Not it-kind-of-looks-like-a-heart-if-you-squint-the-right-way, but a distinctly heart-shaped cloud. I grab my camera. I have no idea what setting to use so the first few I snap are out of focus. But this heart cloud is patient. It doesn't move on to other parts of the sky. It gives me some time to fiddle and experiment until I'm able to capture it just the way I want it.

That night, I meet Maggie's Ben. He's funny and cute, and it's obvious he's falling fast for my best friend. This is about the time I start feeling sorry for Maggie's boys. They usually end up brokenhearted. But the way Maggie looks at Ben makes me think he might have a chance.

I cook a bell pepper risotto for dinner. It takes a long time, risottos do, but it's therapeutic, almost meditative, stirring the rice, adding the broth, stirring the rice. There's enough to share, and we have a tiny dinner party.

A few days later, Petey brings me a small heart-shaped rock she found.

"It reminded me of those cloud pictures you showed me," she says.

I hold it in my hand. It's dark and smooth and heavier than it looks.

"Thanks, Petey," I say, and slip it into my pocket.

Saturday morning I do laundry and find the rock at the bottom of the dryer. The spin cycle cracked it, and it looks like a tiny broken heart. As I stare at it, something clicks in my brain.

I hop online and do some research. I'm not exactly sure what I'm looking for, but I'm hoping I'll know it when I see it.

What I find is a flower, *Dicentra spectabilis*, more commonly known as bleeding heart.

"Hey roomies," I holler. "Who wants to take a trip to a botanical garden?"

I turn in my photo series in the morning and spend the afternoon at Jamba Juice second-guessing my editing choices. *Did the cloud photo need a sharper contrast? But it's a cloud, it shouldn't look sharp.* I'm concentrating so hard I don't notice that Orange Dreamy Dream has walked in until he starts talking to me.

"Hey," he says.

I jump.

"Hey," I say back, pretending I wasn't startled. How is it 3:30 already?

I'm already ringing up his order when he says, "I thought I might try something different today. Do you have any recommendations?"

Oh. That's unexpected.

"Strawberry Surfrider is my favorite," I say.

"Okay, I'll give it a try."

I make him his smoothie, and he pays for it.

"Enjoy," I tell him.

"Thanks," he tells me.

I get my photo series back next class, and I'm pleased to see the red A on the back. Professor Melvin also wrote, "Nice job capturing the different textures of your subjects. I appreciated this fresh take on an old theme."

I'm glowing with pride and can't wait to show Maggie. She's eating sunflower seeds and conjugating Latin verbs when I get home.

"I have something for you," I say.

"Perfect, I'm starving." I've been bringing home leftover Jamba Juices after my shifts, and the roommates have grown accustomed.

"It's not for eating, it's for looking at."

I spread the three pictures out on our beat-up coffee table.

I spent hours working on them before I turned them in, but I try to look at them with fresh eyes.

On the left is my photograph of the bleeding heart flower. It's a vibrant pink and looks young and fresh and delicate. Next to it is the dark heart-shaped rock. I magnified it so the crack through the middle is clearly visible. The third photo, on the far right, is my giant puffy cloud heart. It looks weightless and somehow content.

I only had forty words for the caption, and I tried to make each one count.

"Hearts start out young and fresh like a spring flower. Sometimes they get broken and feel as hard as stone. But time and love can transform heavy hearts into hearts as light and full as summer clouds."

"Do you like it?" I ask.

"I love it," Maggie says.

"It's for you. I couldn't have made it through the last month without you," I say. "Thank you for being there for me and for healing my broken stone heart."

"That's the cheesiest thing I've ever heard," she says, wiping tears from her cheeks.

"I know. Very cheesy. But true."

She gives me a hug and wipes her nose on my shoulder. "I'm glad your stone heart is a happy cloud now."

"It's not quite a cloud heart. That was an exaggeration for artistic effect, but it's getting better."

What I wanted was a perfect beach photo capturing the feel of waves and sun and sand. The kind that makes everyone who doesn't live in Southern California feel stupid for not living in Southern California.

What I have instead is a thundery sky filled with dark purple clouds and an ocean churning like somebody's pissed it off and is about to pay.

I've spent all week trying to capture something amazing for our midterm photography exhibition next week. And so far, I've come up with nothing. I don't know what you call the photography equivalent of writer's block, but I have it. I decide to head home before I get soaked or struck by lightning.

I take a shortcut around the boardwalk, and I end up by some fancy shops and a gelateria. It's been months since I've had gelato. I stop and look at all the flavors, then get a small dish of Nutella and raspberry. I take a seat at the wrought iron table out front. The first bite brings back a dozen memories. The second bite brings back Marco's words. As I think about what they mean, there's a shift in the clouds and a few rays of sun break through.

258 LIBBY TANNER

I take my camera out of its case.

All the roommates come to the photography exhibition. I told them it's not that big of a deal, but they come anyway.

"Don't tell us which one is yours," Petey says when we get there. "I want to see if I can guess."

Petey runs off to look for my photo and Pirate follows her. The exhibition is for the whole photography department, not just my class, so there are hundreds of eight-by-tens on display.

Professor Melvin sees me and waves me over. "I'll be right back," I tell Maggie.

"I'm glad I spotted you," Professor Melvin says. "I was just telling Professor Hendricks that I have a student he should meet."

Professor Hendricks is at least 112 years old and wearing a corduroy blazer that looks even older.

"Professor Hendricks, this is Juliet Evans. Juliet, this is Professor Hendricks."

"Nice to meet you," I say and shake his hand. It's dry and papery with a strong grip.

"I'm the editor of *Lens*," he says. *Lens* is the photography magazine the department puts out each quarter. It's stunning.

I nod, but don't say anything.

"I thought your style of photography might be a good fit," Professor Melvin says. I stare at him blankly. "For the magazine," he says with a small smile. "I'm encouraging you to submit your work to Professor Hendricks for consideration."

"You are?" It comes out as a whisper, and I'm hoping Professor Melvin didn't hear, but he smiles and gives a little nod.

"Shoot me an email," Professor Hendricks says. "Let's see what you've got." He hands me his card.

"Okay," I say. "Thank you. Wow. I will. I will shoot you an email."

"Enjoy your evening," Professor Melvin says, gently excusing me before I do anything else awkward.

I can feel the blood pumping in my cheeks as I walk away. Actual published photos! I try not to get ahead of myself. I'm just going to send him some things, and he'll see what he thinks. But there's already a feeling spreading through me that this is the beginning of something wonderful.

I dart through the displays looking for the girls and find them standing in front of a photograph. I walk over and grab Maggie's arm.

"We found your photo," she says.

"What do you think?" I know fancy photographers aren't supposed to care what people think about their work, but I still do.

She doesn't say anything, just nods and squeezes my hand.

We stare at the photo together.

It's pretty striking, if I'm being honest. And all the credit belongs to the dramatic lighting. The sky is dark, but I was able to capture a beam of sunlight shining down on the wrought iron table like a spotlight. In the middle of the table is my cup of gelato. There's only a little left, chocolate brown swirled with raspberry pink. I shot it at an angle, so you can see the glass case of gelato flavors in the background. There's a mound of orange mango with mint garnish, creamy white *stracciatella* with specks of dark brown, and a soft green hill of pistachio sprinkled with nuts. The table and the cup are in sharp focus and the gelato case behind is soft and blurry.

The title is "Love like gelato."

Pirate reads the caption out loud. "Some love is like gelato. Sweet and wonderful but not made to last. Enjoy the experience, savor the memory."

"That's beautiful," Maggie says.

"I got it from Marco," I say.

"Well, he is very wise."

The next day at work, I'm still flying high from the exhibition. I was too hyped to go to bed and ended up looking through all my photos to find some good ones for Hendrickson.

"Someone's in a good mood," Kevin comments as I restock all the fruits and veggies.

"All right, what's his name?" he asks in a teasing tone.

"Believe it or not, my good mood has nothing to do with a boy," I say. "It has to do with me being an awesome photographer and nailing life."

"I didn't know you were a photographer. I want to see your photos some time."

"Trust me, you will. Soon they'll be everywhere."

He raises an eyebrow.

I give him a cocky smile. "Everywhere."

That's when Orange Dreamy Dream comes in for his smoothie.

"Hey," he says, with a shy smile.

"Hey," I say back, grinning.

"I liked that Strawberry Surfrider you recommended. I'll take another one of those."

"They're pretty great," I agree as I take his credit card. "It's the kick of lemon in there. It keeps it from getting boring."

"Yeah, I noticed that."

I make him his smoothie and hand it to him with a smile.

"There you are."

"Thanks." He stands there like he's going to say something else, but then he doesn't. He glances at Kevin and leaves.

Kevin tries to get me to trade shifts with him so he gets out at six and I stay till closing, but I refuse. I can tell my time of working as many shifts as possible to fill the sad hours is coming to a close. It's Friday night, and I feel like celebrating.

I give him a smug wave as I walk out the door, and he makes a scowly face at me. I scowl back and then turn and slam right into Orange Dreamy Dream.

Orange Dreamy Dream? What's he doing here?

"Sorry," I say a bit too late. "Didn't mean to slam into you."

"It's okay," he says. "No harm done."

He stands there for a moment, not going through the open door, so I finally say, "Well, have a good night," and walk out.

He follows me.

"Actually, um, I came to talk to you."

What? Why? I think. "What? Why?" I accidentally say out loud.

He clears his throat. "Well, actually I was wondering...My name is Kyle, by the way."

"I'm Juliet."

"Yeah, I know. I see it on your name tag every day."

I look at him and nod. It *is* on my name tag every day.

"Anyway, I was wondering if you'd like to go out some time."

"Go out some time?" I repeat stupidly.

"Yeah, like maybe get something to eat or something."

He's asking me out on a date. My palms start sweating, and my mind starts coming up with reasons why I can't go out with him. I'm a vampire. I'm a spy for the CIA. I fell in love and got my heart broken and it sucked.

I take a deep breath. It feels risky. I'm not sure I won't end up heartbroken.

But I say, "Yeah. I'd like that."

Chapter Thirty-Four

The breeze in Sorrento, Italy smells like olive oil and the sea. It's been three years since I left this country. Sometimes it feels like more. Today, with a deep inhale, it feels like less.

The resort I'm staying at opens to the public next month, and I've spent the last four days photographing it from every angle, along with the charming seaside town of Sorrento.

I unscrew the lens on my camera, carefully stow it in my camera bag and then tilt my head to each side, working out the kinks in my neck and shoulders. Tonight, at the hotel, I'll go back through the week's work and make my edits. But I already know my boss Eloise will be pleased.

Henry's packing up his notebooks and recorder. We don't have to file the story until tomorrow, so Henry will spend the evening getting drunk on the company's dime. He's a big guy, mid-forties, heading for his third divorce. This is my fourth assignment with him.

"Care to join me for a drink?" he says, gesturing in the direction of the hotel bar.

"No thanks," I say. "I've got plans."

The hotel calls me a cab, and I give the driver the address for the restaurant. Waiting out front is my Italian bestie, Paolo.

He looks good. He always did.

"Finally, my Julietta Dolcetta has arrived."

I kiss his cheeks, and he pulls me in for a hug. Then he holds me at arm's length.

"Three years and you look just the same." He tilts his head. "Not the same. Better I think."

"You're as charming as ever," I tell him.

We get a table, and Paolo orders for both of us.

"Tell me about work," he says. "You're still at *Conde Nast Traveler*?"

"Yes."

"And they love your photos so much they give you the best assignments in Italy."

"I'm pretty sure I only got this one because having someone who speaks Italian means they don't have to pay a translator. This is my first international assignment."

"The first of many, I'm sure."

"My boss did mention some assignments in South America, so fingers crossed I get put on one of those."

Our food comes, and the first bite has me closing my eyes in bliss.

"You've missed this," Paolo says. "I need to start sending you lasagna care packages."

"You do," I agree.

"Where are you living these days?" he asks. "Still San Diego?"

"For now. But I'm thinking about a move. Southern California's getting crowded, and I can work from anywhere. I think I'm ready for a change." I take a long drink of water.

"Tell me about Valentina," I say. "I was hoping she would be here."

"She wanted to come," Paolo says. "But she can't travel. Doctor's orders." He pulls out his phone and brings up a photo of Valentina. She looks as lovely as ever. And has a full, round belly.

I look at Paolo, and he's grinning like a fool.

"She's pregnant!"

"Six months."

I give him a smack on the shoulder. "And you didn't tell me!"

"We only found out three months ago. It wasn't exactly planned. And her pregnancy's been rocky. For a while we weren't sure...anyway, she's doing a lot better now."

"Wow." I can't stop smiling. "You're going to be a dad. Are you ready for that?"

Paolo gives me a look. "I'm Paolo. I'm ready for anything."

"You nervous?"

"Terrified."

"When's she due?"

"October. Which is when we were going to have the wedding, until we found out about the baby. Valentina doesn't want to get married nine months pregnant. We'll do a ceremony next year."

"Marrying a Northerner," I say. "How does your mother feel about that?"

"She was furious until she found out she was getting a grandson."

"It's a boy?"

"It's a boy. We're naming him Diego."

My heart stutters. "It's a good name," I say.

"He was a good guy," Paolo says. We sit quietly for a moment. There's sadness, but it's not unwelcome.

"How about you?" Paolo says finally. "Marriage on the horizon?"

I laugh and shake my head.

"I liked Orange Dreamy Dream." Paolo says.

"His name was Kyle," I remind him. "And yeah, he was nice."

"Wasn't there someone last fall? With a super preppy name?"

"Brent. That fizzled out before spring. It was fine, I was graduating anyway. And now I'm so busy with work, I haven't been dating much."

"Such a shame for a sweet thing like you."

"I'm perfectly happy on my own for now."

Paolo gives me an appraising look. "I can see that. You look happy."

Dinner passes too quickly, and before I know it, Paolo's driving me back to my hotel.

"I talked to Jake a few weeks ago," Paolo says in a too-casual tone.

"Mm," I say, noncommittal.

"He's doing well."

"Glad to hear it."

"I've got his number if you'd like it." Paolo has offered me Jake's phone number on various occasions over the past three years. And like every other time, I decline.

BETTER THAN GELATO

I invite him to come visit me in California, like I have several times. And like every other time, he declines. He makes me promise to come to the wedding.

"I wouldn't miss it for all the pasta in Italy," I tell him.

The landing into JFK is rough. There's an early season thunderstorm and hundreds of flights have been canceled. Ours is among them. It's only 10 a.m., but the earliest they can get us back to LA is tomorrow morning. Henry calls the office, and they arrange rooms at the airport Marriott.

Henry hands me my key and goes to sleep off the rest of his hangover. I try to nap, but I'm too antsy. After an hour, I give up.

I check my phone. There's a text from Eloise, she's delighted with the sneak peek of the photos I sent her. There's a text from Paolo checking to make sure I made it home safely.

> Flight to LAX got canceled. Stuck in NYC. Won't be home till tomorrow.

He replies a minute later.

> You're stuck in NYC all day?

He sends Jake's contact info "just in case."

I don't bother responding.

I grab my camera and catch a cab for Central Park. The rain has stopped, but the sky is a thundering mass of purple and gray. I wander around taking pictures, and I can't help remembering the last time I was here with Jake.

Spending last week in Italy has made old memories feel fresh. And maybe it's all those memories, or being here in this park, or the fact that I'm jet-lagged and sleep deprived, but before I know what I'm doing, I pull out my phone, check Paolo's text and dial Jake's number.

This is totally normal, I tell myself. *Paolo's an old friend. Jake's an old friend. It's normal to catch up with old friends.* Of course, Paolo and I chat once a month, and I haven't spoken to Jake in close to three years...

He picks up on the third ring. "Hello?"

"Hey. Jake. It's um…"

"Juliet!" That one word, spoken by this voice, has me closing my eyes against the rush of memories.

"Yeah, it's Juliet."

"Wow. How are you?"

"Good. Yeah. I know this is kind of random. I just got back from Italy. I had a nice dinner with Paolo, and he gave me your number, and then my flight out of JFK got canceled, and I just thought…I'd give you a call."

"You're in the city right now?" His voice sounds surprised.

"Central Park."

"When do you fly out? Are you free for dinner?"

"Um, yeah. I don't fly out until tomorrow morning."

Jake suggests 5 p.m. and says he'll text me the address of a restaurant he knows. I hang up and bury my phone deep into my bag, wondering what in the world I've just done.

Jake's standing outside the restaurant when my cab pulls up, and for a quick second, I consider telling the driver to keep driving. But I don't.

I had no good clothing options for an impromptu meet-up with an ex-boyfriend, so I did some Manhattan shopping. This dress cost double what I'd usually pay, but the woman in the shop wasn't lying when she said I looked fantastic. I take a breath and climb out.

Jake's smiles when he sees me and it sets my heart racing. The dimples are out in full force, and his eyes sparkle like stars. I catch my breath.

"*Ciao, bella!*" he says and gives me a kiss on each cheek.

"*Ciao, bello,*" I say.

We stand there a moment, not awkward exactly, but unsure.

"You look incredible," he says.

"Thank you. You look well."

Inside, a hostess leads us to a table for two in the corner. The restaurant is dimly lit and quiet. The chairs feel like real leather.

Jake wants to hear all about my trip. I tell him about my work and my dinner with Paolo.

"They're expecting?" he says, his eyes wide, his mouth slightly open. It's an expression I remember.

"Yep. A little boy they're calling Diego."

He smiles sadly. "That's wonderful news."

Our food comes, and I have a sudden flashback to a hundred meals I've eaten with Jake.

"So, you're working for *Conde Nast Traveler*. Living your dream. I always knew you would."

I smile. "Tell me about med school. This is your last year, right?"

We spend the next two hours eating and catching up. Everything about Jake is exactly how I remember, how I tried not to remember. The animated way he talks about patients and procedures makes me smile. He's doing well. He's happy.

We order tiramisu for dessert and coffee after that. He asks about my parents and how they're enjoying retirement. I ask what Naomi's up to. When the waiter walks by for the third time, Jake pays our bill.

"Thank you for a lovely dinner," I say. "This was nice."

"Yeah, it was."

We stand on the sidewalk, traffic and pedestrians buzzing around us.

"Well...thank you," I say again.

"Would you like to walk?" Jake asks.

I hesitate for a second then nod. We head away from downtown, through Battery Park and along the Hudson.

It's the walking that brings everything back. This is our natural state. We don't hold hands, but occasionally our arms brush and it sends sparks shooting through me. I'd somehow forgotten about this chemistry, the kind that makes my thoughts blur.

We talk a little, mostly just sharing each other's company. Each step seems to erase the time apart.

"I want to apologize for how things ended between us," Jake says.

I was really hoping we wouldn't have this conversation.

"No need for apologies. It all worked out."

"If not apologies, at least explanations." He runs a hand through his hair. "Coming home was a hard transition for me."

"I get it. The switch from *bisteca milanese* to ramen noodles was a rough one for me."

"I was failing my classes."

I look at him, shocked. Jake's the smartest guy I know. He looks straight ahead and keeps talking.

"I was sleeping less than five hours a night, barely eating anything, and failing three of my classes. Everything was harder than I expected. My research in Milan was great, but it didn't prepare me for med school. I'd gotten lazy, forgotten how to take notes, how to prepare for an exam. My advisor called me in and told me I needed to make some big changes, or I wouldn't make it through my first year."

We walk in silence as I mentally search through all our phone conversations, looking for signs he was failing.

"But you made it through," I say finally.

"I did. I stayed at Columbia over Thanksgiving and Christmas to get in extra work time. A resident took me under his wing and helped me out. By spring, I was in better shape."

"I had no idea," I say.

"I was too embarrassed to tell you. I felt like a complete failure. And... well, it's hard to love someone else when you don't love yourself. If I could go back, I would do a lot of things differently."

I'm not sure what to do with this information.

"Well, not to brag, but I killed it my first semester back," I say.

"Did you?"

"Yep. When you're heartbroken and depressed, you don't party on the weekends. You study and get straight A's."

"Were you heartbroken and depressed?"

His voice is full of tenderness and to my absolute mortification, I feel tears coming to my eyes. I cough and wave off his question.

"It was a long time ago. And we both made it through."

"I tried calling and emailing, but you never responded."

"I know."

I don't apologize or explain. I needed him completely out of my life so I could heal. But now...Maybe now things could be different.

"I'm dating someone," Jake says.

I walk into a fire hydrant.

"Ow! Holy monkeys that hurt." I rub my shin and turn my head away from Jake.

BETTER THAN GELATO

"Want me to take a look?" he asks.

"No, no it's fine. I'll be okay." We keep walking. I only limp a little.

"So you're dating someone," I say lightly. I shouldn't be surprised. This is Jake. He loves having a girlfriend.

"Yeah, it's pretty early. We'll see. How about you?"

"Work. I mean, I'm not dating anyone. I've been working a lot. I mean there were some people. Men. There just aren't any right now." *Sweet mother of Moses, stop talking, Juliet.*

I ask Jake about his plans for after med school, and he tells me he's specializing in cardiothoracic surgery, so he's got three more years of training. He's already been accepted to the program at Columbia.

"Good for you. That sounds really cool," I say.

I've got to call it a night. At a certain point, this becomes masochistic. And yet the pull to be near him is so strong I can't bring myself to cut the night short. The rain makes my decision for me. What starts as a trickle turns into a downpour. We take cover under a restaurant awning.

"I'd better go," I say.

"Of course," he says. "You must be exhausted from traveling. Let me get a cab for you. What hotel are you at?"

"The airport Marriott."

He hails a cab, tells the driver my hotel and pays.

"You didn't need to pay for my cab," I tell him. The insecure part of me wants to tell him how much money I make now, but I don't.

"It's my pleasure." I lean in to kiss his cheek, and he pulls me into a hug. Muscle memory kicks in, and I melt against him. It feels so good tears well up in my eyes. We stand there, getting soaked by the rain, neither one letting go. Finally, I take a step back.

"It was so great to see you," Jake says.

"Yeah! Totally. Always good to catch up with an old friend." My voice is over the top casual. Jake looks like he wants to say something else, but I pretend I don't notice and jump in the cab. I give my best happiest smile and wave as we pull away from the curb.

Adrenaline courses through me, and my breath comes out ragged. I squeeze my hands into fists and then rub them into my eyes. Then I whip out my phone and text Paolo.

270   LIBBY TANNER

> He's dating someone.

I don't elaborate. Paolo will know it's Jake. Just like he knew I would call him.

His text comes in when I'm back at the hotel crawling into bed.

> I didn't think that would make a difference.

And it shouldn't. It was dinner with an old friend. No big deal. So why do I feel like such a mess?

I don't sleep well. I stare at the ceiling. I curse Paolo for giving me Jake's number. I curse myself for calling. I curse Jake for answering.

Being with him has stirred up all the things I've been so careful to leave undisturbed. And now I have to face the truth. That Jake is every bit as wonderful as I remember. And being with him feels just as good as I remember. And being without him feels just as terrible as I remember.

Around 4 a.m., I give up on sleep. I shower and stand under the hot water for a long time. When my skin has turned a scalded pink I get out and get dressed. I wear my traveling clothes. Black wrap dress, black sandals, black sweater. It's early, the sky's just barely turning pink, and we don't need to be at the airport for another hour, but I can't keep staring at the same four walls. I check that I have everything from my room, then wheel my carry-on downstairs to the lobby. My phone's dead, and I look for a place to charge it while I wait for Henry.

That's when I see Jake.

He's asleep in a red armchair by the door. His head's bent at a funny angle, and his brown hair has fallen into his eyes. My heart is pounding, and I'm not sure what to do.

"Jake?" I put a hand to his shoulder, and his head snaps up.

"Juliet!"

"What are you doing here?"

He rubs his eyes and then blinks at me.

"I wanted to see you again. I called but you didn't pick up."

"My phone died."

"I didn't know what time your flight left, but I knew it was early, and I didn't want to miss you, so I just came here and waited."

"You never went home last night?"

He shakes his head. "I didn't want to miss this chance..." He glances at a businessman giving us a curious look, then takes my arm and leads me to a couch farther away.

"I've thought about you a lot, Juls. Even when I tried not to. I told myself that I'd embellished what we had. That Italy made things seem special, even when they were ordinary. But seeing you last night. Walking the city together. I know I've been lying to myself. It wasn't Italy. It was you. My memories of you are not embellished. In fact, they don't do you justice. Being with you is even better than I remember."

I try to take this all in and make sense of his words.

"You're dating someone," I say.

"A perfectly nice girl. For someone else. I let her know last night."

He runs a hand through his hair and shakes his head.

"The truth is, I'd forgotten I could feel this way. And if this connection still exists, I can't settle for anything else."

He takes my hand in his. His palm is damp with sweat. "I know this is fast, and I know we just spent one evening together..."

He looks at me, soft brown eyes lit with intensity. "I asked Paolo for your number for years, but he'd never give it to me. He told me you were happy. He didn't want me to ruin it. He said maybe you would call me when you were ready.

"And then yesterday you called. And I guess...I guess I'm wondering, are you ready?"

My brain races to process his words and interpret their meaning. My thoughts are all scrambled. I don't know what to say.

But my body knows what to do. I lean in and touch my lips to his. Tentatively at first, my hand trembling as I press it against his chest. His arm reaches around my waist, pulling me close to him, and all the nerves in my body wake up for the first time in years.

This. This overwhelming feeling of rightness is what I've been trying to forget for years. And I know, with everything in me, that I'll never find anything like it, no matter how long I look.

When we come apart, I'm not scared, or nervous or uneasy. I look into Jake's eyes, and I'm sure.

"I'm ready," I say.

Thank you for reading! Did you enjoy? Please add your review because nothing helps an author more and encourages readers to take a chance on a book than a review.

Want to see what happens next with Juliet and Jake? Join Libby Tanner's newsletter and read an exclusive epilogue at www.libbytannerauthor.com

And then, read 23 AND YOU AND ME, by City Owl Author, Michelle McCraw. Turn the page for a sneak peek!

You can also sign up for the City Owl Press newsletter to receive notice of all book releases!

Sneak Peek of 23 and You and Me

BY MICHELLE MCCRAW

JANUARY, SUBURBAN COLUMBUS, OHIO

This is it. After everything that happened, I'm going to die in a freaking golf cart.

Gabe gripped the steering wheel, his normally tan fingers turning frost-white, all his focus on keeping the vehicle from slipping on the icy curve and spilling out his family.

"I could walk faster than this," Uncle Bobby grumbled from the back.

"I couldn't." In the front passenger seat, Grandpa massaged his knee. "That's why we're riding."

"Leave Gabe alone." From the soft *oof* behind him, Gabe figured Aunt Pat had elbowed her brother. "You know he has—" Her voice faded to a whisper too low for Gabe to hear.

He didn't want to hear it. After five years of therapy, he was well aware of his own issues. He braked—slowly—and brought the cart to a skidding stop in front of the kiddie coaster. Clenching his jaw, he glanced at the low, snow-crusted lift hill, just to show he could. Then he turned his back to the sinuous steel structure and faced the Beach Island Board of Directors, also known as his family.

"We determined this one's in pretty good shape," he said. "The maintenance crew is checking each car and performing minor repairs on the track as the weather allows. Ramirez says they'll be done in about two weeks."

"Kiddie rides," Uncle Bobby snorted. His smooth cheeks were red from the cold. "I want to see the moneymakers. Twister of Terror. The Basilisk."

"Bobby." This time, Gabe witnessed Aunt Pat's elbow. For a woman who had to wear thick-soled sneakers to reach the you-must-be-this-tall-to-ride lines, she had a vicious swing. "We asked Gabe to give us a tour of the winter projects. Let him direct it."

Uncle Bobby muttered something under his breath and crossed his arms over the Beach Island Amusements logo on his fleece jacket.

"Guests under forty-eight inches should enjoy the park, too," Gabe said. Though he wished the kids would stay at home. He wished everyone would stay at home. Then Gabe wouldn't have to worry all the time about someone getting hurt. And maybe he could do what he wanted for a change.

"Right you are," Grandpa said. "Kids who ride this one grow up to ride Twister of Terror."

Gabe shuddered inside his extra-large down coat.

"Plus, they buy plenty of snacks," Aunt Pat said. When she nodded, the flower on her knit hat bounced. "Gabe's a smart boy. He's always done what's best for the park."

Gabe blew out a frustrated breath, which clouded in the icy air. At thirty, he hadn't been a boy for a long time, not since the board had asked him to shoulder the massive responsibility of the park nine years ago.

"Fine, fine." Uncle Bobby pointed over the trees to the wooden curve of Mystery Mountain. "But show us that one next."

Gabe narrowed his eyes at him. "Seat belt."

After Uncle Bobby refastened his belt, Gabe drove carefully along the blessedly straight path to Mystery Mountain. He fixed his eyes on the empty queuing area to avoid the towering hill.

"The team is checking the chain lift, same as every winter. Taking it apart, cleaning it, reassembling it. The cars, too."

"I'm glad we kept this one," Grandpa said. "Not too many wooden coasters left."

"'Cause they suck," Uncle Bobby grumbled.

Gabe silently agreed. The wood warped in the rain and again in the sun. Left unchecked, the coaster would become rough over time, leading to injured passengers. Ramirez griped about it constantly. Year-round, his maintenance chief dedicated a small crew to assessing and repairing this ride. Grandpa probably had no idea how much it cost to keep his pet coaster's ride smooth, even though Gabe called it out every quarter in the financial reports.

His phone buzzed, and while Grandpa and Bobby argued the merits of wooden versus steel coasters, he checked it. Another call from DN-YAY. He hit the Ignore button. He'd deal with that annoyance later. For now, he had a bigger concern: the hill to Twister of Terror.

He cast a glance at his passengers to ensure their lap belts were buckled —too bad golf carts didn't come with beefier restraints—and hit the accelerator. He hoped someone from Ramirez's crew had laid down some ice melt. Despite the cold, his palms started to sweat.

"Gabe, you going to take a vacation this year?" Grandpa asked.

"What?" Was the incline just wet, or was that a thin layer of ice?

"A vacation. You know, sunshine, sand, umbrella drinks?"

"No time," Gabe said through gritted teeth. "Less than four months to opening day." He gambled and accelerated to build momentum to climb the hill.

"It's your turn to go to the Expo this year," Aunt Pat said. "You can get your umbrella drink on in Orlando."

Crap. They'd skipped his turn last time. He'd hoped to pass on the Expo again this year. How was he going to get to Florida? He'd never survive a fourteen-hour drive. He pressed harder on the accelerator, making the tiny engine whine. "Why don't you go, Aunt Pat? I'm more of a beer guy."

"They have beer in Florida. Besides, you know I prefer the snow. I've already got my trip to Whistler planned."

If Gabe hadn't been steering the cart up the hill, he'd have shivered. He'd spent all his life in Ohio, but, unlike the rest of his family, he dreaded every winter. Why would anyone go somewhere even colder and snowier on vacation?

The cart's back half fishtailed, arrowing his attention back to the road. His pulse roared in his ears. *Straighten out. Don't tip.* The adrenaline pumping through him urged him to yank the wheel. Instead, he held it firm, steering gradually in the direction of the skid. At last, the cart leveled out, finally gaining purchase at the top of the hill in front of Twister of Terror. A shuddering cloud of his breath gusted out as he peeled his fingers off the steering wheel. He should've predicted that Aunt Pat and Uncle Bobby didn't weigh enough to counterbalance his mass in the front.

Uncle Bobby chuckled. "Way to give us a little excitement, Gabe." He stepped out of the cart. Gabe did, too, though his legs trembled. He wiped the slick of sweat from his brow.

"Yo, Gabe!" The safety gate clanged shut, and Tony Ramirez jogged out from the maintenance area.

Relief mingled with the dissipating adrenaline. The board would listen to Ramirez. Safety was his job. Gabe's jaw unclenched. "Ramirez. I didn't expect to see you out here today."

"I thought I'd show the board what we're working on here. Give you a break."

Gabe was still too tight-strung to smile at his friend, but he nodded. "Thanks."

Uncle Bobby and Aunt Pat followed Ramirez toward the blue steel monstrosity. Grandpa clutched Gabe's arm, bending him down closer to the old man's height. "I'll drive the cart back with your aunt and uncle. Why don't you head over"—he tipped his chin—"and pay your respects."

The warmth that rushed through Gabe's veins had nothing to do with the weak winter sunshine. Still, he checked his watch, his father's battered old Omega.

Grandpa said, "Don't worry. We'll meet you back in the office in half an hour. Take your time."

"Thanks, Grandpa." Gabe might not have looked much like the short, slender old man, but Grandpa always seemed to know what he was thinking. "See you later."

He meandered toward the circle of trees Grandpa had indicated. Stepping between them into Founders' Park always calmed him, even in winter with ice coating the young trees' branches and the flowers—yellow tulips for his mother—still resting underground.

He avoided the plaque and lowered himself onto his favorite bench, the one that faced away from Twister of Terror's steel corkscrew. He traced the round watch face on his wrist, the smooth, cool glass settling his nerves. He'd never looked much like his dad—too tall, too broad, too dark—so, instead of looking in a mirror to remember him, he came here and dug through his memories for images of Dad's hand clutching his smaller one as they walked through the park, of Dad's almost hairless arm with this watch on it. The watch he'd handed to Ramirez before— Before.

His phone buzzed again in his pocket. Again, he pulled it out. Dismissed another call from DN-YAY. A few minutes of peace was what he needed. No phone calls, no ice, no board of directors. No Theme Park Expo in flipping Florida.

A crack rang out, making Gabe duck his head. When an ice-coated tree limb clattered onto the next bench over, Gabe shut his eyes. Breathed deep to slow his racing heartbeat.

Pushing his hands onto his knees, he stood. He hefted the limb onto his shoulder and headed toward the park's landscaping shed. CEO or not, when there was work to be done, Gabe did it. He might not have his parents' light builds or their cold tolerance, but he'd learned that lesson from them.

If only they'd taught him how to enjoy their legacy, the park, without them.

"Gabe, what are you doing?"

Quickly, he straightened, tucking the snow shovel behind his back. He shouldn't feel guilty. He was watching out for his employee. Employees. "Clearing this ice."

Darlene crossed her arms and shivered. "The maintenance crew's on the way."

"They have important work to do. I've got this." He chipped at a hunk of ice on the sidewalk in front of the administrative office building. What if Darlene had slipped on her way in this morning? Or Grandpa? He'd never forgive himself.

She leaned on the doorjamb. "Tough meeting with the board?"

"No!" But his voice rose in that petulant way he hated. He cleared his throat. "It was fine. They're pleased with the work we're doing. You should go back inside. You're not wearing a coat."

"Neither are you. Come in here. You have real work to do." Carefully, she turned and walked into the Beach Island administrative office building.

Real work. That's what it was. When he was a kid, working at Beach Island, even when he'd been on vomit clean-up duty under Twister of Terror, had been fun. Now, it held nothing but bad memories. And spreadsheets.

Gabe leaned the snow shovel against the side of the building. He sprinkled a last trowelful of ice melt over the sidewalk and followed his assistant.

Darlene leaned on her desk. "You have a call with a new paper goods supplier at one. At two, you're interviewing a candidate for the entertainment director position. In the meantime, you need to review these." She picked up a stack of papers. "Applications for summer jobs. I've already screened them."

Gabe paused before he took the stack. Sure enough, the papers fluttered in her hand.

"You all right?" He scanned her face. She was a few years older than him, in her mid-thirties. Her skin was winter-pale, but it wasn't drawn with fatigue like it sometimes was.

"Course I am." She stared right back. "Are you?"

Shoving the papers under his arm, he looked toward his office door and its brass nameplate that read, *Gabe Armstrong, Chief Executive Officer.* "Of course. Why wouldn't I be?"

"Oh, I don't know. Bobby irritating you again about the safety improvements. Or...Riley."

"Who?" If she could pretend she wasn't having a flare-up, Gabe could pretend, too.

"You might think—"

His phone rang, interrupting her. Gabe pulled it out of his pocket. DN-YAY again. For a second, he weighed his options: another conversation about his ex-girlfriend, or a hassle with the sketchy DNA testing company that'd screwed up his results? "Sorry, I'm going to take this. I'll come check on you after."

"Don't bother. I'm fine." She circled the desk, lowered herself into her chair, and swiveled until her back was toward him.

Shaking his head, he walked into his office and closed the door before swiping to accept the call. "Gabe Armstrong."

"Mr. Armstrong, this is Sunny from DN-YAY. I'm calling about your test results."

Sunny? Was this company for real? Of course not. They'd already screwed up his results, telling him he was seventy-five percent Italian. The Armstrongs were originally from Scotland, and his mother's family was Danish. Who confused northern Europe with Italy? A company that employed *Sunny,* that's who. He should've known a DNA testing firm that advertised nonstop on Riley's favorite fake-reality dating show would be more sparkle than science. Their jingle—*DN-YAY, find out who you are to-DAY!*—tinkled through his mind.

"Did you run the test again?" After he'd gotten his results, he'd emailed Customer Service to demand a retest. Clearly, they'd mixed up his results with someone else's.

"We did, and we confirmed the results. You have two brothers and a sister, all still living."

"That's impossible. I was an only child." He snapped the blinds shut, blocking out the view of the nearby arcade and behind it, Twister of Terror.

"Mr. Armstrong." The woman's voice gentled, like she was talking to a small child. "Have you talked to your parents about the results?"

Kind of hard to talk to someone who'd been dead nine years. His blood went hot, and the peace he'd felt at Founders' Park evaporated.

"Why would I talk to anyone about it?" he snapped. "The results are wrong. You know what? Forget about it. Take me off—"

She spoke over him. "Mr. Armstrong, listen to me." Her voice dropped lower, like she didn't want to be overheard. "I've talked to a lot of people about their families, and things can get...complicated. We found the parents you listed on your information sheet in our database. We have their test results too. I'm sorry, but it's impossible for them to be your biological parents."

Not his parents? And when had they taken DNA tests? And why? His knees wobbled. He flung out his hand for balance and hit the back of the armchair by the window. Gripping the fabric, he eased himself into the seat. "What?"

Her voice went even softer. "You really should ask your parents about the test results."

"They're dead." The words cracked out of him like that snapping tree branch. He straightened in the chair, squaring his back to the window and the view of the roller coaster hidden by the blinds.

"Holy shit! Oh, I mean, I'm very sorry about that." He could almost hear her cringe over the phone line. "Do you want to talk to a genetic counselor?"

"Not unless they're going to rerun the test and explain what the hell happened the first two times."

"Look," she half-whispered, "DN-YAY has some issues, I'll admit it, but they ran your results three times. Your biological siblings are living in Las Vegas."

"Las Vegas?" That broke something inside him. He was from Ohio, the Midwest. He'd never been to Vegas. He slumped in the chair. "I didn't want to take the test. It was all Riley's idea."

"Who?"

"Riley. We had the couple's version. Two tests. A Christmas gift."

"Oh!" When excitement bubbled in her voice, a spark of hope flared in his chest. "Maybe your tests got mixed up," she said. "Is Riley from Las Vegas? It could be his siblings we found."

"His?"

"Shit, I'm sorry. I'm new, and I'm screwing this up so bad." He heard skin slapping on skin like she'd covered her mouth. "I wish I could tell you what you want to hear. DN-YAY has its problems, but it's unlikely they'd mix up a man's test results with a woman's."

The hope fizzled out like the last mortar in Beach Island's Saturday-night Firework Extravaganza.

"We didn't even take them together. She saw all those damned ads. She said it'd be fun." Riley had wrapped the test packages in shiny silver paper with white polar bears wearing red scarves. The bears were doing un-bearlike things like sledding and holding candy canes in their paws.

Gabe didn't have a Christmas tree at his townhouse, but when he'd come home after work a few days after their breakup, Riley had left his kit sitting on the kitchen counter, next to her key to his place. The bears mocked him with their joyful Christmas grins.

"After she—after she left, I, ah, I took the test. Does alcohol affect the results?" When he'd swabbed his cheek on Christmas Eve, his saliva had to have been fifty percent Maker's Mark.

"No." She paused. "I'm sorry she left you." Her voice was so soothing, he almost believed she cared. "Especially at Christmas."

"Doesn't matter. It's a Hallmark holiday, anyway."

"Christmas isn't a Hallmark holiday!"

Who was this woman? She didn't sound like a customer service representative.

"Sure it is," Gabe grumbled. "Cards, wrapping paper, Black Friday. It's all about buying stuff." He'd fallen into that trap. That night at the restaurant, he'd had the black velvet box in his coat pocket. He hadn't had a chance to offer it to Riley before she'd stood up from the table and walked out.

"No, it's not. It's supposed to be about friends and togetherness. Family." Her voice took a wistful turn on the last word. "Oh."

Yeah. Oh.

"No one should be alone at Christmas." Her voice had lost all its former effervescence. "I should know."

In the beat of silence that followed, Gabe heard other, more strident voices over the line. She was in a call center. He didn't know this person, and he shouldn't have been sharing his feelings with her.

"I wasn't alone." Somehow, it was important that she not feel sorry for him. On Christmas Day, he'd dragged his hungover carcass to Aunt Pat's like he'd done as long as he could remember, even before his parents had died. She'd made the same dried-out turkey she always had. No worries about salmonella. Those suckers could've never survived the too-long roast in Aunt Pat's Viking oven.

But if what this woman said was true, Gabe hadn't belonged at Aunt Pat's. Aunt Pat wouldn't have given a Brooks Brothers tie to someone who wasn't her nephew, would she?

Sunny from DN-YAY couldn't hear all the roiling that was going on inside him. "It's good you were with friends," she said. "Are you going to be okay?"

"I'm fine," he said. It was a phrase he'd learned after his parents died. People knew not to push once he'd said that. They knew they'd done their job by asking, and he'd done his by being self-sufficient.

"Are you sure?"

She didn't know the script.

"Positive," he growled.

"On the bright side, this means you have a second chance. At family. At love."

What had this call turned into? First she told him he had family in Las

Vegas he'd never known about. Now she was going off about love? Maybe monosyllables would shut her down. It used to work on Riley. "Sure," Gabe said.

"So are you going to look up your bio family?"

Who was this Sunny person? Did her supervisor know she was so...so... pushy and unprofessional? He'd have sent someone like her to remedial customer-service training. "I don't think so."

"But what if they're looking for you? They all got tested. They checked the box to be notified of relatives we find. You didn't, so we won't contact them, but you should consider reaching out. Look, I..." She lowered her voice to a whisper. "Family's important. I always wished I had siblings, didn't you? Like on that show, *The Brainiac Bunch*. Now you have a chance to meet yours. I'll email you their names. It's public information since they checked the box. You can call them. Meet them."

Meet them? "No. Thanks." He hung up. It was warm in his office, but chills raced over his skin. *Thanks for dropping this bomb on me. Thanks for making me question everything I thought I knew about myself.* Could it be true? DN-YAY's website made all sorts of claims about their accuracy. But couldn't they be wrong about this? Some sort of mix-up. Maybe he hadn't sealed the envelope properly and someone else's DNA had gotten in with his.

But...what if she was right? What if everything he thought was his—his parents, Grandpa, Aunt Pat, Uncle Bobby, his cousins, Beach Island—wasn't?

Gabe stood and shoved his phone back in his pocket. The sweat-dampened sheaf of applications crinkled under his arm. He tossed the stack onto his desk—his dad's desk—*the* desk—and didn't even worry that some of them fluttered to the floor. He flung open the door and strode past Darlene.

"Gabe, what's wrong?"

"Nothing. I'm fine."

He snatched his coat off the rack and flung it over his shoulders, not bothering to change into his boots. He stomped out into the gray January afternoon, past the back of the arcade to the corrugated metal machine shop. Ramirez looked up, but when he saw Gabe's expression, he stared back down into the guts of the Mystery Mountain car he was working on.

Gabe crossed the room to the far corner, where a heavy chain suspended one of the cars from Twister of Terror from a steel beam overhead. He grabbed a wrench from the tool chest and cranked one of the exterior bolts. He didn't need any power tools. His anger would provide the torque he needed.

But even the whine of Ramirez's drill and the hiss of the welder working on the other end of the garage couldn't drown out the doubt that roared in Gabe's ears.

If he wasn't who he thought he was, did he even belong here?

Don't stop now. Keep reading with your copy of 23 AND YOU AND ME.

Don't miss more from Libby Tanner coming soon and grab an exclusive epilogue by signing up for her newsletter at www.libbytannerauthor.com

And then, discover 23 AND YOU AND ME by City Owl Author, Michelle McCraw!

Two strangers on the road to Las Vegas. What could go wrong?

Some might call Gabe grumpy. He prefers safety-conscious. As CEO of the happiest place in Ohio, Beach Island Amusement Park, it's a responsibility he takes seriously, especially since his parents were killed on one of the coasters there years ago.

Sunny has a different legacy: she's Hollywood royalty. Too bad she quit her last acting gig in an award-worthy blowup. But even after being fired from her humiliating job as a DNA testing company customer service rep, she refuses to let real-life drama crush her spirit. She takes one thing with her: contact information for a stranger's siblings – siblings Gabe didn't know he had. She'll give him a second chance at a happy family if she has to drive him to Las Vegas herself.

Which is exactly what she does. On the road, snowstorms, a swoonworthy karaoke duet, and motels with only one bed help these two opposites see they're not so different. But love? That's a jackpot too unlikely even for Vegas. Or is it?

Please sign up for the City Owl Press newsletter for chances to win special subscriber-only contests and giveaways as well as receiving information on upcoming releases and special excerpts.

All reviews are **welcome** and **appreciated**. Please consider leaving one on your favorite social media and book buying sites.

Escape Your World. Get Lost in Ours! City Owl Press at www.cityowlpress.com.

Acknowledgments

If writing a book is like falling in love, getting a book published is like surviving a breakup—best done with help. A huge thank you to all those who helped.

My husband could have been weirded out that I wrote a book about my first time falling in love, and it wasn't about him. Instead, he was supportive, encouraging, and laughed as poor Jake went through much of the same shenanigans he went through trying to date me. My four kiddos are my greatest hype people- telling friends, teachers, and the lady at Qdoba all about their mom's new book. Thank you Eila, Annabelle, Xander, and Gabriella for being such sweet fans.

A huge thank you to my parents Parkes and Christie Tanner. Mom, I've lost track of how many times you've read this book in all of its stages, but I know you made it better each time. Thank you to my siblings Lauren Harter, Nolan Tanner, Julie Dayley, Nathan Tanner, Amelia Christensen and Melinda Tanner for your encouragement, enthusiasm and beta reading.

Thank you Boss Michael for your unwavering belief in me and your strategic plans to make this book a success. To my best friends Jamie Fieldsted and Mariah Reid- your feedback, brainstorming, pep talks, and endless excitement kept me sane through this whole process and made it twice as fun. I love you more than heaps can measure.

Thank you Katie Monson, literary agent extraordinaire, for setting this publishing process in motion. A big thank you to City Owl Press for scooping me up and to Tee Tate for making the editing process way less scary than I thought it would be.

Going through the writing process as a debut author is like wandering New York City as a toddler- overwhelming and bewildering. Writing friends have made all the difference. Thank you Rita Potter and Shalon Atwood for orienting, educating, and beta reading. And thank you to my new Instagram friends for your examples and support.

Thank you to Matteo, Beatrice, and Isa for letting me be your nanny. Isa, you were not half as bad as I wrote you to be.

If you've made it this far you are a true reader and I am grateful for you! As I wrote this novel I pictured someone reading it and giggling and enjoying the magic of first love. I hope that was your experience.

And lastly, thank you to my Heavenly Father for helping all of this come together. I am trying my best to use the time, resources, and energy you've given me for good.

About the Author

LIBBY TANNER grew up in a small town in Northern California that would be charming in a novel but felt suffocating as a teenager. Yes, she left as fast as she could, and yes, she misses it very much.

In college Libby earned a degree in Communications. She wishes she would have studied creative writing instead of playing it safe, but also remembers she had student loans to pay off.

She is the mother of four sweet hooligans and is married to the world's sexiest accountant (the world's only sexy accountant?).

Her dream date would be eating crab legs in a hot air balloon over a vineyard.

www.libbytannerauthor.com

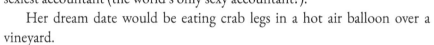

instagram.com/libbytannerauthor

About the Publisher

City Owl Press is a cutting edge indie publishing company, bringing the world of romance and speculative fiction to discerning readers.

Escape Your World. Get Lost in Ours!

www.cityowlpress.com

facebook.com/CityOwlPress
x.com/cityowlpress
instagram.com/cityowlbooks
pinterest.com/cityowlpress
tiktok.com/@cityowlpress